Also by Marie Harte

All I Want for Halloween
The Kissing Game

The McCauley Brothers
The Troublemaker Next Door
How to Handle a Heartbreaker
Ruining Mr. Perfect
What to Do with a Bad Boy

Body Shop Bad Boys
Test Drive
Roadside Assistance
Zero to Sixty
Collision Course

The Donnigans
A Sure Thing
Just the Thing
The Only Thing

Veteran Movers
The Whole Package
Smooth Moves
Handle with Care
Delivered with a Kiss

Turn Up the Heat
Make Me Burn
Burning Desire

BURNING DESIRE

MARIE HARTE

sourcebooks
casablanca

To DT and RC.

Published by Sourcebooks Casablanca, an imprint of Sourcebooks
P.O. Box 4410, Naperville, Illinois 60567-4410
(630) 961-3900
sourcebooks.com

Printed and bound in Canada.
MBP 10 9 8 7 6 5 4 3 2 1

Chapter One

Eight months ago
Seattle, Washington

IT WAS ONE OF THOSE LULLS IN THE SURROUNDING NOISE THAT happen right before a most embarrassing discussion fills the silence. The firefighters in the station house had been talking and laughing, cooking in the kitchen, and coming in from the weight room to check out the kitchen's good smells. Then suddenly, everything seemed to stop, as if the world slowed down in time to hear Mack shoot off his big mouth.

"So, let me get this straight. On your big date last night, the chick *straight up tossed a glass of water in your face*?"

All eyes turned to the conversation happening a stone's throw away in the television area.

"Would you keep your voice down, damn it?" Tex McGovern glared at his buddy and prayed the others on B shift kept their big noses out of his business. He tossed the rest of them a scowl until they finally went back to their own boring lives.

Mack grinned then had the nerve to laugh. A lot.

Texan, firefighter, and former U.S. Marine, Tex sank deeper into the reclining chair, not seeing the game on TV as he relived his pitiful date. He reached for the comfort of his cowboy hat but tugged down the brim of a Seattle FD ballcap instead.

"Yeah, my life sucks." His twang sounded more pronounced, and he did his best to regroup, not wanting the others to know how much he hated what had gone down with a woman he'd grown to like way too much.

"Your life never sucks. You just move on to the next honey." Mack paused. "Why'd she throw water all over you? What did you do?"

Tex glared at his partner, a guy who should have had his back. "Why is this *my* fault?"

Mack raised a brow.

"I did nothin'. Not a thing. And it wasn't my date that splashed me, moron. It was the girl I broke up with two freaking months ago that drenched me. I finally got that date with Bree—"

"Bree of the sunny-blond hair, heavenly blue eyes, and body worshipped by men everywhere? That Bree?"

Tex frowned. Mack sure seemed to have memorized her picture from one shot on Tex's phone. "Yeah, she—"

"The woman you've been dying to go out with finally said yes? I thought she had better taste than that."

Tex flipped him off but lowered his voice when he saw two guys he'd rather not talk to right now glancing over at him. "Yeah, well, after the stunt my ex pulled, I doubt I'll ever see Bree again." He was miserable. "Mack, I'm tellin' ya, I broke it off with that woman two months ago. I had to block her from calling and texting me just last week. I didn't want to, but she wouldn't leave me alone."

Mack shook his head. "Tough being so tall, dark, and dynamic, eh?"

"It really is."

Mack rolled his eyes.

"Woman just wouldn't take no for an answer. Then she shows up outta nowhere at a place it took me weeks to get reservations at and loses it. She calls me a two-timer and a whore and throws my own glass of water on me! All while Bree is watching—"

"In shock and horror."

"—from right across our cozy little table."

Mack shook his head. "Man, that is just… Man."

Tex groaned. "I know. The ex takes off. Then Bree looks at me and tells me I should feel ashamed of myself. She left without letting me explain."

Mack coughed but didn't quite hide his laughter.

"It ain't funny!" Tex wished the rest of his crew could hear him. He knew *they'd* have given him the compassion and pity he deserved. "I mean, I've been trying to get Bree to go out with me forever. We texted and talked, but I had to beg her to meet in person. She has a thing against firefighters, for some reason. And now she probably thinks she was right when she was so wrong."

Mack opened his mouth to respond, but closed it when two of the other guys on their eight-man shift beat him to it. Hell, the two approaching were idiots Tex rarely had patience for on a *good* day.

The ringleader, a guy they called Narc because he never kept anything to himself, smirked. "So, Tex, I hear you blew it with the chief's daughter." Next to him, Narc Jr., a guy who shadowed Narc's every move, laughed like the giant goon he was.

Tex blinked. "What?"

"You know, Brianna Gilchrist, hot as fuck, blue eyes, blond hair, big, ah, dimples?" Narc cleared his throat and looked around. Not seeing their lieutenant, he leaned in closer. "You had my respect for getting a date. God knows we've all wanted to. Couldn't close the deal, though, could you?" He held his phone to Tex, who watched a video of himself getting doused.

Tex leaned forward. "Motherfu—"

"What are you all doing over there? Slacking off?" their lieutenant boomed.

They all jumped. The LT had a mouth that didn't know the meaning of the word "whisper."

Narc turned with a smile. "Not much, LT. Just bonding with the second-best unit in our squad."

"Suck it, Narc." Mack glared.

That earned a scowl, followed by a mean grin. "Say, LT." Narc and Narc Jr. approached the lieutenant and a few lingering guys who gathered to see what the fuss was about. "Check this out." Tex heard him play the video.

Mack shook his head and in a lower voice said, "Seriously, Tex? The *battalion chief's* daughter?"

Tex felt ill. "I didn't know who she was! Hell, I never even got her last name! I swear. We'd just met in person for the first time last night." First time and last time. Tex swore under his breath. As pathetic as it was, he wanted another shot at Bree Gilchrist. He'd had the hots for her since first seeing her picture on a dating app. She'd been sweet and funny online, their conversations never boring. But she'd been even better in person, as brief as their date had been. Just thinking about her made his heart race.

Too bad a petty ex had screwed him over. God, he should have blocked her as soon as he broke off with her.

His LT scowled at him.

Shit.

"McGovern, let's have a talk in my office."

Narc and Narc Jr. laughed at him. The others offered their condolences.

"It won't be so bad," Mack murmured. "Just tell him you're done with her."

Tex stood and sighed. "Not like I'd even started with her to begin with."

He hoped this would all blow over without any major repercussions from his chain of command. And that he'd manage to get over his small infatuation.

Even after the ass-chewing he got from the lieutenant to make better decisions, he still regretted that he'd never gotten a chance to show Bree how charming he could be. But her dad— the *battalion chief*? He shuddered, knowing his track record with women.

Better that it ended way before it had a chance to begin.

Five months ago
The Lava Lounge, Seattle

Hanging with the guys at a bar in Belltown, Tex enjoyed a cool pineapple margarita while his buddies Mack and Reggie razzed him for drinking something fruity. But come on, it was a tiki bar. How could Tex not have something with pineapple somewhere in the title? Brad sipped from a concoction mixed with rum and coconut milk and didn't say much.

The crew of four got plenty of second looks, some friendly and others not so friendly.

As firefighters, they had to stay in shape. But Tex and the guys liked to take it to another level. All prior military men, they knew the value of a good piece of gear on a mission. Hauling around equipment while wearing the fireproof suits and self-contained breathing apparatuses (SCBAs) that helped them breathe through smoke and ash had shown that having a fit body could mean the difference between life and death. For them as well as the public they served.

While they had bonded as brothers, both as firefighters and ex-military, they certainly had their differences. Tex and Brad had served in the Marines, Reggie in the Navy, and Mack in the Air Force. Tex did best with women, though Brad and Mack never seemed to be hurting. For two years Reggie had been in a long-term relationship with a woman. But recently things had grown rocky between them, so they'd gathered for a morale booster for the sarcastic bastard.

They were their own small family, supporting one another through everything, good and bad.

Which made it difficult to remember the good when the idiots continued to throw up to his face the fact that he'd dissed the battalion commander's precious daughter. Damn, but he'd thought that might have died down by now.

"Imagine," Brad said, a grin on his stupid face as he swirled his coconut mambo, or whatever the hell he'd ordered. "In an alternate universe, Tex gets her to go out with him. She ends up bringing him home to meet the parents and he's all, oh, hey, Chief Gilchrist, how's it hangin'?"

Mack chuckled. "So pleased to meet you and the missus. Oh, and I'm sleeping with your daughter. She really is the hottest woman in town. And did I mention I brought my own raincoat to protect my hose? No worries on that score, chief."

Tex glared at Mack. "That was disgusting." To the others he said, "Can we let it go already? How about instead we talk about—" *Brad and all the women he's not dating? Reggie and his ballbuster of a gal?* Tex paused, hearing all that in his head, and knew they needed to change the conversation from women to something else. Reggie didn't look so happy.

Brad must have sensed the same thing, because he slapped Mack in the back of the head. "Idiot."

"What? Oh, come on. I'm kidding." Mack nodded at Tex. "He's been moping for months and needs to get over it."

Brad changed the subject. "You guys still okay with moving to the new station?"

Tex nodded. "Station 44 will be manned by the best and brightest our city has to offer. Of course they wanted us in the new place."

Mack agreed. "Well, that's true. I photograph well."

Tex saw Reggie's look of disgust and agreed. "I still don't know how your ugly face got on all the media stuff for Station 44."

Mack sipped from his beer. "What can I say? The public loves me."

"I mean, I'm much better lookin'." Tex flexed and tilted back his cowboy hat. He liked to think his bronze skin, a shade darker than Brad and Mack's but lighter than Reggie's medium-brown, glowed with sex appeal. His muscles clearly overpowered his buddies'... Well, if he ignored Reggie's huge neck, arms, and chest on account of all his obsessive weight lifting.

Behind him, a few women tittered.

Reggie finished off his beer. "You two make me want to drink."

"Right? God, I feel ill." Brad shook his head at Mack and Tex.

"Probably 'cause you're drinking all that sugar." Tex finished off his margarita and decided to slow down. "I'm with you though. This thing was good but way too strong."

"It's the tequila." Reggie nodded. "We should go work out and burn this off."

"Relax, fun-killer." Mack dodged the play swipe Reggie made. "It's Friday, and—"

"—trouble has once again found us." Brad sighed. "Bridal party, six o'clock."

They turned, and Tex saw what Brad meant. A group of six women wearing feathery boas and a mishmash of headbands showcasing tiaras and one set of demon horns had gotten into a verbal altercation with three large, aggressive men.

Tex could hear the suggestive comments across the bar from the three guys, and as if that weren't bad enough, the bouncer was dealing with two of their friends as well.

"Ah, hell." Tex decided to take one for the team. "I'll do it. Brad, you got into trouble last time."

"By all means." Brad waved him toward the mess.

"I'll go along to help if you need it, lightweight." Reggie smirked.

"This is why no one likes you." Tex walked through the crowd growing around the troublemaking jocks and bridal revelers. "What's up with all the noise?" he asked the woman closest to him.

The bride-to-be—who wore a *Bride-to-Be* sash that hugged her ample chest—was a sexy redhead who looked livid. "These assholes keep trying to take us home. I'm just here with my girl-friends to celebrate my upcoming wedding. Giving blow jobs is *not* on tonight's agenda."

At the word *blow job*, the bar erupted into whistles and shouts of encouraging men, while several of the women in attendance shouted their support for the bridal party.

"I take it a blow job ain't a reference for a drink?"

The redhead scowled. "No, it is not."

Tex turned to the nearest asshole smelling like a brewery. "Look, man, it's obvious the ladies want you to leave them alone." He crossed his arms over his chest, saw the three inebriated fools eyeballing his biceps, and wondered if common sense would win out over lust and alcohol, always a poor mix.

The biggest drunk, a beady-eyed, bald guy who seemed the most vocal of the bunch, shook his head. He either worked out for a living or did some major steroids. He was *huge*. "Look, hayseed, nobody asked what you thought. Fuck off."

"Yeah, fuck off," one of his gym rat buddies seconded.

"You heard 'im," said the third.

A husky, feminine voice swore. "Oh, hell."

He turned to see a familiar blond demon. She wore tiny, red horns in her hair and sported a red feather boa.

Tex smiled widely. "Hey, Bree."

"This is not going to go well," Reggie muttered.

"I said get lost," Bald Guy said again. "Oh, I like red better than white." He goggled at Bree.

"No, *you* fuck off," the bride-to-be said, poking the big guy in his chest. Not exactly a smart move, because the man wrapped his arms around her and tried to get a kiss.

Before Tex could separate them, Reggie was there and shoved the inebriated man from the bride-to-be while steadying her. Tex quickly put himself between Bald Guy's buddies and the ladies before anyone could even think to grab Bree.

"Fellas, I really think you should reconsider," Tex advised in a polite voice, his arms loose, his fists clenched in warning. "Because I have no problem putting you down if you don't."

Fortunately, they seemed to have more sense than their friend.

They took a good look at him, at Reggie, then at their friend sway-ing on his feet and swearing, and left.

"I could have taken him," Bree said, breathless, as she adjusted her horns.

"I'm sure you would have, darlin'."

"My name is Bree, Romeo, not darlin'. Or don't you remember?"

She was *talking to him*. He felt light-headed with joy. "I—"

A scuffle sounded behind him. When he turned to investigate, he saw Mack muscling Bald Guy to the floor, facedown, jerking the drunk's arm behind his back.

Reggie held his hands up in surrender. "It's all Mack. I'm just here looking out for the lovely lady getting married soon."

"Aw, aren't you cute." The bride-to-be had a hold on Reggie's thick forearm and watched him with adoration.

Tex grinned and said to Mack, "Go for it, MP." *Take the military out of the cop, but you can't take the cop out of civvy life.*

Mack sighed. "That's SF, for Security Force. I was Air Force, not a damn… Never mind." He turned to the crowd. "Can some-one get the cops over here?"

"Already on it." The bartender gave a thumbs-up, his phone at his ear.

"I just wanted the demon, to be honest," Bald Guy was slurring from the floor. "But the bitchy bride would have been okay too."

She's my *demon*. Tex glared at the dick on the ground. "Want me to hold him till the cops come?"

Mack shook his head. "Hell no. We are not having any more trouble. We are here to drink and find women. Period." He smiled at the crowd gathered around them. "Anyone free for a beer?"

The bar erupted in cheers as many congratulated them for stepping in. Then talk turned to them being firefighters at the new station.

Tex had been watching Bree, wondering if she'd try to make a break for it before letting him talk to her. As she started to edge away with her friends, he planted himself like a tree in front of her. "Hey, Bree. Can I talk to you for a sec?"

"If you don't want him, I'll keep him busy," a sexy woman with a sparkling, pink tiara offered.

Bree gave him a disdainful once-over. "Trust me, he's no good for you."

"Says you."

Tex winked at Bree. "Well, I say—"

Bree dragged him away before he could finish his sentence, into a quieter area apart from the fracas.

She planted her hands on her trim hips, and he couldn't help noticing her nails matched the horns poking through her honey-blond hair. "Okay, Tex. What do you want?"

He felt suddenly tongue-tied, unable to speak as he drank her in. Damn, but she was pretty, her hair loose and flowing down her back, jeans painted on, T-shirt clinging to her curvy top. The woman was just so tall and toned. Her light-blue eyes shot sparks as she watched him watching her, and he thought the devil horns appropriate.

"Sorry," he said, not meaning it. "But you are rockin' that outfit."

She blushed. "Oh, stop. What do you want?"

"I want a chance. What happened last time wasn't my fault."

"Oh?"

"Darlin'—Bree," he hurried to correct, "I'd broken up with Vanessa two months before we went to dinner. I swear." He crossed his heart, pleased to see her looking at his buff chest. But that didn't seem to impress her enough. She still looked annoyed. "She was stalking me online, so I blocked her. Then she followed me to dinner! That ain't right."

He swore her lips curled into a smile before they flattened. "Okay, so you're not a cheater. You're still a firefighter and serial dater."

"Hey, I never lied. I told you that before we went out." He frowned. "But you never mentioned who your dad was."

"Because I didn't want anyone using me to get up the ladder. You know, in the fire department?"

"Ha ha. Ladder. Funny." He did his best to keep his gaze on her face and not her heaving breasts. Because the girl was breathing pretty heavily, and only a dead man wouldn't notice. "Come on, Bree. I like you. I mean, we connected when we were messaging and talking on the phone, right? I like your looks, sure. You're gorgeous. But you made me laugh, and I thought you liked me."

"I did," she grudgingly conceded.

"Then why not go out for a real date?"

"I've been busy lately."

"With your photography. I know."

"Stalk much?" She raised a brow.

He flushed. "Nah. I just… I looked you up after I found out your name. Same as you did me. Trust me, dating you would not make me popular at the station. I just want to be with you, not your dad."

"Oh, so sex then we move on?" She looked him over. "Sure. When and where?"

"I… Wait." He scowled. "Nope. We aren't gonna just have sex." He felt his face heating and had no idea why, though she seemed fascinated by his discomfort. "Damn it. I just want a chance to get to know you. Is that wrong?"

"I guess not." She still didn't seem sure of him. "We can try again next week, if you want."

"I do." Did he.

Her slow smile mesmerized him. "Okay. I'll unblock you on my phone and message you the details."

"Perfect. See you then."

Four weeks ago

Bree gritted her teeth as she worked the Pets Fur Life calendar shoot, using members of the new Fire Station 44 to make money for the financially challenged charity. She could totally get behind helping strays find good homes. If it took biting back her scathing commentary about Tex McGovern being a no-good liar capable of grinding up a woman's emotions, then so be it.

He lingered near the others, shooting her side-glances but not saying much. Smart of him. She hated to admit it, but in a sea of man candy, Mr. December stood out as the sexiest lollipop of the bunch. She loved his looks and wasn't too superficial to say it. For the shoot, he wore faded jeans, a black T-shirt plastered to his chest, and that stupid cowboy hat that looked way too sexy on him. He might as well have held up a *Ride this Cowboy* sign. Sadly, she'd have to fight herself not to volunteer.

But Bree knew what many didn't—the rest of him didn't match up to the outward hero.

Several inches taller than her own five-eleven, his muscular frame was one anyone would envy. He had shaggy, black hair and light-gray eyes, a square jaw and stubborn tilt to his head. His bronze skin tone only highlighted the brightness of his eyes. She couldn't define one thing she disliked about his looks.

Which she hated.

The blasted man had made her go back on her principles to give him a second chance. She'd let that alleged womanizer back into her life, only for him to show out as someone not worth her time yet again.

She might have believed his ex-girlfriend had set him up on their first date, but Tex standing Bree up on their second date? No warning or explanation of his absence until *two days later*? Who did that? No way she believed that lame excuse that he'd tried to call her and had phone problems.

"Bree?" A pretty woman with bright-blue eyes sidled up to her. "I just wanted to thank you for doing all this. I'm Avery, by the way. I'm doing the pet segment on *Searching the Needle Weekly*."

"Oh, right. I love your Friday morning show. You and Brad are hilarious together." The pair argued with each other and tried to set each other up on a popular streaming channel, as if playing an evil dating game. "And a little more than friends, hmm?" She hadn't missed the kiss Brad had plastered on Avery a few minutes ago. A hop step from beating his chest and proclaiming her his possession, Bree thought, though Avery wasn't complaining.

Avery blushed. "Ah, well, that's new."

"Hey, good for you. But don't stop giving him crap on the show. You ask me, it's good to see a hot fireman taken down a notch."

"You're telling me. Brad's responsible, nice, and handsome. He's a firefighter, a natural-born hero. I'm just a nosy reporter." Avery shrugged. "It's tough going up against Mr. Perfect."

"I'm behind you. Heck, I'd love to adopt one of your strays, that's if I can ever get my schedule under control." Bree had been photographing people and events nonstop for a year. She needed a break, though she couldn't complain the money hadn't been good. "Then again, once the animals appear on your show, they're adopted out pretty quickly. Or is that just made up to look good?"

"No, the animals really are adopted that fast." Avery nodded. "I'm so glad we're helping to find them good homes. I know Pets Fur Life appreciates it. I also know they're thrilled you gave up your time for this. I don't think they could afford to do the calendar without you."

"When Tex mentioned it, I had to help."

Avery studied her. "I didn't realize you knew Tex."

"What gave it away?"

"The way you clenched your jaw when you said his name."

"Ah, that." Bree didn't say any more, and Avery didn't ask.

"Well, I just wanted to come over and thank you for letting me stay through the shoot. It was amazing watching you work."

"It didn't hurt that all my subjects were either cute and furry or handsome, did it?" Bree nodded to the hair stylists busy flirting with several of the guys. She waved at the stylists, who smiled and waved back before turning to the shirtless firemen standing close by.

"Let me add my thanks, boss," her assistant said as she passed. "I love weddings and portraits, but this is why I went into photography. Half-naked men and puppies."

Bree rolled her eyes.

Avery grinned. "I have to agree. Well, I'm taking off. Just wanted to say hi now that you're winding down. Oh, and…"

"Yeah?"

Avery cleared her throat. "This is none of my business. I have no idea what happened between you and Tex before. But he's a great guy. He's genuine."

Bree sighed. "Another one drinking the Kool-Aid."

"I said my piece. And no, he didn't pay me to say that." Avery laughed. "So, now that I've annoyed you by mentioning Tex, how about agreeing to an interview? I don't just do the pet part at *Searching the Needle Weekly*. I run local stories about our community too, and I know our readers would love to know more about you."

"Seriously?"

"Yeah. And with the positive buzz we've been getting, the publicity can only help."

"Sign me up."

They agreed to a time the following week.

Avery left, and once everyone else had cleared out, Bree took one last look around before leaving as well.

The hour had grown dark, but in the parking lot, she spied Tex leaning against his truck, looking at his phone. Her car was the only other vehicle in the lot.

As agreed for doing the shoot, Tex kept his distance. He didn't flirt, and she treated him like a professional model. She'd said the bare minimum, all in regard to the photoshoot, and had been pleasant, if aloof.

In the growing dark, he didn't look at her, and she didn't say anything, just got in her car and left. But in her rearview, she saw him head out after she'd pulled away, turning at the stoplight when she went through.

Huh. What did that mean? And why did it make her heart race that he'd cared enough to see her safely into her car?

Chapter Two

Present day, May 19th

SUNDAY EVENING, AS HE SAT IN HIS LIEUTENANT'S OFFICE, TEX wondered what the hell he thought he was doing. It had been a month since he'd last seen Bree Gilchrist. But not a day had passed that he hadn't thought about the stubborn, leggy blond, wondering what she was up to, if she thought about him, if he had a snowball's chance in hell of talking to her again.

That she'd taken his call about the calendar shoot had been a miracle.

But that hadn't been personal, and he'd contacted her through her business website to set up the project.

A date? Talking person to person? He'd been working up the courage to face her again and to not screw things up a third time.

It was as if fate didn't want them together. The first time, his ex had lied about him being a cheater. The second time, his freakin' cellphone provider had fucked him over but good. His phone had exploded, and they'd given him a real hassle about fixing his service. In the meantime, he'd had no way to get Bree's number to explain the situation—that an emergency he'd encountered had derailed him from their date.

Seeing her at the calendar shoot had been hell. She'd looked even better than he'd remembered, and the station guys had been all over her. Even the married ones had been flirting. *So* not cool. Only Brad had kept his distance, because Brad had Avery.

Sadly, Tex didn't know how to stop thinking about Bree. And now he had an excuse to give in to his urges and be near the woman without being accused of harassing her.

"You're sure you want to volunteer for this?" Ed O'Brien, the C shift lieutenant at Station 44, had proven to be an excellent boss. He had a sense of humor, compassion, and busted his crew's balls on a regular basis. He also had no idea that Tex had a history with the battalion chief's daughter.

Tex cleared his throat. "I'm sure. It's a good opportunity to do something to help the department without looking like I'm sucking up."

"True." Ed studied him.

"I mean, eventually I might want to make it to lieutenant. Doing some quality PR work to help this photographer take pictures for that fancy city grant will give us a good name and make me look like a team player for the higher-ups." Tex couldn't give a rat's ass about promotion. He wanted Bree, and he didn't think Ed would believe he wanted to volunteer his time out of the goodness of his heart.

Ed raised a brow. "So the fact the photographer happens to be an extraordinarily attractive woman has no bearing on your volunteering?"

Tex frowned, trying to appear innocent. "I didn't think about it one way or another, LT."

Ed didn't look as he if bought it, but after a moment, he nodded. "Okay, fine. But we'll pretend I drew names out of a hat. You're the seventh person volunteering to escort this photographer around. But you seem the most honest about your reasoning."

Tex refused to feel badly for lying.

"And if you are lying, at least you've done a better job than Hernandez and the others." Ed sighed. "Look, Tex, this woman happens to be the battalion chief's daughter. He's a friend of mine, as is his daughter."

Tex whistled. "Damn. Really?"

Ed narrowed his eyes and pointed at Tex. "So, you charm the shit out of her and don't even *think* about flirting your way into her bed. You get me?" Ed leaned closer. "Or not only will her father rip you a new one after the captain gets through with you, but I'll be on your sorry ass. And I'm the one you have to worry about every damn day."

Tex swallowed—hard—but forced himself to look casual about the situation. He drawled, "All righty, then, LT." Oh, man, was this turning into a shit show. But then Tex thought about Bree, about how pretty she was, even when mad, and how much he'd missed hearing her laugh or tease him about taking himself too seriously. A few weeks' worth of phone conversations and texts before that date from hell, and he was mooning like a lovesick calf. So pathetic.

Ed was watching him, frowning.

Time to do the smart thing. Tex took a deep breath and let it out, then smiled wide. "Yep, I'm your man."

"You understand this is strictly voluntary? You're off regular duty for the two weeks she's taking pictures. You'll show her around the stations in the city. She can do some ride-alongs if she wants. But you'll be escorting her wherever she wants to go. There's no off duty until her job is over. In other words, this thing is guaranteed to cut into your personal time."

Just what Tex was counting on. "It's okay, LT. It's just for two weeks."

Ed sighed. "Fine. Don't say I didn't warn you." Tex stood, and Ed emphasized, once more, "Keep it in your pants, McGovern. You do *not* want this to blow up in your face."

Tex pulled a nonverbal *aw, shucks* by shrugging and stuffing his hands in his pockets, trying to appear appropriately cowed. "Come on, Lieutenant. It's me."

He was nearly out the door when he heard Ed's muttered, "That's what I'm afraid of."

The next morning during changeover, as Tex was packing up his things to take home for his last forty-eight hours off duty for the next two weeks, Ed called an announcement.

Tex moved with his crew and the rest of C shift, as well as the oncoming D shift, to the main area.

"Okay, people," Ed announced, his hair looking grayer than it had last shift. "FYI, Tex is on the hook for showing the photographer around. To be fair, I drew his name from a hat. I don't want to hear any whining about it. You're welcome." Ed stomped away.

Several turned to Tex to congratulate him while a few taunted him about doing a bang-up job sucking up. Apparently, word had reached the group about the photographer being related to the battalion chief.

Wash, part of the other four-man crew on Tex's shift, said in his trademark Boston accent, "Glad I didn't get picked. Chick is bound to be trouble."

Hernandez nodded. "You and me, brother." They bumped fists.

Tex shrugged. "No problem if I do what I'm supposed to. Show her fires and make sure she don't get burned."

Muttering and teasing continued as Tex hurried without looking like he was rushing out of the station house, hoping to ditch his own crew, who knew the truth.

Unfortunately, Brad, Reggie, and Mack somehow beat him to the parking lot.

Crap. "Hey, guys."

"You are so screwed." Mack shook his head.

Reggie looked sad. "Well, it was nice knowing you." Pause. "Dumbass."

"Hey, I'm trying to be responsible and do the station proud. It's called public re-la-tions," Tex said slowly.

Brad sighed. "First of all, the minute she sees you, she's going to refuse to work with you. And second, you're just going to get your ass handed to you from Ed, because you no doubt failed to tell him you already knew Bree."

"No, no." Tex lowered his voice when a few from his shift passed by them. "That's not it."

Wash shot him a suspicious look and kept on walking.

Tex murmured, "Come on, guys, you know I had to make my move."

"No. Just, no." Reggie shook his head.

"She's gotta know I was straight with her before. This one, she's special."

"Um, her name is Bree, not 'this one.'" Mack rolled his eyes. "Honestly, Tex, if you don't even know her name, this is bound to fail."

"Fuck you."

"Oh, big words." Mack scoffed. "If you were thinking with Tex Sr. instead of Tex Jr., you'd know this is only going to end badly."

Tex *knew* that, but still. It was Bree Gilchrist. He wasn't too proud to admit to himself he had more than a crush on the woman. Even if she did hate his guts. "But she's…" How to explain what he didn't rightly know?

"Her dad won't let her do it. Not with you." Did Brad have *that* right.

"I don't think she mentioned me to her dad, or hell, to anyone. She was pretty serious about not dating firefighters. And now we know why."

Reggie sighed. "Only you, Tex, would be so stupid as to try to make time with a woman who hates your guts *and* has connections. But hey, all for love, right?" Tex heard the bitterness Reggie couldn't hide.

Mack cringed.

"I'll bet twenty on my boy." Reggie wrapped an arm around Tex's shoulders and squeezed before letting go. Guy had a grip like the jaws of death.

Mack shook his head. "I can't take that bet—the money's too easy. Sorry, Tex. But your history says you blow this."

"Thanks a lot." Tex frowned.

Brad held up a hand. "Now hold on. Our Texan has some skills. He just has a messed up idea of how relationships end."

"How's that?" Tex asked.

"The fact that you think they all have to *end*," Brad stated plainly.

"Good point." Mack nodded. "My parents have been happily married for over twenty years. Happy endings aren't just for back alley massage parlors."

Reggie stood with his arms crossed over his chest, his lips toying with a smile. "Mack has a point…about back alleys."

"Well, all of my relationships have ended. I can't help that I have a lot of ex-girlfriends." Tex didn't like feeling defensive. "Not like you losers are all that much better. Brad, you just fixed things with Avery. You don't have much room to talk."

Reggie smirked. "He's got you there."

Brad frowned. "Well, maybe I was a little messed up for a while. But you guys helped me see I was wrong." He smiled through his teeth. "Now I can return the favor."

Mack outright laughed. "This should be good."

"Whatever." Tex didn't have a lot of time to waste. "I have to go home and clean up, then meet the battalion chief at noon. Wish me luck."

"Good luck," Brad, Mack, and Reggie sang at the same time.

Of course, Reggie just had to end it with, "Dumbass."

―――――――――

Monday at noon, Bree chewed her thumbnail, wishing she'd trimmed it this morning instead of forgetting on her way to a late-morning appointment. Fortunately, her client had gotten stuck in traffic, so no one had been left waiting. But now she had a nail that would drive her nuts while having to deal with her overprotective father and the poor schmuck he'd strong-armed into watching over her while she photographed the new fire station and, with any luck, some raging fires that didn't hurt anyone.

Her father sat behind his desk, a tough-looking older man who'd worked his way up from a probie to becoming one of Seattle's battalion chiefs. She was proud of him and loved him dearly. She just wished he'd act a little less smothering in his protectiveness.

"How's your Monday going?" he asked her, leaning back in his chair, his hands locked behind his neck. Still large and imposing, John Gilchrist ran four miles a day, lifted weights religiously, and contended that managing firefighters must be a lot like herding cats that had claws.

"I was running late this morning, but so was my client, so it ended up okay. No problem there. My fingernail is bothering me. My assistant is way too happy to be off for the next month while I do this project. I don't even think she'll miss me. I'm hungry because I haven't had anything to eat yet. And when I called to talk to Charlie earlier, Melissa cut in." She crossed her eyes. "I sense more drama on the home front, Chief."

Her dad sighed. "Yeah. I love your sister, but she's not easy to deal with."

"Gee, that's funny coming from you." How many times had she been scolded to get along with Melissa, her stepsister from hell?

He glared. She glared back.

Bree's mother had passed away when she was just eleven. Two years later, her father had married a wonderful woman who'd always treated Bree with warmth and compassion. Bree loved Charlotte, whom she called Charlie. Unfortunately, Charlie came with baggage—a daughter Bree's age who had major issues with insecurity and jealousy. For a brief time, Bree and Melissa had been like twins, spending all their time together and sharing everything.

The love Bree had for her sister had been wonderful, fulfilling, and all too brief. Sadly, as Melissa had matured, her issues had only grown worse. And the love the two had once held withered, now a bitter thing of envy and loathing, and on Bree's part, wistful regret.

That her father loved his stepdaughter regardless didn't surprise her. John Gilchrist had a huge heart, and he lived to help others. He also had a weak spot for women, treating them far better than many of them deserved. Not that her dad was sexist; far from it. He'd championed her since birth to be whatever she wanted to be. But he couldn't be firm or honest with Melissa, even when she needed it.

"I take it you're doing whatever you can to hide out from the Melissa drama hour." She didn't need him to answer. "Poor Charlie."

He ran a hand over his face. "We're not here to talk about my life. We're here to talk about this project. And again, for the record, I had nothing to do with you being selected to photograph our city's firefighters." He could say what he wanted, but she was sure her connection to one of the city's battalion chiefs hadn't hurt.

John beamed at her. "They chose you on your own merit to win the City Art Grant. That portfolio you submitted to the grant council, who let the chief look it over, was amazing. He's excited that you're going to profile our city's firefighting men and women."

She felt warm all over. "I'm glad you're happy about this."

"Are you kidding?" He sat up straight and pointed at her. "*You* are an amazing artist. But that comes with some pressure. You can't mess this up, Bree."

She groaned. "I know, I know. I need to wrap up my last assignment so I can devote all my time to this project." She glanced at her phone for the time. "Are you sure I need to meet this liaison person now? We can just start up together on Wednesday."

"I want to see how he interacts with you here. Today. With me."

"You mean you want to intimidate the poor guy." Interesting her father had said "he" in reference to her guide. She knew her father would prefer she be guided by a woman. He hadn't been firm with rules while she was growing up, but he'd been adamant that she should *never* date a fireman.

Her dad had a real burr under his saddle about sexed-up

firefighters. Then again, he'd been one until he'd met and married her mother. Since he rarely put his foot down on any subject, she'd been happy enough to accommodate him…until that sexy, obnoxious, dishonest Tex had tried to seduce her to the dark side.

"Intimidate is a strong word," her dad said. "I just want to talk to him."

"Have I met this guy before?" She knew a few of the firefighters in the fifth battalion, but most were older and worked alongside her dad.

Her father glanced at his computer. "His name is Roger McGovern. I don't know him personally, but his reputation is stellar. He's part of a good group of firefighters under Ed O'Brien."

"Oh, I miss seeing Ed."

"Me too. We're going to grab a beer one of these days. Anyway, Ed said McGovern is your guy. I trust you won't have a problem with him."

"So why this meeting?"

Her father put on his stern face. Had she not been his daughter, she'd have been wary. He looked ready to head into battle. "Because I want to make sure I won't have a problem with him."

She groaned. "Dad, I told you. I swear I won't poach your people for my prurient interests." She felt proud about that line, having worked on it for years. "I don't want to get touchy-feely with your peeps."

Her father cringed. "Please. No more."

"I'm not dating right now anyway. I have too much work to focus on."

"Good. Men are assholes."

She chuckled. "You being the exception, of course."

"Of course."

A knock at the door, then the admin secretary popped her head in to say, "Sir, your appointment is here."

He smiled. "Thank you. Show him in, please."

Bree stared in horror as Tex the Almost Ex walked through the door as if he had no idea what awaited him. He wore jeans and a Seattle FD T-shirt, not an official uniform, so he must have been off duty. To her bemusement, he carried a cowboy hat in hand.

He stood before her father's desk behind the chair next to her and introduced himself, not glancing her way. "Sir, I'm Roger McGovern, here about the photographer assignment." His Texas drawl was evident, as was his charm when he smiled at her dad and added, "But please, call me Tex. I only get called Roger when my momma is yellin' at me about somethin' one of my brothers did but blamed me for."

Her father smiled back.

Damn it. Don't fall for his charm, Dad! It's like quicksand that sucks you in until you're dead and gone. And seriously pissed off.

"Tex, please have a seat. This is the photographer you'll be working with, Bree Gilchrist." Her father cleared his throat and in a deeper voice added, "My daughter."

"Ma'am." Tex shook her hand briefly, all professionalism, before sitting. "It's a pleasure."

Her eyes narrowed, sensing his amusement. *Oh, so we're going to play the we-don't-know-each-other game. Fine.* She spared a glance at her dad, who watched her closely, then turned a pleasant face on the jerk. "Tex, is it?"

Tex nodded.

"I'm Bree. I know you've been told what to expect, but we're here to make sure this is a good fit. The City Art Grant is a really big deal."

Tex nodded. "Yes, ma'am. I know. Good coverage is a big deal to all of us, especially at the new station, and we want to do the city—and your dad—proud. I won't screw it up. I swear."

She wanted to slap him, having been burned twice before. "Great." Her grin felt brittle. "Then let me make something perfectly clear. We do this my way. I won't be patronized or worked around. I'm not here to make friends. I'm here to take pictures. Period. You got that?"

"Yes, ma'am." A hard look settled over his features, making him look more like a western gunslinger than a firefighter. "But make no mistake, if there's a dangerous situation, and you want to get closer to snap some shots, it ain't happening. Your safety is my first concern."

She frowned. "Now hold on. I'm in charge."

"Of your work, yes. But when it comes to keeping you fire-free, *I'm* in charge. And there's no question about that."

Surprised he'd be so firm with her in front of her father, she turned to her dad to catch his reaction.

John Gilchrist nodded, and she could see the approval in his eyes. "Sounds perfect, Tex. If you need anything at all, you let me know. And I mean contact me. I don't need you running this up the chain. When it comes to this project, I'm overseeing it."

"Yes, sir." Tex paused. "But I'll make sure to keep my lieutenant in the loop if it's all the same to you. He likes to know what I know."

Her dad grinned. "Yes, best not to keep Ed out of the loop. He's the vindictive type."

Tex laughed. "You should see what he… Um, I mean, yes, sir."

Bree didn't like how chummy Tex and her father seemed, all of a sudden. "Is that it, Chief?" she asked, her sarcasm evident. "I have work to get back to." She stood.

Her father frowned. "Sorry to keep you. Tex, nice meeting you."

Tex stood and reached out to the grab the hand her father offered. "You too, sir." He turned to Bree and held his hand out. "Ma'am."

"Call me Bree, damn it." She shook his hand, hating that frisson of warmth that filled her at the contact, before pulling away and watching him leave.

"What's going on?" her father asked, his voice a little too quiet.

"Nothing. I can just tell this is one of those types you're always warning me about."

"Really?" His eyes narrowed. "I thought Tex seemed reasonable. What did I miss?"

Him ditching me twice. But no way she'd tell her father that. "Nothing. Maybe it's that Southern accent. And all the sir-ing and ma'aming he was doing."

Her father relaxed and chuckled. "Reminds me of my visit to Houston a few years ago. He even had the hat to go with the accent." He shrugged. "If you're that bothered, I can assign someone else, I suppose."

Yes. And bring my personal issues into my professional life—something I swore I'd never do. "No. I've got this. If I have a problem with him, I'll handle it."

"You'll tell me, and *I'll* handle it," her dad insisted.

"Yeah, yeah. I'm twenty-seven, Dad. I can deal with my own problems. Not that good old boy Roger McGovern is a problem." Roger. Ha. He was no more a Roger than she was a Guinevere—the name she'd secretly longed for after watching one too many Robin Hood movies as a kid. Nope. Bree was no damsel in distress, fought over by rival hunks. She made her own way in the world and didn't need a man for anything more than moving furniture or having sex. And even that she usually did better alone than with a partner.

And I'm thinking about sex with my dad right there.

Her cheeks burned. "I've got to go, Dad. A quick lunch then back to finishing up some portrait sessions for Carrie." Her best friend forever, Carrie could always be counted on for a sarcastic quip or laugh. Something Bree needed just now.

"Tell her I said hello." He stood and crossed the room to hug her. "I'll be checking in, so if Tex makes a wrong move, you let me know."

"I will." She kissed him on the cheek and left, quickly exiting the building, a million things to do on her mind.

And ran into Tex McGovern leaning against a wall, waiting for her while wearing that sexy-as-sin cowboy hat and looking like a poster child for male strippers everywhere. Could his jeans be any tighter?

"I can explain," he said in a rush as she pushed past him toward her car down the street. "Come on, Bree. Hold on."

When he caught her sleeve, she stopped and glared at him. "Get off."

He let go and held his hands up in surrender. "I volunteered for this gig of yours."

She watched him, hating that every time she saw him, she found him even more attractive than the last time. Then again, deviant personalities came in all shapes and sizes. The Ted Bundy special on Netflix was proof of that. "Did you know you'd be helping me and not some random photographer?"

He nodded. "Yep. Look, the first time we met, my ex-girlfriend sabotaged me. The second time we met, it was over a fight in a bar."

She waited. "And? Is this a prelude to you standing me up this coming Wednesday too?"

He shifted on his feet. "Look, on our last date, I was on my way to you but stopped to help when a house caught fire. I lost my phone on the property, and it exploded before I could get it back. I swear." He handed her a folded piece of paper from his back pocket. "Proof. Look, those are the emails between me and the phone company. I ain't lyin.'" His accent seemed to grow thicker when he was agitated.

She humored him, reading the conversation between Tex and a superpolite phone company employee who didn't help so much as try to placate a crazy man. "You used the words 'plumb pissed-off' in your email?" She had to work not to smile. "Interesting."

He groaned. "I'm telling you, I wasn't lying. It's like I'm not meant to be with you or something." He sounded miserable. "Every time I try to go out with you, something bad happens. So, when this opportunity to help you came up, I jumped on it. And no, I didn't tell anyone I knew you. I just wanted…"

"What? Another chance to see if you could get in my pants?"

He glared at her, and the menace he exuded turned her on. Oh, great. Tex played the bad boy perfectly. Another way he played to her type. Best not to ever let him know.

"I'm done trying to convince you I'm a nice guy. Proof is in the doing." He crossed his arms over his chest, the corded muscle impossible to miss, especially in that clingy T-shirt.

Bree sighed. "Look, I know I came off as a little bitchy in there."

"A little?"

She scowled. "But my dad has no idea we ever went out. And we're going to keep it that way. Me, because I don't want to disappoint him. You, because you want to keep your job." Ah, that had him looking worried. Good. "This working together is a professional thing, one I can't afford to screw up. I forgive you for before, but we go on as associates. Business colleagues. Nothing else. Got it?"

Tex just stared at her, and the intense scrutiny he gave her face, staring into her eyes, made those blasted butterflies in her belly take rapid flight with no sign of settling down.

"Tex?"

He gave a slow nod. "Got it. I swear not to mess up either of our jobs." He swallowed. "Can I just ask what your dad has against firefighters? I mean, he is one, right?"

She sighed. "I have no idea. I only know that's the one area of my life my dad is insane about. He doesn't want me dating a fireman. Ever. I don't even know why I agreed to go out with you in the first place."

He looked like he wanted to say something but kept his mouth shut and nodded instead. "Where do you want to meet Wednesday? At the station?"

"At Sofa's in Green Lake for breakfast. Be there at nine, okay?"

He nodded. "That's sleeping in for me. No problem. See you then." He walked away, no more innuendo, no sly winks or teasing. And she reminded herself that it was for the best, because no way she and Tex would end well in a more intimate relationship. Which really was too bad.

The butterflies inside her had yet to settle down as she watched that fine ass walk away.

Chapter Three

TUESDAY NIGHT, TEX SAT WITH THE GUYS AT REGGIE'S obsessively neat house for a late-night barbecue. Tex would have managed the grilling, but Mack had volunteered, leaving Tex to enjoy a beer with Brad and Reggie. Talk, of course, centered around his upcoming volunteer work for a certain photographer.

"I hope you know you're putting the rest of us in a bad spot." Brad grabbed a handful of chips. "They're sending over someone from Madison Park to cover for you. And I have to partner with him since Reggie won Mack on the coin toss."

"Not sure that's a win," Reggie muttered. "He talks. A lot."

Brad grinned.

Tex frowned. "Reggie, you and Mack normally pair together. Why did you let Brad sucker you into a coin toss?"

"It just seemed fairer to let fate pick the loser." Reggie shrugged. "Besides, ever since Brad started dating Avery, he's all emotional all the time. He was whining about something or other, then he started crying. I couldn't take it. Frankly, Brad, it was embarrassing."

Tex nodded. "Oh, right. When he was bawlin' his eyes out Sunday night. Damn, son. It was a *Chicago Fire* rerun, and they did save the day."

Reggie laughed. "They always do—no matter how dramatic it is."

Brad growled, "I cried on Sunday because some asshole shoved a handful of jalapeños into my turkey sub without me knowing." Brad gave Tex the eye. "I about had a heart attack."

"Whoa, now. It wasn't me. I'd have used habaneros, maybe ghost peppers. Jalapeños? Please. Besides, we all know you can't handle hot stuff. You can barely handle Avery."

"Truth." Reggie held up a hand, and Tex slapped it.

"It was Wash," Reggie said. "And probably Mack. I swear, our little Air Force is getting way too chummy with the rest of C shift."

"No kidding." Tex shook his head. "Mack and Wash have been working on pranking the lieutenant."

The crew at the station lived to tease each other. It had started innocently enough with one of the firefighters' kids leaving a doll behind after visiting. A Ken doll, which did actually look like Brad, started doing odd things to Barbies and other monstrous action figures found in the station in odd places. Then the station's other lieutenant, Sue Arthur, who resembled Dora the Explorer, started finding Dora stickers on her notebooks and the cute little doll sitting at her desk. Everyone at the station thought it hilarious, Tex included.

"They're pranking Ed?" Brad laughed. "Oh, that's why they were messing around with an old A-Team action figure. Ed does kind of remind you of Hannibal. If Hannibal were twenty pounds lighter, with less gray, and a few inches taller."

Tex frowned. "Hannibal?"

Brad sighed. "He's a character from an old eighties show my mom used to like. Never mind."

Reggie grinned. "It was a great show. Wait. You know, I think they did a skit on *Family Guy* about that."

Tex stopped Reggie before he got on one of his pop culture kicks. "No one cares, Reggie."

"Ass."

Tex ignored him. "Anyhow, ever since Ken left Barbie for Pup Patrol—on your behalf," Tex said to Brad, "everyone's talking about how funny it would be to get Ed. He's the only guy left no one's ever fucked with."

"Yeah, the LT should know better than to think he's immune." Reggie snorted. "Ed needs to realize he's fair game."

Tex liked seeing his buddy in a better mood. His breakup with Amy months ago had left a sore spot Reggie liked to pretend didn't exist, but he hadn't been himself for too long.

"Just don't involve me in it," Tex told them. "I'm on thin ice bein' with Bree and all. Ed warned me not to screw things up."

"You mean, not to screw Bree," Reggie clarified.

"Well, yeah." Tex finished his beer and got up to get more from Reggie's fridge. He returned with seconds for the guys as well. "Bree gave me the speech, like I thought she might."

He'd already told them how his meeting with Chief Gilchrist had gone. "She's pretty serious about me not doing anything to mess with her project. Not that I would." He'd been thinking about nothing but Bree and her ideas since yesterday afternoon's meeting. "But I'm telling you both. That woman is mine."

Mack had returned at that moment, and the whole crew stared at Tex as if he'd grown a third eye.

Mack frowned. "Wait. Say that again?"

"My future girlfriend wants nothing to do with me. I have to trick her into trying me on for size. And with her daddy against her dating a fireman, it's not going to be easy."

Mack frowned. "Did you hit your head or something?"

"Are you drunk?" Brad asked.

"He has to be." Reggie nodded. "Because trying to seduce a woman who continually tells you no sounds a lot like stalking. Or assault. Hmm, and what's another buzz word, Brad?"

"Career suicide?" Mack offered.

"That's two words," Tex muttered.

"Oh, wait, I know a few." Brad smiled, though there was nothing funny about what he was saying. "Hashtag MeToo. Criminal offense. Jail time. Getting fired."

"Whoa, whoa." Tex put his beer down and waved a finger at them. "I'm not gonna stalk her or hurt her. Jesus. Relax, you guys. I'm talking about showing her how great I am then stepping back. That way *she* makes all the moves. See, I'm going to let her fall in love with me. Because a gentleman always lets a lady set the pace."

"Oh, *that's* what he meant." Reggie scoffed. "You are so going to get yourself in trouble from this. Tex, man, we can only cover for you so long before Ed and the captain—and the freakin' battalion chief—fire your ass."

"For what?"

"Being stupid," Mack and Brad said together.

Tex frowned. "I'd never hurt a woman."

"We know that." Brad sighed. "But Tex, you don't seem to be thinking straight about Bree. You haven't been for months."

"I'm crushin' on her. I admit it."

Reggie scowled. "You barely know her. Trust me. Love doesn't guarantee a happily ever after."

Mack nodded. "He's right."

"But if I don't try, I can't…" Tex couldn't explain it to them. Heck, he could barely explain it to himself. He felt things for Bree that made no sense. And he needed to know if he was experiencing infatuation, lust, or something else. Something he thought he might really feel for the woman. And that had nothing to do with sex and everything to do with affection and respect, which usually took a lot longer for him to feel.

And he'd know, having dated. *A lot.*

"Okay, okay." Reggie surprised him by standing and supporting him. "We're behind you, man. But you have to be smart. Go slow. Do your charm thing that doesn't seem like it's intentional."

"And use the hat." Mack nodded to Tex's Stetson sitting on the couch. "Ladies dig the hat."

Brad seemed to reluctantly agree. "Yeah, even Avery likes it. But like Reggie said, be smart. Do all the dancing you want but let her make the first move."

"Fellas, I know no means no," Tex teased. They didn't smile back. "I swear. I'm smarter than I look."

"And thank God for that," Mack said. "Anyway, I came in to let you know dinner's almost ready." He grabbed a platter from the kitchen and went out back again.

Reggie headed toward the dining table. "Look, Tex. If you like the girl, I'm with you. But I'm also worried, because you normally have more sense than to fuck with your future."

"What Reggie said." Brad stood and met with the rest of them around a large dining table, where Mack set a platter of ribs and burgers, joining plates of burger fixings, buns, and some potato and macaroni salads.

As the four of them sat and ate, the familiar camaraderie settled, giving Tex what he'd missed when he'd left home and again what he'd lost in leaving the Marine Corps. He loved all his families: the one he'd been born into, the one he'd served his country with, and the one now seated around Reggie's table.

Though their caution about Bree grated, he knew they cared, which made for frank talk. They shared what they needed to in a safe space, something Tex never took for granted. Maybe because he'd known too many guys who'd had nobody, and he understood the gift of brotherhood he had with these men.

"Reggie, what's up with you? The truth," he said, knowing Reggie needed to do something about his attitude before it ate him up inside. "I've been honest about Bree. I'm love-bit, and I'm stupid. I know. But I won't make the same mistake twice. Then we have Brad, who finally did right by Avery. He's in a good place." Tex glanced at Mack and grinned. "And our car-lovin' brother is content with his Chevelle. That leaves you and your pissy attitude."

Reggie glared, but when Tex didn't break his stare, the big guy groaned. "You guys need to give me some space, okay?"

Brad snorted. "Um, no. We did that for months. Tell us what's up. You need a date? Avery knows people."

"I have a few friends who have friends," Tex said, though he'd been planning to steer clear of his exes on account of his plan to woo Bree. But for his buddy, he'd revisit the past.

"And *I* know women too." Mack scowled when the guys just looked at him. "I do."

"I don't need a hookup, thanks," Reggie growled. "Amy fucked with my head, okay? Is that what you want to hear?"

Tex huffed. "Man, we already knew that. But that was a while ago. What are you thinkin' now, hoss?"

"God, not more cowboy talk," Mack complained. "But yeah, what Tex said. Come on, Reggie. You're no fun anymore. Always mad at everything. And let's all be honest here. The breakup wasn't your fault. You were great with Amy from the beginning. You even loved her kid."

"Rachel." Reggie swallowed.

"Yeah," Brad said, his voice soft. "We know Amy messed you up by leaving. But brother, it's her loss. You still have us."

"And your dad and sisters," Tex added. "You never did tell us what they had to say about Amy leaving." At Reggie's look, Tex stared. "You didn't tell them?"

"No. I just said we were done." Reggie squirmed, which was funny, seeing a guy that big and intimidating threatened by his much smaller sisters. "Lisa and Nadia would kill her. And then Rachel would be without a dad *and* a mom."

"No shit. Your sisters scare me," Mack said and made the sign of the cross. "But tell them I said hi and how much I admire them, just in case 'hi' offends them."

Which had everyone laughing. Reggie's sisters were gorgeous, funny, and mean to anyone who messed with their younger brother.

Tex smiled. "Look, you need to realize you'll find your own Miss Right someday. If Brad can do it, surely the rest of us can."

"Real funny, Tex." Brad didn't look pleased.

"But it's true. You just have to get outta that hero mindset and let some fine woman be there for *you*," Tex told Reggie, which all of them knew but Reggie never wanted to hear. "Amy always needed rescuing. Well, she rescued herself out of a fine man. Now she's done and gone." *And good riddance.* The woman had used

Reggie for way too long. "Little Rachel was lucky to have known you. Now, since Avery and Bree are clearly taken, you need to find yourself some other woman. And that means getting out there again."

"Please, no more." Reggie seemed to sink into himself. "My father is dating again, and he's been giving me dating advice." He looked sick. "If it's all the same to you guys, let's talk about something else. I promise, I'll get back to scoping out women."

"By the end of the month, or I'll have Avery trying to hook you up live on the internet," Brad said.

Tex laughed. "That's the way. Get Reggie on the show to adopt some Pets Fur Life critters. And speaking of which, the calendar was a success, so I hear."

Brad nodded. "I talked to Avery's roommate, who's been taking on more responsibility with the charity. Oscar too," Brad said proudly. His brother had been dating said roommate and getting his life on a good track.

Tex liked the guy, which reminded him to give Oscar a call back. He'd left a message yesterday, but Tex hadn't yet listened to it. "I'll give him a call."

"Why do you talk to Oscar more than I do?"

Because I miss my own brothers, and Oscar reminds me of Wyatt. "Jealous, Ken?" The Barbie/Ken shot was always good for a zing, especially because Brad got that lemon face when anyone used it…like now. Tex grinned. "Don't be. I like to keep track of the animals, is all. Unless you'd rather I talked to Avery more about it. I mean, with her and the adoption show and all. She seems to have a thing for buff guys. Sadly, she settled for you. Imagine what the hottest guy in Station 44 could do for her?" He flexed.

Brad's face turned red, which had the rest of them snickering. "Fuck you. Leave my woman alone. Talk to Oscar all you want." His expression turned sly. "Or, you know, we could have you and *Bree* guest star on Avery's show. I'll bet Avery would love to interview

Bree about how she knows you and what she really thinks of you, Tex."

"Ah, no." He could just see their show getting too much attention…from her father, his captain, and Ed, not to mention everyone at the station. "I'm good. Say, who wants more ribs?"

The others laughed, and talk turned to D shift and who they expected to take Sue's spot when she took her yearly two-week vacation.

But Tex couldn't stop thinking about how to behave the next morning and if he should be cool or turn up the heat with Bree. Hmm. Decisions, decisions…

———————

Tuesday evening, Bree half-heartedly enjoyed a box of caramel corn on Carrie's couch while her best friend stared a hole through her forehead.

Bree squirmed. "Stop. You're making me self-conscious."

Carrie raised a brow, the same one that, when used in the courtroom, often had witnesses spilling the truth to cut through Carrie's awful silences and uncomfortable stares.

"Oh? Do you feel terrible for being a glutton and hogging all the caramel corn yourself? Or because you know that consuming that much sugar means the fat goes right to your thighs?" Carrie smiled, but the barb still stung.

Bree tossed a handful of her treat at Carrie, who watched the caramel corn fall to the ultraclean carpet of her living room floor and scowled. "I'm not cleaning that up."

Bree slouched on the couch, maneuvering to lie faceup while hanging her head upside down over the cushions. Carrie looked less scary from a different perspective. "Relax, neatnik. I'll pick it up in a minute."

"I'm still waiting to hear why you didn't tell your father about that asshole with the nice pecs." Carrie's description of Tex.

Bree sighed.

"You're so pathetic."

"I know." Bree groaned.

Carrie's dark eyes should have been warm, the brown having a deeper richness than her cropped, platinum-blond hair. But the woman had taken the nickname "Ice Queen" to heart. Six-two, white, and rail-thin, Carrie still looked like the runway model she'd once been with an angular face full of contrasts—an irregular beauty that had sold a lot of copy and clothes from all the top designers. For a while, she and Bree had modeled together, touring Italy and Paris before finishing with a stint in southern Germany Bree still thought of with fondness.

But Carrie had bailed from a life of fake perfection at the same time Bree had. For different reasons, but the result had been the same. Carrie had left the looks business for good and focused on her law career instead.

"Do you ever regret that you never went pro?" Bree asked out of the blue, switching topics to Carrie's other career.

Without missing a beat, Carrie answered, "Nope. By now I'd have knee and ankle injuries, and I'd be constantly worried about being kicked off the team." Carrie had played four years of varsity basketball for the Oregon Beavers. But instead of continuing into the WNBA, she'd been discovered by a modeling scout and entered the tricky world of high fashion. "Besides, after my scholarship, the modeling paid for my law school. Cha-ching."

"Paid for my cameras and business start-up too. Another cha in your ching."

Carrie raised a glass of apple juice and clinked glasses with Bree's, which remained on the coffee table while Bree hung partly upside down.

Carrie shot her a look. "So, what's your damage tonight, woman? I thought you said the horny cowboy looked too good to be true and you were glad to be done with him. Now you're telling me you two will be working together for the next two weeks while you shadow the fire department. Why?"

"I wish I knew." Bree slowly sat back up, letting the blood rush from her head and enjoying the dizzy feeling. "Dad liked him, but when he mentioned maybe assigning someone else, I couldn't go through with it. First of all, that would be letting my personal life interfere with my professional one. I mean, Tex's lieutenant gave him the okay. He might be a dick, but he seems good at his job."

"Okay, that's first of all." Carrie nodded. "What's second?"

"Second, there's no way I can let my dad know I even *thought* about dating a fireman."

"So, you're twenty-seven and still being bossed around by your daddy." After a pause, Carrie added, "Having met John Gilchrist, I concede your point. What else?"

"My third and final issue…I still get nervous when he's around."

"Your dad? I know. We just confirmed that you're a twenty-seven-year-old tween."

"No, doofus. Tex." Thoughts of him stirred an odd sensation in her belly, a flurry of excitement she had a hard time ignoring. "He's freaking hot, and he keeps acting like he's totally into me. It's messing with my head."

"You—"

"I know I should kick him firmly to the curb," Bree interrupted. "I meant to. I did twice before. Then he makes these excuses, and I find myself wanting to believe him."

"Hell, I'm just glad I don't have to go up against that charmer in court." Carrie shot her a disgusted look. "I should pity you."

"Shut up."

"But instead, I'm deeply ashamed. Your honor, I call to the stand…"

"No. Please, not the fake court proceedings."

"…Ms. Bree Needs a Man to Be Complete."

"Ambulance chaser."

Carrie chuckled. "So sad."

Bree frowned. Even she knew that corporate litigation was worlds away from tort litigation. "I tried. Lame lawyer. Crooked counselor. Ha!"

Carried rolled her eyes.

"Ack. I know. They're pathetic. Just pick an insult."

"You're out of order." Carrie's dark eyes sparkled. "Now, Ms. Needs a Man, please tell the court why you can't say no to the long, tall Texan."

"I need to get laid."

"Granted. And?"

"And I need to have better standards because I only deserve someone who will treat me right." Bree both loathed and loved these conversations with Carrie. They reminded her of all she'd overcome up to this point in her life. And all she still had to work on. "Why can't I be more like you?"

"The judge would normally overrule this as outside the scope of the question, but I'll allow it." Carrie gave her a smug smile. "Go on. Tell the court why I'm so worthy of emulation."

"You and your million-dollar words," Bree muttered. She cleared her throat, took a sip of juice, and just said it. "You go your own way and fuck everyone else. They tell you you've gained a few too many pounds for a photoshoot? You tell the photographer to kiss your ass. The agent isn't pleased with your attitude? He can go fuck himself. Your boss tries to sexually harass you? You laugh in his face and tell him he's the reason you're a lesbian."

"He's not, but the insult was too good to pass up. What else?" Carrie waved at her to continue.

"Isn't that enough?"

"No. I also don't cleave to put-downs from a jealous stepsister. I'm okay admitting I go to therapy because it's not a big deal. It's called being *normal*." She pointedly looked at Bree's blushing cheeks. "And I'm happily hopping beds at the moment because I can't decide if Cheryl or Mattie fits me best, and until I'm ready to commit, I need to be free to choose. And they both know about it because I'm not a dog."

"A bitch is a female dog, and you claim to like being a b-word."

"I am a bitch, and I wear the moniker with pride. But I'm not a liar or a cheat. I don't have ex-girlfriends throwing water on me in a restaurant. When I say I'll be there for a date, I'm there, or I communicate if I'll be late."

"All good points."

"I know." Carrie flicked invisible lint off her suit jacket, because yes, Carrie liked to relax while still styling. The weirdo.

"I wish I could be so confident."

"Hey, it's taken a lot of years and a lot of wading through other people's bullshit to get this fierce. But at least your parents aren't homophobes. So, I've got that *not* going for me."

They clinked glasses again and finished off their juices. "Am I winning or losing this court case, your honor? I can't remember."

"Well, you're a loser because you threw perfectly good caramel corn all over my carpet."

"Nag, nag." Bree picked up the pieces and tossed them in the kitchen trash before joining Carrie once more. "I know I should talk to a therapist about this new inability to steer clear of problem men." At least she'd been doing better to put her animosity toward Melissa on the backburner.

"It's only one problem *man*, though, isn't it? You haven't been dating in a while."

"True. I've been so busy with work, I haven't had the time." Which should have rung true for the too-attractive fireman. There was just something about Tex McGovern. She wished she could easily forget him. Unfortunately, the memory of him had stuck with her for months. "Like a bad case of the plague," she muttered.

"When you start talking to yourself, I get really worried." Carrie laughed at the finger Bree gave her. "Easy, girl. You know this will work out okay. Just do your job, keep your legs closed, and remember that 'sex' is a three-letter word."

"So what?"

"So, 'love' is a four-letter word. And that's what you really want, isn't it?"

"I hate to tell you this, but 'fuck' is a four-letter word too. And it's the word my brain seems stuck on whenever I look into Tex's lying eyes." Eyes that happened to be silver, enticing, and confusing—that about summed up Tex McGovern in a nutshell.

"For God's sake." Carrie huffed. "Your problem is you're pent up. Go have a nice night with one of the guys in your little black book."

"Um, it's pink. I tossed the black book a few months ago."

Carrie sneered. "Pink. Ugh. Why not add more stereotypes to your life? You're a girl who loves pink. And what, are you a dumb blond too? A daddy's girl?"

"Hey. I like pink. I'm not stupid—"

"Debatable."

"—but I do love my dad."

Carrie paused. "Well, actually I do too. Pink is fun, and your dad's amazing. But we don't want to satisfy anyone's expectations. We mean to break them. No, even better, exceed them."

"Um, er, right." Even for Carrie, her zeal tonight seemed a bit much.

Carrie must have realized it. "Sorry, I'm so buzzy. I won our case today for my client. She kept the majority of the company…worth twenty-five million! Her scum-sucking partner was nearly crying when we were done. My bosses are super happy with me." Carrie beamed. "So, I'm a little man-hating and anti-bad-relationships tonight. I know, I don't do divorce work, but corporate work can feel like a divorce when the company breaks up. And my client's partner was a huge dick."

"Geez, Carrie. Why didn't you lead with your win when I walked in the door?" Bree gave her best friend a huge hug before settling back on the couch. "Instead, you let me go on and on about my pathetic problems. I'm so happy for you!"

"Me too." Carrie smiled, and that genuine joy melted her icy demeanor, leaving her the warm, loving woman Bree had clicked with upon first meeting. Though very different, the two of them were soul sisters. That Melissa hated Carrie only made it more obvious what a gem Bree had found in her best friend.

She firmed her resolve. "I'll deal with Tex. He's nothing more than a blip on my professional radar."

"Good for you. And hey, if it gets too bad, just sleep with him and get him out of your system. Then work the hell out of your new grant project."

"I can do that. Not the sex part, but the picture taking."

"Uh-huh." Carrie gave her the eye. "Just remember that any man who looks like Tex and has that many exes isn't the safest guy to sleep with, if you get my meaning."

"Not going there."

"Right. I'll tuck a few condoms in your bag just in case."

"Do it and die."

Carrie stood and looked down at her.

"Well, you'll metaphorically die from all my loathing and disdain." Bree paused, then muttered, "Not like I could reach that scrawny neck to strangle you."

"It's good to have dreams, little girl."

"You know only three inches separate us, right?"

Carrie's grin looked more menacing than happy. "Whatever. Now quit it with all the chitchat and let me tell you about this hot waitress I was talking to during my lunch break."

"What about Cheryl and Mattie?"

"Hey, I have a lot of love to give. Don't rain on my million-dollar parade."

"And you call Tex a stud? You could give him lessons in breaking hearts."

"Aw, you say the sweetest things."

Chapter Four

WEDNESDAY MORNING, BREE WATCHED TEX STROLL INTO Sofa's Bakery at nine on the dot, swaggering like he owned the place. After having wrangled with one of the owners, a kind though sarcastic friend Bree had known since her modeling days, she now sat with a vanilla latte she hadn't asked for as well as a tray full of goodies. Apparently, a plain coffee and breakfast cookie were "way too pedestrian" for a woman like her. Who knew?

"He makes one wrong move toward you and I'll end him," Elliot, her overzealous friend, had threatened before seating her near the front counter, where he'd be able to overhear everything.

But as Tex ambled—there was no other word for his lazy but controlled stride—toward her table, Elliot muttered, "Holy croissant, but that man is buttery goodness all rolled up into hot crossed buns…of steel. Would you look at those thighs." He winked at her, intentionally overdoing it to make her laugh.

She had to bite her lip not to, though she mentally agreed. She shot the busybody a dark look to let him know what she thought of his comments.

"Sorry, sorry." Elliot left her to help his sister fix a few drinks and serve new customers.

Wearing a working uniform of dark-blue Nomex pants, a button-up Seattle FD shirt, and dark-black boots, Tex looked like a walking advertisement to protect and serve. Or, you know, strip down on a stage.

She itched to take a few photos of him and forced herself to relax. He nodded at her. "Mornin', Bree."

"And that accent," she heard clearly from Elliot's direction. "Cream my bagel and butter my toast."

Bree coughed to cover her laughter.

"Ease up, Elliot." His sister sighed. "It's going to be a long-ass morning."

"Good morning," Bree said to Tex, hoping he hadn't heard or understood Elliot talking about him. The man didn't need another fan in his corner. "Have a seat."

He sat, said nothing more, and waited.

She waited in silence with him.

After a minute, he smiled. Which caused her to smile then try to hide it with a frown.

His smile grew wider.

Elliot brought a coffee for Tex. "Welcome to Sofa's. Any friend of Bree's is a friend of mine."

Where the hell had the threats and taking her side gone? The way of a pretty face, that's where. She shot Elliot another dirty look. He winked and left, whistling.

She glared after him. "I'm not leaving you a tip."

He snorted and turned around to wave at Tex. "Enjoy the food, and don't let Miss Bossy keep you away when you become addicted to me."

Trust Elliot to add his own flavor to her morning.

Tex blinked. "Addicted to *him*?"

"To his food. He takes his catering and baking seriously." She bit into an apricot tart and cursed Elliot for being so good at his job.

When she'd finished the treat, she noted Tex staring at her. "What?"

"I've never seen anyone eat so fast in my life. And I live and work with people constantly on the go."

She ignored the heat in her cheeks. "I like sweets."

He sipped his coffee and polished off his croissant, a blondie, and two pastries before he said, "You broke the silence first, so I win."

"Real mature, *Roger.*"

He flushed. "I hate that name."

"It doesn't quite fit, does it?" She laughed. "Fine, you win." Pause. "Roger."

"Call me Tex, or I'll make the next two weeks miserable."

It took her a moment to process the threat, because it had been delivered so politely in that deep voice. Man, he might be able to hold his own in an argument with Carrie. "Don't get your panties in a knot…Tex." She loved that she'd gotten under his skin. His warm, manly, rough-where-it-counted skin.

She blew out a breath, calming her unwelcome arousal. *Real professional, Bree.*

Tex cocked his head, appearing concerned. "You all right?"

Now feeling like an idiot, she cleared her throat and nodded. "Peachy. Okay. Do-over. *Tex,* for the next two weeks, you're my shadow while we move through the city and Seattle's Fire Department. I'm open to what you have to show me. And I'd appreciate it if you treated this seriously."

"Trust me. I know this is a big deal. With my LT, captain, and the battalion chief watching where this goes, I'll be on my *best* behavior."

She didn't trust that smile. It looked sincere and innocent, but she'd swear something darker lurked behind Tex's silver-eyed promise.

"Okay then. This should go well."

"I hope so." He waited for her to finish a croissant, because what the hell, she needed a boost in fortitude, then left a large tip in the jar on the counter before walking her to her car. "Follow me to the station, and we'll take the 'company car.'" He used air quotes. "I'm authorized to use a battalion vehicle for your project."

"Okay."

He looked her over, grunted, then left for his truck.

"Huh. What did that mean?" She followed after him, focusing

on what kind of shots she wanted to get, pictures of the hardworking firefighters of Seattle doing a sometimes thankless job. Of them interacting with the community, surely. And with any luck— and she felt terrible hoping for it—some really big fire (where no one got hurt) that she could capture on film.

She arrived at Seattle's newest fire station and parked near Tex's truck. Station 44, part of her father's battalion, sat between the Beacon Hill, NewHolly, and South Beacon Hill areas, providing greater assistance to Fifth Battalion's responsibilities.

The outside looked typical: a large, two-story, brick building situated on a busy road. The attached bay, otherwise known as a garage, housed the engine and medical vehicles. The building itself provided a large area for the thirty-six firefighters and administrators who worked there—not all at the same time, obviously.

"You ready to go inside and look around?" Tex asked, now wearing a Station 44 ballcap.

"What is it with you and hats?" she asked, gripping her camera bag. "You going bald or something?" Not that a lack of hair would harm his good looks.

He held a hand over his heart. "Words can wound, Ms. Gilchrist. Bald? Please. We McGoverns never go bald. Gray, sure. But that's on account of the women in our lives."

"I dare you to say that to your mother." She squelched a tingle of excitement when he put a hand on the small of her back to guide her inside the open bay housing the engine truck, E44. Several men were cleaning Aid 44, one of the medical trucks beside it, and stopped to stare.

"I'm not as stupid as I must look," Tex said with a grin. "No way in hell I mess with my momma. She's got a mean right."

"No, he really is as dumb as he looks." Mack came forward, all smiles. "I just want to apologize in advance."

She took a cautious step back and bumped into Tex. Mack, with that large grin and bright eyes, was a hunk of man candy for sure. And an all-around nice guy she'd enjoyed during the calendar shoot a month ago. "Apologize for what?"

"That you have *that* guiding you around." He nodded at Tex. "They didn't choose me to show you around, I think because the LT was afraid you'd be too distracted by all this"—he waved a hand at himself—"to get your work done."

She laughed; she couldn't help it. "Oh, right. All of you are this bad. I'd forgotten."

Reggie walked around the medical truck, rubbing his hands with a cloth. "No, that's just Thing One and Thing Two. The rest of us are normal."

"Yeah, right," Mack huffed.

"Nice to see you again, Bree."

"You too, Reggie."

Talk about a heartthrob, flashing those pearly whites, a smile in his kind eyes, and those biceps. She had to take a few shots. Quickly digging in her camera bag, she pulled out her Nikon and started taking pictures of Reggie and Mack. A glance down at her view screen showed lighting issues, and she hung the camera around her neck by its strap as she jotted down some notes in a notepad.

"Um, do you need any help?" Tex asked after a moment.

She glanced up to realize a few more firefighters had joined them. "Oh, sorry. It's going to be like this for the next two weeks. I'll need to figure out lighting and timing, maybe take some photos from different perspectives, add some filters… Hmm." She was talking to herself, ignoring Tex, but this time not on purpose, fully immersed in her work.

Enthused all over again about the project, she walked deeper into the bay, looked around, then lay down on her back and looked up through her camera at a world that needed to be captured.

Tex watched as Bree lay down on the cement floor and cringed, hoping she didn't get any stains on her clothes. Then again, her canvas jacket looked as if it had taken a beating or two in its life, the darker brown able to hide a few stains.

Bree looked damn good. Dressed in jeans, knee-high, chocolate-brown boots, and a plain red shirt, she looked both casual and chic lying there. Her hair wasn't spread around her head though, the way he'd imagined it looking over his pillow when she finally realized the error of her ways and stopped resisting him.

"What the hell is she doing?" Hernandez asked, having joined them to wash the engine.

"She's looking amazing, that's what she's doing," Mack murmured. "Wow, I had no idea how much I loved blonds."

"Shut up, Mack." Tex shouldered his way past the gaping men around him. "Um, Bree, how much longer you think you'll be down there?"

She seemed lost in her own little world as she snapped picture after picture with that camera that had to cost a fortune. At his voice, she turned to him and kept taking pics.

He didn't know if he should strike a pose or what, but he didn't want to look cheesy in front of the guys, so he kept his game face on and waited for her to answer.

When she continued to say nothing, he frowned. "You in there or what?"

"Talk, dark, and annoyed. I love that look. Keep frowning."

The others guffawed.

He shot them *that look* before extending a hand to her. "Okay, photo lady. Let's get you up and inside before you get run over on a call."

She took his hand, hers so much smaller than his, and accepted help to her feet. "Thanks." She waved at everyone. Heck, the only people on shift *not* down here were Brad, the LT, Marcus, and... nope, Beanie just entered the bay.

Bree smiled. "Hi, everyone. I'm—"

Tex interrupted. "Ma'am, this is *my* job." Her brows drew close in a scowl, so he hastened to say, "Fellas, this is Bree Gilchrist, the professional photographer assigned to take pictures for the next two weeks. She's gonna be in and out, so let's extend her every courtesy." He focused on Hernandez and Wash. "You get me? Or heads are gonna roll."

Wash snorted. "Whatevah." He smiled at Bree, all warm and personal, his northeastern accent thick. "Hey there, Bree. We know you from the photoshoot you did for Pets Fur Life. Remember us?"

Hernandez scooted past Wash and let loose a wide, welcoming grin. The bastard. "Yo, Ms. Gilchrist, nice to see you again."

Bree smiled back sunnily at everyone, chatting about how much fun she'd had on the calendar shoot, how lovely it was to see them again, and how excited she was to blah, blah, blah.

Tex lost his patience when Brad joined them and had the nerve to start flirting. And he had his own woman to think about!

Cutting through the herd to guide her where she needed to be, Tex gave his old border collie a run for his money by separating Bree from her many admirers. *Fuckin' sheep.*

Reggie didn't smile, but his eyes were laughing as he met Tex's gaze.

Jackass, Tex mouthed. He cleared his throat and said to Bree, "Well, we'd best see you to the lieutenant so he doesn't think I'm not doing my job." He tried his best not to appear annoyed with his friends and the rest of the C shift dicks.

"Oh, sorry. Yes, let's go see Ed. I mean, Lieutenant O'Brien."

He knew the LT had a deeper relationship with Chief Gilchrist than mere professionalism. Proven when Bree called him by his first name. Tex and Bree walked to the stairway, and Tex shot the others the finger behind his back as they went, ending with some unfortunate name-calling aimed his way.

Bree paused on the stairs. "Did someone just call you a diesel dick?"

"Nah. That's just the guys messing with each other. Not me. I get along with everyone."

She shot him a disbelieving glance but didn't call him on it. "Yeah, sure. Though I'm not sure what a diesel dick is."

"Me neither." They continued up the stairs. "So how do you know my lieutenant?" Ed wasn't funny about what the guys called him, as long as it was mostly clean. But Tex had always felt weird about calling the guy by his first name. Years in the Marine Corps had made working within a chain of command a natural state of being, and he'd never called a superior officer by his first name.

"Oh, he and Dad have been friends for years. They were in the same squad for a while, I think, though my dad had more time in service. If Ed decides to try for promotion to a battalion chief or higher, I bet he'll get it."

"Yeah, but I can't see Ed wanting all that goes with the position. I could be wrong, but I don't think so."

She agreed, coming to the top of the stairs. "He's more of a hands-on guy. My dad is too. It kills him sometimes that he's not in the thick of things. Running the scheduling and training for the battalion takes all of his time."

"I'll bet." Nah, Tex wouldn't want that headache either. Though the commensurate salary would be nice. "So, before we get to the lieutenant, this hallway leads to the common area and kitchen. And farther down is the weight room. But if you go this way"—he turned them left instead of right—"you get LT and the admin office. Down the hall that wraps around are the sleeping quarters."

She nodded. "And you guys have four shifts, eight people per shift, right?"

"Yep. Lieutenant O'Brien leads A and C shift. Our other lieutenant, Sue Arthur, leads B and D. Sue's great." And not his commander, thus he had no problem calling her by her first name. "She's pretty tough."

"She'd have to be, surrounded by so much testosterone." Bree snorted and turned to see Ed coming from the kitchen. She brushed by Tex's shoulder, and a waft of floral shampoo washed over him, stirring a predictable warmth within.

Ed saw Bree, and pleasure lit up his usually hard-nosed expression. "Well, well. Bree Gilchrist. You get prettier every time I see you."

Tex watched in awe as Ed had Bree blushing and protesting his compliment, her sweet side out in full force. Ed kissed her cheek and led her into his office, completely ignoring Tex standing right behind her.

He sighed and followed them inside.

"Shut the door, would you?"

After shutting the door, Tex sat next to Bree, across from Ed.

"This is a real pleasure. We're excited to have you featuring the department for your project. Would you like something to drink? Coffee, water? I just made a fresh pot of coffee, if you want the good stuff."

Tex grimaced. Who the hell had let the LT near the coffee machine?

Bree settled her camera bag gently on the floor beside her. "Well, I had coffee earlier, but I could go for another."

Ed snapped his fingers and pointed at Tex. "Grab her a cup, would you?"

Bree gave him her prettiest fake smile. "With cream and sugar please."

I got something sweet I'd love to give you, sprang immediately to mind, his thoughts around Bree never far from sex. But a glance at Ed's narrowing gaze had him biting back anything but a polite, "Sure thing, Bree."

Fetch this. Do that. He could tell it would be best for him if they did a lot of their picture taking on the go, away from the station house. "You sure you want our coffee? It's pretty strong."

She raised a brow, her attitude condescending. God, she made him hot. "Thanks so much, cowboy, but I can handle manly coffee. Who the heck do you think made the stuff while I was growing up? My dad."

"Suit yourself." He left and returned to find them discussing the station and its inner workings.

He handed Bree her drink and sat down to watch. She didn't disappoint, her eyes wide and watering as she forced down a large gulp.

"Good stuff, eh?"

She cautiously glanced at Ed and worked up a smile. "Oh, great."

Ed nodded. "Told you I know a good cuppa joe."

"Huh. Seems to me her eyes are watering." Tex fought back a grin.

"Right." Bree coughed. "Okay, so, Ed, you were telling me about C shift and why you think they're the worst of the bunch."

Tex frowned. "Come on, LT. You don't mean that."

Ed chuckled. "Well, I guess I don't. Maybe. What with Brad getting us all that publicity with *Searching the Needle Weekly*, the calendar with supposedly 'hot' firefighters, and now you helping Bree out, C shift does seem to be the most popular group at the station."

Bree eased her camera out and took a few shots of Ed, who flushed.

"Don't take pictures of me. No one wants to see that."

Tex nodded. "Yeah, no one wants to see that."

"Shut it, McGovern."

Bree couldn't hide her grin as she stood and moved around the office, taking photos of Ed…and Tex. "Don't mind the camera. I'm taking a ton of photos today. Probably ninety percent of which I won't keep."

That relaxed Ed. "Good. Although the boss would love to see me in a picture not holding a beer."

"By 'boss,' he doesn't mean the captain," Tex explained. "He means the woman he married."

Ed winked at Bree. Ed's wife had Ed by the 'nads. A funny woman, but damn, Tex understood why the lieutenant had to bring the heat at work. He needed to be in charge somewhere in his life.

"What do you guys think I should concentrate on with my photos?" Snap. Bree took another photo of Tex, and this time he smiled at the camera.

Ed shrugged. "You're the artist. You tell us."

"People," Tex said.

She turned to him and lowered her camera. "Which people? C Shift?"

He shook his head. "Our job is helping people, being a part of the community. Hell, tying the community together. Sure, take shots of Mack doing CPR or Nat hosing down a fire. But get the old lady who needs her cat out of a tree—and yeah, that actually happens. Or the kid crying because he broke his arm and didn't catch the ball. Get the public in your shots, because without them, there's no us."

Ed stared at him.

"What?"

"I can't believe all that came out of your mouth."

That Bree looked just as amazed annoyed him. "I keep telling everyone I'm not just a pretty face," he grumbled.

Bree blinked. "Huh."

"What now?" he snapped.

Ed's gaze narrowed.

"You might actually be smarter than Mack and Brad said you were."

Tex sat up straighter and cocked back the brim of his ballcap. "Just when did they tell you I had rocks for brains? I'm a dang genius."

"So succinct," Ed muttered. "Wait, don't answer him, Bree. This sounds like a lengthy conversation if it involves Tex's brain capacity."

Tex held back a snarl. Barely.

Ed smirked at him. "I actually need to get back to work. I just wanted to welcome you to Station 44 and let you know that we're here to help. Anything you need, anything at all"—he paused to eyeball Tex—"and we'll get it for you."

"Even one of your burly guys' phone numbers?" Bree wiggled her brows.

"Who?" Tex asked.

Ed's expression grew dark. Really dark.

Bree had the temerity to laugh. "God, I'm kidding. If you only knew how many times my father has drilled into my head to keep away from flirty firemen." She chuckled. "Sorry. That wasn't professional at all. But Dad did tell me he'd give me twenty bucks if I could shake the unshakeable Ed O'Brien."

Tex felt weak from relief and refused to consider why. "Good one. I'll be your witness. The LT can't seem to close his mouth."

Ed's jaw snapped shut. He pointed an accusing finger at Bree. "Just you watch your step, missy, or I'll tell Charlie you're misbehaving."

"Charlie?" Tex looked from Ed to Bree. Shoot. Was Bree dating some civilian?

"Her stepmom." Ed looked smug. "She's as protective as John." Ed chuckled. "I aim to follow the Gilchrist way as my kids get older. No dating and nothing but straight As and schoolwork to keep them happy and healthy."

"Poor kids," Tex drawled.

"And you, keep your distance. Already Ed Jr. is begging for his own Stetson and going around the house saying howdy and calling me 'hoss.'" Ed rolled his eyes.

Tex laughed. "That's what you get when you bring your kids

around on field trips. We educate 'em somethin' good. Wait till he tells you what I told him about girls and cooties."

Ed tried to stifle a grin, but Tex saw it.

Bree shook her head. "And we're done here." She was laughing as she stowed her gear. "Thanks for lending me one of yours, Ed. I'll make sure I don't get him in any trouble."

"See that you don't." He harrumphed. They all stood, but before Tex could follow Bree out the door, Ed snagged his arm. "And you don't get *her* in any trouble. Clear?"

"As mud. Ow. Easy, LT. I got you. Damn."

For an older guy, Ed still packed a punch. Tex rubbed his arm, tipped his hat at his boss, then scooted after the fast-moving blond.

Chapter Five

THE NICE THING ABOUT HAVING A FIREMAN FOR A FATHER WAS that Bree didn't need Tex to explain everything about how the units functioned. For example, she knew that every firefighter in Seattle had to be an emergency medical technician, an EMT, first. They did BLS—basic life support—and used the aid vehicles, what looked like ambulances but were assigned to the station houses, not hospitals. Paramedics, on the other hand, were sparse and served in the medic trucks, doing ALS—advanced life support.

Seattle had five battalions of firefighters and thirty-three stations—now thirty-four with the addition of Station 44—around the city, plus Medic One at Harborview Medical Center, which housed the paramedics.

The city didn't use volunteers, and all the men and women in service had worked their tails off to get into the fire department, which held an impressive wait list of people wanting to serve.

"So why firefighting?" she asked as Tex pulled them back into the parking lot later that night. They'd spent the day driving to several stations, letting her look around, play with the angles and lighting, and try to get a feel for what she wanted to do. No big fire emergencies had been called in, so she'd laid a rough groundwork for what she wanted to do the next day.

He parked and looked at her. "You really want to know?"

"I asked you the question, didn't I?" They'd had a mostly pleasant day, all of it professional—if she discounted the way he studied her when he didn't think she was looking. They'd shared a lunch at a popular sandwich shop, but other than that break, they'd been either driving, stuck in traffic, or at different stations.

"How about we do dinner and I'll tell you all about it?"

Since Tex was on a special duty with her for the next two weeks, he'd be working her hours, mostly nine to five or six in the evening, unless she wanted night shots or a major fire happened.

"Dinner sounds…"

"Not too personal," he finished for her. "You heard everyone warn me to be good, right? No screwing around. I'm here to help you do your job and to make us look good in the process." He smiled.

Her heart raced. Damn it.

"You can say no, obviously, and I'm fine with going home alone."

"Alone, really?" Had that just popped out of her mouth? Really?

"I'm normally working today and off for the next ninety-six hours. But now I have to readjust. Dating's the last thing on my mind, darlin.'"

She should have corrected him on "darlin,'" but he'd been so good all day. It had unnerved her. She kept waiting for him to try to con her into a kiss, a date, or something more inappropriate.

And damn it that she felt upset he hadn't tried anything. So contrary to feel so stupid.

"Actually, I'm going to go home and take a look at what I shot today."

He cocked his head. "Really? More work?"

"This is the fun part. Well, taking the shots is fun, but looking through everything and culling the worst gives me a clearer picture."

He frowned. "I thought you were just playing around today. You're gonna keep some of those pictures?"

"I don't know. Maybe."

He just looked at her, and she wondered how he felt about being the star of several of her shots. Not because she had the hots for him but because the camera did. Having been on both sides of the camera for a good portion of her life, she knew when a person had "it." Tex definitely had it in heaps and bounds.

"Huh." He scratched his temple, then set his hat firmly over his head. "Well, I won't keep you. Nine again tomorrow morning?"

"Yes."

"I'll swing by to pick you up, okay? No reason to bring your car. I'm not even using my truck. I'll be using this in case a major call comes in."

"Oh, right. Please call me if something happens."

"That's the idea."

She felt like an idiot for stating the obvious and felt her cheeks heat. "Yes, well, um, I'd better go."

"You sure you don't want dinner? It's on me."

She wanted to say yes. She said no instead. "Another time."

"No problem."

He waited until she'd gotten in her car and pulled away before leaving. But he sure didn't seem too upset that she'd rejected his dinner plans.

In fact, he'd been polite and charming, but not too charming, all day long.

Maybe her father's warning had done its job.

And she wondered why she found that thought so depressing.

Tex sat with Brad's brother, Oscar, and Oscar's girlfriend, Gerty, at their place for dinner while he played with their puppy, a three-legged Lab mix named Klingon.

He laughed at the dog's antics as it raced around on wobbly legs trying to get its tail.

"Man, this guy is so dang cute. He just gets cuter every time I see him."

"Like some firemen I could name." Gerty appraised Tex sitting on the floor. "Oscar, if you weren't so fine, I might have to see what Tex looks like as an orc king."

"Over my undead draugr body!"

"Gamer nerds." Tex sighed.

Oscar looked a lot like Brad. Same sandy-brown hair, same facial features, same annoying tendency to try to boss Tex around. Gerty, though, looked like a hundred pounds of tiny, blond fairy. Her pixie haircut, red jeans, and neon, striped shirt seemed to be making some kind of statement. The burn-out-your-retinas kind.

"How's it going with your übernemesis?" she asked him.

"Who, Bree?"

"Yep. The photographer with a grudge."

"She likes me. She just won't admit it to herself yet."

Oscar grinned. "Admitting her problem is the first step."

"Yeah, well, I don't think she's wanting any coins for completing her recovery process."

"Coins?" Gerty looked puzzled.

"For completing a step in AA," Oscar informed her.

"Oh, right. So, what's she addicted to?"

"Hating me," Tex muttered.

Gerty laughed. Oscar coughed to hide his mirth.

"It's all fun and games until I'm no longer helping you two with your adorable strays," Tex growled, a reminder of why he'd come to visit in the first place.

Gerty cleared her throat. "Sorry, Cowboy Carl."

"Huh?" Gerty was so weird.

She continued, "We've homed so many strays thanks to you guys. Heck, with Avery's show, Brad's work with it, and the rest of you holding adoption days for Pets Fur Life, we're able to accept more strays than ever before."

Oscar grinned at Tex. "You have to admit it's a great way to meet women."

"It is better than the bar scene," Tex admitted. Especially

because the only woman he wanted didn't seem hang out at bars unless with a bridal party, and she seemed to have no interest in flirting at work. "Anyway, what's your emergency?"

Oscar and Gerty looked at each other.

"Well," Oscar started, slowly. He reminded Tex a lot of his own older brother back in Texas. Wyatt was funny, sarcastic as hell, and a homegrown lothario who liked to pretend he could get more girls than Tex. But Tex had outgrown stupid dating competitions after high school. And it wasn't a competition anyway, since Tex had bigger muscles and a helluva lot more sex appeal than stupid Wyatt.

"I'm still waitin'…"

Klingon jumped on his leg and tried to nose under it. Then Tex realized he'd been sitting on a pretzel someone must have dropped. Loud crunching clued Gerty in to the fact her pooch had found treasure.

"See, Oscar? I told you you missed some," she scolded before picking up Klingon and hugging him. "You are so cute." The dog licked and licked her.

Too bad Bree wasn't close by to snap a picture of that.

No, she'd spent her day distanced behind her lens, taking pictures of him while barely talking about anything substantial. Questions about firefighting, Fifth Battalion, and what a great Cuban sandwich the deli shop made. But not one answer to any question he'd hedged about her personal life or hobbies.

Maybe he'd been too vague. He hadn't wanted her to think he was trying to find out more about her, just being friendly in a non-threatening way.

"Hello?" Oscar waved a hand in front of his face. "I think we should talk after we eat."

"Yeah." Tex yawned. "My blood sugar's low. Feed me, and I'll respond."

Gerty snorted. "Men."

They ate a great deal of pizza. Between Oscar and Tex, they polished off a pizza apiece.

Gerty ate her fair share, but filling up her tiny body didn't take much.

"You two are monsters. Come on, Klingon. Let's go for a walk."

It was still light out, and they lived in a decent enough area in Fremont, so Tex didn't worry for Gerty's safety. Not that he'd have to with Oscar around, but still. His daddy had ingrained into his brain the need to be protective.

Gerty left them with a wave.

They sat in silence at the table as Tex drank down the rest of his root beer. "Well? I ain't getting any younger, son."

Oscar flushed.

Tex chuckled. "It's like looking at a younger, more agreeable Brad Battle."

"Be nice, Tex."

Tex loved his firefighting brother, a former Marine and an all-around amazing guy. But Brad was hardened. Oscar was not.

"I, ah, I think I might need some help."

Tex's smile left him. "You been going to meetings?"

Oscar nodded. A recovering alcoholic, he'd been sober for close to two years and occasionally leaned on Tex for emotional support. Since Tex had been there for Wyatt, providing help and tough love when needed, he'd seen the same vulnerabilities in Oscar upon first meeting the guy. Brad had tried to help, but Mr. Perfect didn't know what it was like to fail and fail again.

"I'm doing more meetings, hanging with my sponsor when I need to. And, well, there's another guy in the program. He has a dog."

"Aha." Pet service needed.

"I'm really asking you to help me with that, not the drinking part."

That made a heck of a lot more sense than that Tex could solve all of Oscar's problems.

"The dog is older and neglected. I finally managed to talk Scott into giving her up for adoption instead of just setting her free to live her own life." Oscar scowled. "He's got some weird idea the dog would be happier by itself, alone in the city."

"What a dick."

Oscar nodded. "I promised I'd come get Bubbles before the end of the week. He's got it in his head that if he takes her to a shelter, they'll put Bubbles down."

"Seattle is a no-kill city." Tex paused. "Hold on. The dog's name is Bubbles?"

Oscar sighed. "He named her after his ex-girlfriend...a stripper."

"Oh, okay." Tex pictured some yappy little dog with pink sweaters and a rhinestone collar pining for attention.

"I told Scott the dog would be fine at a shelter. He doesn't care. I'd go over there and grab the dog, but I kind of don't want to be around any drunk people just now. And I don't want Gerty over there with him alone. Scott can get weird when he's hammered."

"No, keep Gerty away. Yourself too. Good call." Except some poor, older dog was stuck with an asshole on a bender.

"I really am sorry about this." Oscar glanced away. "I would have called Brad for help, but I don't want him to think I'm having problems. It's... I just..."

"No, man. I get it. It's your business anyway. Don't worry about it. You're being smart about things. Gimme the address and a time to get over there to get the dog. I'll bring her back."

"Well, that's the other thing." Oscar swallowed. "We're only allowed one dog here."

"And?" Why did this problem seem to have no end?

"And I need to find a place for Bubbles to stay. And, well, since you have a yard..."

Tex groaned. "You're killing me. I want to help, but I'm not home enough for a dog."

"It's just temporary," Oscar jumped in. "And for however long you have the dog, either Gerty or I will come over to walk it or let it out to pee. Please, Tex? It's just sad, what this dog has been living with. For years."

Tex wanted to say no, but he couldn't. "Shit. Fine. But I'm only keepin' this dog until you find her a good home. And fast. Bubbles," he said with a huff. "Who names a dog Bubbles?"

———

Tex spent the next two days carting Bree around, showing her how professional and distant he could be while slowly worming his way under her skin. Oscar had yet to call him about picking up Bubbles, so he focused his efforts on winning Bree over.

He couldn't say for sure, but she seemed to respond to him easier, not looking so guarded all the time. She even smiled more, especially when he offered suggestions on shots she might like, from different perspectives at places he'd been before. As a firefighter, Tex saw a lot of the city most folks never did.

Bree seemed like such an artist. He'd seen her work in magazines and galleries, having followed—not *stalked*, thank you, Mack—her online and looked into her endeavors.

He didn't figure he had much of an artistic side. He didn't like to draw or write, could take decent enough pics with his cell phone but normally only snapped them to make fun of the guys doing stupid things, and had no flair for domestic arts. He could cook so-so, but though the food was edible, it was short of spectacular.

Tex might not be artistic, but he gave his all to everything he attempted. At the age of ten, his father had taught him how to hunt. Shooting a gun had been fun, but he'd had no desire to kill anything with it. Shooting with a bow, however, had been thrilling. He'd won several competitions shooting at targets. Unfortunately, his time in the USMC hadn't been dicking around with a bow and arrows. He'd kept his rifle by his side through thick and thin, fortunately only needing to fire on the range to qualify each year for promotion. An expert on the rifle with ease.

Maybe he could consider his love of hitting the target a form of artistic expression and impress upon Bree that he was pretty good at something other than annoying her.

He glanced next to him in the truck as he and Bree readied to end their Saturday spent driving around the city. The evening hadn't yet arrived, the sun still bright overhead, but Bree had decided she needed a break. He agreed.

They'd spent the past three days together, from morning through evening, taking pictures of the many firefighters all over the city in their home stations. But much of her time had been spent on the technical aspects of her shots, not just taking the photos themselves.

Today they'd followed a pair of paramedics out of Harbor Station on a ton of calls, the last one an ugly car crash downtown. One driver had been listed as critical, his passengers—two small children—nearly as bad. Fortunately, they'd been wearing their seat belts when they'd been slammed into by a woman texting on her phone. She had walked away with a few bruises, but he wouldn't want to be her when the cops came calling. She'd for sure get more than a ticket for texting while driving.

Tex and Bree had been on Pine when the scanner had broadcast the emergency. Flashing lights, he'd gotten through to the mess and parked out of the way. It had itched at him not to provide assistance, but he'd stayed back and let the others do their jobs, keeping Bree close while protecting her...without acting like he was protecting her. She'd done a great job of being unobtrusive while still taking shots.

"I don't know how journalists do it." Bree shook her head. "All that tragedy. I had to block it out to shoot, but I felt sick at all the blood and pain. Those poor kids and their dad." Her brows drew close. "I hope they throw that woman in jail. She caused that accident."

"I know. It was a mess." He sighed. "I hate when kids are involved. It's always bad, but the little ones really get to you." He could feel her studying him, her gaze penetrating.

"Thank you for helping me back there. You made sure I got through and kept me out of the way."

"Just doing my job." He spared her a grin while working like a demon to devise a way to turn this into an opportunity for more Bree time. "You sure you want to end tonight? It's gearing up to be a full moon. A lot of crazies coming out soon."

She chuckled. "I'll bet. I'm tired though. We'll do more tomorrow." She paused. "I never asked, but tomorrow is Sunday. Do you do church?"

He nodded. "But I've been known to skip. A lot, sorry to say. My schedule isn't always the most flexible. Though sometimes I go and sit in the back in uniform if I'm on duty. Brad's okay with it, but Reggie and Mack get annoyed. So I try to partner with them when I can on Sundays so we can *both* sit in church together."

She smiled. "You like getting under people's skin, hmm?"

How to answer that one? "Only my buddies'. Trust me. They do their best to get under mine, and on a daily basis."

She laughed. "Which one's the worst?"

"Brad's too stern to really let go. But Avery has him smiling a lot more. Then there's Reggie, another Mr. Serious. But he's a sneaky cuss. A lot more sly and tricky than you'd think. I like fuck—er, messing—with him the most. And Mack, because he's a huge pain. Like me, he has a lot of brothers. You kind of grow up knowing how to needle people when you have brothers."

She was staring at him, he could feel it. "I have one stepsister, and she and I don't get along."

"Older or younger?"

"Same age." She sighed. "What about you? I remember us

talking about your family a little, mostly about your life growing up on the ranch. Was it three or four brothers you have again? I forget."

"Wish I could," he teased. She laughed, and he felt tingly hearing it. "I have three older brothers. All perfect children, to hear them tell it." He chuckled. "The oldest two are both married, and I have a four-year-old nephew. I'm the best uncle, honestly."

"I imagine you're the fun one who always got his brothers in trouble when younger."

"No way. I got saddled with all the guilt for stuff I ain't never done." He deliberately thickened his accent and winked, and she laughed with him. "I might have done a few things, but my brothers were hellions. I'm respectable."

"Please."

"I am. I joined the Marines, and now I fight fires." He frowned. "But I don't live at home anymore working the ranch, and I'm not married. So those are two big points against me." They'd been having such a great conversation, so he took a risk and asked, "What about you? You live near your parents, so you're still in good with the family, right?"

"I love my dad and stepmom, sure. But I'd be lying if I said they weren't always asking who I'm dating." She glanced out the window. "My dad is way too interested in my social life, but if I ask him to leave it alone, his feelings get hurt."

That, Tex couldn't fathom. Chief Gilchrist was built like a tank and had a glare like a priest catching a kid chugging the communion wine. His feelings hurt?

"So, everyone in your family is married but you, huh?" she asked.

"No. Wyatt, my older brother, is still single. But he works on the ranch with the family, so they cut him a break." Tex grimaced. "I'm not looking forward to Christmas this year. I'm due to go home, and I know they're going to eat me alive. Wyatt will get a girl just to spite me. I know it."

"You're weird. No one dates just to get back at a sibling." She paused. "Then again, my stepsister once dated one of my exes and brought him to a Christmas Eve party. So maybe you have something there."

"That's not cool."

"No, it's not."

"Wyatt's never done that. But it's tough for me because I'm the youngest. My momma worries about me so far from home, so defenseless."

She shook her head. "You're shameless. How old are you, anyway?"

"Twenty-nine. Thirty in December. You?"

"Twenty-seven. Just turned in March."

"Oh, so just a baby in this rough city, filled with scary Starbucks and wild Nordstroms on every corner. No wonder your daddy is scared for ya." He chuckled when she shot him the finger. Now they were getting somewhere. Bree was acting feisty and giving back as good as she got. Not so distant now.

Their gazes met, and the air thickened between them. Tex quickly looked back at the road as he turned toward Capitol Hill, where Bree lived.

Bree cleared her throat. "You never answered about tomorrow. Do you need extra time in the morning?"

"If you're okay with it, I wouldn't mind hitting an earlier service."

"No problem at all. Who would have thought Tex McGovern answered to something other than T and A."

He blinked. "*What* did you say?" He stopped at a light and stared at her.

She burst out laughing. "Oh my God. You are so red right now."

"Shut up." He was not.

"You're acting like my grandma did the one time she farted in church."

"Dear Jesus."

"That's what she said!" She laughed harder.

Tex found it difficult not to yank her into his arms and hug her, wanting to feel some of that joy. But he sat there, a stupid grin on his face. It took the guy beeping behind him to force him to look back at the road and drive.

She wiped her cheek. "Sorry. That was so funny. You crack me up, Tex."

"Glad to be of service. You know, after these two weeks are up, I should ask for a raise."

She snickered. "I hope it's a big one."

"That's what she said," they said at the same time and broke down laughing even more.

"Sorry," he said. "It just slipped out. And do not say 'that's what she said' to that."

Bree twisted an invisible lock over her lips then ruined it by speaking. "Sorry. I shouldn't have said that either, but it was too funny."

"I agree."

"So, uh, do you have plans tonight?"

He froze but tried to act nonchalant. "Just gonna go home, lift, watch some TV probably. You?"

She shrugged and glanced out the window again. "I figured I might cook something. And since you've been so nice, maybe you could come over to eat. Just for dinner," she emphasized. "Not for any other reason than to be nice."

"Must be killin' ya."

"Oh, trust me, it is." Her eyes sparkled.

Tex wanted to kiss her so bad. Instead, he gave a slow nod. "I suppose that might be all right. Can you cook?"

"I can. And by the look of you, I'd say you like to eat."

He patted his flat stomach, pleased when her attention centered there. "I sure do." But he didn't want to ruin things between them, so he gave her an easy, nonthreatening smile. "Thanks, Bree. I'd love dinner—and just dinner—at your place." His cell phone rang. "Mind if I answer this?"

"Sure."

He hit the Bluetooth feature in the car to answer, the caller coming through the car speakers.

"Tex?"

"Yeah. Who is this?"

"It's Gerty, silly." Her bubbly laugh came through. "So, any thought to posing naked so my friends can make a virtual duplicate of you for my game? Hubba hubba."

He could sense the tension now in the truck's confines. "Uh…"

"Kidding, handsome. Just kidding. I'm calling about Bubbles, you know, the sad woman in your life you promised to take care of?" Gerty sighed. "Bubbles. Worst stripper name of all time. Maybe Candy or Lady Ta-Ta. But Bubbles?"

Bree's brows rose, and he could all but feel his invitation to her house being withdrawn bit by bit.

"Hey, ah, Gerty, I'm in the car with—"

"Shoot, gotta go. It's in West Seattle. I'll text you the address. Love you, cowboy." She hung up.

A pregnant pause filled the truck.

"You do have plans after all," Bree said.

Tex swore. "Damn it. That's not what it sounded like."

"Bubbles?"

"No. No way. Not tonight. You're gonna see the truth if I have to drag you there and make you." He turned the wheel, ignoring her protests, which soon turned to threats, and instructed Siri to take him to the address. "Geld me later, darlin'. Right now we have a hairy non-stripper to save."

Chapter Six

BREE WANTED TO SMACK HERSELF FOR BEING SUCH A DUPE. Twice before he'd burned her, and though she'd later found his excuses to have some merit, she should have learned her lesson. Inviting him to her house for dinner? She'd been clear the meal would be in the name of friendship and no more, but surely he could feel the sexual tension between them. She sure the hell could.

Except once again, some supposed female disaster needed Tex's help to handle. It would have been laughable if he hadn't forced her to come with him.

"Tex, I want to go home. Now."

"Later. After you see the hell that is my life," he said brusquely.

She studied him, interested despite herself. "Really? A stripper, Tex?" Not that she had anything against them. She'd modeled some scanty outfits in front of hundreds of people for money, though no one had tucked any bills into her G-string.

He barked a short laugh. "Trust me. She's not a stripper. She's a dog."

"That is both cruel and insensitive." She'd thought better of him.

"Damn it. I'm serious."

Confused, Bree didn't know what to think. "Fine, Tex. Have it your way. Let's go meet Bubbles. Then I'll get my dad to assign someone else to shadow me around."

She hated to be like that, but he shouldn't have strong-armed her into going. And she should never have invited him over in the first place.

His lips firmed. He glowered at the road and turned on the radio to a country station she sometimes listened to.

Twenty minutes later, they pulled in front of a house that had seen better days. Tex looked at his phone again, grimaced, and turned to her as he removed his seat belt. "Do me a favor and stay here. I have no idea what I'm walking into."

She frowned. "You don't know Bubbles?"

He rolled his eyes. "No, I don't."

"Then why are we here?"

"Because I'm a sucker, that's why." He opened the door. "Stay here," he ordered and left.

Bree didn't have long to fume about his command. Moments after he knocked on the front door, the door opened, and Tex pushed himself inside. The door closed. Minutes later, it opened again, and Tex led a huge dog outside by a leash. The shepherd-retriever mix had a dull gold coat and had to weigh close to eighty pounds, all of it lean muscle. The poor thing looked dejected, walking with its tail tucked, its ears low, as it followed Tex toward the truck.

He opened the door.

Bree blinked. "That's a dog."

"Meet Bubbles."

"Bubbles is a dog." She couldn't say why she was so surprised. Tex had told her Bubbles was a dog, but she'd thought he was being discourteous calling her that.

"Yes, Bree, she's a canine," he said slowly. To Bubbles, he crouched and stroked her gnarled fur. "You poor thing. Someone's been doing a piss poor job of takin' care of you. Come on, girl. Get in the truck." It took a little coaxing, but the dog eventually leaped into the back seat of the truck and lay down, her head on her paws, facing the seat back.

"She's so…"

Tex sighed. "Sad. And miserable. I'd be miserable too if I'd lived with that prick." He shut the back door and entered the front. "Sorry." He clenched the steering wheel. "I mean, sorry about all of it. I should have simply dropped you off at home, but you seem to think the worst of me, and I don't like it. I'm not a liar, Bree. I just have weird shit happen to me when you're around."

"I'm sorry too." She reached back to pet the forlorn dog. "What's the deal with Bubbles?"

Tex started the truck and pulled away. "She belongs— belonged—to an alcoholic who never played with her, took her out, or did anything with her. For the past two damn years! I guess when he broke off with his ex, he decided to be a dick and keep the dog to hurt her. And his ex was no better because she left the poor thing with him. Once his girlfriend left, the jackass stopped caring for the dog. She looks underweight to me, and she's lethargic. He didn't hit her or anything, but he ignored her and barely fed her. No vet visits, no playing, no belly rubs." He glanced in the rear-view and angled it down to see the dog. "You poor thing."

"Oh, that's so sad."

"Yeah. I grabbed some dog food for a little dog a few days ago, thinking I'd be picking up a tiny thing for a few days. I had no idea Bubbles wasn't some teacup poodle." He grunted. "Oscar and Gerty owe me big for this."

"Wait. You're going to take care of her for them?"

"Only until we find her a home."

Bree stared. "Tex, that's…" Heroic, sweet, so incredibly caring. "I tell you what. Let's stop at a grocery store on the way back to your place, and I'll make you a nice dinner while you spoil Bubbles." She sniffed. "But maybe give her a better name. That is not a bubbly dog."

A slow smile worked its way over his lips. "Yeah? Well, then, that's okay. You hear that Bubbles? We're getting dinner tonight."

She didn't wag her tail, but Bree didn't stop petting her.

Once settled into Tex's two-bedroom cottage in Beacon Hill, Bree watched him show the dog his nice-sized yard, letting her do her business. "You sure you're okay if I get her used to the house and yard?" Tex called from outside through the open back door.

"No, please. Go ahead. I'll just make myself at home in your kitchen, if that's okay."

"Cool. No problem. Thanks, Bree." Tex remained outside with Bubbles, who'd finally seemed to come to life, sniffing around his yard. He had a good space of fenced-in privacy, though his neighbors on either side weren't that far away.

The house itself felt like him. It was pretty enough on the outside, a one-story cottage with white, wooden siding and black shutters up on a slight hill, so they'd had to climb stairs to reach it from the street. Old beechwood floors covered the living and dining rooms, with a large, black-and-white ceramic tiled kitchen. The walls had been painted a light gray, the furniture sturdy enough to fit a man of Tex's frame and surprisingly tasteful in a Shaker style. Once, she might have guessed it would resemble a frat house, but the inside was warm and inviting, much like the man outside, taking care of a neglected dog.

The off-white kitchen had a small, butcher-block island in its center, the only dining area a round table between the kitchen and living room, the space open yet sectioned off by the archways in the ceilings, denoting each area.

Bree's own home boasted more modern furnishings, but this fit Tex: earthy and down-home.

She started on a simple meal of already-baked chicken, some fresh boiled beets, and a nice salad.

By the time the chicken had warmed up, she'd prepared the beets and salad as she watched Tex and Bubbles through the kitchen window, overlooking the backyard.

That poor dog. She still looked sad, yet she seemed to come to life under Tex's gentle guidance.

Watching him with the animal had opened a whole new side to the sexy cowboy, showing he had depth under the playboy exterior.

After setting the table and pouring them both glasses of water to go with dinner, she stepped through the doorway onto the porch to find the dog lying belly down next to Tex while he brushed her with slow strokes.

Bree quietly left him to grab her camera from her bag and snapped several photos from behind the pair, the sunset giving the shot a glow.

"All ready?" Tex asked, not turning around, and put the brush down to stroke the dog's ears and muzzle with a gentle touch. When he stopped, Bubbles nudged his hand to continue. Tex chuckled. "See, now, girl? I knew you'd come around."

Yeah, apparently, we all do. Bree didn't say it, but she wondered what the heck she was doing making Tex dinner. *We're friends,* she told herself. Just friends. *He's sweet, and he's saving a senior dog.* "Hey, Tex, how old is Bubbles, anyway?" She walked back inside and stowed her camera.

"I think Oscar told me she's seven."

"Really?" Yet as the dog entered behind Tex, her golden color shone, and only the hint of gray under her chin and above her eyes showed her age. Her tail wagged, and she looked up at Tex with love.

"It's so weird," Tex was saying as he washed his hands in the kitchen sink. "She's the sweetest thing, doesn't shy away when I pet her, so I don't think she was ever beat down. But there are so many ways to abuse that don't leave a mark, you know?"

She nodded. "On people too. That's not just limited to animals."

After a pause, he asked, "You know that from personal experience?"

"Oh, me? No." She shook her head. "Can you imagine what my dad would do to anyone who tried to hurt me?"

Tex eased up. "Good point."

"But I had two friends when I was in high school. One of them had an abusive boyfriend. He used to beat her, leaving marks where they wouldn't show. The creep. The other had a pretty rough upbringing. So sad. Her dad used to beat her mom in front of her, but her mom was too scared to leave him."

"I just don't understand that." Tex frowned. "Hell, in our house, you *never* hit a girl. Even if she wallops you with a two-by-four."

"Really?"

"That's actually how my oldest brother met his wife, but that's another story."

"One I want to hear." She grinned.

Tex laughed. "I'm sure Liam deserved it." He stood in the dining room, staring at the set table. "Holy crap. That looks amazing. Smells even better."

"Let's eat."

She noted that he waited until she sat before he did, which made her feel a little funny. Good funny. His manners and chivalric tendency threw her. Made her like him a little bit more.

For all her need to be treated equally, she didn't mind being catered to. Oh, not all the time, but the little things he'd been doing since Wednesday, when they'd started her project, had been about seeing to her comforts before his. She'd been on plenty of dates with guys who, though nice enough, didn't hold a chair out for her or didn't let her go first through the door. And that habit of putting a hand on the small of her back while he waited for her to precede him… At first it had been annoying, that shocking connection. Now she looked forward to it.

Man, I need to be super careful with this one.

They dug into the dinner, which had been easy enough to prepare.

"This is so good." Tex ate slowly, savoring each bite. She wished he'd stop looking so…satisfied. Because she kept imagining him making that face in a bed. On top of a woman. Like her.

"It's just baked chicken. And all I did was spice it up and reheat it." She kept her gaze on her plate, trying to focus on her food.

A paw landed on her lap, followed by a whine.

"Now, Bubbles, behave." Tex shook his head. "No, girl. Nope."
The dog glanced at him then looked back at Bree.

"No," Tex said, his voice firmer.

Bubbles dropped her paw and crawled under the table.

"I think you scared her," she said, feeling terrible.

"Dogs should have manners. And beggin' from the table is a no-no. Something my momma taught me and my brothers early on."

"Not to feed the dog, huh?"

"Nope. Not to beg for seconds till everyone else finished their firsts." Tex chuckled. "We ate a lot growing up."

"I'll bet."

"I sure do miss Momma's cooking." He sighed and took another bite. "But this makes up for it."

"Yeah, sure." She felt herself blushing under his compliment. "So why did you become a firefighter?" She'd been dying to know, and he never had answered her question before.

"Simple, really." He shrugged. "I grew up on a ranch but wanted to see more than Houston. So, I joined the Marine Corps, like my daddy and his daddy before him—we boys all spend a few years in the service before we find a civvy job—and I realized how much I liked helping people."

"You helped people in the service?"

He nodded. "I know a lot of Marines who had trouble overseas. We're in some real shit nowadays, you know?" At her nod, he continued, "Fortunately, I had a good tour and didn't have to shoot at anyone. Anyway, my time came up to reenlist or get out, and I knew I was ready to get back to normal life. But I just couldn't go back home for good. It didn't feel right." He tapped his chest. "In here, I knew I needed to do something else. After visiting at home a few months, I ended up following a few friends out this way. My best bud went to Portland, so I went with him. While there, I watched a fire rescue. It hit me that I wanted to do that, make people safe. But then I moved around, found out I liked Seattle better—and yeah, there was a gal involved."

She sighed. "Of course there was."

He laughed. "She was just a friend, and it was years ago. She's now happily married—to that best bud I mentioned. They live back in Portland."

"Huh. Wouldn't have thought that would work."

"Right?" Tex shrugged. "It's a wacky world. But I stayed here, became an EMT, met Brad and the guys, clicked, and kept on as a firefighter. It's even better than being a Marine—but don't quote me on that, or the guys will give me grief."

"Did you like the Marines?"

"Loved it. Didn't like how cut-and-dried it was though. You're all good until you get a bad commanding officer. Then life can get sticky."

"Makes sense." She poked at her chicken, her appetite fading as her interest in Tex grew. "I mean, I've had some bad bosses. But I had the option to quit. You can't do that in the military."

"No, ma'am." He sat back and patted his belly. "Damn, that was good."

"Want more?"

"I will." He winked. "But not yet. Gotta let my food settle first. But don't let me stop you from eating."

She forced herself to take another bite, not sure where her appetite had gone, and focused instead on the beets, which were amazing, if she did say so herself.

"What about you? What's your story?"

Since he'd shared his own, she thought it only fair to share hers. "Well, I didn't join the military. I had a pretty nice life with a great family—minus the stepsister." She wrinkled her nose, wishing she could stop feeling the hurt that always accompanied the anger at thoughts of Melissa. "I was lucky enough to model for a few years out of high school. I learned a lot, living in Europe on my own."

"I can't believe your dad let you go."

"Right?" She laughed. "I couldn't either, but I wanted to go, and he'd promised my mom he'd always support my dreams." She missed her mother sometimes, so much. But Charlie had helped fill a maternal role with love and support, balancing Bree's father. "My mom passed away when I was a kid. Totally random accident."

"Oh, man. I'm sorry."

"Me too." She liked that his empathy wasn't over- or underwhelming. It just was. "Anyway, my mom had done some modeling, and she said she'd learned a lot from the experience. I did too."

"All good?"

"And bad. Heck, I was eighteen in a foreign city on my own—Paris. Trust me when I say I learned a lot." She smiled. "I made great friends. I met my best friend, Carrie, through our time modeling. We roomed together over there. They take a bunch of girls and put them together in cheap apartments. You live in a big group while you do smaller shows and magazines. It was fun, but man, a lifetime ago." She laughed at herself. "People seem so impressed by it. It wasn't easy, but it was something I did that made me enough money to come home, get a loan for a house, and figure out how to make a living as a photographer. I learned a lot being on the other end of a photoshoot."

"Makes sense." He nodded. "Probably why you're so good at your job now."

Pleasure made her smile. "I hope so."

"Yeah, you did a killer good job on the calendar for Pets Fur Life. And it ain't easy to make Hernandez and Wash look good," he teased. "Hell, you even made Reggie look human."

"Oh, stop."

He laughed. "Okay, now I'm ready for more food."

He polished off any leftovers she'd hoped to leave him for the next day then fed Bubbles, who only nosed at her meal, more interested in watching them. They did the dishes together, which annoyed him because he insisted the guest, who had cooked, shouldn't be dirtying her hands with dishes.

She really wanted to meet his mother to thank her. Tex might still be a playboy with a lot of exes, but he was courteous when it counted.

The sun had set, the dishes sat in the drying rack, and Bree needed to figure out how to gracefully go home. Especially because she didn't want to. Her traitorous body kept trying to figure out how to get in Tex's way so he'd have to touch her. Or, maybe, to somehow trip and fuse mouths so she could finally get that kiss she was dying to take.

But she wouldn't, because that would be the surest way to screw up their working relationship. Not to mention send mixed signals, considering all she'd said and done to convince him to be "just a friend."

"Well, Bree, that was super." Tex stood very close to her, drying off his hands at the sink. "I can't thank you enough for that meal."

"S-sure." She blinked up at him, thinking his eyes had never seemed brighter.

He took a step closer, looked as if he meant to reach out and touch her, then shoved his hands in his pockets instead. "Um, well, I, uh, should probably go get changed out of my uniform. And, uh, let you go to finish up your night." He gave a weird laugh, a shaky chuckle that turned into a cough. "I doubt you want me to take up all your Saturday."

"No." *I want you to kiss me.* "I mean, thanks for today. And for dinner."

"You cooked it."

"You paid for it." She couldn't stop staring at his eyes.

He leaned closer, his gaze fixed to her mouth.

She felt the heat between them, the feather of his breath over her lips.

Bubbles whined, and they both jumped back.

Tex shoved his hands deeper in his pockets.

She gave the dog a thankful glance and moved to her camera bag. "Oh, you have to drive me home."

He nodded. "Sure thing. You mind if I change real quick?"

"Sure."

And he meant quick. Tex returned to her in a blink wearing a pair of sweats and a T-shirt that clung to his broad chest.

"You must lift weights a lot. You look huge."

"If I say that's what she said, are you gonna crack me one?" He bit his lip to keep from laughing.

And that easily, the sexual tension that had been building eased into something not as hot, but something deeper and more confusing. "Okay, Romeo. Drive me home."

He hurried to grab his keys and wallet, then opened the door for her and Bubbles, whom he brought along on her leash.

"She's coming?"

"I don't want to leave her all alone in a strange place."

She watched him.

He flushed. "What?"

"Nothing." *God, what a nice guy. And he'd hate for me to say that.*

"I don't trust that look." He stomped over to the truck, scooted Bubbles in, then opened the passenger door for Bree.

"Why, thank you, kind sir."

"Cut it out." Tex's mouth quirked. "I ain't no sir."

"You mean you're no gentleman." Though she wasn't so sure on that. He'd been gentle and kind as could be with Bubbles. And with her.

"Potato, po-tah-to. Let's get you home."

He dropped her off, and not content to leave her at her walkway, he left the truck to walk her up to her door. "I'll see you tomorrow. Ten okay?"

"Sure." On impulse, she suggested, "I usually meet my friend

Carrie for Sunday breakfast. Would you like to join us, and we could get to work after that?"

Tex watched her, looking for what, she couldn't guess. "Sounds good."

"Okay. I'll text you the place. See you then." When he made no move to leave, she frowned. "I'm okay. You can go now."

"I will, just as soon as you get inside. I'm not leaving until you're behind a locked door." He waited while she looked for her keys. "And before you say I'm being all protective, I do the same for Mack when I take him home." Tex grinned. "He's all fragile and stuff, not like you though. I'm watching out for you so the chief doesn't chew me a new one. With Mack, it's out of pity because the boy can't hold his liquor."

She wanted to be annoyed that he wouldn't do what she said, but he made her want to laugh. "Stop talking, and go home." She patted his cheek, because she couldn't help herself. To her delight, he froze. "And I'll see you tomorrow, Roger."

His eyes narrowed, but he still smiled. "Sure thing, Miss Gilchrist. Ten o'clock. I'll be there. No doubt waiting for you to be five minutes late."

She unlocked her door, walked through, and closed it behind her.

A quick peek out the dormer showed Tex strolling away.

Just as easy as you please.

She sighed, watching those buns until he left the glow of her porchlight. Then she swore, realizing she'd have to tell Carrie who would be joining them for breakfast tomorrow.

But watching Carrie try to get Tex to crack before he charmed her into a smile would be worth the fallout from her BFF. She just had to make sure she kept her wavering feelings for Tex in check. Let Carrie even get a hint that she was starting to feel affection in addition to any sense of lust and Carrie would give her a huge lecture Bree could do without.

Carrie could be brutal that way.

Nope. Not gonna happen. Because Bree didn't feel anything but physical attraction to Tex. And maybe a small case of the likes. Yeah, very small.

Chapter Seven

SUNDAY MORNING, TEX SPENT HIS TIME IN CHURCH PRAYING he could keep his feelings for Bree in his pants. The previous night, he'd had to take himself in hand, so worked up from being near Bree, he'd been horny and miserable until he'd taken care of things. Twice.

The church service went well, and he took a selfie of himself after it ended and sent it to his mother, who swore he'd be losing his soul in a city of sin like Seattle. But she just said that stuff to get a rise out of him, he knew. His mother had never been a holy roller. More like a hell-raiser who thought she hid her past behind Southern manners. Ha. As if his daddy would have married a nice girl.

He grinned, feeling the love of his family as she texted back a picture of Oliver and Wyatt behind her, making faces.

He signed off and left to meet Bree and her friend, trying to calm his nerves. But it was important that Carrie like him. If Bree's friend liked him, Bree might be more inclined to let him into her world. As it stood now, they were associates and close to being real friends.

Last night he could have made a move. He'd seen her response to him, had felt the mutual attraction. But he'd stuck to his guns, wanting *her* to make the first move. She had to like him as a person and not just the extraordinary lover he knew himself to be.

A stroke of luck that she'd softened after seeing him with Bubbles, the poor thing, though that hadn't been his intention. He'd just wanted her to know he wasn't lying, and his focus had been to rescue the dog from a bad situation.

Last night, Bubbles had followed him everywhere in the house, looking so hopeful. He'd paid her attention and tossed a ball for her that she'd expressed little interest in. So, he'd simply let her follow him everywhere. Into the garage while he lifted weights. Sitting on the floor with him while he'd watched a movie on TV before going to bed. Then, of course, she'd snuck up on the bed, at the very edge, and just watched him with those soulful eyes until he fell asleep.

The little darlin' had looked so dang sad when he'd left her that morning. He had no idea how he was supposed to keep a dog, even for a few days, until Oscar and Gerty found her a home. She needed love and attention, more than he could give her. But after just a day, he started to feel attached. Not good.

Yeah, and not just about the dog either.

Tex knew this fixation on Bree would be a problem. He wasn't good at relationships. Her father didn't want her dating him. And Bree frazzled him. He had a tough time being smooth and cool in her presence, feeling more like a dippy teen wanting a shot at the prom queen.

He ran a hand over his face, silently apologized to God and his momma for being so hung up on sex, and talked himself into being relaxed as he charmed the hell out of Bree's best friend.

But when he got to the restaurant Bree had texted him, he realized Carrie was going to be a huge pain in the ass. She sneered his way, not smiling, and clearly had intimidation down to a science with that stare. Like a snake that didn't blink, was all he could think, feeling like a field mouse.

"I still can't believe you won that settlement. I should have been a lawyer," Bree said to her friend as he approached their table at a popular diner in Queen Anne.

She practiced law. He now understood the scare factor. Woman had brass balls…and a familiar face. He knew her from somewhere. Good-looking, stern, and icy. Now where had he met or seen her before?

"Ladies." He sat across the booth from the pair. Even seated, Carrie looked tall. "Well, how tall are you? I gotta know."

"I'm six-two. Want my weight and other stats?" Her husky voice surprised him, coming from a woman who seemed comfortable being aloof.

Oh, yeah. Now he remembered her. He smiled, recalling her being competitive…and a lawyer, like his sister-in-law. He knew exactly how to handle Carrie.

Bree looked lovely as usual, her hair resting over her shoulders, a honeyed yellow with streaks of burnished gold. Her light-blue eyes laughed at him while her full lips curled in a smile.

Carrie raised a brow and said to Bree, "I thought you said he was charming."

"Oh, I am. Just after a cup of coffee goes down." He smiled, putting his all into the expression.

Carrie didn't blink.

Tex waited for Bree to introduce them. When she didn't, he held out a hand across the Formica table. "Howdy. Carrie, is it? I'm Tex McGovern, Bree's chauffeur for the next two weeks. Nice to meet you."

Carrie met his handshake with a firm grip. "You too." Her sly smile warned him to be wary. "I've heard *so* much about you. It's good to put a face to the name."

"Heard what about me, exactly?" he aimed at Bree.

Carrie answered, "Well, first there was the ex-girlfriend. Then ghosting Bree when she gave you a second chance. And of course, your legendary charm, which has been clearly shown to be less than successful." She glanced at Bree. "Or not, since you did wrangle an invitation to brunch."

"But is it brunch? It's only ten in the morning, so technically this is breakfast."

Her eyes narrowed, and he could see her scenting the opening of an argument. Hell, she really did remind him of Liam's wife, an assistant DA back home. Nothing made that woman happier than to argue.

Carrie had been cut from the same cloth.

A waitress came by to fill his cup. He'd barely taken a sip of coffee before Carrie insisted it was brunch and proceeded to list several reasons as to why she was right.

"Well, I'll tell you something else," Tex said once she'd wound down. "It's not brunch in Germany right now, is it?" She frowned at him. "But hell, it's after five somewhere, right? So, keep on drinking your cocktail. Who am I to judge?"

"Cocktail? You mean my mimosa."

Bree glanced at her glass. "Second mimosa."

"That's obvious, isn't it?" Carrie handed her empty glass to their approaching waiter.

He left after taking Tex's order and confirming the usual for the ladies.

Bree's eyes widened. "Are you really going to eat an omelet, three pancakes, and two sides of meat?"

"I'm a growing boy, Bree. I need my protein." He looked over the ladies. "You two look like you're in shape. What are you getting?"

"Our standard order," Carrie said. "Bree gets French toast, and I get the classic benny."

"Good choice for you. But Bree... French toast?"

Carrie turned on her. "See? Too much sugar."

"Hey. Be on my side." Bree frowned.

"Now hold on." Tex held up a hand. "I was just going to say that you should have ordered the chocolate chip pancakes if you want sweet. French toast is pretentious."

The ladies blinked.

"That's a pretty big word, Tex." Carrie snorted.

He sighed. "Let's not with the stereotypes, Miss Legal Eagle."

"Say what you want, I solve problems and put out fires."

"I put out *actual* fires," he reminded her.

"Oh, right." She waved him away. "That's important, I guess."

Tex met Bree's amused gaze and winked.

Carrie raised a brow. "But have you ever made a grown man cry?"

"Yep."

"I, oh." Carrie frowned. "When?"

"I don't suppose we could talk about something nice?" Bree suggested. "The weather's amazing, isn't it?"

Tex leaned forward. "I'll tell you when. When I bet my friend the Ducks would overtake the Beavers in a long-ago basketball game. Ha. 72–57 win for me. Beavers bit it big time, and I made a hundred bucks."

Carrie glared. "That had to have been a lucky win."

"But was it really?"

Bree frowned. "You like Oregon basketball?"

Tex shrugged. "It's okay. I just wanted to get her goat, is all." To Carrie he said, "You played center for OSU ten years ago, right? I was a sophomore dating a girl who went to Oregon State, and I visited for a bit. I swear I saw you play."

Carrie blinked. "You saw me play basketball?"

"I never forget a pretty woman, especially one who can dunk." Tex chuckled. "Sexiest thing I ever seen." He glanced at Bree. "I mean, back then it was. Not now or anything."

Bree was flabbergasted. "You really saw her play?"

She looked at Carrie, who seemed nonplussed.

"Yep. I don't think you can forget a six-two woman who dunks through her opponents. It was poetry. Absolutely amazing. You guys lost, but not on account of your playing. And, like I said, I won a hundred bucks off that game, so thanks."

"Are you seriously saying you saw me play, and you remember me today?"

Tex nodded. "Carrie, I never forget a face. It's a gift."

"Wow. That's some gift." She seemed intrigued, and that chip on her shoulder seemed to slide, slowly, to the wayside. "Do you play basketball? Or I should say, *did* you play?"

"Some when I was in high school. A little in college for fun, but I left my studies to enlist in the Corps. Sometimes the guys and I play a little ball. But I lean toward soccer or football as favorite sports. Now *watching* college and professional basketball, on the other hand, is something I love to do."

"Yeah?" Carrie's eyes glowed. "Who's your favorite team?"

―――――――――

Bree watched and wondered what had happened. Carrie had sworn she was going to grill him, to make Tex realize how ridiculous it would be to think he might have a chance with Bree. Even though Bree wasn't at all interested… Carrie hadn't seemed as if she believed Bree on that score, but Bree would rather have Carrie focused on Tex—the enemy—than her, so she hadn't protested overmuch.

But to see Carrie so animated, talking about basketball with a man who'd complimented her play… Wow. Tex was *good*.

They ate while talking about sports, including Bree in on what she liked to watch, which oddly enough was soccer, but mostly for the women's skill and the men's lovely bodies, until Tex excused himself to use the restroom.

The moment he was out of sight, Bree poked Carrie in the arm. "What the hell?"

"Ow. Sorry." Carrie rubbed her arm. "God, he's good. I mean, really good. He charmed me, and I was on my guard! Bree, you didn't tell me about the dog."

Tex had mentioned Bubbles in between references to the Trailblazers and greatly missed Supersonics.

"I know. But you like animals, and I didn't want you softening toward him. Weakling."

"Yeah. I don't know how you're holding out. The first two times with you two were legit misses. But rescuing an older dog? Liking basketball? Looking like a stunt double from *Magic Mike*?" Carrie grinned. "And Bree, he likes my dunk. I have to say, I like him."

"You disgust me."

Carrie sighed. "I know. I disgust myself. And I'm not even into guys. But I like him."

Bree gaped. "Seriously?"

Carrie frowned. "What? Oh, gross. No, not like that. I mean, I think he's a lot better than his first impression. That or he's really good at bullshitting. Tex seems genuine. Nice."

"Too nice." Bree looked back at the restroom. "We had dinner together last night, after he saved Bubbles."

"On a date?" Carrie shook her head. "You're supposed to keep your distance."

"He'd just rescued Bubbles. I couldn't say no to that."

"Oh, okay. So?"

"So nothing. He didn't make a move. I felt like he wanted to, but he didn't."

"Hmm." Carrie watched the hallway by the restroom. "Well played, Tex McGovern."

"What? You think he's playing me?"

"It's what I'd do. I can tell he's still into you. He's talking to me, but he keeps looking at you, involving you in the conversation. And you're lame when it comes to basketball."

"It's boring."

"Sacrilege!"

Bree laughed. "You're a goof." After a pause, she said, "How is he playing me?"

"I don't know exactly. He might just be giving you what you asked for. But if it was me... I'd do what you said, keep my distance, and make you want me more."

"But he can't know I want him."

"I can tell."

"Yeah, but you know me."

"Aha! I knew you still wanted him."

"Damn it. I mean, I'm attracted." She lowered her voice. "He's Southern and sexy with a deep voice and big old body. He's hot. But I'm being careful. Professional. No sex or kissing. No touching. Just friends."

"Sure you are. That or you've come over to my side of the fence."

"Nope. I'm just focused on work right now."

Tex left the restroom and headed toward them.

"I'm not into guys, and I can't focus on anything but his body as he's walking toward us. Maybe it's the model in me. I don't know. I do know the man is pretty, Bree. As an artist, you should be appreciating his body."

"Oh, I am."

"And I have to say, even if he's bad at sex—and with the smooth way he moves, I doubt that's the case—you still can't go wrong. His bad will still be pretty good for a normal guy, I'd imagine. At the very least, he'll look good while he's being bad in bed."

"Shh. He might read lips."

Carrie hid her mouth behind her mimosa. "And if he can't read my lips, he can always hear your loud voice, moron."

Bree blushed as Tex rejoined them and tried to hide his smile by taking a sip of coffee. "What's this about me being bad in bed?"

———

Half an hour later in his truck, Tex apologized. Again. "I'm sorry I made you spit coffee all over yourself." His voice, still tinged with laughter, sounded gritty. "I had no idea my sex life was so interesting. But I'd really like to know who told you that. It's not true at all." He didn't seem bothered by a need to defend himself. He kept laughing at her.

Since Carrie had driven her to the restaurant, Bree had ridden with Tex when they'd swung by his friends' apartment to give them a key along with some details about poor Bubbles. Now they headed to Occidental Square so she could take shots of the Seattle Fallen Firefighters Memorial.

She wanted to change the subject of why she had been talking about his prowess in bed. "I've never taken pictures of the memorial, believe it or not. I know it was built to honor four firefighters who died in the line of duty, but that's about it."

"The tribute is pretty cool, actually. The four died while fighting a warehouse fire. Floor dropped out beneath them. Happened in 1995 in the Chinatown district. Really sad. I like that the city remembers them."

She liked that too. "It makes you realize how scary your job is. I'm glad my dad isn't running into fires anymore. It's got to be hard for you."

"It's not easy. But it's worthwhile. That's how I know it's the job for me. And let's be honest, most of our time is downtime— cleaning, resupplying, training. When we do go out, eighty percent of our calls are medical. They're mostly stressful for the patients. Not us. I just get worried we'll lose someone. Hasn't happened yet, but I know it will." He paused. "Brad and Mack lost a kid last month. It really hit them hard. They did everything they could to help, but it was too late."

"How do you do it?"

"It's the job. I try to focus on the ones we save." He shrugged. "How do you do what you do?"

"It's not the same at all. No one dies if I wear the wrong dress or use the wrong exposure."

"True. But what you do is still important, and it feels right to you. Doesn't it?"

He continued to surprise her with his insights and acceptance. A lot of people scoffed at modeling, as if she had to be an empty-headed woman in love with her looks and the idea of fame to get paid to wear clothes. But modeling had been hard work. Long hours, maintaining poses, watching her figure constantly. It had been a challenge to maintain any kind of ego with too many people eager to point out her flaws.

"Hey, you okay?"

"Yeah. Thanks." She put a hand on his knee and squeezed before putting her hand back in her own lap. "So many people make fun of modeling. It's not easy. Photography isn't easy either. It's an art, and like art, it's tough to make a living at it. But you're right. I love it. There's nothing I'd rather be doing."

He nodded, his gaze approving.

She liked the warmth he instilled, how natural it felt to simply talk to him. He listened to her and made eye contact when not watching the road. She just hoped it wasn't all a ploy to get into her pants.

After Carrie's comment in the restaurant, now she was wondering about the meaning behind a lot of what Tex had to say.

"Anyway, maybe we'll—"

The scanner interrupted. A serious fire had broken out in Greenwood.

Tex turned the wheel and flicked on the sirens. "This could be bad. Get your camera ready, and listen when I tell you to fall back, okay?"

"I will. Trust me."

Tex parked down from the fire and rushed over to one of the officers in charge. He checked in and returned with a handheld radio, likely set with the operational channel and a comms link, through which the firefighters communicated.

The engine unit had the fire contained within an hour. Bree managed to get several shots while Tex stood with her, helping her past the police barricade but still back from the action.

She did her best to focus on the actual fire and not the terrible sight of burn victims and crying.

Three stations had arrived to take the fire in hand. She took as many pictures as she could, convinced several of them would make it into her project. The fire had shattered several windows on the second floor of the building, fortunately not a large building, so less people would have suffered.

The ladder unit that swung by had been put into use, rescuing a few families that couldn't access the stairs.

Tex's blow-by-blow as he listened to the comms unit in hand filled her in on everything while she took pictures.

A ruckus in the crowd had her turning, taking more shots, but this time of a heartbroken teenager. "Mom! Grandpa!"

"Bobby!"

The officer there tried to keep the teen back, but the boy got through.

"Shoot. Stay here," Tex said and darted to intercept the boy before he could reach the responders.

Bree couldn't help herself and snapped a few pictures, watching. Tex physically held back the teenager, who stood only a few inches shorter than Tex and looked like a high school wrestler.

"I live here! My mom and gramps are in there!"

"Hold on. Stop." Tex issued commands like a whip, and the boy stopped trying to push past him. "What's your name?"

"Bobby Childers."

"Okay, Bobby. What's your mom and grandpa's name?"

Bobby told him, and Tex brought the handheld up. "Mallory two, this is McGovern. I have a relative asking about Mona and Todd Childers. Any word on them?" He paused, nodded, then turned to the teen. "Come with me, Bobby. I'll take you to your mom." He shot Bree a look, and she nodded.

"Go." She waved at the circle of chaos where several medical trucks worked with the victims. In the middle of everything, Tex gave the appearance of surety, of safety. He didn't waver as he guided the young man toward his family, and she couldn't help snapping pictures of him working.

He returned a few minutes later. "Damn. That's so sad. The boy's mom is okay, but his grandfather started the fire. Guy had dementia, it seems. They were planning on moving him into an assisted living home next week."

Bree blinked back tears. "That's awful."

"Yeah. They were a tight family too. That poor kid is crying his eyes out."

She sniffed. "How terrible."

He shrugged. "It is what it is."

She'd seen that same stoic response from her father after many a rough day at work. She understood. A need to separate from too many negative emotions allowed her father to do his job and help those he could.

"Do you need to go back in there and help? I'm fine here. I promise I won't go anywhere near the action."

"You're close enough as it is." He looked down at her, and something in him seemed to ease. "You okay, Bree?"

"I'm good. It's not my house and family in danger."

He stroked her cheek once before losing that gentle mien. "I'm just going to let them know I can help if they need it. You sure you're okay? My job is to take care of you."

"Please, go. Helping them is much more important than my pictures."

He left but came back soon after. "They have it handled. I'd only be in the way, and I don't want to step on any toes. Greenwood and Ballard have this. You ready to head home?"

She sighed. "Yes. It's been a long day."

"And it's only seven." He sighed with her. "Some days are longer than others."

They took the truck back to her place so he could drop her off, and she unbuckled her seat belt, her hand on the door to leave.

"I smell like smoke." To her embarrassment, she teared up, memories of those poor people suffering all she could think about.

"Hey, hey. It's okay, Bree." Tex removed his belt and dragged her closer. He fiddled with the seat and had her in his lap, braced in a hug.

She felt silly but couldn't stop crying. "I'm s-sorry. I feel s-stupid." She sniffled.

"Aw, darlin'. It's good to cry. Get it out. You felt for those people. Ain't nothin' wrong with that."

She tentatively reached up to hug him back, and he squeezed her tighter. The hug felt comforting, not oppressive, and she let herself cry it out, wetting his shirt.

After a moment, he handed her a handkerchief. "Here. Probably smells like the fire, but it'll do."

Bree gave a hoarse chuckle. "Thanks." She blew her nose, now extremely embarrassed for having cried over the poor man while he'd been out there actually helping people, doing real work while she just took pictures. "I'm sorry, Tex. I don't know why I lost it. I've never been that close to a real fire while people were hurt, I guess."

He leaned back so he could look into her face. "Don't apologize for having feelings. It's not easy for any of us, and we're used to it."

She looked into his eyes, seeing the man behind all the come-ons and flirting.

Time stopped as she tugged him toward her, saw him close his eyes and part his lips. She kissed him, the connection clear and warm. His lips, though firm, felt soft against hers, and she sighed into him, content to sit with him like this forever.

But an intense need filled her, the desire to deepen the contact overriding sense. She pushed closer, angling her mouth to deepen the kiss. Then she slid her tongue over his lips, into his mouth.

He gripped her, holding her waist while tentatively kissing her back. He shifted under her legs, and the brush of something firm nudged her thigh.

Bree's mind shut off as her body took over. She wanted

nothing more than to take him inside her, right here, right now. Overwhelming lust removed any hints of sadness she'd been feeling, and she knew only Tex could satisfy her.

She felt his heart racing against her palm and smoothed her hands over his chest. She nipped his lip, and he growled, but he still held back.

"Tex?" she whispered and pulled back to look up at him.

His eyes had turned dark, his expression tense, his breathing harsh. "Bree... Not...now." He leaned his head back and swore, long and loud.

She debated asking then decided to go big. "Did you want to come inside?"

Tex didn't give her the yes she'd hoped for. He laughed like a crazy man.

The prick.

"Fine." Now near tears once more, but for a different reason, she made to move from his lap and found he wouldn't let her.

"No, wait." He opened his eyes and stared, and her embarrassment turned to wonder. "We go into your place, I'm gonna fuck you raw. All night. I'm not kidding. I want you." He drew in a breath when she unconsciously moved against his erection. "But not like this."

"Like what, then?" she asked, fascinated. She would have sworn Tex would jump on the chance to have sex with her. Was he that afraid of her father? Perhaps that was it. Ah, well. "It's my dad, isn't it?"

"No." He dragged her close for a kiss that turned her brain to mush. "Baby, when you and I are together, it'll be right. Fun, sexy, and lasting a very long time. I fuck you now, I'm done in seconds. You got me too worked up. And you're still kinda sad." He wiped her wet cheeks. "God, you're pretty, Bree." He kissed her lips once more. "I've wanted you since the day I first saw you. I still want you. But I don't want to take advantage. I like you. A fuck-ton."

She blinked. "That's a lot, right?"

"Hell, yeah." He shifted under her and grimaced. "This isn't a game. I'm not trying to yank you around. But I think we should both go home and think on this. I'm being honest."

"I know." She marveled at this Tex. Serious, handsome, and so dear.

Then he opened his mouth and ruined everything.

Chapter Eight

TEX SAT GLUMLY WITH BUBBLES AND THE GUYS AT HIS HOUSE Wednesday night, drinking beer and listening to some terrible alt-rock crap Mack insisted outsold Brad Paisley any day of the week. He'd held them off with the truth of his disastrous Sunday night with Bree. But after three days of arctic silence with the chick, he knew he needed help.

They sat around his dining table, the cards and chips out for a night of beer and poker while he tried to figure out how to fix things with Bree. He only had another week of being paired with her, and he knew if he didn't set things right before they parted, she'd end up never talking to him again.

"Hold on." Brad grinned as he petted an enthusiastic Bubbles, who'd taken to his friends as if they'd always been one big, old pack. "You had her on the ropes, the mood was set."

"You'd been honest," Reggie added. "Talking things out."

Tex nodded. "I was trying to do right by her."

Mack's brows shot up. "By telling her to really think about what she wanted, because once she had a taste of Tex's testicles, she'd fall in love and be ruined for all other men?"

Tex flushed when they laughed at him. "Fuck off. It wasn't like that." He paused. "I mean, I did warn her she'd fall for me. They all do."

More laughter, which had the damn dog baying. Huh. First time she'd ever done that.

"I just wanted her to be ready in case we hook up and it fails."

Reggie scratched his head. "That's kind of like proposing by saying, 'I want you to marry me, and here's the prenup for when it falls apart.'"

Mack hooted.

Tex groaned. "Honesty gets you shit."

Brad set his beer down to shuffle the cards. "Tex, you are so much better than that. What happened to you?"

He wished he could say. It was like his balls had fried the circuitry in his brain. Kissing Bree had been better than he'd expected, and he'd been expecting some explosive chemistry. He'd been close to shooting his wad just from her sitting on his lap. He wanted her with every breath, heartbeat, and blink of her pretty eyes. And that scared the crap out of him.

Once with Bree wouldn't be enough. He knew it. He wanted her to know it too before she committed to sleeping with him.

"Hell. I should have just slept with her. She'd be hooked on me, and I'd be a happy man now instead of hanging with you pricks."

"Real nice." Reggie glared at him. "Hey, it's not our fault you stepped on your own dick."

"I know, damn it." Tex dropped his head to the table.

Mack snickered. "I never thought I'd live to see the day that Tex couldn't make the magic happen. My world is so much brighter now."

"Well, Tex, if it makes you feel any better, we miss you at the station," Brad said. "The new guy we've been training has no sense of humor."

"Truth." Reggie sighed. "And he's a kiss-ass."

Tex lifted his head. "You're miserable without me? That helps."

Bubbles left Brad to nuzzle Tex's hand. He stroked her. "Hey, girl. At least you love me."

"She's so cute." Mack left his seat to pet her. "But how can you keep her?" He gave her a final pat and sat back down.

"I can't." Tex felt a bellyful of regret. "She needs a yard and kids. People around her a lot." He frowned. "You know, I wonder if my family would take her."

"You don't think she'll get adopted here?" Reggie huffed. "Tex, there are like four million people in Seattle. Someone will take her. She's a sweetie. Aren't you, Bubbles?"

Bubbles grinned, her tongue hanging out, and barked.

The guys laughed.

"Yeah, but how will we know she's in a good home?" Tex worried. "My family's got a ranch."

"In Houston," Brad said. "That's kind of far, you know."

"I'll think of something." Tex hated to let Bubbles get adopted by someone who'd ignore her. Dogs were special. Hell, he preferred them to people a lot of the time. Maybe he'd call down to the family and see if one of them could make a road trip. Wyatt was nutty like that. Maybe he'd take some time to drive up in his RV and take Bubbles back home.

"So one lady who likes you." Reggie rubbed Bubbles's ears. The dog was in heaven. "And then there's another lady who wouldn't bat an eye if you disappeared off the face of the planet."

"Thanks, man." Tex glared.

Brad dealt the cards. "You ask me—"

"I didn't."

"—you need to up your game. Bring her flowers. Grovel a little. Women love that."

"You'd know," Mack muttered.

Brad glared at him and finished dealing. "Just be sincere without all that beating your chest crap."

"I tried. I really like her. I don't want her to hate me." *When it's over. Because it's always over.* Tex wanted so badly to have a lasting relationship like his parents. Like his eldest brothers. But he'd been dating for over ten years, and nothing stuck. It freaked him out. McGoverns weren't supposed to divorce. So, when he felt a relationship wasn't going anywhere, he ended it, and better sooner than later. He'd never once experienced that spark with another like his parents talked about.

Well, not counting Bree. But with her, that spark felt more like buried frustration. God knew they had sexual chemistry. A fuck-ton, as he'd said to her. But that kind tended to fizzle out fast, and he wanted to savor his time with Bree.

Maybe he should just let her have a taste of him and see for herself that he'd been telling her the truth. He was plumb amazing.

"Hey, Tex, how many can you take?"

"Huh?" He looked down at the cards he'd been dealt. "I thought we were playing Texas Hold'em."

"Nah, Spades," Mack said. "Weren't you listening?"

"Fine." He preferred Spades, having played plenty in the Marine Corps. "Me and Brad versus you two."

"Again? You guys always pair up." Reggie frowned.

Both Marines, Brad and Tex generally whipped the others. Reggie wasn't too bad, but Mack sucked. And he knew it.

"Stakes?" Tex asked.

"Losing team has to wash the winners' cars," Brad said.

"That's not fair. Mine is spotless." Mack scowled.

"Maybe if you got a girl and spent less time in that car, this could be a win for you too." Tex frowned at his buddy. "Dude, you need a girlfriend. Seriously."

"Shut up. Seems to me all you guys with girls have girl problems."

"Amen." Reggie nodded.

Tex scoffed. "Yeah, the anti-dater backin' you up really strengthens your argument."

Reggie didn't look too pleased with him or Brad when he laughed.

"Fine." Mack shrugged. "But loser *also* has to bring in a baker's dozen from Sofa's. Mix and match on the treats."

"That sounds fair." Brad nodded. "I mean, since you'll be paying."

Tex agreed. "Brad, you have to let me know when they come in and save me a few. I'm with Bree till next week."

Mack smiled. "Look on the bright side, Tex. You keep pissing her off, and you'll be back working with us that much sooner."

"Hurray," Reggie said without inflection.

Tex laughed. "Oh, come on, Reg. You know you miss me."

"Like I miss your cooking."

"Aw, see. You do miss me."

Reggie rolled his eyes. "Thick like a brick."

"Like a brick wall." Tex flexed. "And strong as one. Check me out."

Brad and Mack were laughing.

Reggie just sighed. "Okay, Mack. It's time to finally beat the Marines. How many bags can you take?"

The bidding got underway. Brad and Tex took the first four rounds. Mack and Reggie managed to take one and got cocky. They then lost the rest of the game.

Tex brought out more snacks and beer. Even Bubbles got a new bone.

"I want it to shine, Mack. Yeah, I want *you* cleaning my truck. You know how to take care of your wheels. Reggie…not so much."

"Up yours." Reggie flipped him off.

"But if I can make a recommendation, at Sofa's, make sure you get a few of their apple fritters. And some blondies. They're amazing."

As they settled down to finish their food and discuss the goings-on at the station, Tex peppered them with ideas about how to win Bree over.

To his surprise, Mack, of all people, came up with the best one.

"I do have hidden talents," Mack said and took a bow from the couch.

"Yeah, who knew?" Brad grabbed the chips. "But seriously, Tex. Mack has a good point. Try it his way. What have you got to lose? She already seems to hate you."

Reggie clapped Tex on the shoulder in sympathy.

"Ow." Tex rubbed his shoulder. "Easy. I'm fragile."

Mack pointed a chip at him. "Exactly. Fragile. Vulnerable. Just pile that shit on. Women love trying to fix us."

"I thought honesty was best."

Reggie snorted. "Yeah, right. Because telling her you're scared of commitment is a lie?"

Brad agreed. "Seriously. Lay it on the line for her. That's after you hit her with the flowers. Just try it. Like I said, what have you got to lose?"

———————————

But Tex played it smart the next day. He kept quiet, was polite, and did whatever Bree told him to instead of trying to charm her into forgiving him. She kept giving him looks he ignored. By lunchtime, he could see the politeness getting to her.

"Okay." She let out a loud breath. "Let's talk about what you said the other day."

"I apologize."

Her eyes narrowed. They sat outside at a park in Queen Anne, enjoying sandwiches on a picnic table. The sky overhead was a robin's-egg blue. Wispy, white clouds fluttered in the cooling breeze while the sun smiled down on the city. The mild temperature hinted at the coming summer, not too cool that Tex couldn't enjoy his Seattle FD T-shirt with his Nomex pants and a ballcap to keep out the sun.

Bree wore sunglasses, masking her eyes, and a pink tee and jeans with sneakers. He thought she looked beautiful, and when piqued, adorable. But no way in hell he'd mention that. He was keeping to the plan. Being courteous yet slightly distant before taking the blame for everything. Even the fact that the earth was round, if it would make her happy.

He still didn't think he'd been wrong for being honest before, but perhaps he could have stated his position a little more gently.

"Sorry for what, exactly?" she asked before biting into a ham and cheese sub.

"I had no intention of hurting your feelings or coming across like an ass, which I obviously did." He gave her a self-effacing smile. She didn't react. "Look, you want the truth?"

"I thought you already gave me the truth." She smirked. "You remember. When you said all women fall for you, and the sex makes it worse. That I'd be hurt if I expected too much." She snorted. "As if your penis should be gold-plated."

It really should. He swallowed that response. "No two ways about it, that sounded pretty cocky—no pun intended." Ah, there, she had to bite back a smile. "And condescending. I didn't mean it to sound that way." He frowned and tipped up his hat. "You know, after it came out of my mouth, I just sat there, stunned. I wanted to say that I want you, I think you're too beautiful and way too good for me, and that I prayed I wouldn't screw up a good thing." He'd practiced that line over and over again. She had yet to blink. "But instead, I messed it up so I wouldn't be surprised when I messed it up later, I guess." *Wait, that feels like it might be a little true.*

"Oh?"

She needed more groveling.

"It's just… I've dated a lot. I never lied about that. But I never liked a gal the way I like you." He felt the blush from his neck to his ears. Talk about corny.

"Really?" She sounded partially skeptical. He'd count that as a win, because that meant another part of her might believe him.

"Yeah. Sounds dumb, but when we texted and talked, even briefly on the phone, I felt like you saw the real me. And I thought you were as funny and as smart as you are pretty. Then all that crap happened with my ex and my exploding phone. Like, the worst luck a guy could possibly have."

"You're not wrong."

He sighed. "I know. I just couldn't let you blow me off a third time, not when once again I was just trying to help somebody. You know, Bubbles."

"Well, technically you kidnapped me. But it was for a good cause."

He groaned. "You see? This is my life when it comes to you. I want to look good. I come across as a jackass. I finally get the green light from you, and I'm so afraid of fucking it up—excuse my language—that I fuck it up anyhow. I just… I can't lie. I want you real bad." His voice thickened. "But I like you. I don't want us to be over. I'm killer good in the sack, by the way. So that's not the problem."

"Then what is?" Her blue eyes shone with mirth and more than a little interest.

Thank God.

"You have to ask? It's my foot. And my mouth. Together."

"True." She nodded to his sandwich. "You going to eat?"

He had lost his appetite, so nervous she'd refuse to deal with him on any kind of friendly level again. "I will. Just…forgive me, okay? It would mean a lot. I swear I won't bug you anymore, and I'll keep my hard-ons to myself."

"Well, now, don't be too hasty."

———————

Shoot. Not how she'd meant to put that.

Tex blinked. "What?"

"I just mean, we've become friends. Getting to know you better has shown me you're actually a pretty decent person. *Person*," she emphasized when he appeared to get his hopes up. "Not boyfriend or lover."

"I can live with that." He smiled. "So, do I get a do-over for Sunday?"

"Um, okay." She studied him, thinking he looked tired. "I also wanted to apologize for kissing you. I mean, I guess I started it, and—"

"No, no. It was a rough day, and then we got emotional. I might not show it, but I feel it, Bree."

He sounded so earnest.

"Okay."

"I mean it. That fire and that poor guy dying, that was awful. I'm sorry you had to see that. The pictures alone tell a story, and it's tragic. I hope you can use that in your art."

"I will," she said softly, glad he didn't consider her the worst kind of voyeur, trying to take advantage of other people's pain.

"Good. Now that kiss… That was something we both wanted. I'm telling you true, if we'd gone into your house, things would have ended differently. I don't want to tell you how to feel. But I've been around a lot of trauma, and it can affect you even when you don't think it does." He glanced at his water, breaking eye contact. "I don't want you to regret being with me. If you ever decided we should be together, I'd want you to be glad. Not upset with yourself."

Bree just stared. That was one of the nicest explanations for a rejection she'd ever heard. And it made a lot of sense. "I think you're right."

His gaze shot up. "You do?"

She nodded. "I was pretty emotional after the fire. It's no secret we seem to click, physically."

"Hell, yeah. I love the way you look." He kept his gaze on her face, to his credit.

Hers slipped to his broad chest before flying back to his face. "Me too. The way you look, I mean." She coughed. "I think we could be compatible in a lot of ways."

He nodded.

"I'm not looking for anything long-term right now. And with my dad's stance on firefighters, it's tough to go there with you."

"Go there?"

"Sexually."

He flushed. "Yeah, right."

She'd give money right now to see if he felt the same butterflies she did just talking about it. But she appreciated him coming clean. "I do like you, Tex. I'm sorry we never got that good first date."

He nodded. "So, uh, do you think that maybe after this working thing is over, we could have a date? A real one, just you and me? No firefighter. No daughter of the chief. No job between us. Just a guy and a lady hanging out."

Excited at the prospect, she thought about it.

"And Bree, no pressure, okay? If you say no, I totally respect that. No hard feelings. I know you're in a tough spot with your dad. I love my career, and I could get a lot of flak from the higher-ups for asking you out. But damn, girl, I just want to be with you. Without all this." He pointed to his hat. "It's not about the station, the guys, Carrie, your dad, photography. It's you and me and enjoying some time together. In public or not. I don't care. I'd just like to be with you. That's where I'm coming from. But if you don't feel it, I respect that. Just think about it, okay? Like I said, for real, no pressure."

He bit into his sandwich, finally dropping his eyes.

She let out a silent breath, totally enamored with this man's words. She already loved his body, but she had never been treated to such an intense declaration before. He wanted Bree for Bree. She knew he wanted her. But he'd had the opportunity to have her Sunday and had said no. A user wouldn't have done that. Also, he knew Bree couldn't help his career. Quite the opposite, in fact.

"Tell me more about Carrie," he said between bites. "She hates me now, right? Because I mentioned she was pretty, and I never forget a lady's face?"

"Yeah, right. I think she wants to challenge you to a basketball game. She still plays now and then. I'd advise against it."

"No kidding?" He smiled.

God, shoot me now. That dimple is killing me. "Yep. She's hell on wheels on the court. And in the court*room*." *Ha. I have to tell her that one.*

"You guys have known each other a long time, eh?"

"She's amazing. I told you we roomed together a long time ago. She kind of took me under her wing when I was starting out modeling. She's a few years older but worlds wiser. We hit it off in Paris. That's where I met Elliot too."

"Elliot?"

She felt rather than saw his tension. "Yeah, the cutie at Sofa's bakery? My friend who called me bossy?"

"Oh, that guy." Tex frowned. "He looked like he was into you."

She was right. He was jealous. In her mind, she gave herself an air high-five. "I hate to tell you this, but he was into you."

"What?"

"Elliot likes men. He's gay."

"Oh. *Oh.*" The second "oh" sounded much lighter. "Well, I am hot. So I've been told."

"I'm going to refrain from any fireman jokes, Mr. Hot."

"And hose jokes. Don't make those either. That would be inappropriate."

She bit her lip to hide a smile. "Right. Especially since your hose is apparently addictive. And most women can't get off the Tex train once they jump on." And yes, he'd really said all that.

He cringed. "I didn't mean that the way it came out."

She laughed. "You totally did. You have an ego."

"Hell, Bree. I'm damn good in bed," he growled. "That's one area I never get complaints."

Complaints—from more than one person. Bree didn't begrudge Tex his past personal life, but she reminded herself to be cautious. "Tex, let me ask you this. Why did you break up with the lady who threw water at you?"

He groaned. "Do we have to talk about this?"

"Please." He wanted her to forgive him. Fine. She'd get all the info out of him she could. "It would go a long way toward building trust."

"Vanessa was clingy, okay? I couldn't breathe without her all over me." He shifted on the bench, clearly uncomfortable. "I think a couple should do things together. Sure. But she wanted to hang with me and the guys. Every. Night. Weekends were for us. Nights off were for us. Days off were for us. I mean, I'm all for being with the person you like or love. I liked Vanessa. She was a sweet gal."

"And pretty." Bree couldn't forget the blond beauty.

"Well, yeah, but not so pretty inside." He sighed. "I'm not one to talk behind people's backs, but you did ask. She was kind of mean about other women. She'd say stuff to me about people when we were out. And she had some issues about me hanging with just the guys. Brad, Reggie, and Mack are my brothers. You know?"

"My dad is still tight with his firefighting buddies. They do a twice-monthly poker night."

"You get it." He nodded. "I wasn't fooling around. I don't believe in cheating." He looked her right in the eye. "My parents have been happily married for thirty-four years. I learned a lot watching them. Hell, I want what they have. Maybe that's why I'm so cautious about the ladies. I'm looking for the same magic."

"Me too. My dad and mom really loved each other. And my dad was so lucky to find a new love with Charlie. She's the best." Charlie's daughter, not so much.

"It's hard. McGoverns don't do divorce. And in this day and age, with everybody breaking up, that's a lot to live up to."

"You mean no one in your family has ever gotten divorced? What if you got married and broke up? Would your parents disown you or something?"

"Heck, I don't think so. I hope not." He frowned. "It's just, I feel like I'd be lettin' them down if I brought home the wrong girl. I haven't been home in a while, and I moved out at eighteen. Never brought a girl home to Mom and Dad yet."

"What?"

"I'm not talking about high school dating. Think about it. I was briefly in college then the USMC away from home. I got out, went home for a little, then moved out here. When would I bring a woman home?"

"But you must have had some long-term relationships, right?"

"What's long term to you?" He cringed. "I sound like a bad bet, don't I?"

"Not exactly." She pondered his question. "To me, long term would be six months or more, I guess. I mean, I've introduced my parents to guys I've dated for longer than a few months."

"Nope. Longest girlfriend I had was four months, back when I was stationed in Camp Pendleton." He shrugged. "Long distance is rough when you get deployed. Like I said, I'm not one for cheating. The longest I ever had a girl, it ended when I found out she was seeing other guys when I was out of the country. I mean, I understood she was lonely. I just never understood why she couldn't have broken it off with me first. To be honest, it didn't bother me like it should have." He frowned. "Can't believe I told you that. I never think about her, honestly. But you asked, so..."

"Wow. She cheated on you?" The woman must have been insane.

"Can I pick 'em or what?" he teased and glanced at his phone. "Heck, we're wasting daylight. Eat your sandwich, and we'll get back on the road. Any idea what you want to shoot next?"

"Yes. I want the building that burned on Sunday. I want to see the aftermath."

He nodded. "Can do."

"Great. Now let's enjoy the rest of our lunch, the birds, and the nice weather. But if you wanted to continue to apologize, in many different, colorful ways, for being such a jerk the other day, I'm all ears."

"Huh?"

"I'd love for you to extrapolate about what a complete dickhead you were. And feel free to use four-letter words while doing so." Heck, yeah, she'd milk his need to make things right with her.

He flushed. "Look, I was a total douche. A real jerk."

"You know, you're pretty good at this." When he just sat there, she motioned for him to continue.

He rolled his eyes but gave her more of what she wanted to hear.

And she'd never had a better lunch.

Chapter Nine

Tex had been so grateful that Bree had forgiven him for being "a total dickhead with delusions of grandeur, barely good enough to suck her toes" that he agreed to whatever she asked for all day long.

That night, he left her at her house with a pleasant goodbye and waited in the truck for her to go inside. She'd made no more mention of them having sex or agreeing to a date night after the two weeks ended. But he had hope. Now he just had to stop being so honest with her and keep his big mouth shut.

Although...Tex's speech about being afraid to mess up a good thing had worked perfectly. Yet the more Tex thought about what he'd said, the more he wondered if he'd ended up stumbling upon a deeper truth. He *had* been worried about messing up a good thing. And he *did* often flake on relationships once he realized they had no spark instead of trying to make the spark happen. It was like his parents' perfect marriage impacted him in a negative way. Instead of having a great example of a relationship to strive for, he constantly feared he'd never live up to grand expectations and ended everything before it could really begin.

Damn. He should charge himself for his own therapy.

He sat, his mind loopy, and watched as Bree picked up the bouquet of flowers by her door before letting herself inside her house. He drove home, ignoring the ringing of his cell phone and the beeping of several texts.

Once in the door, he gave Bubbles some love and went outside to throw the ball for her. The dog had started to lose her reserve, finally, her tail wagging like mad when she saw him after an absence. She didn't jump up on him, a polite gal. But she refused to leave his side when he was at home.

And that level of attention made him sad for her, that she'd been so lacking for God knew how long. His old dog had followed him around, sure, but then the pup had done her own thing. Hanging with his brothers or just chasing crickets outside in the yard.

Not Bubbles. She wanted nothing but to be with Tex, and he felt awful for leaving her alone whenever he went to work. At least Oscar and Gertie had been giving her love when he hadn't been by to do so. He called Oscar.

"Yo. It's Oscar. Speak to me."

"Oscar, it's Tex."

"I know. And I still picked up! Imagine that."

"Asshole. Any word on a home for Bubbles?"

"Not yet. We've had a few folks interested, but they didn't check out. Bubbles needs caring and outdoor space. Stimulation with lots of love."

"She follows me all over the place when I get home. It's not fair to her to be alone all day. I know you've been swinging by to let her out and play with her. Hey, if you want, you can stay at my place with Klingon when I'm not home. I just… I don't want her to be alone so much."

The dog kept looking at him, her dark-brown eyes huge with love and need. Tex felt suffocated, the same way he had with so many of his exes.

He wasn't doing right by the dog, and both Bubbles and he would be torn up when she left.

Oh my God. I'm a basket case. "I'm going to try to see if I can find her a place."

"Whatever you can do, man. We're also going to put her on the show next week. You know, Avery's show for *Searching the Needle Weekly* with the pet adoption segment. It would be great if you could show up too."

"Maybe." Yet as much as Tex wanted Bubbles to find a good family, the idea of her leaving hurt. Bad. "Fuck. I don't know."

"Tex?"

He felt jumpy. "I gotta go. I'll talk to you later about it, okay?"

"Sure, man. And seriously, thanks so much. She's already *worlds* better living with you. You have no idea how withdrawn she was with Scott." Oscar disconnected.

Great. More guilt.

Bubbles stared up at him and smiled, panting, her ears perked as she watched him.

Tex stared back. "You're emotionally needy and physically challenging." He stared at the dog hair on the floor. "You're shedding, Bubbles."

She didn't blink.

"Where's your ball?"

She barked. Ball—her new magic word.

After twenty more minutes spent playing fetch, she caved to taking some water while he set some ground beef in a pan to go with the leftover veggies he'd made the other night. Tex could cook okay, but he wasn't a genius in the kitchen.

His phone vibrated again, and he checked, seeing a message from Brec. Several messages, actually.

His heart raced. He dialed her, his voice calm while the rest of him buzzed with excitement. "You called?"

"You got me flowers?"

He grinned. "You like them?" Considering his luck with Bree, he worried he'd made a mistake. "Oh, man, you're not allergic or anything, are you?"

"No. They're great." She paused. "You didn't have to do that."

"I did. I was a horse's ass. A huge jackhole. Remember?"

"'Jackhole' is a new one. I like it." She laughed. "Thanks, Tex. The flowers are really sweet."

They hadn't been cheap, but Bree was worth it. "I said it, and I'll say it again. I'm really sorry about before."

"Stop it already."

He pumped his fist. *Yes.*

"Look, we'll let bygones be bygones. Why don't you come over for dinner tomorrow? And bring Bubbles. How does steak sound?"

"Great. I can pick up a few before—"

"No. This is on me. We're good, Tex. Relax."

"Just good, not great?"

She snorted. "One step at a time, cowboy. Keep being a stand-up guy—don't hurt yourself, now—and we just might get to that date when we're done."

"Hot damn. Okay. And yeah, dinner tomorrow sounds great. I'll pick you up in the morning at nine for work, okay?"

"Yes, but feel free to wear casual clothes. Unless you're partial to your uniform. I want to do some work in my office, and I'd like your input on some of my shots."

"Me?"

"Yes. Some explanation about some of the shots I took would help. And I'm curious as to what photos pop out at you."

"Okay. Sure. See you at nine."

But the next morning, Bree didn't answer her door. He knocked. No answer. He pulled out his phone, thinking maybe she'd slept in. He called but she didn't pick up. Odd. He stood there and thought he heard something. He knocked again. "Bree?"

The door flew open, and Bree yanked him inside. He stared at her in shock.

She wore nothing but a drenched, knee-length, terrycloth robe that clung to her.

"Bree?" came out as a croak.

"Help me!"

He followed her to her bathroom, the floor covered in sopping towels. The shower sprayed into a full tub, which was overflowing.

"I have a slow drain, and I can't get the water to turn off." She flipped a hank of wet hair back.

He couldn't help grinning. "You look like a drowned rat." A sexy rat. Her robe really showed off her assets, plastered to her as it was. His mouth watered as he raked his gaze over her breasts and thighs.

"Help. Me." She planted her hands on her hips.

He held up his hands in surrender. "Okay, okay. Where's your water shutoff valve?"

"How the hell would I know?"

He sighed. "Where's your water heater? Any valve-looking things?"

"That's all in the garage." She muttered, "I think."

"Show me." He followed her into the garage, spotted a valve he hoped would turn off the water to the house, and shut it off. "Tools?"

She pointed to a toolbox that looked as if it had never been opened. "My dad gave it to me years ago."

"Right. Go check to make sure the water's off in the bathroom, would you?"

"Okay." She left.

He dragged the toolbox inside and paused in the hallway to remove his shoes and socks and roll up his jeans.

"Water's off," she called from the bathroom.

He entered, walking over the wet floor. The tub continued to drain, the water now below the edge and sinking. He rolled his pants higher and waited until it had gone halfway down before stepping in the tub.

Bree hovered nearby. "Can I help?"

"I'll let you know." He'd propped the toolbox on the counter and leaned over to grab a flathead screwdriver. He popped off the cover plate to the shower handle and pulled the knob assembly off the valve stem. Then he fetched a pair of pliers from the toolkit and used them to turn the stem counterclockwise. It wouldn't go any more.

"Okay, this should do it. The water is off, but you might need to replace the cartridge inside. Only reason I know this is that my parents had this exact same problem last year, and I watched my dad fix it. One heck of a Christmas, I can tell you, four of us sharing one shower."

She smiled. "Thanks, Tex."

Her robe gaped, and try as he might, he couldn't help looking. She had the *nicest* breasts…

He glanced up to see her following his stare. "Oh, uh, sorry."

She looked at him with a frown.

He blurted, "I can't help it. You're all wet, and they're right there. It's like they're begging me to get closer." *Stop. Talking.* He turned mute, but he couldn't blink, his entire being focused on her wet, stacked chest.

"You like my rack, eh?" Bree was smiling at him. "Are wet T-shirts your thing?"

He found it safe to smile back.

Mistake.

She turned, grabbed a bowl that for some reason sat in the bathroom filled with water, and tossed it at him, hitting him right in the face and chest. And it was *cold*.

"Damn it." He staggered back, slipped, and nearly fell on his ass in the tub, then said to hell with it and plopped down in the inches of water remaining.

"Oh, shoot. Are you okay?" She leaned forward with concern, and he yanked her down on top of him.

"There you go. Now we're both miserable." And he had an armful of Brianna Gilchrist.

Which was not at all a good idea.

He no longer felt the cold. Her robe gaped, leaving a wealth of her slick, wet skin visible and so close… He had his hands on her thighs, holding her over him, her legs spread as she straddled his hips in her unusually wide tub.

"It's like a spa tub," he said, the inane words not connected to the spike of blood pressure rushing below the belt. His jeans felt way too tight, her legs way too smooth.

"I like to take baths a lot."

"Yeah?" He had trouble breathing, his focus on her proximity.

"Your T-shirt is all wet. Sit back and lift up your arms." Oh, shit. Her voice had gone husky.

He sat up for balance, careful not to move her off him, and lifted his arms.

She drew his shirt off and tossed the sopping fabric. Then she looked at him. Really looked.

The air thickened. His body felt sensitive all over, and when she stroked his chest, flicking her fingers over his nipples, his desire shot into hyperdrive.

Fuck. Me.

Bree stared, her mouth open in a sexy O.

He felt so hard, he hurt. "You're all wet."

The pause between them gave more meaning to what he said.

She bit her lower lip, and Tex felt like he'd entered another dimension, one where his porn fantasies meshed with real life.

"I am wet. All over. Want to see?"

What the…? "Jesus. Are you kidding?"

"I want you. Do you want me?"

He dragged her down and kissed her, which was all the answer she needed.

———————

Bree couldn't handle the pressure any longer. She'd been lusting after this man for months. And the past week and a half had been frustrating, because even when she wasn't sure she liked Tex, she wanted him.

She sure the hell hadn't planned to wake up late then deal with a possessed shower, but to get Tex McGovern wet and half-naked? Priceless.

She ground over that large bulge between his legs, sighing when he parted her robe and put his hot, callused hands over her breasts. He cupped her and took over the kiss, grinding up against her while he fondled her into a fevered arousal. And his hands had nothing on his mouth.

His tongue filled her, stroking and persuading, his moans more than setting her off. She wanted him inside her. Now. "Tex, I—" she started as he ran his mouth across her cheek and down her throat.

The wet robe slid down her arms and stopped at her elbows, the fabric parted so that she was all but naked on top of Tex.

"I knew you'd be hot as fuck, but this is insane," he muttered and latched onto her breast.

She gasped as he teethed her, sucking the nub with a roughness that turned her into a mindless, needy creature. She was drenching his jeans, and it wasn't just water messing the fabric.

He turned to her other breast, and she could only hold on to him, running her hands through his hair, keeping him where it felt best.

"Need to be in you," he said as he drew back to stare at her. He looked her over, lingering on the junction of her thighs resting over his groin. "You got any condoms?"

"In the bedroom, I think." Honestly, she found it difficult to do more than feel. She used birth control and always practiced safe sex, so she was safe. But was Tex?

He startled her into a gasp before she could ask, easing her over his shoulder as he stood. He left the bathroom with speed. "Which way?" he asked as he grabbed a dry towel from the rack.

Are we doing this? Oh my God. We're really doing this! "To the left." Anticipation made her light-headed, that or the fact she slumped over Tex's shoulder, staring at his tight ass as he high-tailed it to her bedroom.

He set her down gently and removed the robe from her. "First time's gonna be fast," he said, staring at her. He unzipped and pushed down his clothes, then kicked them off. "Grab a condom."

She hurried to her nightstand and came back with one. "Here." She handed it to him.

"Not yet." He stalked her, and she backed away before she realized it. The back of her knees hit the bed. "Tex?"

"You say no and I'm gone." Tense, he waited.

"Yes. I'm saying yes."

"Then get on the bed and spread your legs. You clean?"

She blushed. "Yes."

"Me too." Then he was all business, his body tight, his muscles huge, and his cock…magnificent. She wanted so badly to take his picture, right then and there.

"Bree?"

"Tex?"

"Darlin', my eyes are up here." He sounded amused.

She blinked and met his gaze. "Sorry, it's just so big."

"I know." He chuckled. "Now if you want to see how good it feels inside you, lie back on the bed and spread those gorgeous legs. I can't wait anymore."

"Me neither." She hurried, not feeling self-conscious as much as dying to feel satisfied and praying he wasn't a dud in bed. Still, even if he was, he was dynamite to look at—Carrie had been correct in that.

But instead of covering her and thrusting deep, Tex blanketed her with his body, leaning up on his elbows so as not to crush her, and kissed her. He kept on kissing her while that thick cock brushed against her belly, so incredibly thick.

She moaned, needing him, her body on fire to have him.

Then his fingers were there, skimming her clit, and she shot up against him, on edge.

He moaned and thrust his tongue in and out of her mouth, following with his fingers in and out of her body.

To her embarrassment, she teetered on the verge of orgasm already. "No, Tex, wait," she said when she could catch a breath. "I'm almost there."

"So why stop?" He continued to kiss her throat, his fingers now toying with her belly while he angled his cock between her legs. Not penetrating, just resting against her. And each time he shifted even the littlest bit, she shivered, ever closer to orgasm.

"I want you in me." She gasped and closed her eyes. "In me, Tex."

She heard rusting, felt him move off her, and then he was back.

"Condom's on. I'm so fuckin' hard, Bree. I promise, next time will be longer."

"You with all the talking. Get to it already," she ordered, not needing a play-by-play.

He chuckled before positioning himself, prepared to enter her. "You ready for a hard fuck, Bree?" He leaned forward to kiss her again, making love to her mouth until she was begging him to take her.

"Please, Tex. God, now."

"That's it, darlin'. You need me, don't you?" The jerk gave her little bits of himself, driving her crazy.

Her body hummed, close and then not close, edging too slowly toward climax. He grazed her nipples as he moved, and he whispered dirty things he planned on doing to her the next time.

Then he lifted up on his hands to look down at her. She blinked up, watching him as he pushed inside her, inch by inch. So damn big. And so incredibly good...

"Tex," she breathed, electrified when he pumped and grazed the sensitive bundle between her legs. "Oh, yes, *yes*." She couldn't stop the orgasm that rushed through her, nor could she stop seizing as he shoved hard and continued to fuck her.

The pounding took her to new heights, so big and wonderfully raw. He didn't last much longer than she had, and before she knew it, he'd thrust one final time and jerked inside her, moaning her name.

She'd closed her eyes, because she had to open them to see him. He shuddered over her, small pumps of his hips as he emptied into the condom. She shivered, the pleasure awe-inspiring. She'd never had an orgasm last so long. Or been so loud about it. She recalled shouting his name as she came.

Tex looked down at her, and his intensity had yet to dim.

He gave one final push before easing out of her and cringing. "Sorry. I'm a little sensitive. I think you made me see black there for a minute."

She grinned, feeling too good for any recriminations or self-doubt. "Me too."

"Be right back." He returned without the condom, his cock still half-hard.

"Does that thing ever go down?"

"After a workout."

"You mean at the gym, it gets hard?" Odd.

"What?" He stood next to the bed and stared down at her in question. "No, darlin'." He chuckled. "I meant after having sex. A workout. With you though, it's going to stay hard until I take care of this need. You and me got some more to *work out*."

"Again? Now?" She looked at him, and it appeared he'd need more time.

"Give me a little room to breathe. I'm good for it. Besides, I didn't get near enough time with those breasts and that pussy."

"Tex." She blushed.

He grinned and settled next to her on the bed again, this time resting on his side as he studied her body. "I'm just gonna say it. You are the most beautiful woman I've ever seen." His accent thickened. "I've imagined this in just about every way possible. But doing what we just did didn't come close to what I thought it would be."

"It was worse?" Great. Now she felt self-conscious.

"No, dippy. It was fucking fantastic." He frowned. "But if you have to ask that, I musta done something wrong."

"No, it was great. It..." She watched him draw closer to her breasts. He closed his eyes as he sucked her nipple, making love to her body. She bit back a moan, wishing she didn't respond so readily. But the man had it easy with her. He had only to look at her and she was aroused.

"Tex, *oh.*"

He continued to kiss her while he cupped and toyed with her other breast. Then he swapped the attention, his hands all over the place.

She needed to touch him as well, so she ran her hands over his shoulders and pecs, down his nipples to his belly.

"Yeah, touch me like that. Fuck, Bree. You feel so good." He moved over her and kissed his way steadily down her body.

Would he keep moving lower?

Why, yes, he would indeed.

She sucked in a breath when he blew over her sensitive flesh. Then he put his mouth over her—licking, sucking—and added a finger inside her. She groaned and arched into his touch, exhausted yet wound up at the same time, letting him lead her all the way to a loud, moaning climax.

But instead of shoving up inside her, he kissed his way back up her body, then turned to lie on his back beside her. She caught her breath and looked at him, only to see him thick and hard once more.

"Touch me." He drew her hand to his erection, and she could barely wrap her hand around him. "Oh, yeah. That's it." He closed his eyes as she pumped him, marveling at his size.

She wanted to feel him again inside her. "Reach into the nightstand for another condom. I think I have more."

"Oh, God, please." He sounded desperate.

She chuckled.

He found one and handed it to her. "Put it on me."

She did, taking her time to roll it down. He writhed, and she loved it. Despite being sated, she wanted to feel him stretching her out, filling her up. She straddled him and took him in hand, then slowly sank over him until she rested against his pelvis.

"You feel so big," she said on a breath, incredulous at the fullness inside her.

"This." He reached up and held her breasts in his hands. "Fucking this. I want you to ride me. Yeah, up and down. Let me watch those tits bounce." He continued with even dirtier talk, and hearing him say such blunt things excited her to no end.

Before she knew it, she was slamming up and down over him, encouraged by his moans and pleas for more. He pinched her nipples, so she did the same to him. Then the tricky devil slid a hand between her legs to rub her while she rode him. And her unstoppable libido raced him to the end, their speeded coupling growing more intense.

"That's it. Fuck yourself with my dick. Up and down. Yeah, more." He sounded hoarse, his body taut, his face tight with agony.

Then he shouted and seized, and she jerked against him, coming once more as his clever fingers and thick shaft brought her to a foggy state of ecstasy.

When she'd finally wound down, she felt as if she'd run a marathon. Weak and trembly, she eased off him, taking the condom from him and disposing of it. She returned to the bed and crawled over it to lie next to him, her heart taking its own time to slow down.

As the minutes passed, the awkwardness she'd been hoping to avoid settled over them.

"So, um, I didn't plan this," he said, staring at the ceiling.

She looked up as well, finding a pattern in the texture. "Me neither."

A pause.

"What do you want to do about it?" he asked.

A good question.

"How about we pretend it never happened? We continue to work together, finish up the project. Then when it's over, we have that date."

He rolled over to look at her, his face slack with repletion, his eyes hazy with a satisfied smile. "I can do that. I can't swear I won't envision you naked. Or not think about this every damn second until that date. But I won't tell a soul, and I won't act any different at work. Deal?"

She nodded, relieved. He wasn't making a fuss, and he seemed to understand. She held a hand toward him. "Deal."

"Oh, hell, no. We just fucked, baby. No handshake seals our deal." Tex leaned over and kissed her until they were both panting.

"Nope, nope." Tex pulled back. "Sorry. I can get carried away. If it were up to me, we'd spend all day in your bed. I have so many more fantasies with you to fill out. Say, you don't own a cheer-leader outfit, do you?"

She flushed. "No, you big ass. I do not."

He chuckled. "Kidding. Kind of."

She sighed.

"Okay, I'll go get dressed in my…well, my clothes are wet."

Your pants are a little wet from me as well. She felt her cheeks heat. "How about we give them a quick run through the washer and dryer? I'll get dressed, and we'll have breakfast while your clothes dry."

"That's a deal." He smiled, traced her lips with his finger, and kissed her again. "One more week. I can handle that. Just friends, no sex. This never happened."

"Right." She kissed him back. "Okay, getting up, here. Because if I don't, I might never leave."

Sadly, he had no idea she meant that.

Chapter Ten

TEX SPENT FRIDAY IN A KIND OF DELAYED SHOCK. HE'D HAD SEX with Bree, and he worried it had totally ruined him for any other woman. Period. That stupid claim that *he'd* ruin *her* had completely backfired, rooting itself in reality.

She'd been sexy, hot as fuck, and giving. Kissing her made the world fade away, with Bree at the center of his universe.

And she wanted to pretend it had never happened.

He would have been hurt if he hadn't understood why she needed that boundary. And if he hadn't seen how much she wanted to fuck again but had to talk herself out of it.

They spent the day at her studio looking through her computer at the many shots she'd taken. She had her laptop plugged into a wide, flat table that allowed her to see multiple shots at a time. He'd seen so many that made him proud to be a firefighter. And no one looking at them could doubt Bree's talent as a true artist.

He'd chosen a few that stood out, ones she'd agreed with, and they'd spent the rest of the day not talking about the incredible sex they'd had. Instead, they'd scouted more places to take pictures in addition to finally getting to the park to photograph the fallen firefighter memorial.

By mutual unspoken agreement, dinner had been canceled, each needing some time and space to regroup.

Saturday seemed to be much the same as the previous day, minus the sex. They'd just reached a late lunch when Bree took a call that had her looking spooked. She walked away with the phone, her movements agitated, while Tex sat at their table waiting for the food to arrive.

She came back and put her hand over the phone. "Tex, are you busy tonight?"

"No, why?"

"I'm sorry about this, but my dad wants you to join us for a family dinner. To hear about our progress."

"And check me out." He grinned. "No problem. It's all going great, right?"

She went back to her conversation, not answering him. "Sure, Dad. He's happy to come. Seven thirty? I'll let him know. And… Oh. Melissa's coming too? Does she have to?" Pause. "Kidding. It'll be fine, Dad." She disconnected and groaned. "I'm sorry. But this way he'll know we're on track and there's nothing to worry about."

"It's fine. Plus, I get a free meal out of it."

She smiled, but he saw her strain. "My stepmom and stepsister will be there too. Melissa. Ugh."

"The sister you don't get along with?"

"That's the one." She waited for the waiter to set their food on the table before saying, "I know I keep repeating myself, but Tex, we need to keep yesterday to ourselves."

"What are you talking about?" he asked, all innocence, and winked. Then he dug into his burger, famished.

"Right." She sighed. "I hate having to deal with Melissa, so I usually keep my family visits brief if she's there. She was awful when I was younger. She's not that much better now. And then my dad will be giving us the third degree about work. He's going to dig at you to make sure you're 'taking care' of me."

"Not a good time to say that I took care of you just fine, right?"

She blushed, as he'd known she would. "Look, I love my dad, but he can be overprotective. I don't want you to have any problems at work because of me."

"What can he do?" In honesty, though, John Gilchrist could do a lot. The battalion chief could easily make Tex's life miserable. "I'm union. I'm good." At her frown, he said, "I'm kidding.

Honestly, yesterday was a one-timer. Just between you and me. We're good, Bree." One-timer? Man. So much for being honest with her. If up to him, that one time—technically, they'd done it twice—would turn into an unending schedule of sex, sex, and more sex. And cuddling. He'd liked holding her yesterday, brief though it had been.

"I'm not trying to hide you," she was saying. "I mean, I am, but I'm not. Geez, I feel like I'm back in high school keeping my boyfriend a secret again." She turned scarlet. "Not that you're my boyfriend or anything. You know what I mean."

"I do." *Boyfriend.* Oddly enough, the term didn't bother him. Not with Bree. The more he considered it, the more he liked the notion.

But she clearly needed to ease into the idea.

"I swear, Bree, I'll be on my best behavior. Your dad will see nothing at all between the two of us but mutual admiration and professional conduct."

"Thanks." She fiddled with her knife and fork.

"Bree?"

"It's just... If my stepsister is bitchy or comes on to you—she's done this to other friends of mine—can you ignore her?"

"Damn. That's cold. And yeah, I'll ignore her. Now stop fretting about dinner. Eat your lunch so you have the strength to deal with your family tonight. Let me get Gerty and Oscar to dog-sit." He made a call and confirmed Bubbles had her own date with Klingon later that night.

The rest of their afternoon went well. They followed a medical emergency calling for an aid vehicle, and the patient received treatment. Following that, Tex and Bree had some interesting talk with the guys from Station 28. Bree asked intelligent questions, he noticed.

In addition to being beautiful, Bree had a brain that fascinated him. Tex was at first a superficial kind of guy, he admitted. He liked women who appealed visually. Something physical about them had to attract him. Eyes, breasts, butt, a terrific smile. Bree had all that. But she had the one thing that was guaranteed to keep him around longer—intelligence. Talking to her wasn't a chore. She made him laugh, and the more he watched her interact with others, the more he respected her.

"You're really good," he said once they drove away, heading back to her house.

"Oh?"

"With people. You're smart, and you never talk down to folks. I like that."

She blushed. "Thank you. I could say the same about you."

"Could? Please. You *should* say the same about me. I'm ah-mazing, and yeah, there's an H in there." He grinned when she made a face at him. "You like board games?"

She eyed him with curiosity. "Um, yeah." He had no idea where that question had come from. Then he realized it came from the idea of fitting her in with the crew, seeing how she'd act with them. Something he'd rarely done with his exes.

"The guys and I like to hang around together away from the station sometimes, when we're not there working out. We play a lot of board games and cards." He shrugged. "Sounds stupid maybe, but it's a great way to de-stress."

"It doesn't sound stupid at all." She turned to face him and tucked a strand of hair behind her ear. He could feel her attention, and he basked in it. "I kind of envy you. You have a great bunch of friends you're close to. I have Carrie. She's like a sister, and I love my parents. But I don't have a crew of people, if you know what I mean."

"A crew?"

"Now I sound stupid." She huffed. "I mean, a group for sup-port. People who love you and accept you and help when you need it. And even if you don't think you need it, you have them there for you. I have that with Carrie, but sometimes it would be nice to be with a group and feel that kind of energy."

He shrugged. "I can't say I looked for it. Though maybe I did. I don't know." He turned toward her neighborhood. "I had three older brothers growing up, so we had a tight family. Lots of love at home, and I know I'm lucky to have it. Then I joined the Corps, and I had that same belonging there." A lightbulb went off in his head. "And maybe that's why I turned to firefighting. Not only could I help people, but it felt familiar. Kind of like the military yet different. And there's that physical aspect to the job that I love, but also the people." He smiled. "A better bunch of guys I couldn't hope to have by my side in the thick of things. Mack's a motormouth, funny and obnoxious. But he'd never leave a man behind. Same with Brad and Reggie. They push and prod if they think you're not okay."

"That sounds...interesting."

She'd heard his *tone,* obviously.

"I'll let you in on something. I was so down after I blew it with you Sunday that I told the guys what I said. After laughing at me for being a moron, and smacking me around and calling me names, they helped me realize I should just be honest and grovel a lot. But the flowers is all me." Brad had mentioned buying her some, but Tex had already been thinking along those lines.

She chuckled. "They did good. I truly love the flowers. I have them in a vase on the dining room table." She paused. "Want to see?"

"Sure." *Not smart, Tex.* The vibe in the truck was changing, growing more intimate. She kept shooting looks at him. And he, as safely as possible while driving, returned them.

He parked and locked up, feeling nervous, which was very unlike him. They walked into her house, and he couldn't help watching that ass move. He all too clearly remembered plunging into her wet heat, and the hard-on from hell assumed the position of attention, making it uncomfortable to walk.

Inside, Tex closed the door behind him. She dropped her camera bag on the table and showed him her flowers.

"Pretty, aren't they?"

He spared them a glance before focusing on her. "Beautiful."

She took a step toward him, her eyes bright. "Thanks again for sending them."

He moved toward her. "You're welcome."

And then he was kissing her, and she was kissing him back, desperate with desire and unable to stop.

"Just one more time," she said as he walked her back against the wall.

"Yeah. Once." He ravished her mouth, need spiraling until he could think of nothing but getting inside her.

He yanked her shirt over her head and made short work of her bra. Then he took her nipple in his mouth, sucking hard while she moaned and yanked at his jeans. She had him unbuttoned and unzipped, a small hand wrapped around his cock, then stroked a thumb over his wet tip.

He groaned and kissed his way to her throat, then up to her mouth. He freed himself, throbbing, and helped her get rid of her jeans and panties.

Naked and backed against the wall, she looked like a pinup.

"Gotta fuck you, now."

Not the most romantic words, but she must have felt them because she reached up and put her hands around his neck. "Fuck me." She bit his lip when they kissed. "Right now."

"Bree," he sighed. "Baby, I don't have a condom on me." Stupid, stupid Tex.

"I don't care. I'm on birth control, and I'm safe. You said you're safe, so..."

She didn't need to say any more. He kissed her and drew her as close as possible. She wrapped her legs around him, shifting to take him between her legs. He used a hand to guide himself to her core and hissed in pleasure to feel her so wet.

Then he took her in a savage kiss as he thrust hard inside her.

She gasped and ate at his mouth, wild and growing wilder when he used his thumb to grind her clit. Her fingernails bit at his shoulders and raked his upper back.

He pumped, glad for the wall for support, because he couldn't stop. He prayed she'd get off soon, because his end was coming. And coming hard. The feel of her around him was unlike anything, and he couldn't believe how close he felt to her, as if they were riding one giant wave of pleasure.

He ripped his mouth free and moaned as he came, pouring into her so hard, he shook. She ground against him, intensifying his climax, and cried out, coming with him, her body like a vise.

Tex couldn't stop pumping, loving the fact he'd come inside her.

And freaking the fuck out when he thought about what he'd just done and how he hadn't been in control. At all.

Lost in floating pleasure and panic, he just stood there, shivering when she clenched her body around his cock, jerking another bit of seed from him.

"Jesus." He leaned his forehead against her shoulder and felt her stroking his back. Her caress made him feel cared for, even though they'd just kicked it like two feral cats in heat. "Oh, man. I don't wanna move."

"I know." She sighed, kissed his shoulder, stirring more warmth, and eased her legs from around him.

He withdrew and gently let her feet fall to the floor.

"Bree, I..." He had no words.

"I know. You're addicting."

"You're addicting."

They stared at each other and started smiling. At the same time, they both said, in saccharine voices, "No, *you* are," and burst into laughter.

Feeling lighter, Tex tilted Bree's chin up. He kissed her lips, felt something in him give, and cupped her cheeks. "I should get home and clean up. For dinner tonight."

She nodded, then her eyes widened. "Oh, man. Dinner with my dad." Great, now she looked rattled. "This never happened."

"Nope. Never." He paused. "Because we're friends. But I still get that date when we're done." He kissed her again, because he had to. "I'm on your side, darlin'. Don't worry about tonight. It'll go down easy. I swear it."

———

And boy, had Tex spoken way too soon.

While Bree waited for Tex to arrive, she smiled at Carrie. A smart move on Bree's part, actually. Carrie made a nice buffer in dealing with Melissa, as her parents well knew. Carrie handled Melissa better than anyone else in the family, something for which Bree's father had always been grateful.

Now, freshly showered and relaxed thanks to fifteen minutes of breathing and meditation exercises, she chatted with her step-mom, Charlie, while Carrie kept Melissa occupied and her father finished up a phone call in his study.

Once again, a pang of regret filled her, that she couldn't laugh and smile with her best friend *and* her stepsister. There had once been a bond between Bree and Melissa, a strength forged from mutual pain at a loved one's loss, and from a need to connect. For such a short time, Bree had had someone she loved with her whole heart, a sister to just be with. Melissa had been funny and fun, sweet yet sarcastic, and she'd made Bree laugh.

Then something had changed. Bree had never been able to put her finger on it, but her stepsister had grown distant. She'd pulled away to the point where they didn't speak, and when they did, Melissa had been biting and bitter, fracturing what could have been a loving, tight family of four.

"I'm excited to meet Tex," Charlie said, bringing Bree back to the present. Charlie stirred the bisque she'd made for the meal. A lovely woman with frosted, dark-brown hair and a sincere smile, she wore love well. Charlie made a house a home, her father liked to say, and it was true. Charlie always had a kind word for others, her gaze warm and soft, and perfect for a man used to dealing with life-and-death decisions. Her father didn't deal with too many of them now, but he'd been through hell several times in his life, including losing a wife, a partner, and dealing with danger.

"Tex is an acquired taste," Bree teased. "I'm kidding. He's a charmer. He's big, handsome, and smart. You've been warned."

Charlie snuck a look toward the hallway and, not seeing John, leaned close. "How good-looking are we talking?"

Bree fanned herself.

Charlie nodded. "Ah. I see." She glanced again at the hallway. "Do you like him?"

Though Charlie shared everything with Bree's father, Bree knew the woman could keep her secrets. "I do like him. As a friend." She paused and whispered, "And maybe something more. Except..." She nodded at the hallway.

"I know." Charlie rolled her eyes. "The man thinks everyone is a dog just because of what happened with your mother."

Bree frowned. "What?"

Charlie blinked. "He never told you that story?"

"No. I don't think so."

"Well, he should have. Just as he should stop with all this anti-firefighter and anti-cop nonsense."

"Wait. I can't date cops either?"

"That would have come up had you ever mentioned being interested in one." Charlie sighed. "So the story goes...your mother was dating someone else in your father's unit when the man cheated on her and broke her heart. She turned to your father for sympathy, and that was that." Charlie smiled, not bothered at all by John's first love. She'd always claimed Bree's mother had helped make him into the wonderful man he was today. "His story about love at first sight is probably true, but maybe it happened when your parents *really* saw each other. I know your father always loved her, but I think your mom needed to leave a bad relationship to know a good one. And of course, your father is not only wonderful under all the bluster, but he's easy on the eyes. That never hurts."

Bree gaped. "He never once told me all that. Just that mom had a few doozies of bad dates before she met him."

"Hmmph. Well, bring out those guns if you need to, that is if you and Tex are more than just friends at some point."

Bree hugged her. "I love you."

Charlie hugged her back and laughed. "I love you too, sweetheart."

"Where's *my* hug, Mom?" Melissa said sweetly from the other entrance into the kitchen. She held out her arms. "I've missed you."

Behind Melissa, Carrie held a finger gun to her temple and pretended to pull the trigger. Bree coughed to hide laughter.

Like Charlie, Melissa had rich, sable hair and brown eyes, but hers showed a brittle anger that never seemed to fade. Over time, Melissa had grown to resent the stepsister who took her mother's attention.

Her father, ever the optimist, kept throwing Bree and Melissa together, as if one day, by chance, all the Scrabble tiles would fall together to spell "friends."

Yeah, right.

Charlie hugged her daughter. At least Melissa remained steadfast in her love for Charlie and John Gilchrist. She'd had no problem treating him like a dad. Bree? No longer a sister and certainly not a friend.

Her father stood behind Carrie. "You getting shorter, Counselor Norris?"

She turned to give him a hug. "You wish. Oh, and I'm game for a rematch on the court whenever you are, Chief."

He frowned and set her back. "I thought I told you not to mention my embarrassing defeat in front of family."

Carrie snickered. "It was so, so sad."

"You can still dunk. I want to say I'm impressed, but you did it in front of my friends. That's all I ever hear about at poker night, you know."

She grinned.

Bree grinned with her, surprised to see Melissa laughing as well. Bree had always thought Melissa loathed Carrie. But maybe Melissa was starting to change since dating Bill, her steady boyfriend. She'd become quieter, for sure, and didn't come by the house as much, for which Bree remained grateful.

Carrie too seemed surprised, but she said nothing about it.

"Bree, honey, you look lovely."

She accepted her dad's hug, not bothering to look for the sneer Melissa would be wearing.

He smiled and pulled back to ask, "How are things going with Tex?"

"The guy's name is Tex?" Melissa blinked. "Does he wear a cowboy hat and spurs?"

An image of Tex in a hat, spurs, and nothing else appeared in Bree's mind. That would definitely demand film.

"You'd have to ask him that," Bree said, trying to be pleasant for her parents' sake. "Though I have seen him in the hat. He's been really helpful, Dad. And he helped out at the apartment fire. I got plenty of shots. From a safe distance, don't worry."

Her father frowned. "He was supposed to be watching you, not assisting. I'm sure we had plenty of men and women on the scene to handle it." It had happened in Fourth Battalion's area, or her father would have been there.

"He was watching out for my safety, Dad. A teenager broke through the barricade and was rushing toward the ambulances, but Tex caught him before he could go into danger. Then he helped the boy find his mom, who had been caught by the fire. That's it. I stayed where he told me to, and he was right back to make sure I was fine." And honestly, she wasn't a toddler. She didn't need a man to hold her hand and tell her what to do around a fire. But to make her father feel secure about her project, she let him fuss.

"Oh, okay. Good." John nodded, looking stern. Something about him reminded her of Tex, and she stared at him. Maybe that breadth of shoulder? The way he made her feel safe?

She felt a bit icky to be looking for a man like her dad in a relationship then realized some women did, on some level. Or so she'd once heard.

The doorbell rang. Everyone froze until Carrie offered to get the door.

"No, I'll get it," John barked. "This is my house, and I don't want you scaring him off before I get to talk to him."

"Talk? You mean interrogate. Sure." Carrie waved her father in front of her. "It'll be like the Spanish Inquisition. But will Tex leave with his head? That's the real question."

Charlie laughed. "Oh, Carrie. We've missed you."

"Yeah, we have." Melissa raised a brow. "Nothing like the comic element to make sure we have peace at dinner." She shot Bree a sharp smile.

Melissa stirred the bisque without having been asked, and Bree left the kitchen right behind Carrie. Avoidance would be the name of the game tonight. Now if only things worked out with Tex...

Chapter Eleven

BREE FOUND TEX INSIDE THE FOYER WITH HER FATHER, shaking his hand. In his other hand, Tex held flowers and had a bakery box tucked under his arm. His eyes lit up when he saw her, but he only nodded.

"Hi, Bree."

"Hey."

He turned to Carrie and gave a mock grimace. "Oh, it's you. The lawyer."

Carrie snorted. "And the cowboy. Where's your Stetson, cowpoke?"

"It's in the car, Stretch. Why? You wanna try it on for size?"

John laughed. "Thanks for coming, Tex."

Charlie entered, and when she saw Tex, her eyes widened. She glanced at Bree, who gave a subtle nod. *Told you so.*

Tex had arrived in jeans, work boots, and a dark, button-down shirt, which made his gray eyes pop even more. His hair had been combed, taming the shag he normally wore. He'd shaved, though she preferred his stubble, truth to tell. But that beautiful smile he used to charm the ladies left and right was in full force. Damn, but even her father seemed to be caught up in Tex's spell.

Charlie turned back to Tex and smiled. "Welcome, Tex. Come on in."

"These are for you." He handed Charlie a lovely spring bouquet, one smaller than the one he'd given Bree. Bree noticed and felt petty for being glad. "This too," he said, handing her the bakery box. "But that's really for your whole family."

"Tex, you didn't have to do that." Charlie blushed. "These are beautiful."

"Now, Mrs. Gilchrist, I had to." His accent seemed a bit thick to Bree, but Charlie was eating it up. Carrie too, the traitor. "My momma would whoop me if she knew I'd been invited to your home and didn't bring anything."

"Tex, call me Charlie."

"Yes, ma'am. Ah, Charlie."

"I have to meet your mother," Bree's father said with a grin.

"You'd like her. She's not one for sass." Tex winked. "The box is full of sweets." He met Bree's gaze. "Don't tell Elliot. I didn't get them at Sofa's."

Carrie's eyes widened. "You know Elliot?"

"Bree and I met at his bakery before we headed out for our first day of work. He seems like a real character."

Her father snorted. "Oh, he is."

"Dad." Bree shook her head. "You just don't like it that he called you cute."

John flushed. "I'm old enough to be his father!"

"But still a looker," Charlie teased, and the rest of them laughed.

They moved deeper into the living room, where John invited Tex to a beer.

"Sure, sir, thanks."

Bree took a spot on the couch next to Carrie, nervous about tonight's entertainment—the Big John show.

"You've obviously met Carrie." Her father sipped his beer and studied Tex.

"We met over breakfast. Something I have a problem with lately." Tex patted his nonexistent gut. "I've been meeting Bree out for breakfast before we get started, and I haven't been hitting the gym as much. She's hard on a guy, Chief. Especially when she insists we meet at Sofa's. How can I not have a blondie and a coffee? Then she made me eat with her and Carrie at a place that serves the best pancakes."

"EggsNCheeze?"

Tex nodded. "Yeah. They kill the flapjacks."

"He made fun of me for getting French toast," Bree said, pleased with the way Tex was behaving. Nice and friendly, but not overly so.

"Bree's taken some amazing shots of the city and plenty of the department hard at work. She makes us look dang good, and I don't know squat about art."

John watched Tex. "You saw her photos pre-edit?"

"SOOC—straight out of camera. See, Bree? I'm learning the jargon."

Bree chuckled.

To her father, he explained, "She also took me by her studio and asked me to look at a few. I wish I had an eye like she does."

Carrie nodded. "She's got an eye, all right. When I first met her, we were modeling together, getting our pictures taken. One day she took me aside, and we looked at our shots. She pointed out a dozen they should use, saying they should scrap the rest. The photographer's assistant had a hissy and threatened to never let us work with them again. But the photographer listened and agreed. He also told her she had a good eye for angles and color."

Bree blushed. "You always tell that story."

"It's true."

Her dad nodded. "It is. I'd love to see some of what you're shooting if you—"

"Nope."

He blinked.

Tex glanced from her father to Bree and took a long drag of his beer.

Carrie shook her head. "Here we go."

"Now, honey, I just want to—"

"Nope. I'm not ready yet."

Her dad looked hurt. The faker. He was just nosey. "You let Tex look."

"Dad, he'd already seen what I shot. He's been guiding me, remember?"

"Such a hard-ass," her dad muttered, but he sounded half proud.

"You're tellin' me," Tex just had to say.

Her father laughed and slapped him on the back. "Tell me about your time in Station 44, Tex. How are you liking the new place?"

"It's great. The facility has an updated kitchen and gym, which is just outstanding, and the sleeping quarters are pretty decent."

Carrie turned to her and whispered, "He's holding his own with your dad. So far. Five bucks says he does or says something to get your dad scenting blood."

Bree subtly leaned closer to her friend and whispered back, "What do you mean?"

"I mean if you don't want to give me five dollars right now, stop looking at Tex as if you want to do him. Again."

"*What?*"

Her father looked over at her. "You okay, honey?"

Tex just sipped his beer and wandered to the fireplace mantle to study some family photographs.

"Carrie's sharing gossip. I'll be right back."

He chuckled and rejoined Tex, pointing out a few pictures of himself and his station house back in the day.

Bree tugged Carrie with her down the hallway into Charlie's crafting room. "What are you talking about?"

"You have that 'I've been fucked by a cowboy' look." Carrie shrugged. "Meh. I figured it would happen. Just not this soon."

Bree felt hot and cold at the same time. "Seriously? You can tell?"

Carrie smirked. "And now I know."

"Damn it! This isn't funny. My dad will have a fit if he finds out. And then he'll do something nasty to Tex's career."

"Nah. Your dad is way too professional to let personal feelings interfere with his work."

"You're not that dumb."

"Hey."

"He once almost got my PE teacher fired for flirting with me, and the guy was only trying to correct my form playing tennis."

Carrie shrugged. "If you say so. But you can never be too careful with predators in high school."

"Seriously, Carrie. Help me out here."

Carrie leaned closer. "Fine. Then tell me. I want details."

Bree confessed, "On a scale of one to ten, he's a twenty. And he's huge. Happy now?"

"Like, he's a big guy? Or he's a *big guy*?" She pointed at her crotch. Bree just smiled.

"Man, if I were straight, I'd totally hit that."

"Hit what?" Melissa asked, finding them huddled by the crafting table.

Carrie didn't miss a beat. "I was telling your sister about the sexy barista who served me today. Had she been a little older, I'd totally have hit that."

Melissa frowned. "You're so crass, Carrie."

"Crass my ass. I'm honest. I can give oral like nobody's business. That's truth, sister. That barista would have been lucky to have me. In so many ways." She wiggled her brows.

Bree tried not to laugh at the way Melissa's eyes bugged out.

"Maybe you should try me before you get all offended. Bet I can make you scream my name in less than five—"

"Carrie really!" Melissa darted out of the room.

"—seconds. And see, I was right," she yelled after Melissa.

Bree tried to muffle her laughter but found it difficult to calm down. Soon she was snorting with Carrie, the pair trying to contain themselves.

Charlie found them and frowned. "Why are you two in here? Someone needs to go rescue Tex from your father, Bree. Oh, and dinner's ready." She turned around and left.

Bree was still laughing when Carrie murmured, "I think Melissa wants me. You okay if I make a move?"

That sobered Bree right on up. "Oh, yeah, Lady Loves a Lot. Go for it. She's all yours, even though I'm pretty sure she's never dated a woman before." If she'd had one thought that her stepsister might take a liking to Carrie, or that Carrie actually meant it, she'd never have suggested it.

Carried hooked a thumb at herself. "It shouldn't have to be said that once you sample a taste of this, you never want to leave."

"Oh my God. That's who Tex reminds me of. You!"

Carrie grinned. "Aw, shucks, ma'am."

They snickered as they rejoined the family, now gathering around the dining table.

Dinner passed nicely, though her father continued to grill Tex, who managed to fend off the heavy-handed interrogation with aplomb.

"So, the Marine Corps, hmm?"

"1st Marines, 1stMarDiv. Alpha Company." Tex speared a hunk of salad and chewed with pleasure on his face.

Bree made sure to keep her attention on her plate, especially when Carrie nudged her leg under the table and muttered, "O-face alert."

When she glanced up, she saw Melissa watching them.

Melissa sat next to Tex across from Carrie and Bree, with their parents on either end of the table. Used to entertaining, Charlie cooked and served with the ease of long practice, and any attempt to try to help normally earned a subtle scold. She must have really missed Melissa to let her help with the bisque.

Melissa hadn't protested sitting next to Tex, though she remained quieter than usual throughout the meal.

"Did you like your time in the service?" her dad asked.

"John, really." Charlie harrumphed. "Let the boy eat."

"It's okay, Charlie." Tex wiped his mouth. "I expected the

grilling. I am taking his daughter around town, after all. I have to say, though, the one who's scaring me is you."

"Me?" Charlie blinked.

"I don't think I can stop eating. You even make salad taste good. And I'm more a meat and potatoes or shrimp and lobster kind of guy." He smiled at her. "This seafood chowder is dang amazing. My momma would want this recipe for sure."

"I'm happy to give it to you." Charlie glowed with pleasure. "I like to call it Charlie's Superb Seafood Bisque."

"Superb is right." He winked at her.

"Oh, you're good." Bree's father sighed. "But you're not wrong. I'm going to need to hit the gym tomorrow for sure."

"You should swing by Station 44 and work out." Tex gave John a wicked grin. "Challenge Lieutenant O'Brien to meet you for reps. He needs the workout. The guys say he's a little too fond of his wife's banana bread, and it's starting to show."

John's face lit up. "Jan's making him banana bread? And he brings it to work?"

"He sure does brag about it, I can tell you that." Tex chuckled. "But the last time, he wouldn't let me have any. Told me I was gettin' fat then made me do twenty push-ups just to get a piece. And he gave me the butt."

Bree frowned. "What?"

"You know the end of the bread. The butt. And it was still delicious."

"Jan can bake." John cleared his throat and darted a sheepish look at his wife. "But, uh, not as good as you, honey."

Charlie shook her head. "You should take lessons from Tex on how to charm a lady."

At that, John raised a brow. "So that raises the question. Just how many ladies are you charming at present, Tex? And is my daughter one of them?"

Such a great question. Tex had been prepared for something like it, though he hadn't thought the chief would be so direct. Bree looked like she wanted to crawl under the table. Carrie and Melissa watched, wide-eyed. Charlie, the sweet woman, audibly prayed for her husband's manners to reemerge.

"Now, Chief, a gentleman never tells. I make sure to keep my private life private, so it never interferes with work. And Bree is straight-up professional. We don't mess around at all. Especially not when I'm technically on duty for these two weeks. Right, Bree?"

"Oh, um, what?" She glanced up, looking guilty. "I'm sorry. What did you say?"

Her daddy sighed. "Have you heard anything we've been saying?" His eyes narrowed, and he glanced from Tex to Bree. "Or is there something I should know?"

"I don't know if she's been listening, but I sure have, John," Carrie cut in with a wide smile. "You pretty much said that Jan bakes better than Charlie. Then you asked if Tex was shacking up with any women lately, a not-so-subtle hint to keep his junk in his pants around your daughter."

Charlie choked on her water. Melissa gaped at Carrie, and Bree just covered her face, clearly used to Carrie's antics. But Tex laughed so hard, he cried. "Hot damn, that's a fine recap of the conversation, ain't it?"

John tried not to laugh, but he couldn't help it. "You, young lady, are a menace."

"Only because I work so hard at it."

Bree interrupted before her father could browbeat Tex some more. "Dad, did I tell you Carrie won her last mediation? And get this, to the tune of twenty-five million for her client!"

"Wow. That's fantastic," John gushed, and Carrie, wicked, cool-as-a-cucumber Carrie, blushed with pride.

Charlie toasted her, and even Melissa chimed in with a, "Wow, that's pretty amazing, Carrie."

"That's more than my fingers and toes can count," Tex teased.

Carrie chuckled. "Whatever, cowboy. You're a lot slicker than you give yourself credit for. I can tell."

"Hmm."

Great, now Bree's dad was looking at him with suspicion again.

It was taking all Tex had to play the friendly guy when he kept remembering taking Bree against the wall, all heat and need and hunger. Best damn sex of his life. And that was saying something. He spared a short glance her way then drank more beer.

To his horror, he felt himself getting hard and willed his erection away.

A glance next to him showed Melissa watching him. When he met her gaze, she smiled.

The chief sure had a handsome family. Charlie was beautiful, kind, and cooked like a dream. Tex could understand the attraction John had for his wife, and Melissa looked just like her. The woman was gorgeous, stunning, but in a different way than Bree. Melissa appeared harder, sharper, where Bree exuded sexuality. He could see Melissa wielding a whip and stilettos, whereas Bree would be the sex kitten in a baby doll teddy.

Nope. Stop thinking about sexy clothing. Don't go there.

He focused again on his bisque, enjoying a second helping and trying to stop from needing a third. "I don't mean to hog all your food."

"Don't worry about it. She made a second batch for the crew at work." John smiled. "I'll be pretty popular tomorrow."

Heck, the chief was popular with or without Charlie's fine cooking. Tex only heard good things about the guy. He treated everyone fairly, didn't play politics so much as had earned a sterling reputation, and had started at the ground level, so even the newbies recognized the chief had their best interests at heart. Tex couldn't see the guy yanking him around just for dating his daughter. Then again, everyone had warned him away, and Bree seemed pretty freaked about coming clean.

He'd already messed up around her enough; he'd take her lead in dealing with her dad.

"What about your family, Tex? What do they think of your job?"

"Dad." Bree groaned. "Is this a dinner or a shakedown?"

"He's just being friendly," Melissa said, her first words at the table. "Don't mind Dad," she said to Tex. "He asks pushy questions to everyone who comes over for dinner." She smiled.

Tex smiled back. "I don't mind. I'm an open book."

"A picture book for kids, I'll bet," Carrie added.

Tex laughed. "You know, you'd fit right in with the guys at the station. C shift all the way, Carrie." He turned to the chief. "To answer your question, my folks miss me, but they like what I'm doing with my life. I have three older brothers. All of us joined the service before we decided what we wanted to do. Only one of my brothers mistakenly joined the Air Force. The rest of us are Marines."

John grinned. "So was my dad. Once a Marine, always a Marine."

"Yep." Tex nodded. "But when I got out, I felt like I wasn't done serving my country. I just needed another angle. And I found it here."

"Why so far from Texas, if you don't mind me asking?" Charlie asked. "I assume Tex is short for Texas."

"It is. I came out here with a Marine buddy. He ended up getting married and moved to Portland to be near family, but I stayed here. Fell in love with Seattle. I really like the Pacific Northwest."

Thankfully, talk turned to the area and weather, as well as great places to hike or ski, should he be so inclined. Which he was not.

He did his best to act natural, but between the chief questioning him, Bree doing her best to ignore him, Carrie watching as if sitting at a damn movie, and Melissa staring a hole in his head, he felt pretty stressed throughout the meal.

When it ended, he stood to help clear his plate and found the chief doing the same. Charlie darted toward the kitchen to fetch dessert.

"I need to call your parents and tell them what a fine job they did raising you," the chief said with a smile. "You ate all your food, cleared your plate, and called me 'sir'. You're either one polite young man or one hell of a liar and a suck-up."

"Geez, Dad." Bree groaned. "Ignore him, Tex. He's still testing you."

Tex snorted. "I've been through the wringer before. This is no different. And I have nothing to hide. Ask me anything you want." *But don't ask if I'm sleeping with your daughter. Please don't.*

He didn't look at Bree but instead looked at Carrie, who was frowning at Melissa.

"Hey, where's your engagement ring?" Carrie asked.

All eyes turned to Melissa, who froze then promptly burst into tears and darted from the room.

Everyone stared at one another, confused, Tex especially.

Charlie rushed back in from the kitchen and looked around. "I heard crying. What happened?"

John shrugged helplessly. "No idea."

"Wait. She was *engaged*?" Bree's eyes grew wide. She turned to Carrie. "How did you know?"

Carrie looked smug. "I hear things." To Charlie, she said, "Melissa's not wearing her ring. And the fact she raced from the table probably means things aren't going well with her Mr. Right."

Charlie frowned. "*Was* engaged? Oh, no." She followed after her daughter.

Bree gaped. "She's engaged?"

John sat back down. "I need a drink." Then he looked at Tex. "How about you join me for a scotch in my study?"

"Don't mind if I do." He sent an apologetic glance to Bree, but she looked too stunned to accept it. He followed the chief into his study and sat when motioned to the seat across from a huge desk.

"Sorry for the family drama. We normally don't have all that much."

"Everyone's got something. You should see my family. I have three brothers. One of them is married with a kid, the other is married and expecting, and my other brother is a handful, according to Momma and Daddy. Family dinners can be a nightmare."

John smiled. "I'll bet." He poured a glass of scotch for himself, but Tex politely refused. Then John sat and sipped. "Ah, that's nice."

"I'll take your word for it. I'm a hops man, myself. And I'm driving tonight, so I'm good with what I already drank."

"Tex, I apologize if I came across as invasive, but I love my daughter. Daughters, both of them, but you're only involved with one of them at present." The chief sighed. "I've been around firefighters my whole life. My father was a volunteer, you know. In northern Washington. And I've been around a long time. I know how men think. My daughter is beautiful. I think we can both agree on that."

"Yes, sir."

"And I'm protective. I don't know if she told you this, but I pretty much forbade her from dating anyone in our profession a long time ago."

"She mentioned it."

John nodded. "I just want to protect her. Our job is dangerous, and a lot of us act out. With women, with alcohol or drugs, and all-around tough family dynamics. There's a reason we have a high divorce rate." He sighed. "I mean no offense, but I want Bree to have a happy home life. And that's hard enough as it is these days. Adding more stress from our line of work makes it worse."

"I hear you. I know what you mean." Tex should have let it go.

But he couldn't. "But, sir, that's Bree's choice to make. And this has nothing to do with me at all. I mean, it's her life, period."

The chief looked taken aback.

"My uncle tried this same tactic with my cousin. She's a total cutie, sweet as can be, the whole package. And it blew up in his face. She married that bull rider and divorced his sorry, cheating ass two years later, after she'd gone and had a kid with him. But she learned, and now she's married to a terrific guy on a neighboring ranch. My point is, nothing was going to make her stay away from the rodeo. Not Uncle Owen's warnings or trying to scare away anyone who sniffed too close. I know I don't have a dog in this fight, and I don't have daughters. But I watch and learn, and I know for a fact telling a body not to do something is a surefire way to get them to do just that. If Bree wants to date a firefighter, she will, I'm sure. One thing I've learned about your daughter—she's headstrong. All I'm sayin'."

Tex thought that had gone rather well.

The chief leaned forward, his gaze piercing, and a little scary. Bree's dad was a big guy with the brawn to back up that fierceness. "Well, let me tell you something, son. I *do* have daughters. And I have seen a broken heart or two. I can't control what others do, but I'll tell you this. If you want a career in this department, and you want to go far, you'd do wise to steer clear of Bree. Because even if you do end up stealing her heart, you'll always have her bear of a daddy to deal with at work. You get me?"

Well, fuck. But Tex couldn't back down now. He leaned forward as well. "Sir, I respect the hell out of you. And this conversation really isn't one worth having with me. But I'll tell you the cold, hard truth."

"Oh, what's that?" The chief leaned back and sipped his drink, imposing without trying to be.

"That if I fell in love with a woman like Bree, nothing—not her daddy, my job prospects, or threats of any kind—would stand in the way of me courting a woman I loved. Period. And if that stuck a craw up her daddy's ass, so be it. Because any Texan worth his salt loves a challenge."

He sat back and laced his fingers over his lap, wondering if he'd just flushed his career in the toilet with a hypothetical threat aimed at the big boss.

I am so fuckin' stupid.

Gilchrist watched him for a moment.

A tense moment that had Tex's insides cramping and sweat dampening the back of his shirt.

But the chief only laughed. "You know, Tex, I like you even more right now. I don't agree with you, but I love that conviction. You, Tex McGovern, will go far in the department with that kind of will. Just so long as you don't piss off the wrong people."

"Ah, well. It was nice workin' here while it lasted."

Gilchrist laughed harder.

"You think I'm joking? You should talk to my lieutenant. I get him ass-mad just about every week."

Charlie knocked and stuck her head past the door. "Drama averted. We're all happy and having apple crumb cake."

Tex let the idea of sweets override this dreaded conversation. "Really? Apple crumb cake? Ma'am, are you sure you're happily married to this guy? I'm younger, and I really love a woman who can cook."

She laughed prettily and left.

The chief stood, rounded the desk, and slapped him on the back. "Nice try. She's mine. Get your own girl."

I'm trying, guy. But you pretty much just warned me off her. Tex shrugged. "Can't blame a fella for trying. If I can't have Charlie, is the apple cake still on the menu?"

Chapter Twelve

TEX WAS OUT THE DOOR AND HALFWAY TO HIS TRUCK WHEN Melissa called out and asked if he could drop her off at her condo. She'd arrived via Uber but didn't want to take one home in the dark.

He looked over at Bree, standing outside with the others, who was shaking her head no, same with Carrie. Both of them stood behind everyone else, so only he could see them.

"Oh, that would save me a trip. If it's not out of your way?" John asked.

A glance at the chief, after that huge warning to steer clear of his other daughter, reared its head.

The man stood with an arm around his wife and nodded. "Really, you'd be doing us a favor, Tex."

A second request from the old man. Well now, Tex couldn't rightly refuse. "No problem. Thank you again, Charlie, Chief. I had a wonderful time. I'm finding it a problem to sit comfortably with my belt about to bust, but I'm full of good food. Can't complain."

He waved, helped Melissa into his truck, then hurried around to his side and started it up. He watched as she buckled up. A glance at the house showed Bree and Carrie hadn't stuck around to watch him go. The chief and Charlie waited by the front door for a beat then went back inside and shut it behind them.

"Where to, Melissa?"

"Thanks so much, Tex. I really appreciate this." She gave him her address, not too far from Bree's, and they headed her way. "I'm so sorry for that scene at dinner."

She said nothing more, though she watched him, and he took that as his cue to ask about what had made her so upset at the table, even though he really wanted nothing to do with her. What would Bree think of him taking her home? Oh, man. He hoped she wouldn't blame him for this.

"So, uh, are you okay?"

She blinked. "No." Then she started crying.

Shit got *awkward*. "There's some tissues in the console." He gestured to the space between them.

She removed a travel pack and wiped her eyes. "Thanks. My fiancé, Bill, broke it off with me. I'm devastated, of course."

"He must be crazy."

"Thanks." In the flash of oncoming lights, he saw her watery smile. "I guess we weren't meant to be. But it hurts. We were supposed to get married next year."

"Better to know now, I always say."

"Yeah." She sighed. "Bree's never been engaged, you know. I would have been the first one down the aisle."

He said nothing to that, glad to hear it, actually.

"But then, she's always had problems. You know. With relationships. Too busy jet setting around the world. Living it up with men, partying, and—sorry. That's none of my business, or yours." She cried again.

But these tears sounded a little forced. *Bree? Men? Partying?* What Bree was Melissa talking about?

"Hey, now. You're a pretty gal, smart, and you have people who love you. You'll find someone easily."

"Know any hunky cowboys who fight fires?" she teased, sounding…flirty?

"Nah. They broke the mold with me." He smiled, but inside he cringed. *Get me out of this truck!* "You might want to keep your interest just to cowboys. I get the feeling your daddy doesn't want you out with any firefighters."

"He just likes to talk. I've dated firefighters before. We even christened a new engine a few years ago." She giggled, and all he felt was creeped out.

"They don't like us to do that." He sounded prudish. Now, if he had an engine all to himself with Bree, he'd find some way to get her into the cab and under him. Or on top of him, would be better...

A hand fell on his knee.

He jerked and forced himself to keep the wheel steady. "Melissa?"

"I'm sorry you're having to take me home. But can I ask you something?"

"Ah, sure."

"Do you think I'm pretty?"

"Yep."

"Fun?"

"I don't rightly know you."

"Am I prettier than Bree?"

Rough terrain, here. He sped up to get her home faster.

Instead of answering, Tex asked a question of his own. "What's really going on, Melissa?"

She leaned her head back and took her hand from his leg. *Thank God.* "Bill and I had no spark. No chemistry. He was boring. And he said I didn't interest him."

"Nah. You're great. Be honest. Something had to be missing. No spark?"

He felt her looking at him. *Shut up, you idiot. Just take her home and stop talking.*

"I don't know. In all my relationships, there's always been something lacking." She turned to face the window. "I never had a modeling contract. I didn't go to Europe and party with CEOs and dignitaries. I was never in a magazine." She sounded bitter. "My experience with men is different than my sister's." She said "sister" without a sneer, so that was something. "And sometimes I'm angry and petty, and I wonder if that bleeds into my relationships with men."

"Have you tried women?" *God, what is wrong with me tonight?*
"*What?*"

"Sorry, I just meant…"

"What?"

"What I meant is that I should stop talking, because what the hell do I know?" *That's right. That's it.*

"But you're a guy. You have some insights I don't. Oh, there. That's my building."

Yes, almost done…

He pulled in front of her building and put the truck in park, waiting for her to leave. Instead, she looked at him expectantly.

He sighed. "Look, none of this is my place to talk. Ask your daddy."

"Are you kidding? My father still likes to think I'm a virgin, I'm sure." She snorted. "I'm not asking for the answer to my problem. Just… If you're not feeling a spark, is it worth chasing? From a guy's perspective?"

"It's all about the guy in question, I'd say. Look, if this Bill guy left, you have some choices. You think about life without him." Without Bree, he'd be empty. Bored. Unhappy. "And you wonder why. What is it about him that made you so happy to begin with?" A sense of humor, kindness, a rockin' body. "Now that he's gone, what will you do with your life? Are you really that unhappy he's gone? Or is it just that you're lonely? What spark do you mean? A sexual spark? An intellectual compatibility? Or maybe it's both or neither, just something you know deep inside. Nobody has the answer but you, Melissa. And something I've been told too many times by well-meaning friends—if you have the same problem with everyone you meet, maybe it's not about them. It's about you."

She stared at him. "Hmm. That was pretty darn insightful for a Southern boy."

They both laughed.

"Can I give you a hug?" she asked.

"Um, er, I…" He swallowed. "Okay."

She didn't get grabby or kissy. She just wanted to be held, apparently, and Tex felt the need to help her feel better. A few seconds later, she let him go and wiped her eyes.

"Oh, hell. Forget my bitchy comment about Bree. Her wild ways were all in the past. And thanks for being so nice, Tex. I promise not to tell my dad you have the hots for Bree."

"I—*what?*"

She left the truck, and he hustled out to walk her to the front of her fancy condo. He left her once she'd walked inside, where he saw someone in uniform sitting behind a desk. The man nodded to her and hurried to press a button for her at the elevators.

Tex got back in the truck and stared at the dash, not seeing it. Melissa thought he had thing for Bree? Bree's dad warning him off? What the fuck? Bree was twenty-seven years old, not a young girl needing her parents' permission for anything.

He groaned, reading a text from Bree stating she'd talk to him on Monday, giving him the next day off. He didn't know how to feel about that. Good or bad? Had he ruined things or not?

And why did all of his advice for Melissa sound more about how *he* should think about Bree? Because no two ways about it, he'd become obsessed. He liked her. A lot. And he wanted her even more. Bree was the best sex he'd ever had.

But that sex made him feel emotionally closer, so the fucking was turning into making love real fast. Good or bad, it just was. Now what to do about her? And what to do on their first date, which he hoped he'd get in just five more days? He could go without sex until then. They would keep all that desire in check until they figured out this new relationship. Because it wasn't a fling, but a beginning.

He just had to convince Bree of that.

Bree watched her stepsister leave with Tex and had to stop herself from kicking her dad's ass. She didn't say anything until they were all inside and she'd had a minute to think about how not to sound too upset. Half-teasingly, she said, "Yo, Dad, way to throw Melissa at Tex."

"Seriously, John. Not cool." Carrie crossed her arms over her chest.

Charlie frowned at him.

Her father sighed. "Go ahead, hon. Get it out."

His wife scowled. "What they said." She sniffed. "I'm going to clean the kitchen. And I for one really liked your friend, Bree. Your *professional*, not *personal*, friend." Charlie left.

Her dad winced. "I wasn't throwing them together. She has the same rules as you, you know. No firefighters. And no cops."

"When did the no-cops rule apply?" Bree blinked.

"Now you're taking it too far! What about handcuffs? Those are necessary in any given relationship." Carrie stomped her foot. "I'm so done with this conversation. I'm going to help Charlie in the kitchen." She left father and daughter alone.

Bree chuckled and saw her father's amusement as well. Carrie had a knack for diffusing tension—when not trying to outright stir trouble. Then Bree and her dad locked gazes, and their mutual mirth faded. "Geez, Dad, what is going on with you? You used to be so much more open-minded."

"I'm aware that I have two lovely daughters. You look more like your mother every day." His eyes shone suspiciously, as if holding back tears.

"Dad?"

"Did I ever tell you that your mother had a fiancé before me?"

"No, but Charlie filled me in. You can't seriously expect me to believe your bias is rooted in Mom's heart being broken. Hello?

I'm standing right here. She obviously chose you. Or are you not my dad?" Man, that would throw her for a loop.

He scowled. "Of course I'm your dad. But—"

"But nothing. I'm twenty-seven. I can choose my own boyfriends. And this has nothing to do with Tex—my *professional* guide. It has to do with me, Dad."

He gave a harsh laugh. "Your 'professional guide' told me the exact same thing when I warned him to keep his distance. Said I should let you be you. Then he had the nerve to tell me that he would do whatever he wanted regardless of any threats." Her dad watched her carefully.

A trap. "Good for Tex. If he fell in love with a woman, I bet he'd date her regardless. Dad, what if I find a guy and his parents tell *him* never to marry a model? But we love each other. Doesn't that mean anything?"

"I'm tired, honey." He kissed the top of her head. "Let's talk hypothetical love stories tomorrow, okay?"

"Dad! You can't walk away while we're talking."

"I can and am." He patted her shoulder. Hell, he might as well have patted her on the head. "And just so you know, I'd never tell you who you can and can't date."

All the anger in her defused. Good. He wasn't as insane as he sounded.

"*But* I would make it impossible for any firefighter not respecting my wishes to go far in the department. He'd get frustrated and bored and either quit or remain at the lowest rung on the ladder forever with no chance of advancement." Her dad waved. "Good night."

She stared, not sure what to think. Had he just threatened Tex's livelihood? Or had he meant firefighters in general? And what the hell, exactly, had Tex said to her father?

She found her stepmom and Carrie chatting in the kitchen. They stopped when she entered.

"Dad just threatened to not promote anyone at the department interested in me."

"Wow. Pulling out the big guns." Carrie whistled.

Charlie frowned. "There has to be more to this than how he and your mother first met."

"You'd think." Bree sighed. "But none of it matters. Tex and I aren't dating, and I'm not keen on finding a firefighter to shove it in Dad's face."

Carrie shook her head. "Yeah, imagine how much more awkward dinners could be then. Not only will Melissa be breaking up with a new guy each week, but John will glare holes into your fireman while your fire-babies suffer his wrath."

Charlie and Bree just stared at her.

"What? Too much?"

Charlie chuckled, and Bree thought she'd stayed long enough. She said her goodbyes and left with Carrie, heading back to her place in Carrie's car since her best friend had driven.

"What the hell happened tonight?" Carrie asked as they entered Bree's house. "Holy drama, Batman. That was fucking *awesome*. Why do you think Melissa and Bill broke up? My money is that she's secretly lesbian."

"Your money on anyone breaking up always rides on the secret lesbian card." Bree rolled her eyes. "What I want to know is what Tex and my dad talked about in his study." She told Carrie what her dad had said. "Tex never said he was dating me."

"Dating? Is that what you call one morning of fucking?"

Bree blushed.

Carrie, that shark, homed in. "More than one morning?" Her voice rose. "Hot damn! We have a winner!"

"Stop it." Bree laughed. "Okay, but don't judge me."

"I've seen his thighs and biceps. No judgment here."

"We were going to leave it as one temporary morning of insanity. You know, hormones. And then he asked me on a date. Not sex, but going out together after the photography is done. After this coming Wednesday." Excited at the prospect, she still intended to go out with him. That was, if her father hadn't ruined everything. "And then, well, he got me flowers."

"How sweet. That's all it took? You're easy."

Bree pointed to the bouquet on the table. "Shut up. I made the mistake of inviting him in to see them this afternoon. And, well, it happened." She groaned. "Carrie, it was so sexy. He's so strong. Against the wall!"

"Wow. I've never done it against the wall." Carrie frowned. "Maybe I should date a bodybuilder. I'm not that heavy for my size, but I'm tall."

"I should take some time and space. Maybe he and I should take a break tomorrow. I'll take my own pictures and give him the day off." She texted Tex, intent on finding out what Melissa had said to him later, after she'd had a chance to settle. "Hey. Can you do me a favor?"

"After tonight's stellar meal and entertainment, I owe you."

"Can you find out from Melissa what the hell is going on? And what she said to Tex in the truck? And how did you know she and Bill were engaged?"

"She talks to me sometimes. We text."

Bree stared. "Really? But…why? I though she hated you." *You're* my *friend. Not* hers.

"I did too." Carrie shrugged. "You ask me, I think she's lonely." Carrie paused. "And a lesbian."

Bree groaned.

"One of these days, I'll be right. If nothing but for the sheer fact probability makes it so."

"Whatever. I need sleep."

"And to rest that magic between your legs, I'll bet." Carrie cracked up. "Dudette, just say no. It's not that hard."

"That's what she said." Bree snickered.

"Weak." But Carrie was smiling. "Okay, I'll get the goods and let you know. And try to get along with your family so Tex isn't out of a job anytime soon."

That worried her. After Carrie left, Bree tried to sleep, but she kept thinking about her dad's threats. That couldn't be legal, to mess with someone's career. And that was totally beneath her father. He'd never do that.

Then again, when it came to her personal life, her father had never been all that rational.

She settled in her bed and thought she'd be up half the night worrying. To her surprise, she dropped off like a rock and missed the text Carrie sent hours later.

———

Carrie had just changed into a tank and boxers, her idea of pajamas, when someone knocked on her door. To her shock, Melissa stood outside, looking peeved.

Upon opening the door, Carrie stared.

Melissa stared back. Several inches shorter, curvy, and with dark-brown hair and eyes, the woman was a knockout. If only someone could curb her wicked tongue and resentment of all things Bree.

"Come in, princess."

Melissa flushed. "Thanks. I would have called, but—"

"You wanted to catch me in my undies. No problem."

Melissa glared. "Look, can we talk?"

"Sure." Carrie felt incomplete, so she fetched a silk, designer robe from her closet and returned, chic and fabulous. "Ah, now I feel better. Thirsty?"

"Water would be great." Melissa sat on the couch, her eyes puffy from crying, her pert nose red. And still she could have walked on any runway Carrie once had. Well, maybe if she'd been a little bit taller.

"What's up, buttercup?" Carrie sat next to her, leaving a full cushion between them as she turned to face her guest. "And what did you and yummy Tex talk about on the way home?"

Melissa looked at her, and Carrie had the odd sensation of being fully dissected. "He's into Bree. I can tell."

"Really? I don't know. Maybe." Best to act as if she had no idea.

"They have something between them. I could feel it."

Honestly, so could Carrie. It was in the way the pair *didn't* look at each other so damn hard. Tex had tried, but his gaze had sought Bree's too many times. And Carrie's dunderhead friend had memorized the contents on her plate instead of being normal and making eye contact with anyone other than her stepmother—or quick glimpses of Tex—throughout the meal.

Carrie shrugged. "What's your point?"

"I wanted to see what she liked about him, so I had him drive me home. And he was nice. He didn't hit on me or talk bad about anyone. Not even Bill. He gave me some excellent questions to ask myself."

"Ah, okay." Even for Melissa, she was acting weird. "What do you care about what Tex is like? You hate Bree."

Melissa looked uncomfortable. "I'm trying to be a better person. I'm seeing a therapist about my issues."

Holy crap. Talk about life changes.

"What exactly did Tex say that helped?"

"Carrie, have you ever felt a spark with your partners? Like, a sexual spark, or more?"

"Sure."

"I never do."

"Never?"

"The good sex is never great, and it wears away from good after a few times. Then we have nothing in common. And it's not just Bill. It's all of them." She sighed. "I'm not that big a bitch—"

"Oh, no?"

Melissa glared. "—that I think I'm better than everyone else. I just act that way." Tears filled her eyes. "It's like I'm in this never-ending jealousy loop with Bree, and she's clueless about it, which makes it worse."

"Explain."

"She's the pretty one. The successful one. The smart one."

"Hey, moron, you have an MBA from Stanford and make six figures plus a yearly bonus at your job."

"But it doesn't matter. Mom and Dad love her more."

"Oh, wow. You really are that immature."

"What?"

Carrie felt bad for her. "Melissa, you and Bree were never close. I get it. You were jealous of her, and she had no idea why you hated her."

An odd look crossed Melissa's face. "Yeah, yeah. I'm a petty bitch. Let's move on."

Carrie grinned, liking this Melissa. "Why are you here?"

"I never have that spark with anyone. But I have it with you."

"I—*what?*"

"I think I might be gay."

"Wait. Hold on." Carrie wondered, "Did Bree put you up to this? Because statistically speaking, I had to be right one of these days."

"Huh?"

"You're telling me you like girls."

"Women, and I'm not sure."

"You know what I mean. Have you ever been with a woman?"

"Sexually? No." Melissa flushed.

Carrie was suddenly, shockingly, incredibly turned on, and feeling so unlike herself. *Whoa. Totally not the time to be attracted! This is Bree's sister. And she's very confused.* "Melissa, just wait. I get that things with Bill didn't work out. And your other relationships haven't either. But that doesn't mean you're a lesbian." Carrie tried to be kind. "Or maybe you are. Or you're bisexual. Or asexual. Or some other type of sexual. Who knows? You don't need labels to be happy. You just need to be happy inside. The rest comes when you center yourself. And that is thousands of dollars of therapy talking, so believe it."

Melissa smiled.

Carrie felt uncomfortably drawn to that smile.

"Will you help me answer a few questions?"

"Um, I guess. Just please tell me you aren't out to sabotage my best friend and a sexy Texan she's not interested in."

"I'm not." Melissa laughed. "They're pretty dopey thinking no one would see how much they like each other."

"That's what I said." Carrie sighed. "Okay, so ask your questions. I'll answer them if I can."

"That's what I was hoping you'd say." Melissa smiled.

And Carrie forgot all about Bree and focused on what a spark really meant. And why it mattered.

Chapter Thirteen

TEX SPENT SUNDAY WITH HIS FRIENDS AT BRAD'S MOM'S HOUSE for a picnic. Oscar and Gerty were there, as was Avery, Brad's girlfriend. Bubbles tentatively nosed Klingon when the puppy wasn't too busy bothering an older Maltese. Otherwise she lay under a table, waiting for someone to drop food.

Tex had missed his buddies. They ate hot dogs and burgers and harassed each other over cornhole, only the best darn outdoor game to be created. Unfortunately, Avery was pretty damn good and a sore winner.

"Hey, Tex." She smiled at his defeat. "Who's the dog you brought with you? Bubbles?"

Hearing her name, Bubbles ambled over to Avery for some welcomed belly rubs.

"Oh, she's so cute! How old is she?"

"Seven, I think." He sighed. "I want to keep her. I already love her, but I have no time to give her the attention she deserves, and it's killing me."

"Could she maybe be a station dog?"

"I thought about that. I'd have to get permission, but I just don't see that for her. She's still a little timid with crowds. This picnic is as busy as we've been, and she's been under the table for most of it. She's sweet but likes it quiet." He checked his phone. His brother hadn't texted back about Tex's plan for the family to take her. "I want my family to keep her down in Texas. She could live out her life on the ranch or with my folks. She'd be outside a lot or could have plenty of quiet indoors. They'd love her." He knew they would, his momma especially.

"We can try to home her here. I know we could get her with a good family."

"I know, I just don't want her to go." Christ, he felt tears in his eyes looking at the damn dog, who looked at him with so much love. He blamed his emotional state on Bree, who was stirring him up in weird ways.

Avery patted his arm while he blinked away useless emotion. "It's okay. I feel the same way when I see all these lonely animals that have no place to go and no room at Pets Fur Life."

Just then, his phone buzzed. "Hold on."

Yo, loser. We're making a road trip. We'll take the dog home with us. Wyatt shot him a thumbs-up emoji.

His heart lightened. *Who's we?*

Me, Oliver, and Josh. Uncle Owen wants our idiot cousin to do something useful, and he's got another month until boot camp.

Tex breathed easier, feeling less guilt for finding Bubbles another home. *Awesome. Let me know when. You can stay with me.*

Duh. Later, little guy.

Tex looked down at Bubbles. "Hey, good-lookin', I think I got you a new place to live. And it's full of Southern dogs, so you'll have a great place to lay down your head begging for ribs."

As if she understood him, Bubbles barked and grinned.

If only all females were this easy to manage. The guys heard the good news and cheered, Oscar especially, as he looked forward to meeting the brother Tex had told him so much about, Oscar and Wyatt having so much in common.

Brad's mom made the party complete with some dance moves to technopunk that had everyone laughing.

The hours passed. Tex hated to leave but had to get in a workout. He hadn't been lying last night about all the good food putting some sag on his wag. Reggie agreed to go with him, so after stopping by his place to grab his stuff and drop off Bubbles, Tex joined Reggie in some running gear and took a five-mile run around Reggie's neighborhood. They talked as they ran, the workout good for breathing control but not too strenuous.

"So, you and Bree, huh?" Reggie commented.

"It's not going until we finish her project. Then her dad will try to demote me for looking at her or breathing her same air."

Reggie raised a brow. "That's not right."

"I told him that. Not exactly about me and Bree, but in general." Tex relayed his conversation from the previous night.

"Fuck, that's rough. You can say what you want about HR and the union, but Gilchrist is smart. He'll find ways to keep you under his thumb. And you can use your union rep forever, and it still won't help. Networking, son. It's all about who you know."

"And who you *don't* blow, apparently." Tex groaned. "Reggie, I really like her. I'm not out to fuck and fly. I want to be with her. But I love my job. I don't want to lose it."

"So maybe you're no longer the love-them-and-leave-them-eventually type?" Reggie put on a burst of speed that Tex easily matched. Reggie started breathing hard. "I hate that you're fast."

"And sexy and smart and strong. I know."

"I can out-bench you."

Tex smirked. "If it makes you feel better, yep, you sure can." The reality was Reggie could lift more. The strongest in their group, the guy surely looked it. His arms and chest were bodybuilder-huge. Of course, he'd only gotten that big since breaking it off with Amy.

"You can haul my big ass out of a fire without too much of a struggle." Tex gave him a thumbs-up, and Reggie flipped him off. "You have that going for you, Reginald." He laughed at the face Reggie made. "But I'll outrun you any day of the week. Comes from chasing after stray cattle as a kid. I used to run for miles instead of going to preschool. That's how they raise ranch kids."

"No kidding?"

"Of course I'm kidding. Duh. Wrangling cows as a toddler?" Tex laughed. "Yeah, right."

"Sometimes I hate you."

"Only sometimes. I'm making progress now, ain't I?"

After having to run *from* Reggie on a sprint back, Tex eventually made it to his truck and parted ways from his buddy. He went home, did some much-needed laundry, and played with Bubbles before giving in and texting Bree. She'd asked for a day's space, but he missed her. And if she didn't want to talk to him, she could ignore her phone, he reasoned.

She texted back right away, which made him feel better. Melissa is being weird. Not sure what's going on.

She ok? U ok?

Bree called him. "Sorry. I can't text all this when my brain is on overload. Melissa is acting really strange. Carrie too. She hasn't called me back, and I left three messages."

"Um, maybe she's busy?"

"It's me, Tex. When I call, Carrie answers. Something's up. Plus, I can't stop thinking about my dad. He's insane for actually thinking he can still tell me who to date."

"I'm sorry. Hope I didn't make things worse when I talked to him. All I said was that you should be able to decide who you go out with. I never said or hinted it might be me."

"Well, all I know is, if he tries to make your life miserable for any reason, you let me know. That's *not* happening."

"Yes, ma'am."

She chuckled. "What did you do today without me ordering you around the city?"

He told her about his picnic, the run with Reggie, and doing chores.

She had done her own set of chores and made her dad apologize by fixing her shower.

"Nicely played." He paused. "Did he ask how you knew to stop the water?"

"I told him I'd googled it. After the crap he put you through at dinner, I didn't want to let him know you'd been in my—gasp—house. I'm telling you, Tex. It makes no sense. My dad is a good guy. He's just not rational about my social life."

"He's a dad. They're known to be odd. My dad once dumped a load of manure in Liam's bed to make a point about his room looking 'like a shit house'—his quote. Needless to say, my brother kept his room neat from then on. But my momma was *not* happy about Dad's way of handling things."

She laughed. "I can imagine."

They chatted about more family experiences, and he told her his brothers and cousin would be making an appearance in a few weeks. He wondered what they'd think of her.

"Oh, wow. More McGoverns. I can't wait to meet them." She paused. "I mean, if they're around when I'm around."

"I'm sure that can be arranged." It warmed him that she thought about a future with him in it. Then he worried what that might mean. Reggie's comment about Tex being a love-them-and-leave-them-eventually type hit home. Was possibly ruining his career worth a month or two of being with Bree? *No way*—that was normally what he'd say before cutting himself loose. But he couldn't. Not yet. Should he say something about his uncertainty? Or wait?

"Oh, man." Bree let out a breath. "It's getting late, and I still have some things to do before tomorrow. Can you swing by to get me at eight? Or is that too early?"

"No problem. I plan to get in a workout before I grab you. Back to getting up early. You've been spoiling me."

"Good. No more sleeping in for you."

He sighed. "You're a morning person. I thought you were just a perky blond, but now I can see it's in your DNA. You like getting up early."

"Yep." She sounded cheerful, and that made him smile.

"See you tomorrow then. It's supposed to warm up to seventy, so be prepared to sweat."

"Ha ha."

Seattleites prized their warm temperatures and considered anything above sixty to be hot.

"Sweet dreams, Bree."

She paused. "You just had to say that, didn't you?"

"Huh?"

"Never mind. I'll see you tomorrow, Romeo. Be prepared to find us a fire. I need more heat for my photographs." She hung up.

Confused yet charmed, Tex did his crunches before hitting the sack. And damned if he didn't dream about Bree doing all manner of things without clothes on.

He woke to a raging hard-on and took his fantasies of her to the shower to work them out. He'd always been a sexual guy, but he'd never jerked himself off so much when dancing around a woman. He and Bree surely had some intense chemistry.

When he met her Monday morning, it was business as usual. They cautiously handled each other in a polite yet friendly manner, Bree sticking to her photography and Tex doing his best to keep it professional. Being near her caused everything inside him to stand up and shout, but he figured he'd keep it cool and focus on the job.

The day went well, and he felt proud for being able to pull back and view being with Bree as a job. Well, except for those small smiles she had just for him or the flirty way he kept teasing her, complimenting her, and using any excuse to touch her. The hand on the small of her back. Helping her out of the truck. Helping her into the truck. Leaning close to smell her shampoo.

God, he had it bad.

He promised himself he'd be better the next day, and to give himself a break, he decided to take her to Station 44.

After picking her up Tuesday morning, he informed her of the plan. "Okay, we haven't taken a lot of shots of my station since the first day, so I thought we could follow the gang today to see what's what around town."

"*We* haven't taken shots?"

He flushed. "I mean you."

"Ha. You're blushing. So cute."

"Hush, woman. You're distracting me."

She chuckled.

"I talked to the guys, and I'm calling in our bet."

"What bet?"

"Brad and I beat the pants off Mack and Reggie at Spades last week. It's sad really. In the Marine Corps, you spend a lot of time waiting around and end up playing a lot of cards or dominoes. Brad's almost as good as I am."

"He was in the Marines too, right?"

"Yeah. All four of our crew are prior service. Mack was in the Air Force as military police. Brad and I were infantry. Reggie was a sonar tech in the Navy. After we got out, we all met at one point or another and got assigned together, and we stuck. I guess it helps we all did time in the military first. We've been together for years. Anyway, that's not what you asked. Point is, Mack and Reggie still don't get that they just can't beat us, and I like to remind them as often as I can."

"I'll bet you do."

"They lost, and now they have to clean our cars and bring in treats from Sofa's."

"Sofa's? Sure, let's hit Station 44 today. Great idea."

He grinned.

When they arrived, Brad nodded at them to join him by the engine in the vehicle bay.

"Why aren't we going upstairs?" Bree asked.

"Because Hernandez and his cronies are circling like buzzards." Brad glanced around to make sure they had the bay to themselves. "LT brought in his wife's banana bread, and the guys are all over it." He grinned at Tex. "Poor Ed has to take a break from the magical bread to work out with the battalion chief this morning."

"My dad's here?" Bree blinked.

"Good." Tex grinned. "Let him compete with Ed and keep them all busy kissing ass. That leaves us with Sofa's."

They met Mack and Reggie at a counter along the wall. Today it held a carafe of coffee, paper cups, and plates and napkins to go along with the delicious aroma of baked goods in a box Mack opened.

"Here. You win." Mack's sour expression made everything sweeter.

"When are you and Reggie cleanin' my truck?"

Mack ignored him. As did Reggie. "Hi, Bree." Mack took her hand and kissed the back of it. "Don't you look like a fresh spring daisy today?"

She laughed. "Flatterer."

Reggie smoothly cut in front of Mack and guided Bree to the treats. "Ladies first."

"Right. Brad, after you." Mack bowed.

"Asshole," Brad muttered.

Bree grabbed a blueberry muffin and coffee while Reggie chatted her up.

"How's it going?" Brad asked in a low voice as he joined Tex a few steps away.

"Okay, so long as her dad stays off my ass." Tex sighed. "I'm really confused, man." He made sure Bree couldn't hear him. "I want to be with her. Like, dating and shit. But that threat from her dad, screwing with my job? This is my life, you know?"

"The guy's probably just messing with you. Chief Gilchrist is a good guy. Everyone knows it."

"Yeah, maybe."

Mack had hung back and said in a low voice, "You know, you're making too big a deal of this. Just hang out with her in private. See where it goes. Then if it's serious, you make some decisions. If not, you two crazy kids have fun, and no one cares because no one knows."

Tex tried to consider taking things one step at a time, but for some reason he kept envisioning a future with the sexy photographer. "Oh, ah, yeah, that's a thought."

Brad left him to flirt with Bree, or be personable, as he liked to call it. Bree didn't seem to mind being surrounded by his friends as they let her inside the engine to take all the pictures she wanted. Mack held her coffee for her, and Reggie guarded her muffin in the event the idiots upstairs came down.

They ate and drank, enjoying the lovely morning. The food really hit Tex's happy spot, and he made a mental note to visit the bakery to tell Elliot how much the firehouse enjoyed his food. Maybe he'd bring Bree with him when he did.

That would be fun. But not a date. Their date would have to be enjoyable and creative while also being private. Hmm. He'd have to think on that.

Reggie called out, "Yo, Tex, get your head out of your ass. Bree wants us to pose for a picture."

"You mean she wants to frame me with you less-than-handsome bookends."

"Oh, whatever." Mack huffed. "I'm the centerpiece here, Tex."

"Gentlemen. You are all drool-worthy." Bree gave them directions, moving them just so, adjusting her camera and fiddling. She shot a few pictures before the alarm sounded. The guys shot to their lockers to get their gear on. And man, did they move.

Bree continued to take shots as they geared up and got ready to leave.

Excitement filled him even though Tex wouldn't be taking part. "Okay, guys, we'll follow along." Then he realized they were missing a body. "Where's the new guy?"

"We left Rob upstairs with the others." Brad rolled his eyes. "He's got the personality of a rock."

"And not a pet rock, because they're fun," Mack said.

Bree bit her lip. "They really are. I had one as a kid."

"I'm coming," Rob said as he raced into the bay followed by Hernandez's crew hopping into the aid trucks.

Wash frowned. "I didn't know the photographer was here."

"Why should you?" Tex asked.

"Do I smell food?" The giant homed in on the Sofa's box like a bloodhound. "Yo, Hernandez. They had food and the pretty lady and didn't share."

Hernandez flipped Tex off before heading into Aid 44. "I'll remember this, McGovern."

"Whatever." He turned Bree's attention to both trucks. "Aid 44 and Aid 45 are going out with the engine on this one. Sounds like we need to follow."

"Uh-oh." Daughter to a firefighter, Bree would know the seriousness of having everyone out on a call.

He hustled with her to the battalion truck outside as the engine screamed out of the bay, followed by the aid vehicles, and flashed the lights as they headed out.

With the scanner on, Tex picked up the information. A bad fire in an abandoned building that used to be an auto shop not two miles away. Bad news, as the place hadn't been completely cleaned out yet and likely still had oil and chemicals inside.

As they neared, an explosion rocked the air.

"Shit." He followed the sirens and pulled in a bit behind, away from danger should another explosion happen but close enough to feel the heat.

"Oh my God." Bree gaped, her camera in hand, as she left the truck with Tex.

"Shoot, woman."

"I know, I know." She snapped photos fast, moving closer and around while Tex continued to guide her back, away from the blaze and responding personnel.

There had to be an accelerant in play, because the fire had spread rapidly and continued to burn like crazy.

The lieutenant was directing people, making sure they established command, an ops link, and had people on the hoses. Brad and Mack were already on one of the hoses to water down the blaze closest to them while Reggie and Rob readied to head inside. Hernandez and Wash suited up as well, two more ready to go in and scope things while the other two on Hernandez's team remained with the aid truck.

Tex listened to the handheld and said to Bree, "Station 28 is on the way. They had something come up, or they'd have been first on scene." He steered Bree back when she wanted to move closer.

"But I need that shot."

"Come on. With me." He hurried them around the action toward the back of the warehouse, which hadn't yet burned like the front, though smoke poured from the broken windows on the second floor.

Bree gasped.

"What?"

She zoomed in on the building with her camera. "Tex, I see people inside!"

"How many? Can you tell?" He radioed the lieutenant and told him what Bree relayed.

"Looks like three people, no, four. Two older women, a teenage girl, and a young man. They don't look so good." An odd mix of folks to be hanging around an old, empty auto shop.

"LT, Bree can see four people. Two older women, a young man, and a teenage girl. Stuck on the second floor. Wait. I can see the girl waving." He waved back and yelled, "Stay there. We have help coming," though he didn't think she could hear him over the noise of the fire and more sirens. "Make it fast, LT. The smoke is bad."

"Roger. Out."

It killed Tex not to go inside and help, but he waited while Rob and Reggie rushed around the back, found an open door, and headed inside. Hernandez and Wash stood by outside. Tex changed the channel on the handheld to listen to the operation inside. The guys would communicate via their breathing apparatuses on the ops channel.

He listened as Rob and Reggie scoped the area and were able to locate a set of stairs that hadn't yet been touched by the fire.

Bree listened with wide eyes, her camera lowered as the action unfolded. Hernandez and Wash continued to wait. The two-in-two-out rule applied, making safety a priority not just for the victims but the responders as well, so one team always had the other's backs.

"This is scary," Bree said, her voice quiet. "I mean, I know the job. I've seen my dad do this, but it's still hard."

He put a hand on her shoulder as they watched and listened.

Rob and Reggie reported they had the two older women, but the younger pair had decided to try to get out themselves.

Bree left Tex behind as she darted to the other side of the building.

"Damn it, Bree. Wait."

She kept running then stopping to look up through her camera, and he realized she wanted to see if she could help from a better view outside the building. A different perspective.

"There. I can see movement inside. But it's on the ground floor, and I can't be sure…"

Tex called it in. Hernandez responded, still waiting for Reggie and Rob to exit. The other two on Hernandez's crew pulled an aid truck around back as well, so everyone was ready. More firefighters joined the team, waiting out front.

Tex heard through the radio that Rob and Reggie had exited with two women needing medical attention for smoke inhalation but no burns or obvious injury otherwise. Hernandez and Wash then went inside and quickly found the two younger people and escorted them out, the teenage girl in a fireman's carry.

They put her in the aid vehicle and rushed away while the others helped the older women to medical attention.

Invested in the action, Tex hadn't realized Bree had kept taking photos. He hoped she got what she needed. He knew he hadn't, wishing he'd been inside with the others. That desire to help, to be a part of it all, only emphasized that firefighting was in his blood. These men were his people, and he could allow nothing to come between him and his passion.

He glanced at Bree and sighed, wishing his life could go back to being uncomplicated. "You did good, Bree." He escorted her around to the front of the building, where the captain and her father stood watching as Ed took charge. Her father gave her a sharp look before giving Tex a short nod.

As if Tex would let Bree fall into danger. The thought of that happening didn't comprehend.

And Tex realized his grand passion might not just be for firefighting, but also extended to one gorgeous blond with a caring heart.

Chapter Fourteen

WEDNESDAY, THEIR LAST DAY TOGETHER ON THE PROJECT, HAD come and gone, and by Friday, Bree had butterflies of steel warping the inside of her stomach as she waited for Tex to pick her up for their first official date...not at all counting the one where Bree had thrown Tex's water in his face. They both pretended that one had never happened.

They'd decided to go out at the end of the week. Bree and Tex both needed the break from the constant work on her project, and Tex had off until his regular rotation began again the next week. They could, ostensibly, relax and just focus on enjoying each other.

They'd both agreed to make the date a low-key affair as well as private, away from prying eyes. Tex thought he had the perfect solution. He called it a getting-to-know-you date. And he'd said he'd take care of all the details.

Sadly, the only detail she wanted had to do with whether he wore boxers or briefs and how long until she could get those suckers off his glorious body.

Bree groaned. *Do not think about sex. Try to get to know more than his package, doofus.*

To take her mind off her date, she called Carrie, sadly not expecting an answer. As she waited to go to voicemail—again— she plucked at her silky shirt, wondering if she'd dressed up enough for her date. Tex had said to be comfy casual, so she'd worn a sporty skirt that reached her knees, a comfy but stylish tee, and cute sneakers with sparkles, because, you know, sparkles.

The air felt cool but not cold, and she had an insulated though lightweight jacket for warmth.

To her surprise, Carrie actually answered the call, and it took Bree a second to respond to the unusually meek hello.

"What the hell, Carrie?" she snapped. "You've been ducking me with stupid texts. Are you okay? What's going on with you?"

Carrie blew out a breath. "Okay, you can't freak out."

"Oh, no. What? *What?*"

"You're freaking out."

"Damn it. Talk, or I'm coming over there."

"No, you aren't. You're waiting for Tex for your big date. That's why I answered your call now, actually, because you can't come get me."

"Wait. How do you know that?" Bree had been keeping her date with Tex a secret, planning on sharing with Carrie *after* it was over since her best friend couldn't take it upon herself to talk on the phone like a normal human being.

"I made out with Melissa."

Totally not what Bree had been expecting to hear, and she had no idea how to respond.

"I know." Carrie groaned. "I didn't mean to. She had questions. Now I have questions. And that's it though. It was just a kiss. Nothing else."

"Wait. Nothing else?" Bree's brain was on pause. "What?"

"It's too early to tell, but my lesbian theory might just hold water."

"I'll cancel my date with Tex. We need to talk about this."

"No, *we* do not need to talk about this. This business is between Melissa and me. You got a courtesy answer because I love you. And because I know what a pain in the ass you can be if you think someone's keeping secrets from you."

"Not true." She paused. "Well, kind of true. You could have called and told me though. You didn't have to hide it."

"I totally did. I'm not handling this well myself. It's…weird."

"Yeah." Bree cringed. "Please, just don't become a couple with her or anything. You're *my* friend. And yes, I heard myself say it and know I sound like a terrible person. But we're talking about Melissa."

"I know. But Bree, she's hurting. She's pretty messed up. And I'm not sure how she feels about all this, so you really can't say anything."

The perfect revenge for all of Melissa's bitchiness over the years. And something Bree would never in a million years do. Gay, straight, and whatever else her sister might be, her personal life belonged to no one but Melissa. Heck, Bree wished Carrie hadn't told *her*.

Bree heard Tex's truck pull up. "She's actually talking to you about her issues?"

"Yeah. I think it's about time too. But enough about me, what about you? What are you guys doing, besides each other, for this date?"

Bree appreciated the change in subject. "We're not having sex."

Carrie laughed.

"We're going to *try* not to."

"Why not?"

"Because we want to get to know each other beyond how we look naked. We need to have more than sexy times to be a couple." She blinked. "Oh, wow. Are we trying to be a couple? I don't know. The sex makes me want that, but there are problems. My dad, Tex's many exes, my best friend kissing my sister..."

"I'm going to pretend you didn't mention that again and that you aren't freaking out. Okay, while you're dealing with your sexed-up Texan, I'm going to drink. Heavily. It's been a tough week."

"Sorry, Carrie." Sometimes Bree spent so much time bitching to Carrie that Carrie didn't get a fair shake. Then again, Bree seemed to have a messier life. "Want to hang out this weekend?"

"Sunday brunch?"

"Deal. And I promise not to go wacko on you about Melissa. Okay, he's here. I have to go."

"Later. Try not to be too easy."

"Idiot."

Carrie laughed, and Bree disconnected. She answered the door, only to see Tex standing with a large, black duffel bag.

She stared at the bag, trying to focus past the handsome cowboy wearing tight jeans, an even tighter T-shirt, and a cowboy hat. Because the hat really did quadruple his sex appeal. *Oh, mama.*

He tightened his hold on the duffel, and she said the first thing that popped into her mind. "I hope that's not for my body when you're done with me."

"What? No. Wait, what?"

"I like to watch true crime on TV. Best way to move a body is to chop it up into smaller pieces for ease of movement."

Tex frowned. "O-kay. And see, this is why we needed a date. I had no idea you were so into crime shows." He paused. "Or crime. Should I be scared?"

"Maybe." She grinned. "So where to?"

"Come with me…"

Half an hour later, she stood over the plate, ready to swing again. "This is actually a lot of fun. I haven't been to a batting cage in almost twenty years."

"A little birdie told me you liked softball and tennis. I have the perfect night planned."

"Would that little birdie be six-two and have very scary eyes?"

"That's the one." He grinned. "Carrie told me I'd owe her big, and she'd make me pay. I'm officially frightened."

"You should be. But I'm flattered you sold your soul to make our date fun."

"What can I say? You're worth it. Especially when you wriggle as you wind up. Nice ass."

"Tex." She shushed him. "There are little kids around here."

They were at a fun center that catered to games for the younger crowd and a few brave older souls who didn't mind whack-a-mole, birthday parties, and cosmic bowling. With any luck, she'd get a shot at the retro arcade before they left.

"It's eight o'clock, and we're surrounded by teens and old guys like me, in case you hadn't noticed." He chuckled. "Man, you're brutal, Bree. These poor kids are going through puberty and dealing with your skirt. That's gotta be tough."

"What's wrong with my skirt?"

"Don't look at me. Look at the pitch."

The ball shot out of the machine and flew right by her.

"Strike one." Tex laughed at her angry face. "The only thing wrong with your skirt is that it shows your legs. Your very long, very smooth legs." He sighed. "And on that note, I should stop talking. This is a fun date. With our clothes on."

Two teenage boys walking by overheard and glanced at Bree, then at Tex.

"Guy has no game," one muttered to the other as they passed.

Tex shook his head. "He's not wrong."

Bree blushed. "Would you keep it down?"

He glanced down at himself. "I'm trying, okay?"

"Not that…just…never mind." He was making her laugh despite her embarrassment. And it made her feel better that he still desired her as much as she wanted him.

They each took turns batting, and she'd managed to really smack the ball a few times. Tex, of course, hit home run after home run according to the digital scorekeeper.

"Do you come here to practice on your days off?" she asked, suspicious.

He laughed. "No. But I've always been good at baseball. I was an athlete back in the day."

"And now."

"Kind of. I do like playing in our county league. You should see us play soccer. It's brutal, like a death match with a ball. Come see us sometime. We're the Burning Embers."

"Lovely."

He grinned and bought them sodas to go with their cheesy nachos. They ate inside the facility, overlooking the indoor bowling alley. The fun center also had bumper cars and miniature golf.

"So, do I get the whole treatment?" she asked. "Bowling? Golf? Bumper cars?"

"We'll see. Depends on how many of my questions you answer correctly."

"Oh, a quiz. How fun."

"Question one: How do I feel about music?"

"The questions are about you?"

"No, you don't get to ask them, I do."

"Well, hmm. You like to listen to country music in the truck. And I've heard you singing under your breath. I think maybe when no one's with you, you sing along to the radio."

"Good answer. Okay, you win a round of miniature golf."

"Yay, I win." She clapped like a child and saw him try to hide a laugh. "Next."

"Question two: Am I a cat person or a dog person?"

"Both. You love animals. And you love people. In fact, I'd put you as an extrovert."

He blinked. "Ah, yes. Good. And you get extra credit. After golf, we'll hit the arcade."

She made gave an exaggerated fist pump. "*Yes.* That's what I was hoping to score. Okay, my turn."

"What do I win if I guess right?" The expression on his face, especially when his gaze moved from her eyes to her lips and stayed there, told her exactly what he wanted.

"Tex, behave."

"Aw, shucks."

She laughed. "*My* question number one is: True or false? I am afraid of clowns, gum, and spiders."

"Oh, that's a tough one." He studied her, his eyes clear, his lips curled. "I'm going to go with false. Clowns and spiders, sure, but gum?"

"You are correct. And you are wrong. Ha! You forfeit a point."

"Wait. You're afraid of gum?"

"I had a bad incident in second grade. Got gum in my hair and had a hideous haircut because of it. It left lasting scars." She ran her hands through her hair to remind herself she had length.

He laughed. "Okay, no gum. Not even to chew, ever?"

"Nope. I don't do gum and don't like people chewing it near me. I know, weird. Oh, but I do hate clowns. Spiders, however, I have no problem with."

"Wow. A gal who likes spiders. How about that?"

"Stereotype much?"

"Quit harrassin' me. What's the next question?" He grabbed some nachos and chowed down. But he didn't make a pig of himself and made sure not to take more unless she took some as well. Always the gentleman…

"Question two: What is my least favorite food?"

"Aw, come on. These are hard questions."

"Suck it up. Guess."

"Um, well, how about onions? Or liver? Maybe brussels sprouts?"

"Wrong. That's two points you're in the hole for. I hate pudding, Jell-O, and anything mushy. I can't stand the texture."

"Seriously? No mashed potatoes? No peanut butter?"

"Nope and nope."

He stared at her, his eyes wide. "Are you even human?"

She laughed. "What about you?"

"I like all food, can't you tell?" He rubbed his stomach. "What's your favorite color?"

"Pink—and don't say a thing about girls liking pink."

"Not a word. I like pink too. But I like blue best."

"Favorite animal?"

"Probably dogs or horses. I like cats too, but they seem kinda evil to me." He studied her. "I bet you love cats."

"I do." She shrugged. "What can I say? I love their predatory nature."

"Says the woman who talks about dismemberment and my duffel bag—that held bats, might I remind you."

"So sensitive. I didn't accuse *you* of being a killer. I just asked if maybe you had leanings that way."

Tex finished his beer. "You scare me a little."

"Good, just what I was going for."

"Another important question: How competitive are you?"

Bree showed him by kicking his ass at miniature golf, and she talked a lot of smack while doing it. After they returned the putters, she apologized. "Sorry. My dad taught me how to play a few sports, and he instilled a nasty competitive streak."

"Blaming your dad for that, huh?" Tex walked with her back inside toward the arcade. Her body hummed, and she subtly inched closer, loving the heat he generated. "Well, then, sweetcakes, prepare to eat up what you just dished out."

Tex then proceeded to destroy her at *Donkey Kong*, *Space Invaders*, and *Frogger*.

"Fine. You win." Bree didn't like losing. "But I totally rule at *Ms. Pac-Man*."

"Double or nothing?"

"On what, exactly? You lost two points from the quiz, and I think you cried when I sank my ball under the windmill."

"I had a bug in my eye," he grumbled, but she could see his amusement. "I don't know what to think about this killer side to you, Bree. It's…interesting."

"I hope it's still interesting when I mop the floor with you and Blinky."

"Huh?"

"He's the red one."

They found the *Ms. Pac-Man* machine empty and stood by it while Tex forked over the change for the game. "Ladies first," he said with a flourish. "That you know the names of *Pac-Man's* ghosts—"

"*Ms. Pac-Man*," she corrected as she chased energy pellets and a bouncing cherry.

"—disturbs me. I can't believe you know their names."

"I can't believe you don't."

The game surprised her by being close. Bree normally crushed the competition. When younger, she'd been addicted to the game, and as she'd gotten older, she still cherished remembrances of her mother taking her to the old-fashioned arcade downtown, which unfortunately had become a shoe store a few years ago.

"Finally. I win." She turned, exhilarated by her victory, and found herself kissed breathless.

"Sorry, but you're irresistible when you're gloating." Tex sighed and kissed her once more. "Okay, I'm done."

I'm not. She cleared her throat. "Well then. Time for you to pay up."

"Yeah?" He smiled. "I'm happy to do whatever you want, darlin'. As fast or slow as you need…"

———————

"What the heck kind of pay-up is this?" An hour later, standing in Bree's garage, Tex glared at the busted lawn mower sitting near her barely used toolkit. "This is evil, even for you."

"Not my fault you assumed I'd want you to sex me up."

"But…" He looked at her. Then he sighed. "Fine. But I think you're missing out on some of my greatest talents."

"I'm not going to ask." She wanted to. Badly. But tonight had been so much fun, and they'd spent it getting to know each other outside a bed. She felt so proud of herself for resisting temptation. "Can you come back tomorrow to fix it? I don't want to ruin your Saturday, but my lawn is getting out of control."

"Being with you isn't ruining anything." He stuffed his hands in his pockets and regarded her with a frank gaze. "I liked being with you tonight. I learned a lot. Like the fact that you cheat at mini golf."

"I do not."

"And you're a sore winner. It's kind of cute how you rub my nose in it, so angry-like. Especially when you know I could carry you like a human duffel bag with only one hand."

"What does that have to do with anything?" She frowned. She couldn't help her size compared to his.

"See? That bit of fire in you. It's sexy. And cute. And you're gettin' madder." He chuckled. "Easy, Killer. I'll swing by tomorrow to fix your damn mower. What time?"

Gratified by the "Killer" reference, she let out a little breath. "Would eleven be okay? I want to sleep in tomorrow. And I'm sure you do too."

"Sounds good." He followed her from the garage out to his truck in the driveway. "So, um, are you busy tomorrow? After I fix your mower? You probably are."

"Not really, no." She should have made up something, to seem like she had a super exciting life outside of work. But all she could think about was the possibility of spending more time with Tex. She liked him. He made her laugh, and they could talk about anything, agreeing or arguing, and she felt energized and thoughtful after.

"Maybe we could hang out or something. And that's not a sly way to ask for sex," he said before she could accuse him of that. "I like spending time with you."

She blushed. "Me too."

He took a step closer to her. "Can I hug you good night?"

"No kiss?" she teased.

He looked serious. "Not if you want to keep your clothes on. I don't have that much willpower."

"Oh." She smiled and held out her arms.

He hugged her off her feet, and his body felt like a slab of granite. He was so strong.

"You smell good." He groaned and set her down. "I'd better go before I do something I won't regret but you probably will." He got in his truck, waved, and left.

Bree stared until his lights faded and went back inside. After closing the garage, she got into her pajamas and flicked through the channels on cable and streaming on the web, not seeing anything of interest despite hundreds of options. Though it wouldn't have mattered if she had, her mind full of Tex McGovern. She really, really liked him.

Personality, brains, looks—he had it all. Now if she could just figure out if she could trust him. And she had no idea how to gauge that.

With a sigh, she turned off the TV and headed for a glass of wine and a bath instead. That would have to do until tomorrow.

When she'd have Tex all to herself. She bathed and plotted. And couldn't wait to put her devious plan into action.

———————

Tex picked up Bubbles from Oscar and Gerty's place, went home to let her out for a few tosses of the ball, then locked up the house and went straight into a cold shower.

He froze his nuts off for a good minute, seeing how much he could take.

But when he went to bed, he stared down at a tentpole in his shorts.

Swearing, he left the bed—because he couldn't do what he needed to with Bubbles staring at him—and hid himself in the bathroom in the dark. The lights off, the house quiet, he let himself imagine Bree naked, seeing those full breasts with their tight little nipples, the hollow in her belly, the soft, rounded curves of her waist and ass. He remembered how it had felt to plunge into her wet heat, to feel her coming around him and see her face as she lost herself in his arms.

It took him no time to get off, and after cleaning up, he went back to bed and wondered why a simple choice of Bree or his career had suddenly grown complicated.

Chapter Fifteen

TEX SHOWED UP AT BREE'S PLACE AT ELEVEN WITH BUBBLES BY his side and his own tool kit at hand, determined to pay off his debt, no matter how pedestrian the challenge.

When she opened the door, her expression broke into a delighted grin. For Bubbles. "Hey, sweetie, come here. Oh, and come on in, Tex."

Bubbles grinned and went right in, leaving Tex to fend for himself. He followed and closed the door behind him. "Why, thanks for the warm welcome, Bree."

She snickered and knelt to give Bubbles a good pet. When she straightened, she looked him in the eye. "You fix my lawn mower, we're even. And I promise not to tell anyone you cried when I beat you."

"For fuck's sake, it was a bug."

"So you say." She sniffed and turned to lead Bubbles outside into a perfect, late-June morning. She had a patio table and a few chairs accessorized with throw pillows and a matching umbrella. The small yard had enough space to keep Bubbles happy under the sun that drifted in and out of the clouds. Birds chirped and insects buzzed. It was like a movie set of what a summer day should feel like.

"Love those shorts," he commented, his gaze on her shapely legs, trying to pretend her skimpy tank top didn't showcase her breasts to perfection.

"I like yours too." She gave him a heated once-over that predictably affected a certain part of him. "You're so...athletic. And big."

"Stop it, you little witch. It's not fair. I'm hard and you can tell. Only way I know if you like me is if your nipples get hard. Which, thank God, they are." He took a step in her direction, and she held up a hand.

"Stop right there, mister. Lawn mower first."

"First?"

Her lips twitched. "No guarantee of anything, but maybe, just maybe, I'll be so impressed with your work, I might have to offer a more substantial reward."

"Shit. What else you need fixed? Your fridge? Car? Air conditioner? I'm your man."

She blinked. "You can fix those?"

"Honey, I grew up on a ranch in Texas. My daddy didn't believe in hiring folks when he had big, strapping sons to do ranch work." He grinned. "Of course I can fix stuff."

"So, you're like a handyman, a fireman, and a hunk all rolled up into one human being?"

"Hunk. Yep. That's me."

"Hold on." She closed her eyes, parted her lips, and made soft, breathy sounds.

He froze in place. She used that face when she climaxed.

"*Bree?*"

She wiped her expression and looked back at him. "Sorry. I just had a mini-orgasm. I'm good now. Get to work." She petted Bubbles before moving to the caddy of yard tools near her garden. The dog looked from Bree to him and followed Bree outside.

Tex both laughed and cursed the woman under his breath then set out to fix her mower.

It took some doing, but he got it cleaned up and working again. Her garage retained heat, and the weather had warmed, which made him hot enough to take off his shirt, leaving him in athletic shorts and sandals. He'd also gotten grease all over his hands.

He turned to go inside and saw Bree watching him, her expression inscrutable.

"It's fixed."

"Can you show me?"

He nodded and wheeled the mower outside around the house to her backyard. He showed her the issue and started the lawn mower for her, then mowed a small strip, which showed how much she'd really needed it fixed. The grass around it looked impossibly high.

Bubbles hid in the house.

"Damn. Bubbles." He left Bree to find the dog lying down in the living room, asleep. "So much for being afraid."

"Stop it right there."

He froze at the command in Bree's voice.

"Your hands are dirty."

"I was working with greasy parts." He turned to see her crooking her finger at him.

"Come with me, cowboy."

She had a look on her face he couldn't read, but his body tightened up when he got a good look at her. Seeing Bree in shorts and a tank, now without a damn bra—he noticed—was like walking barefoot over hot coals to get to heaven. He'd do it and like it no matter how much it hurt.

He rose and followed her into the bathroom. "Shoot. I left my shirt in the garage."

She put his hands in the sink, took some soap, and lathered his fingers and palms, standing so close, she had to see him poking into the washstand. And her hands... She was sliding her hands over his, tugging and stroking his fingers until he couldn't contain his groan of pleasure.

"Bree, honey, I'm sorry, but you—" He froze when her hands ran over his shorts and down to cup his balls. He rinsed off and dried in hurry.

"I think you deserve a reward for such a good job." She turned him so that his tailbone rested against the sink.

He stared down at her in awe. "Holy fuck, this is like every porn fantasy I've ever had. Except normally I'm the plumber, not the repair man."

Her throaty laugh made him even harder. Then she let go of him to grab one of his hands and put it on her breast. He felt hard nipples, and the sight of her full breasts unencumbered by a bra really got his motor running.

"I'm hot. Are you hot?" she asked, running a hand down his chest and over his erection barely constrained by his shorts.

He had to clear his throat to answer. "Yeah."

She guided his hands to the bottom of her tank top and lifted her arms.

He followed her unspoken request and removed her shirt, leaving her topless, clad only in silky, blue shorts.

But before he could take them off, she stepped out of her shorts wearing a white thong that barely covered her pussy. A fucking *thong.*

"*Jesus,* Bree." Who the hell was this woman? And what had she done to his brain? Because he couldn't think of one damn thing to say or do to make sense of the situation but fuck her until they couldn't breathe.

"Oh, my hardworking handyman. I owe you a great, big tip." She winked and licked her lips.

Sweat broke out on his brow, and he felt his body jerk toward her in anticipation of what she was selling.

She slowly moved to her knees.

"Motherfucker. I am just… I can't… I need…*you.*"

She winked. "I know." Then she reached for his shorts and briefs and tugged them down. His cock bobbed, thick and slick with need.

She blew a breath over his cockhead that had him shaking. He watched, his eyes narrowed, committing this to memory. Bree parted slick lips and put them over him.

Tex swore his eyes rolled back into his head, especially when her strong hands gripped his hips and held him still. Her mouth moved over him, taking him in, slowly, her talented tongue slithering over his rod with a finesse that had him swearing under his breath, praying he wouldn't lose it so soon.

She pulled back and kissed him the tip of him. "You taste good, cowboy."

"Bree," he groaned. "You're killin' me." He noticed her tight nipples, her breasts swaying as she leaned closer and kissed his dick again. She prodded his legs farther apart and cupped his balls, rubbing the hard knots.

Then she moaned and started sucking him, taking him in and out as she expertly worked him to orgasm in no time flat.

"Baby, I'm so close. I'm gonna come so fuckin' hard."

She only doubled down, taking him deeper. Tex couldn't help pumping into her mouth, though he did his best to be still, not wanting to gag her when she was taking him to heaven by way of the express lane for sure.

Then she grazed his balls and ran her clever hands between his legs and sucked like a damn vacuum.

Tex shattered. He yelled out and came, emptying inside her as she swallowed him down. He saw bright colors and felt his legs shake, his knees—hell, his whole body—weak.

Bree just knelt there before him, his blond angel licking her lips as she glanced up at him and winked. Then she shocked him by taking his cock in hand and licking him clean, which caused another burst of seed to shoot out over her lips.

She licked it off, and he dragged her to her feet and kissed her, full of thanks and affection and something deeper he couldn't yet name. He tasted himself on her lips and groaned at the sexy evidence of her care.

"You are the fucking best girlfriend in the world," he muttered and could have kicked himself when she tensed. "Shit. I mean, well, you, I…"

Her slow smile relieved him. "Blew your brains clean out, huh?"

He laughed, simultaneously exhausted and energized, which made no sense. But then, nothing of this morning did. "Where did all that come from?" he asked in amazement.

And now she blushed. "Well, I—"

"Because I want more. And this time, I get to be the house-husband and you're the sexy plumber. Now where can I unclog you, ma'am?"

───────────

Bree had never felt so turned on and sexy in her life. Watching Tex goggle over her, giving her 110 percent of his attention, and knowing she'd been in control of all of it had been as much her fantasy as his, apparently.

She'd always been partial to oral, though she couldn't have said why. Bree thought it a part of intimacy that only belonged with a committed couple. And she'd wanted to share that with Tex.

His reaction made it all worth it. As did his immediate need to give her an orgasm as well. An unselfish lover, her cowboy.

"Bree, someday you have to give me a naked picture."

"No way in hell."

He laughed as he looked her over, his gaze smoldering though he remained half-hard, despite being spent.

"I know, but a guy can dream. You are the fucking prettiest, sex-iest, just…the best. The fucking best. Sorry for swearing, but fuck. You destroyed me." His accent had turned thick, his face ruddy with repletion. "And you're gonna get rewarded, trust me."

She winked. "I can't wait."

Tex couldn't either, apparently, because he lifted her in his arms and walked them to her bedroom, then closed the door, setting her down gently. "Sorry. Can't have Bubbles seeing this."

She grinned.

He drew her into his body. The feel of his muscles against her breasts captivated her. As did his large hands on her ass.

"Those panties should be illegal. They make you look fuckable. And that on top of the way you already look is hell on a guy. Just sheer torture."

"Oh?" She toyed with the nape of his neck, and he closed his eyes, as beautiful as he'd said he thought her to be.

Before she could kiss him again, however, he turned her around, controlling her movements with force. "Now, now. You've been a bad girl, haven't you?" He took her hands and put them behind her back, holding on to her wrists with one hand, caught between her back and his front. She couldn't move them, and she couldn't see him either.

"Do you know what bad girls get?" he whispered and nipped at her ear.

Oh, wow. If he liked her on her knees, she had a feeling that having Tex act the dominating lover would outdo her performance.

"What?" she gasped as he used his other hand to play with her breasts and pinch her nipples. The small bite of pain was there and gone but fired up her libido as if setting her ablaze.

"They get fucked. Hard."

"I like this."

He smiled against her hair. "I thought you might. You bad, bad girl. Stay put." He left her and returned with a small foil packet.

He took a firm grip on her hands behind her back once more, positioning himself behind her. Kissing her neck, her ear, and whispering naughty things he planned to do with her, he refused to let her move while fondling her. The forced restraint made her crazed with desire.

When he reached between her legs and grazed her sex, she jerked.

"Hmm. You don't seem to be getting the message. You don't move unless I let you. I think you need to be punished. Look at how wet you made my hand. Are you sorry?"

"Nope."

He chuckled and ground against her ass, growing aroused again. She decided to help by stroking any part of him she could reach with her hands behind her back. And he let her, gliding into her palms and giving small thrusts to get himself nice and hard.

Then he shoved her forward, toward the bed. She stumbled, shocked at the sudden change of pace. She heard the packet rip and waited while he donned the condom.

He didn't let her think about it. Instead, Tex muscled her to the floor and had her on her hands and knees. Instead of smacking her on the ass, which she waited for, tense, he stroked her flank and ran his hands over her hips while he nudged her knees wider.

"Time for the boss to fill you up, missy."

"Oh, wow." She tried to back into him and felt a light slap on her butt. "Sorry."

"No, you're not. You little hussy." He chuckled. "Gotta ride the fight out of you, I guess."

He slipped a finger inside her with ease, her body definitely ready to accept him.

Then he removed it and, without warning, plunged into her.

The force hit the exact spot she needed. Shocked into a climax, she cried out her pleasure while he plunged in and out, taking her to new heights. His hands clung to her shoulders, pulling her tight against him, his intrusion deep yet welcomed, and so incredibly wild.

Bree had never experienced anything like it, and she had no idea how to process such pleasure. Her body, so slick, easily accommodated his size, which only made him move faster, harder. He kept thrusting in and out, and she kept squeezing to keep him inside, clenching in ecstasy as he pistoned before finally groaning and jetting into her.

He held her tightly, their bodies as deeply joined as they could be.

"Bree. Fuck, baby. So good." He rotated his hips and jerked, then swore as he withdrew. "Honey? You okay?"

"Yes. No." She sighed, dreamy and panting as she hung her head, trying to come back to earth. "You wrecked me."

"Back at ya." He sounded excited. "Damn, Bree. Didn't know you could drain me to the point of exhaustion."

"Huh?"

"Exactly." He groaned. "I need to ditch the rubber. Think we can shower?"

"Yes, please."

He took care of the spent condom and helped her into the shower, and they hugged as they stood under the hot spray.

"Look, Bree, I gotta say... I have no words for what we just did."

She opened her eyes and saw him looking concerned. "What's wrong?"

"Nothing, that's what's wrong." He scowled. "You're making me crazy, making me come so damn hard, I saw stars. Acting sexier than a woman has a right to be. I like you too much. Too soon. And now I sound like a fuckin' moron."

Bree watched in awe as Tex looked worried. Heck, he seemed almost nervous. "Tex?"

"I can't do this."

She didn't like hearing that. "What?" She wondered if she'd disgusted him by being too needy or too into his domination. "Sorry, I—"

"Nope, *I'm* talkin' now." He had the audacity to cut her off.

Her empathy for his feelings took a dive.

"I thought maybe we could be fuckbuddies. Good friends at least." The water ran over his face and body, and he looked both powerful and vulnerable. He cupped her chin and kissed her, the touch gentle, then firmer as his tongue pushed through and tangled with hers. He pulled back, breathing hard. "I've never felt like this with anyone. It's sexual. It's fuckin' emotional, and I'm not all that great with that."

She hugged him, and he hugged her back. Just the two of them alone together.

She'd never felt such a perfect moment in all her life.

"We should date," he blurted.

She pulled back, now feeling her own nerves. "For how long? When do I get to be added to your list of exes?"

He flushed. "I can't help I dated a lot. I never cheated, and I was always honest. I wanted that with you, to just fuck and be friends. At first. But the more I get to know you, the more I like you." He looked adorably defenseless as he smiled at her, and she saw a little glimpse of the boy he must have been. "Yesterday was a blast. I mean, nonstop fun. I haven't been on a date like that ever. Like, I didn't have to be anything other than me to have a good time with you." He sighed. "That sounds dumb. But it's like I know you get me. And you like me, right?"

"I do like you." She couldn't help herself and ran her hands over his fine body. "It's not just about your body either."

"That's what's so great. You're hotter than I am. I like more than just your body too." He sounded so proud of that fact. Bree had to laugh with him. "I know this is probably all coming out wrong. Your dad is on your ass about not dating my kind of people. And you have a busy life with the photography." He swallowed. "But, Bree, when we're not together, it's not the same."

She felt the same way but hadn't wanted to be the first to say it.

"I realize we're new, and we just spent two weeks in each other's pockets, but maybe we can keep going out. Just you and me doing fun stuff. Well, and fuckin'. Because, honey, you have rocked me so damn hard." He grabbed the soap and lathered her up, paying a lot of attention to her breasts.

"What are you saying?" She ended on a gasp when he turned her around so he could soap up the rest of her. He followed the path of water with his mouth and soon had her back to the wall while he licked between her legs.

Bree should have been too tired to want more sex. Her body, unfortunately, hadn't gotten the memo.

He pulled another orgasm out of her and smiled. "So, can we?"

"Huh? Sure. Yes. Whatever you want."

It was only later that she realized he'd committed them to dating exclusively, and that he now had the right to secretly call her his girlfriend.

———————

Tex spent the next few hours with Bree in a marathon of sexcapades. And wonder of wonders, she'd said they could forego protection. She was protected from pregnancy, and she trusted him with her safety. He'd never felt so good.

He had her in different positions. He dominated. Then she dominated. They played different roles, and he loved that she seemed up for anything. And that she blushed and confessed how much she'd loved going down on him.

It felt as if he'd won the lottery on life.

Poor Bubbles had to endure the indignity of listening to him groan, yell, and gasp Bree's name as he continued to enjoy her delectable body.

He wondered if this starry, wondrous feeling he'd found was the same thing his older brothers had with their wives, that his daddy shared with his momma. And what it meant that the thought of not having Bree in his life didn't make a lick of sense.

He didn't want to leave her, but he didn't want to overstay and have her kick him out. By dinnertime, he'd done enough sexing and cuddling to have exhausted him. With a kiss, he left and took Bubbles home for some rest. And rest he did. He slept through to the next morning, worn out and, to his astonishment, still satisfied.

He sent Bree a text with a few flower emojis, laughing when she sent him back a bunch of eggplants and hearts. He never would have imagined she'd be so sexual or so into playing games and making sex fun.

Bree this, Bree that. He couldn't think of anything without remembering Bree's smiling face and smiling along with her.

Even his run to the grocery store didn't bother him, until he ran into Becky, an old flame, in the snack aisle. She'd been nice but clingy a year ago, and he'd ended things before they could get too uncomfortably close.

"Tex, hi." She smiled and held open her arms.

He gave in to the hug she expected, keeping it brief. "Becky. Nice seeing you here."

"God, it's been a while." She seemed happy, her brown eyes sharp, her dark-red hair pulled back in a ponytail. Her yoga pants and instructor shirt gave testament to the fact she continued to teach yoga. She sure had been flexible, that he recalled. As he studied her, he wondered why he'd ended things with her so soon. Probably because she'd been nice but nowhere near as funny or smart as Bree. Pretty, but not a woman he had trouble not touching or looking away from. Like many others he'd dated.

Huh. Must have been Bree that was different.

"You look terrific," he said, hoping she hadn't noticed him cataloging her assets and finding her lacking in any way.

"Thanks. You too. Still a firefighter?"

"Yeah, at the new station. What about you?" He waved at her getup. "Still teaching yoga at your studio?"

She nodded and shyly flashed him an engagement ring. "And I'm seeing someone wonderful."

He gave her a sincere grin and hugged her, this time the one to initiate the embrace. "Damn, girl. That's terrific! How'd you meet him?"

She gushed, as if having been dying to be asked. "He's a trainer at an exclusive studio in Queen Anne. We ended up meeting through a mutual friend, a client, actually. And sparks flew."

"I hope he knows what a lucky guy he is."

She grinned. "If he doesn't, I'll swing by your station house and point you out. I mean, if you're the caliber of my ex, he should count himself lucky."

They made small talk for a few minutes before they left with grand smiles and waves. Tex wished Bree could have seen him, to know that not all of his ex-girlfriends threw water at him or called him names. He started to text her about the incident, then stopped. He knew it was a point of contention with her that he'd dated a lot. Not his fault, but he could see her point. He didn't think he'd like it if he constantly saw or heard about fellas she'd dated.

With a sigh, he pocketed his phone and finished shopping. Then he headed home and enjoyed a bit of solitude. Though Bree had correctly guessed him to be an extrovert, every now and then he needed to recharge with some alone time. For fun, he lifted weights and went for a run. Then he took Bubbles on long walk, talking to her as they explored the neighborhood in the growing dark.

"Yep. Those are the people who do a lot of stuff they shouldn't at night with the blinds up and the lights on. And that house has a cat that's awful cute. Don't think you'd like him much though." He noticed she looked at him when he spoke, and though she did her business, nosing around, peeing everywhere she could, she didn't tug at her leash or stop the walk. She just had minor periods of pausing.

"You're the best dog, you know."

She trotted, a sniff here, a sniff there.

"You're a good listener, aren't you?" When she gave him a soft woof then kept sniffing, he continued. "Bree likes me." He smiled, feeling that connection deep inside. "She's different, Bubbles. I mean, seeing Becky, comparing her to Bree, just showed me how great Bree is."

He kept thinking that, but he meant it. Bree seemed to take him at face value. Though it was early in their relationship, he didn't get the sense she wanted to change him. He hadn't lied about his life. She knew he'd dated a lot and that he was in high demand. But hell, so was she. Successful, intelligent. She was a professional model turned professional photographer, and she'd nabbed a coveted City Arts Grant over several thousand applicants.

But she had issues if she let her father dictate who she could or couldn't see. The problem being that the man had influence over Tex's career, one that he'd already established meant the world to him. Oddly enough, despite being with him for only a short time, Bree had started to mean the world to him too.

Mack, though, had given him advice to think about. Best not to rush things and take his time. Perhaps the newness of their relationship made it seem so wonderful, as if Tex was stuck in the honeymoon phase. That would make sense.

Still, he didn't think he'd ever been as gaga for any of his ex-girlfriends the way he was for Bree.

Perplexing.

Chapter Sixteen

TEX SPENT EARLY MONDAY MORNING IN ISSAQUAH, ABOUT half an hour outside of Seattle, on the Chirico Trail to Poo Poo Point. It was a terrific if steep hike that gave the best views. Luckily, he had another cloudless day off to enjoy.

The late afternoon he spent on a Pets Fur Life adoption with the guys and Bubbles as his sidekick. The pet store holding the adoption had been terrific about donating money to the charity as well as some pet food for foster families. Tex also turned down a few invitations to grab coffee or drinks from a few happy animal lovers.

People seemed drawn to him. They always had. It had made more than one relationship in the past tricky to navigate. But he'd been honest with Bree. He needed a woman who would trust him, no matter how many women came on to him.

Fortunately, with Brad, Reggie, and Mack along for the adoption, he wasn't the only guy getting chatted up by the ladies. Brad stuck closer to him, though, not wanting to give his girlfriend any issues, since she'd arrived to show her support.

They got all but one older cat adopted, and the crew considered it a huge success. He bought Bubbles a bandana to celebrate, and the crew plus Brad's girl decided to adjourn to Tex's house for a celebration dinner.

As they readied to leave, Reggie elbowed him.

"Ouch." Tex glared.

Reggie shook his head. "You're getting soft. Too much time spent ogling a pretty woman and not enough time in the gym."

"I still outran your sorry ass."

Mack overheard and raised his brows. "What's this? Slow man

Reggie Morgan losing *again* to speed demon, Tex McGovern? Brad, did you hear? Reggie lost another race."

"What's that make you?" Brad asked Reggie. "Zero for twenty?"

"Everyone's a comedian," Reggie grumbled. "Not like *you* can beat him."

"But we're not talking about me. We're talking about you," Brad countered and winked at Avery.

His girlfriend laughed. "Ignore him, Reggie. He's just jealous of your looks and strength."

"I knew I liked you." Reggie smiled at her.

"Wait. You think I'm jealous of Reggie?" Brad frowned.

"You're jealous of everyone," Mack muttered.

Brad ran a finger across his throat, then pointed at Mack while he let Avery drag him away to his car, much to Tex and the guys' amusement.

Mack elbowed him. "So, I'm thinking pizza?"

"It's the best thing I know how to make." Tex nodded.

"Yeah, takeout is your thing," Mack agreed. "My man with the plan. I'm game. See you losers there." He headed for his car with a swagger in his step.

Reggie shook his head. "Guess that means I'm riding with you."

"Where's your car?" Tex unlocked the doors of his truck.

Reggie got in. "I wanted a break. I'm sick of parking in this city."

"I hear that."

They drove to Tex's house with the usually taciturn Reggie playing twenty questions.

"Did Mack and Brad set me up for this?" Tex wondered aloud, under his breath.

Reggie heard him. "What? No. I just want to know. So, Bree. When do we get to all hang out together?"

"Never."

"Come on, Tex. You know she has to pass our test before you get the okay." Reggie gave him a firm look. He'd already learned about Tex's date at the ball cage, as well as a sanitized version of Tex hanging with Bree on Saturday. "Besides, you're in the early stages of young love. You can't just bang and bail. You have to pay her attention."

"Who said anything about banging?"

Reggie just looked at him.

Tex felt himself turning red. "We might have hooked up. But you can't say anything. I mean it."

"Who am I going to tell?"

"Mack, Brad, Wash, Hernandez, Nat, Lori…"

"Okay, okay." Reggie grinned. "I swear, I won't tell anyone outside our circle."

"Reggie."

"Brad and Mack probably already know. You've been *way* too happy today. It's your own fault."

"Shit."

"Yep. You have a certain glow about you when you have a new girlfriend." Reggie paused. "But Bree is a lot more than that, isn't she?"

"Maybe. I don't know."

"You like her a lot. Hell, you about had a fit when you blew that first date. And that was what? Like, seven months ago?"

"Nine and a half months and a few days. Technically speaking."

Reggie sighed. "Yeah, you have it bad."

"I can't help it." It felt good to get the words off his chest. "She's special. I like her. Like, all of her. Not just her body. She's the real deal." Every time he thought about how he might screw up a good thing, he started to sweat…and wondered if he should bail early before he ruined things for good.

"Uh-huh. Well, it's still new. Who knows? But the nice thing is that I like her. She's not some beauty with no brains. We both know you've gone there before."

"And you haven't?"

Reggie shrugged. "Well, sure. I'm a guy. But dating for me isn't a pastime like it is for you. I'll eventually find some girl, we'll date, end up getting married, and settle down. The idea of having a steady woman in my life doesn't give me hives."

Tex stopped scratched his arm. "Aren't you funny. And now who's telling stories?"

Reggie had the grace to look abashed. "So I'm taking my time after Amy. But I know the world keeps turning. My time will come."

Tex didn't have the heart to tell him how unsure he sounded.

"Question for you," Reggie continued.

Tex groaned.

"Why not invite her over to hang with us some time? You're being smart by taking things slow, but it's time to step it up."

Tex didn't think he'd been slow with Bree at all, but he had no intention of prolonging the discussion.

Reggie, however, did. "You and Bree are learning about each other. Privately, right? Where no one but your buds know you're seeing the battalion chief's daughter."

"Thanks for reminding me. I forgot about her dad."

Reggie ignored the sarcasm. "Now it's time to slowly insert her into more of your life. Have her meet your friends in a social setting. See how she fits in with us." Reggie, like the others, knew that the ultimate girlfriend test was in how well she tolerated their four-man crew. "Then, of course, you have to work in a sleepover. But that's a whole other level."

"I have dated before, you know."

"Not someone like Bree."

Reggie had a point.

"What makes you an expert on women, anyway?"

Reggie snorted. "Besides my overbearing older sisters, my father has been on my ass for months with unasked-for tips about dating. I'm thinking a few of them might be legit. Consider this my taking a bullet to share wisdom. You should count yourself lucky my father isn't sharing details of his social life with you." Reggie grimaced.

"Thanks."

"You're welcome." He paused. "Back to the advice… After you and Bree share a sleepover, move on to the meet-the-parents thing, but that's way down the line."

"Oh, uh, well, I already met her dad and stepmom."

Reggie frowned as they pulled into Tex's driveway. "When did this happen?"

"You remember my mandatory I'm-checking-you-out dinner at Chief Gilchrist's last week."

"Oh, right. But that was work-related. Not boyfriend-related."

"Of course not. He doesn't know we're dating." *He can't know, not yet. Not ever—and how realistic is that for a lasting relationship?*

"I'm still not sure how you're going to bridge that one."

Tex sighed. "Me neither."

"Well, that's more worry for another night. Now, let's go eat and enjoy ourselves. We've only got one more day before we're all back to work."

Tex gave a high-pitched squeal as they headed inside his home. "Oh, I'm so excited!"

"I knew you missed us. Brad owes me ten bucks."

But as Tex laughed and enjoyed his time with his friends, a part of him missed Bree, the night incomplete without her by his side.

He wondered if she missed him as well, and why the thought of reaching out to ask had him even more anxious about reinforcing their exclusive relationship—that he wasn't exactly sure Bree wanted.

━━━━━━━━━━

Bree had a tough time getting used to being by herself in her studio Monday, but she made it with only one smiley-face text from Tex to hold her over. And not to be the needy one in their new relationship, she focused on herself and her job—what really mattered, ignoring silly emotional needs.

Since he texted her first thing Tuesday morning, she let herself relax about their newness. She hadn't appeared insecure, letting him talk first to her. Should she chat him up when she had some free time? Or should she remain somewhat distant, still a prize needing to be won? *Wait. I'm a prize? I mean, I am amazing. But we're just two people dating. Why is this so hard? Should I…?*

Bree blew out a breath. *I'm such a nutcase.* She wished she could stop thinking about the man and focus on work. Which shouldn't have been difficult since she'd sequestered herself in her studio to finish the grant.

Her project was really coming along. She'd taken all the shots she'd needed, and now came the hard part. Figuring out lighting, any filters—if she decided to go that route versus a more purist form of expression—and framing.

Her phone buzzed. An incoming call. Immediately, her heart raced, that Tex might be on the other end of the line. She'd been planning to invite him over for dinner but didn't want to initiate. Except he'd asked her to dinner last time, so maybe…

She answered the call with a breathy, "Hello?"

"Hi, Ms. Gilchrist? This is Stefanie Connor from IAG—Illuminae Art Gallery."

Bree's heart raced for another reason. "Oh, hello. What can I do for you, Ms. Connor?" IAG had a reputation for making or breaking an artist's career, and they'd been instrumental in making the careers of some of the country's top photographers.

"We're interested in showing the work you're doing for the city. Congratulations again on winning the grant."

That was unexpected and completely awe-inducing. "Thank you so much. I've been working for years with photography as an artistic medium, not just as a way to pay the bills." *Shut up, Bree.*

Don't bring up your commercial work when she's offering you a showing! "Not that I'm ashamed of my studio work, but it's not the same," she ended feebly, making it worse.

Ms. Connor laughed. "Hey, artists need to eat. And please, call me Stefanie."

Relieved, Bree chatted with Stefanie for a few minutes, firmed down some dates, and hung up with an internal squeal. Then she shouted and pumped her fists, jumping around like a fool.

"Um, is this a bad time?"

She turned around, feeling foolish, as Tex wandered into her studio. Her cheeks hot, she answered, "Oh, ah, no. Not at all."

He smiled, and that grin added to her already great day. He wore jeans and a T-shirt, his usual wear, combined with boots and a ballcap in hand. This one had a Seattle Seahawks logo on it. "So, what's with all the cheering?"

"I just got an invitation to show my work at Illuminae!"

"I take it that's good?"

She grinned. "That's *great.* That's like getting drafted into the major leagues!"

"Well, hot damn." He rushed to her side and drew her into a hug, whirling her around until she grew dizzy. Then he kissed the breath out of her, leaving her seeing stars.

"Sorry, Bree. I couldn't help it. You look so pleased and pretty."

"I am happy. Aw, you're such a sweetie."

He blushed, and she wanted to kiss him until their clothes melted off. Instead, she led him to the pictures she'd been editing.

"Those are great." He seemed to really like the shots of his fellow firefighters working to save lives and of the obvious heartache she'd highlighted in the survivors' faces. Having gotten everyone's signed permission, she'd finally decided on what shots to use.

"So honest. Hurting," Tex said. "You captured the emotions of what it's like going through a real fire."

Then he frowned at a picture of himself—her favorite, because

it showed him in an unguarded moment laughing with his crew.
The four of them, with Tex highlighted because he'd been closest
to her shot, together at the station in the engine bay. A picture of
togetherness, a band of brothers who fought fires and saved lives
at the threat of their own safety.

"I think this one really encapsulates what it's like to be a firefighter." Next to it, in a separately framed shot, she planned to add
a photograph of men and women in uniform covered in smoke
and dirt, working tirelessly to save lives. She told Tex, and he
argued she should leave the picture of him and the guys out.

"Why would I?" she asked. "It's okay to be seen having fun and
living life, especially with all the grim stuff you guys have to deal
with."

"I guess you have a point." He shrugged and gave her a smile.
"You're the artist getting her work hung in a big-shot gallery, after all."

She still couldn't believe it. "It's so incredibly awesome but also
nerve-racking. Now I really can't screw up this project."

"You won't."

She felt his hand on her cheek and glanced up at him, away
from her photos.

His soft kiss, surprisingly tender, moved her.

Oh, wow. She blinked up at him. "So, um, what are you doing
here?"

He straightened and shoved his hands in his pockets. "I figured
to stop in and visit. I won't stay long. I don't want to take you away
from work. Just wanted to say hi."

"Hi."

"Hi." He gave her a goofy grin. "I guess I should leave. But, ah,
I was also gonna ask if you wanted to do dinner. I have to be in
tomorrow, early, but I'm off the rest of today. I would have called
before, but I didn't want to bug you." He frowned.

She snorted. "I was going to call you, but I thought the same
thing. I didn't want to bug you."

He shook his head. "Nah. You never get on my nerves. Well, except now that I know you like true crime and serial killer stuff. But that's mostly because you scare me. Not because it's annoying."

"Muhuhahaha."

He gave a mock shiver.

"Dinner sounds great. How about we eat at my place? Is that okay? And bring Bubbles."

"How about I bring dinner too? Chinese work? I have a hankering for Mother's Chicken."

"Sounds great." She pulled him down for a kiss that satisfied but still left her wanting. "Seven o'clock sharp?"

"Sure," he said, his voice hoarse. "I'll get outta your hair." Quietly, but she heard it anyway, he added, "Damn, girl. Setting me on fire." He left in a hurry, and she did nothing but smile for the rest of her day.

———————

Tex arrived at seven on the dot. Bree opened the door and gave Bubbles some loving attention before turning to him.

"I see you dressed up for the occasion."

He wore a Stetson instead of the Seahawks hat. "Yes, ma'am." He also carried a paper bag filled with good-smelling cartons.

He set the food out while she grabbed dishes, and they had an awkward silence before she blurted, "I missed you."

He gave a slow smile. "I know." Silence. "About time you admitted it."

"Shut up."

He laughed. "I missed you too." He waited for her to finish with the rice before scooping a ton on his plate. "So, what have I missed? What's going on with Carrie? Your dad and Charlie? How about Melissa?"

As usual, mention of her stepsister's name annoyed her and

added to the ache of regret, deep inside. That ache Bree refused to acknowledge. "Well, not much else is going on with me but work. Dad is still Dad. Charlie said to tell you hello if I see you again. So, hello."

He groaned. "That woman is the best cook. And so pretty. Your dad's a lucky man."

She agreed. "Which brings me to your question about Carrie and Melissa."

After a moment, he prodded, "Well?"

"I don't know. I talked to Carrie once since our date. She's been hanging with Melissa, and it's freaking me out."

"Why?" he asked between bites of an egg roll. He'd purchased four of them. She wondered if she'd get one or he'd eat them all. Talk about an appetite.

"Carrie's my best friend. For ten years we've been tight, like sisters. Then there's Melissa." She paused, the hurt festering. But this was Tex, and he wouldn't tell anyone. "She's the sister I always wanted, got, then turned into a bitchy nightmare." High school had been hell. "And it's going on fourteen years."

"Ouch."

"You met her. You talked to her."

"Yeah, but she was nice to me. I mean, she was kind of vulnerable, and it was a little awkward, her asking if I thought she was pretty and all, but—"

"*What?*"

He flushed. "She was bummed about her boyfriend dumping her."

"Fiancé." Bree fumed. Had Melissa put the moves on Tex, knowing Tex belonged with Bree?

"Right. Fiancé. It wasn't flirty or anything," he hastened to add. "She was just feeling down. Probably ugly and dumb, all the things you feel when you get dumped."

"Have you ever felt those things?"

"Well, no. Not really. Once, back in middle school, a girl chose my older brother over me. That hurt. But then I discovered baseball and never looked back." He grinned.

She didn't.

Tex groaned. "Come on, Bree. Let it go. Your sister didn't mean nothin', and you know I'm only looking at you."

"Are you?" Oh, man. Her insecurities were showing.

"You have to be kidding me. I know I'm lucky to be dating you." He pointed from her to him, his finger going back and forth. "Us, together, is the best thing ever. You think I'm going to mess that up by coming on to your sister?" He cringed. "I'm not a dog, Bree. No offense, Bubbles," he said to the canine under the table.

Bree couldn't help a grin when Bubbles gave a soft *woof*.

"I'm so into you, the guys are making fun of me," Tex admitted. "And you don't make it easy. I have to work for you."

"Oh?"

"See? There's that snippy tone. Now I need to work back into your good graces."

"Hmm. I think I like that."

"You're hot, smart, and forbidden. How can I look away?"

She laughed. "So, I'm forbidden fruit?"

"If I say you're ripe fruit that I want to peel and bite into slowly, will you deck me?"

"Probably."

"How about if I just take a bite anyway? I promise you orgasms if you smile at me pretty-like and forget what an asshole I can be."

"How many orgasms?"

"Two? Three?"

"Well, we'll have to see about that. After dinner."

"Best. Girlfriend. Ever."

She laughed. "Let's not talk about Carrie and Melissa anymore. Tell me something funny instead."

After swallowing a mouthful of chicken, he said, "Okay. How about a joke? Mack and a hot chick walk into a bar..."

"And?"

"That's the joke. Mack and a hot chick." He laughed. "How about, how many Marines does it take to piss Reggie the hell off?"

She chuckled. "I'd say one, but this sounds like the beginning of a good story. I give up. How many?"

"Well, it all started out with a misplaced cell phone…"

Chapter Seventeen

TEX HADN'T WANTED TO SEEM LIKE A HORNED-UP JERK, SO HE'D decided to let Bree set the pace when it came to sex. But seeing her smile and hearing her laugh got him worked up, hence the teasing offer of a few orgasms.

And now, for dessert, he got to make his girlfriend come.

Naked and flat on her back on her bed, Bree looked like a centerfold. She had the best damn body. Those bright-blue eyes, those plump, rosy lips…

He groaned and joined her, naked, on the bed. "I love lookin' at you."

"You too, cowboy." She ran her hands over his thighs as he straddled her waist and palmed her full breasts. "Oh." She closed her eyes and tilted back her head. If she bit her lip, he'd…

She bit her lip.

He swore to himself and moved so he could lean down to kiss her, lost in her taste, the sweet scent of honey from the tea she'd had at dinner. He was addicted to the softness of her lips, the delicacy of her touch as she stroked into his mouth with her tongue.

Like steel, his body had little give, growing harder as she seduced him.

He pulled back to watch her while he caressed and kissed her breasts. He loved her body, and she liked when he touched her, especially when he kissed her nipples.

She moaned and arched up into his mouth as he sucked one bud into a taut point. Then he teased the other before kissing his way down her body.

He spread her thighs and looked up, loving the way she opened for him, not holding back.

Planting his hands on her legs to keep them wide, he nuzzled her folds and sought the very heat of her.

When she moaned his name and twisted her hands in his hair, he smiled and kissed her in earnest.

Giving Bree pleasure gave him pleasure in return. Her responses weren't faked, and he liked knowing what made her feel good. He added a finger, caressed and thrust, and soon she was crying out as she climaxed, her tense muscles easing in repletion.

Tex kissed his way up her body, hungry for more of her but needing to see her smile once more.

She wound her arms around his neck and pulled him close as they kissed. He wondered if she liked tasting herself, because he found her sexy as hell.

"Mmm. I guess you do make good on your promises," she whispered between kisses.

"Darlin', one thing I can promise. You'll never be disappointed in bed." In other parts of their relationship, probably. But never between the sheets.

"Good to know." The kisses went from easy to deeper, and he had a tough time not moving as she kept rubbing against him.

"Bree, honey, slow down."

"Why, cowboy? You ready to explode?" she teased.

"Yes." Not a lie. "You taste so good. Got me all riled up."

She gently bit his lip and kissed her way to his ear. "Then what are you waiting for?" She nibbled his earlobe, and he jolted, close to coming.

"No condom?" He sounded gritty but couldn't help it. He still had a tough time believing she trusted him enough to forego protection.

"Just you and me." She tongued his ear, driving him wild. "Fill me up."

"Fuck." He kissed her, angled himself between her legs, then pushed.

She moaned into his mouth as he thrust inside her, the warmth his undoing.

Bree's body clasped him tight when he stilled, reveling in the feeling of her. But then he had to move. He wanted to go slow, to savor the moment. Every time with Bree got better than the last, and knowing she'd already found her pleasure enabled him to let go and find his.

"That's it," she crooned as he sucked at her neck, riding her faster, plunging deeper. "God, Tex. That feels so good."

They were both panting as the climb toward orgasm grew more intense. Her hands roamed over him, the strokes of her palms and the bite of her nails igniting trails of fire along his flank. When she gripped his ass and clamped him deep inside her body, he lost it.

He groaned her name as he jerked and poured into her, the release overwhelming.

She stroked his back and shoulders, planting kisses along his chin and jaw. He came back to himself and kissed her with thanks, then rolled them both over, still connected, and cradled her to him.

"So good," she murmured, petting his chest.

"Oh, yeah." He never wanted to move again. "I…you…"

"I know." She sighed, still touching him. "Nothing matters but us in bed."

"It's the best."

"Yeah."

They lay in quiet for some time, but he could feel something bothering her.

"Bree, you okay?"

"I was just a few seconds ago. But now my brain is firing again, and I'm still annoyed with Carrie." She vented, and he listened. "She and I have been friends forever. When we find someone new we're dating, we can get distant. But it never lasts very long. Lately, I've been consumed with my project."

He'd been hoping she'd been consumed with him.

"And you."

"Yes, and me," he said proudly.

She laughed. "What an ego." She paused. "It's just… Carrie's my best friend. We share everything."

"Then I hope you tell her how big and amazing I am in bed."

"Hush. I meant we share good times and bad, not all the sex stuff."

"Too bad. She could learn a thing or two from me."

As intended, his words had her laughing.

"It's just, lately Carrie's been quiet. She knows how I feel about Melissa. It's petty of me, but I don't want my best friend being friends with Melissa."

"Wow, that is petty."

She slapped his chest.

"Ow."

"I'm sharing here," she growled.

He trapped her hand beneath his. "Look, I obviously don't know your sister or Carrie the way you do. But Carrie's a grown-ass woman. A mean woman, I might add. She can more than hold her own with your sister."

"Stepsister," she corrected absently. "I always wanted a sister. Even more when my mom passed away. Then I got Charlie *and* Melissa, and it was so great. Charlie's kind and lovely. Melissa was too. At first."

"What happened, do you think?"

"I have no idea. She turned into a monster of a teenager and hated me."

"You steal her boyfriend or something?"

"Not to my knowledge. But she stole mine. Twice, actually. It hurt at the time, but I got over it."

Seemed to Tex like maybe she hadn't.

"But Carrie. She's mine."

"I'm pretty sure she's her own person."

"Oh, you know what I mean." She shifted, forcing him to leave her body. After cleaning herself up, she rolled to her side and propped her head on her elbow, watching him while she unloaded. "I hate feeling small and jealous. But Carrie's *my* friend. Melissa has her own life. Hell, my parents drop everything when she needs something. She's never wanted for anything."

"Don't they do the same for you?"

"They do, but I don't need them the way she does."

He hated to be devil's advocate, but he found himself saying, "Maybe she needs Carrie more than you do right now."

"Stop acting so sensible."

He drew her close for a kiss. "Sorry, Bree. You're happy, healthy, and hell, you got me. What does Melissa have?"

"A six-figure career in business, tons of men at her feet, and my parents who give her whatever she needs."

"Yeah, but she ain't happy. And you are, right?" He rolled to pin her under him.

"I guess when you put it that way, I'm worrying for nothing. My life is pretty great."

"Huh. You don't look too great."

She crossed her eyes and made an awful face. "You mean, I look like this?" Ugly-cute.

He did his best not to laugh. "Then again, I only gave you two orgasms, and we did agree to three."

She put her arms around his shoulders. "That's true. Three is the magic number."

He smiled down at her, pleased she seemed to be out of her mood and back into the fun they'd been having. "You really can talk to me about serious stuff. But tonight, I want you to be happy. You got a deal with that gallery and a great dinner I made myself."

"You mean bought."

"Same difference." He kissed her. "And you're fucking me dry. It's a perfect night. Don't let anyone ruin it for you."

"You're right."

"Always."

"Let's not get cocky, cowboy." She paused as he nestled himself between her legs. "Well, let me rephrase that…"

———

Bree didn't know how he'd done it, but Tex had sexed her out of her funk Tuesday night. They spent their evenings together all week, enjoying themselves with or without sex. He liked movies, taking walks, and playing cards. Quite the card sharp, was Tex McGovern.

Since he went back to work Saturday, she'd rescheduled her Friday night movie with Carrie. Bree and Tex had been spending a lot of time together, but the few times Bree had reached out, Carrie had been busy, so she didn't feel too badly for being preoccupied.

Saturday evening, as she stood in front of Carrie's door, she kept going over her conversation with Tex about her best friend. Tex had been correct; Carrie was her own person. If she chose to *ruin her life*—strike that—if she chose to *make odd choices* in her friendships, that was Carrie's business, not Bree's. After all, Carrie had been dating a stream of women, many of whom Bree had never met, and it had never affected their friendship.

Why should Carrie's new association with Melissa mean anything had to change with Bree? And there might not even be anything to worry about. Just because her friend and stepsister had talked and kissed meant nothing. Nope. Not a thing.

God.

When Carrie opened the door, Bree put Melissa out of her mind and gave Carrie a hug. "Hey, slacker. How have you been? Besides ducking my calls, I mean?"

"Ducking your calls? Please." Carrie raised a brow. "I fear no woman. No man. No animal. Only roaches and pineapple on pizza, because both are just gross."

"Now that's just mean." The smile on her face froze when she heard a toilet flush and Melissa walked into the living room and settled on the couch. In Bree's spot.

She looked comfortable there, wearing dark yoga pants and a pink top that slid off her shoulder, exposing the strap of an athletic bra. "Hi. Don't mind me. I'm here for girl time."

Bree looked back at Carrie, who managed to avoid making eye contact as she shut the door behind Bree then scurried into the kitchen.

Bree walked with patience, not sure what the heck was going on. Carrie never moved as if nervous. She didn't avoid confrontation. Yet she was acting totally out of character.

"What's going on?" Bree asked, having pinned her friend in the kitchen.

"I'm just an innocent bystander." Carrie seemed more like herself as she held up her hands. "Don't shoot the messenger. I'm neutral ground, where you can come to a peaceable solution with Melissa. Get back together as sisters who don't hate each other. Think of me as brokering a treaty."

"Are you serious?"

"I know, right?" Melissa tossed her hair. "Imagine a real conversation between the two of us." She tittered from her cozy seat on the sofa. "Maybe you should run back to Mom and John and tell them how hateful I am. Again. Or, I know, you can avoid me for another ten years."

"Fine. Let's cut out the middleman."

"Thank God," Carrie muttered.

Bree walked back to the living room and studied Melissa.

Her stepsister looked beautiful as always, not a hair out of place. If she'd been doing yoga earlier, she hadn't been sweating or contorting in positions to affect her perfect hair and perfect outfit. Still striking, curvy, and a man-magnet. Or was it woman-magnet, now?

"Why are you here?" Bree asked.

Carrie watched from the kitchen, drinking a bottle of fruity water.

"Why is that your business?" Melissa studied her nails. "This is Carrie's home."

"And you and Carrie have never gotten along. So again, why are you here?"

"People can change, you know. I never hated Carrie." Melissa shrugged. "I like talking to her. *She's* real." Her tone implied Bree wasn't.

Carrie rolled her eyes and drank.

"Can you for once just say what you mean instead of being so passive-aggressive? What exactly is your problem with me? It's been years of you being a bitch and me having no idea why." Might as well get it all out in the open. "You want to know why I go out of my way to avoid you? Well, there you go."

Melissa laughed, but the sound held little humor. "You're kidding, right? The princess, the suck-up, the never-puts-a-foot-wrong daughter wants to know why *I* might have issues?"

"Seriously? It all boils down to jealousy?"

"I can't believe you." Melissa shook her head, finally sounding annoyed. "It all started at the end of eight grade, when you stole Kurt Johnson from me. And it got worse. All my friends flocked to the fire chief's golden daughter. I was nothing but the pathetic stepsister."

Bree gaped. "Are you kidding? First of all, I was dating Kurt, and you tried to take him from *me*." Blasted Melissa had kissed the boy. Bree had broken up with him. Bree had also lost more than a few friends to her pretty, funny stepsister. "And you were more popular in high school than I was."

"Because I put out, sure." Melissa had no problem admitting it.

"You go, girl." Carrie toasted her from the kitchen.

"I got what I wanted by doing what you wouldn't. It never bothered me, not even when you'd call me a slut."

Bree blinked. "What are you talking about?" Sure, she might have *thought* that, especially when Melissa had stolen Doug McKinney from her in tenth grade, but she'd never said it aloud.

"I know what you thought. And our friends told me what you said."

"*We* didn't have friends. Whoever you're talking about lied. I might have hated you for being such a bitch, but I never talked about our family with anyone." A firm rule her father had taught her growing up and laid down from day one of his new marriage. Family came before anything. A rule she'd tried to subscribe to, despite Melissa saying all manner of things. "I was also smart enough to figure out that if a guy would cheat on me with anyone—even you—he wasn't worth having."

"Point to Bree," Carrie announced.

"Shut up, Carrie," Melissa sneered.

To Bree's surprise, Carrie didn't respond.

"I had a horrible time in high school," Melissa continued. "Then you left for modeling overseas, and my life got worse. John and Mom bragged about you all the time. I could never compete. And when you'd come back for brief visits, you always acted as if we were friends when I knew all along you hated me. Even when you came home for good, you put on a show, making me look like the bad daughter."

Huh. Bree hadn't realized Melissa had caught on to that. Still, Bree was tired of being blamed for so many other things she hadn't done. "All this time, you've let your petty anger and bitterness turn you against me. I never did or said anything to anyone about you. Well, except for Carrie."

"Oh, please. You might not have said anything, but you were just as passive-aggressive as you accuse me of being."

"How's that?"

Melissa stood and pointed an accusing finger at her. "You never included me in anything growing up. Mom had to make you invite me anywhere."

"Yeah, because you stole my boyfriends and my friends!"

"See? You admit it. And when you could have helped me get a modeling contract, you didn't. You kept me away from anything that might have given me a better life."

"For fuck's sake, I had no control over that." She looked to Carrie for backup.

Carrie shrugged. "I don't know. Maybe you could have introduced her to Marcel or something."

"Bull." Bree saw red as she glared back at Melissa. "You're too short, and that's not me being passive-aggressive."

"Short women model all the time."

"But not for Marcel or the others I modeled for. If you wanted to do what I was doing, you should have gotten a contract on your own."

"I couldn't. John was heartsick missing you. And Mom asked me to stay around."

"She did?" He was?

"So, for them, I stayed. And I took boring business classes."

"And you're a boring CEO." Boring *rich* CEO.

"Who makes more than you." Melissa gave Bree a smug smile.

Carrie cleared her throat. "For the record, Melissa, that's a pretty self-satisfied tone you're using."

"I'm not done."

Bree sighed. "What else are you going to blame on me? The fact that the sun set today? That your last relationship failed? And for the record, I'd never even met the guy."

"No, none of that is on you. That's all on me." Melissa sounded bitter about that. "But once again, I came to dinner to be with Mom and John, and you were there. This time with a hunk of a fireman. Have you ever had a rough patch in your life? Ever had a tough time getting something you wanted? Jesus, I'll bet when you get sick, you vomit rainbows and shit unicorns. You can do no wrong. Nothing bad ever happens to you."

Bree knew she'd lived a charmed life. But how was that her fault? "But none of my good fortune had to do with you. I never stepped over you to get anywhere." Now hurt, Bree shot back. "I wanted a sister so bad. From the first time I met you two, I loved Charlie and I loved you. We had good times before you turned on me and never told me why. How can I fix what's broken if I don't know what's wrong?"

Melissa frowned. "I never thought you'd care."

"Maybe if you'd talked to me, like you're talking to me now, we could have salvaged our relationship. I would have worked harder to include you." Though thinking back on it, perhaps Bree *had* held back a bit with Melissa. Even in high school, her stepsister had been popular with Bree's friends. Had she, without realizing it, kept Melissa at a distance?

"Well, here I am, Saint Bree. Why don't you, Carrie, and I be a new set of BFFs?" Melissa asked, her voice sickeningly sweet.

Bree turned to Carrie, wondering what her friend would say. Surely, she could see the venom beneath Melissa's stupid request.

Carrie just watched them, saying nothing.

Bree turned back to her stepsister. "If I thought you really wanted to be friends, I would. But you can't even apologize for being a shitty sister all these years. Everything is always about you. You can't do anything in our family without clamoring for attention. And it's just pathetic."

Melissa's cheeks flushed. "Fuck. You."

"Oh, yeah." Bree gave a hollow laugh. "You really want to make peace and be friendly. That 'fuck you' says it all." She turned to Carrie once more. "Well? You're the mediator here."

Carrie looked sad but firm. "I'm glad you two got all that off your chests. But you're nowhere near to finishing this."

"Finishing what? The Melissa pity hour?" Bree snorted. When Carrie crossed the room and sat next to Melissa, Bree couldn't believe it. "Oh my God. Don't tell me you're falling for her shit?"

"Come on, Bree. You know I love you. Let's sit down and talk this out."

"Great. Now I get a lecture from the lawyer."

Carrie's eyes narrowed.

"No thanks. Fine. Have your girl's night with your new best friend. I guess I'll talk to you whenever." Hurt, angry, and unsure of how she'd lost her best friend to her manipulative stepsister, she slammed out of Carrie's apartment and headed back home.

And if she cried a little on the way and wished she had Tex to talk to, that was no one's business but her own.

———————

Carrie sighed.

Melissa patted her on the shoulder. "That could have gone better."

"Ya think?" Carrie glared at Melissa. Now that Bree had gone, she wouldn't tiptoe around Melissa any longer. She'd tried to be impartial, hoping it would help her doofus of a best friend mend fences. Bree had been so happy lately. It had seemed the perfect time to heal old wounds.

Melissa glared back, her brown eyes sparkling and so darned pretty. "What did I do?"

"Please. You gave her your bitch-goddess-does-no-wrong impression."

"To a T." Melissa looked pleased with herself.

"Stop being such a selfish bitch."

Melissa blinked.

"I tried to help you two meet in the middle. And you used tonight to get back at a girl who stole your middle school boyfriend? Get over yourself."

"How's that?" Melissa glared. "I said the truth."

"Melissa, I've known Bree for years. She tells me everything."

Or at least she used to. Carrie could only hope this bad patch proved a mere bump in the road. "I can honestly tell you she had no idea why you stopped being friends—sisters—so long ago. She used to tell me how much she wished you guys could get along."

Oddly, the stepsisters were more alike than they knew. Neither had close friends, were devoted to their careers, and loved their parents. They both wanted a closer relationship but would do nothing to fix the problems of the past.

And now that Carrie had developed...feelings...she needed this to work, damn it. *Stupid Melissa! Stupid Bree!* Argh. If her hair hadn't been so wonderfully styled earlier by Giorgio, she'd have yanked at it in frustration.

The hard veneer faded from Melissa's gaze. "She really wanted us to get along?"

Carrie sighed. "Before tonight, yeah. If she stole friends or guys paid attention to her, I doubt it was her fault. She's gorgeous and oblivious. It's one of the things I like most about her. Despite what you said, she's real."

"Maybe." Melissa bit her lip. "But Carrie, she did used to shut me out. And it hurt."

"Then why not say that instead of saying... What was it? That she vomits unicorns and shits rainbows?"

"No, other way around."

"Still gross."

They smiled at each other. And that tension between them rose again, pushing Carrie to let Melissa get closer.

Instead, Carrie leaned back, crossed her arms over her chest, and scowled. "You fucked this up."

Melissa tried to look uncaring. Her face crumpled. "Crap. I know. I have been working really hard on not being the Melissa I used to be. But tonight, it was like everything came rushing back. Once again, Bree is the amazing one and I'm the bad one, and nothing I do really matters. I want to be nicer and apologize and not be so nasty." Melissa sniffled, and her eyes welled. "I just don't know how."

"Geez, Melissa. You were the one who wanted to talk to her." Not that Carrie had been against it, but she'd thought it best if they'd kept her out of it. But for Melissa to reach out to Bree meant someone had to make the first move. Carrie had tried to help. She couldn't understand why it had gone so wrong.

Melissa groaned. "I'm sorry."

"Sorry has two syllables, not four."

Melissa snickered and wiped her eyes, those shimmery brown orbs that sparkled in the light.

Carrie cleared her head. "Look, let me talk to her again. I'll make her see reason."

"Not if she cuts you out of her life too."

"Me?" Carrie snorted. "Honey, you are out of your mind if you think Bree can hold out against all this." She waved at her body. "I am sincerely amazing and smarter than both of you put together. You two need me."

"We do, huh?" Melissa twirled a lock of her hair, her gaze soft and surprisingly needy with a vulnerability that hit Carrie right in the heart.

"Oh, and way to go sitting in Bree's spot." Which Carrie had asked her not to do. "Classy way to rile things up before they got started." Carrie deliberately moved to the seat nearby. And ignored Melissa's pout since her mask of strength was back in place.

"Okay, I was being a bitch." At Carrie's look, she amended, "Am still being a bitch. But she gets me so mad, acting all clueless."

"She didn't used to get you mad. Maybe you should remember those times, when you two got along. And that's all I'm going to say about that. Now it's time for *Firefly*."

"Is this a rom-com?"

"Oh my God. You need help. It's only the best cancelled science-fiction series on TV ever."

"What?"

"Shut up and watch. And then we're going to work on your people skills. Because they need a lot of work." *And I need a miracle to make my best friend not hate me.*

"Yes, ma'am." Melissa gave a mock salute with one finger.

"I'll ignore the gesture, but the sentiment… First intelligent thing you've said all night."

Chapter Eighteen

SUNDAY MORNING, AFTER LEAVING THE STATION FOR THE FIRST of his next ninety-six hours off, Tex ran next to Bree at a slower pace than he was used to, but he loved watching her body move. Even clothed.

Tall and toned with curves in the right places, Bree looked amazing in shorts and a T-shirt as they jogged part of the Lake Union Loop, passing fellow runners and outdoor enthusiasts. The weather had warmed. The sun overhead shone brightly through spots of fluffy, white clouds, and birds chirped while squirrels raced up and down trees.

"It's so nice out," he said, confused, because Seattle liked to tease glimpses of the sun before whisking it away behind clouds and rain that came and went all day long.

"I mean, how hard is it to just save a small amount of time for your best friend?" Bree groused and picked up a little speed.

He kept pace, not liking all the attention she earned as they ran on the popular trail. He'd felt jealousy before but never so deeply.

"Right?" she asked, breathing harder.

"Huh? Oh, ah, right." He nodded. "Why did Carrie ask her over?"

"She's playing peacemaker. And taking sides," Bree bit off and sprinted ahead.

Tex wondered if he should let her win, enjoying watching the back of her. Then his competitive nature kicked in, and he caught up with her.

She glared at him.

He smiled back and increased his speed.

She swore at him and ran faster.

They dodged a few fellow runners and walking groups before she started to slow. Tex kept pace, loving the burn of muscle, and finally stopped to walk with her when she moved to the side and bent over, breathing heavily.

"I hate you," she wheezed while he stretched his neck and took in a nice breath, letting it out easily.

"Many do. It's not easy to be this beautiful." He posed with his left leg behind him and flexed his calf.

Two women running by whistled.

He laughed.

Bree shot him the finger.

He laughed harder.

When she stood and started jogging again, slowly, he fell in step next to her.

"It's my job to be fit. Don't worry. I bet you're better than me at other things." At the look she shot him, he bit back more laughter and said, "Okay, you're better than me at everything. Let me have this. And weight lifting." He paused. "And maybe drinking. I'm pretty sure I can drink more than you."

She clamped her lips tight, but he saw the grin.

"And I'm funnier," he just had to say.

"Shut it, Roger." She chuckled. "You're such a pain."

"It's like you're channeling my brothers."

They headed toward her car, having completed their run. The lake mirrored the sky, boaters enjoying the nice weather as well. Sailboats, paddlers, and a few motorized boats traveled the light waves while more people parked and came out to enjoy Lake Union and the sunny skies.

"Didn't you say your brothers were coming soon?" she asked as they headed to his truck.

"Yeah. I think they'll be here next week. I sent Wyatt a few messages, but he hasn't returned them. The ass."

She smiled. "I can't wait to meet him."

Tex considered her for a moment, and his smile left him.

"What?"

"I don't want them liking you too much."

She frowned. "Why not?"

"Because Wyatt's an easy guy to like," he growled. "At least Oliver's married."

Her frown cleared. "Well, now. Who's feeling jealous?"

"I am." He wanted to take her in his arms and kiss her in front of all the jackasses looking too hard at her in that thin tee and those short shorts. But she'd get mad, accuse him of acting like an idiot, and then he'd be in the doghouse. And he'd been doing so well, lately.

She watched him, nodded, then waited by the passenger side of the truck.

When he unlocked it for her and held it open, she winked. "Good."

"Good?" Man, he planned to make her eat those words later on.

"Now you know how I feel when we go somewhere and the women are eating you alive with their grubby little stares."

"What about the men?"

"Them too."

"Oh, well, that's flattering." He couldn't help laughing. "I meant, how the hell do you think I feel when I see men gawking at you? You're gorgeous and mine, and I can't tell anyone about it." The light moment turned dark, fast.

She sighed. "It sucks."

"You don't like it either?"

"No." She shrugged. "But what do you want to do? Tell everyone we're dating?"

Everyone meant Battalion Chief John Gilchrist.

"I do, except, I think, maybe..."

"Exactly. We're still new. We need to take it slowly."

"I agree."

"I mean, we're being smart, right? We spend time at your place or mine a lot. But when we go out, we usually go to places where most of your friends don't go. Or we go out on a Sunday morning, when most people are still in bed."

Or in church. Dang. He'd say a few prayers later for missing.

"Yeah. We're being smart." He started the truck and headed for his place. Bree had packed a bag and planned to spend the day with him. Just the two of them being together.

Tex didn't know how it had happened, but he enjoyed their downtime. Whereas before it had been all about getting down with a woman in bed, with Bree, he wanted to do things *with* her. Not just *to* her.

Today she'd promised to teach him how to make a six-tiered hazelnut chocolate cake. He couldn't wait. And if they had extra frosting, he had plans to show her how inventive he could be with leftovers.

"Tell me about your brothers," she said as he drove.

Immediately killing the need between his legs.

"Buzzkill," he murmured.

She grinned.

"I told you about them."

"Not details."

They'd swapped a lot of stories about her family and his fire-fighter brethren but not so much about his family in Texas.

"Fine. I'm the youngest of four. There's Liam, who's thirty-four. He's married to Nat. She's the lawyer who reminds me of Carrie. Their boy is Jonah. He's four." Tex loved that kid. "He's my mini-me. Got a mouth on him."

"I'll bet."

"Next is Oliver. He's a year younger than Liam and married to Sierra. They're plannin' on a baby in another six months. Just married too. Can you believe they had sex before saying I do?"

"The shock. The horror."

He laughed. "Maybe you are funnier than me."

"No maybe about it." She stuck her tongue at him.

"Promises, promises."

"And there goes our conversation. Right into the gutter."

"Then there's Wyatt," Tex said, doing his best to ignore thoughts of Bree's tongue when talking about his family. "He's only two years older than me. He's pretty bossy; probably why he's still single." Tex paused. "Wyatt and I are closest." He didn't mention his brother's drinking problem, because that was Wyatt's to share or not share. "I love my family."

"And your mom and dad?"

"You mean Peter and Sara Ann McGovern? The patriarch and matriarch of the McGovern Ranch?"

"Oh, like, a real ranch? With cowboys and horses and everything?"

He glanced to see her eyes wide. "Yeah. Now how sexy am I? A real cowboy for you, darlin.'" Shoot. He'd left his hat at home.

"A cowboy in Seattle. Not as sexy as you think."

"That hurts."

She jabbed him in the side and grinned when he started. "Oh, ticklish."

"Don't even try it," he snarled. "I'm driving." He hated getting poked.

Her eyes twinkled. "Sure thing, cowboy. Safety first. Eyes on the road and all that."

"Smart-ass."

"So does your whole family work on the ranch? Are you the only one who got away?"

"We all get away and end up comin' back, working at the ranch." He paused, missing his family a lot all of a sudden. After clearing his throat, he continued, "It's tradition that when we graduate high school, we hit the service. It's our choice, though to hear Daddy tell it, only a real man goes into the Corps."

"Corps?"

He sighed. "Marine Corps. Come on, Bree. Keep up."

"I'll give you something to keep up," she muttered.

He bit back a grin. "So Daddy, like his daddy and granddaddy and so on before him, signed up. Got out as a gunnery sergeant years later, then settled down on the ranch and married my momma. Liam and Oliver both did their time in and got out after four years, though Liam rebelled by going Air Force. Wyatt served for six years before he got out. Had some hard times over there, but he's straight and all now." He glanced over at her.

Bree nodded, her eyes soft with concern. "What about you?"

"I played for a year in college, knowing I wouldn't stay. Did my tour in the Marines. Six-year contract. Loved the hell out of it too." He smiled, remembering his friends, his time served with pride and dedication.

"Why did you get out?"

"I felt it wasn't gonna be my everything, you know? I was a grunt. Basic infantry. The hard work, the backbone really, of the USMC. I was good at it."

"I'll bet, Mr. Muscles."

He grinned. "But then I moved out here and fell in love with firefighting. My parents weren't happy I didn't come home to stay." He pulled into the driveway, and they left and locked up the car. "But what can you do? Texas is my home, my family. But so is Seattle." He smiled at her.

"Do you think you'll move back any time soon?" she asked, though he thought he heard something deeper in the question.

"Who knows? Not anytime soon, for sure. This is a good life. I have great friends, a kick-ass girlfriend, and a dream job. Hell, I might even get my face in an art gallery. Can't be doing that in Texas now, can I?"

She laughed and slung her bag over her shoulder. "No, you can't. But you know what you can do?"

"What?" he asked as they walked into his home and were greeted by an enthusiastic Bubbles.

"You can get that water running. I need to clean up before I make you the best Sunday brunch cake you've ever had."

"Brunch cake. Sounds perfect."

Except he didn't get the dessert he'd really been hankering for—a side of wet, naked girlfriend in the shower. Bree insisted on bathing alone, despite his wheedling, and forced him to clean up after she'd finished first.

When he returned, fresh as a freaking daisy, she was at work in the kitchen making him a hell of a breakfast.

"Surprise." She smiled. "I know you hate mornings. And you listened to me rant for a good mile."

"More like two."

She continued to smile. "Don't be an ass. As I was saying, this breakfast is for you." The pancakes had been decorated with eggs for eyes and a strip of bacon for a mouth. A cup of fresh fruit sat to the side.

He looked at the food, back up at her smile, and felt his heart race off the cliff and break at her feet. The warmth of her care had him feeling so much, and he had to take a step back from the emotional precipice for fear of making a terrible leap before she was ready to catch him.

What had he told the guys? That he'd make *her* fall in love with *him*?

Yeah, right.

"Tex?" She frowned.

"I just…" He coughed to clear his throat. "I'm so disappointed."

"You—*what*?"

"I was expecting a naked Bree covered in a half apron serving me cake. Like, cutting it and feeding it to me." He sighed. "I guess this is good too."

He laughed when she balled a towel and threw it at his head.

Hurrying around the kitchen island to hug her in thanks, he muffled her anger with kisses.

She pulled back, grumbling. "That's a little better."

"If I tell you how amazin' you are right now, your head will get too big. Then you'll leave me for a prettier fella. And I'll never be the same."

"You got that right." She poked him in the side, and he flinched. "Ha. I know your vulnerable spots, buddy. You just watch yourself."

"Yes, ma'am." He kissed her again and sighed against her mouth. "Thanks for the happy pancakes, Bree." He pulled back. "Can we eat together now? We can talk about how awful Melissa is and how much my brothers are going to like you."

"Oh, well, that sounds like a plan. And don't think the chocolate cake is off the table. I'm making that after we're finished here."

Tex tucked away a stack of pancakes and could have eaten more. "Woman, you can cook. This is even better than your baked chicken."

"Wow, that good, huh?" She laughed, still working through her breakfast. She paused before taking the next bite. "Can I tell you something?"

He sipped his coffee, wondering if taking a few more pancakes would make him look like a pig. Probably.

"Tex," she said.

"Huh? Sorry. My brain is full on pancakes."

She smiled, but the expression didn't reach her eyes. "Can I tell you something?"

"You can tell me anything. I mean it."

"I'm worried."

"About…?" Him? Her dad? Their relationship? Carrie?

"The art grant."

He frowned, not having considered that. "Why?"

She put her fork down and ran a hand through her hair, which she'd left down. It was so pretty, a curtain of gold framing the most interesting face in the world.

Tex loved watching her, not just to take in her beauty but to study the expressive way she reacted to things. And then she'd talk, and he'd hear all that intelligence and think what a hell of a package Bree Gilchrist really was.

"Sometimes, I don't think I can do it. I'm not that good, and people will find out."

"Not that good?" He blinked. "Are you kidding?"

She blushed. "No. I'm a good photographer. I can capture a smile, a pose, an aspiration of art. But the real emotion, the life behind the still, sometimes I think I'm only seeing what I want to see. And I want to be a *great* photographer, not just good. A true artist. So, tell me I can do it. That I have it in me to be great." She looked at him for hope. Guidance. Advice, maybe?

He had plenty. "You're on crack."

"I—what?"

"Bree, everyone can see the way you work. You have an eye for it. Even Carrie said so."

"She's my friend."

"She's also known for telling the truth. And honey, you're hot as hell. But no way they gave you twenty-five grand because you're pretty when you hold a camera."

She flushed. "No, I earned that grant."

"Then why the lack of confidence? I understand nerves. It's a big fuckin' deal. But come on. You're the one telling me how lucky I am to have you. Are you telling me you're not worth it?"

"This isn't a relationship thing, Tex." She flew out of her seat and started pacing. "Don't you get it? It's such a *huge deal*. Everyone I know, who knows me, who knows my dad, will see my work. And that's just at the showing. Then there's the gallery. The. Gallery. What if my project isn't up to IAG standards?"

"Then fuck 'em."

She stopped pacing and stared at him. "That's your answer? Fuck 'em?"

"Look, you're an artist. And you're blond," he said to get a rise out of her. "It's pretty much a given you're going to be flaky."

Her eyes narrowed.

"But, honey, no way anyone is going to blow smoke up your ass and call it a masterpiece. If that IAG chick called to ask you to show your stuff, it's because she knows you're a quality date."

"Huh?"

A quality date: you'll blow and swallow, and that don't come cheap—a phrase his brother had once used on his fiancée as a compliment. That Natalie still married Liam had baffled everyone. But for some reason the phrase made sudden sense to Tex.

"What I'm trying to say is you're smart and talented, and you don't seem to know how rare that is. That you're not all conceited and bitchy." She just stared at him, so he tried again. "Ever heard the phrase 'you'll blow and swallow, and that don't come cheap'?"

"I… I want to say you're complimenting me, but I can't figure out how." Her eyes narrowed.

He flushed. "I know that was crude. But I'm trying to make a point."

"That I'm weak-willed because I'll swallow on the first date—which I didn't, by the way? Or that I'm a dumb blond?"

Well, at least now you look pissed at me and not scared of the heavy weight on your shoulders. "I'm *saying* the IAG lady knows art. She knows what an honor it is to get that grant. And she's seen your work. You've been around long enough for people to know you with or without this huge hairy deal. And damn, girl. I've seen your stuff, and you're the Ansel Adams of people."

"You do know there's more than just Ansel Adams who's known for photography?" Her lips twitched. *Finally.*

"Who cares? I only know I like you. And so does the art council."

"Council?"

He shrugged. "The fancy folks who voted you in to do the project. They believe in you. I do. You should believe in you."

"I do."

Annoyed, he glared at her. "Then why all the drama?"

"I just had a moment of insecurity. I have those. I'm an *arteest*." She moved closer and poked him in the side. "Deal with it."

"I will. But you better quit poking me."

"Or what?"

"Or I'll poke you back."

———————

Bree felt like a complete idiot. She'd let her self-doubt get to her, and she'd told Tex. And like a big doofus, instead of listening and nodding and letting her get it all out, like Carrie usually did, he'd tried to solve her problems by telling her…something about being a good date?

Now Tex glared at her, her sweet, manly boyfriend with bulging biceps and a heaving, broad chest, offended because she hadn't wept in his arms and thanked him profusely for giving her that pat on the back she needed. She wanted to both thank him for his support and correct him for not listening. All she'd wanted was a simple "you can do it."

Instead, she poked him again.

His eyes darkened…in both anger and lust. A glance down his glorious body showed her how much he wanted to set her straight.

He wore a T-shirt and athletic shorts that reached his knees. Thin, cotton shorts that lovingly clung to every part of him.

"You poked the bear, baby. Now prepare to pay the price."

"Bear?" She blinked as he got naked right in front of her.

Bubbles, she noticed, slunk away and buried herself in the living room under a blanket. At least one of them had some dignity. Bree wanted to mount his maypole. And it was June.

"A hungry bear. I was going to wait for chocolate cake, but I think it's time you learned your lesson, Goldilocks."

She bit back a laugh. "Oh. But which bear are you?" She couldn't look away from his erection, even as she mock-cringed and taunted, "Baby bear?"

"You know, you really aren't funnier than me."

Then he pounced.

She shrieked and laughed, not having expected the fast move. Darting around the counter in her attempt to evade him, she feinted left then right and raced down the hall.

Tex caught her easily and pinned her against the wall in the middle of the hallway.

"Pay up, or shut up."

She closed her mouth, zipped her lip, and tossed an invisible key.

He loomed over her, grinning. "Nah, you need to pay."

She opened her mouth, and he kissed her.

His hands were moving, her clothing flying one way then another, but he kept kissing her.

She groaned and twined her arms around his neck, hugging him closer, and sighed when her bare breasts grazed his chest. His mouth trailed to her throat, his hands busy touching, exploring.

Then he lifted her, and she wrapped her legs around his waist. God, the size of his erection against her belly was massive.

"You need something to help you feel better, Goldilocks?"

"What do you have in mind?" she said between kissing his chest, his neck, anywhere she could reach.

He slid his hand between them, angling down, and his finger disappeared inside her.

"Oh," she gasped, staring into his eyes as he moved the digit deeper, grazing her clit with his thumb.

"Yeah, so hot for me." He smiled, his expressions mesmerizing. Satisfied, turned on, and intense. "I think what you really need is a good fuck."

"I think you're right."

He removed his finger and replaced it with something bigger. "Let's see if this size fits *just right*."

"Oh my God, stop talking."

His laughter turned to a groan as he sheathed himself inside her. In one fast, deep thrust, he filled her completely. But her big bear didn't give her time to get used to him. Instead, he gripped her ass and moved. In and out, deeper, banging her into the wall.

The fast, hard thrusts hit her in just the right spot time after time, until she was seeing fireworks behind closed lids and screaming her pleasure.

He followed not long after, jetting into her as he ground against her.

After some time, he leaned back to look down at her. His face flushed, his eyes dark and sleepy, he smiled. "You know, with all your insecurities, we should probably do that again. I mean, we need to find a bed that fits you, right? Because this wall just won't do."

"You have totally ruined fairy tales for me."

He chuckled.

"When do you play the Big Bad Wolf who eats Little Red Riding Hood?"

"I should say I'm full from breakfast. But actually, you're the one who's full, aren't you, Goldie?"

"Just stop. Please." She tried not to laugh. Then she started and couldn't stop.

He watched her slide down the wall in tears. "And think, we can add more innuendo on top of all my hose jokes. Man, this day just keeps getting better." He pulled her to her feet, then hefted her over his shoulder in a fireman's carry.

"*Oof.*" So much for a romantic carry to his room. Dangling over his shoulder, she slapped him on the ass. "I've got one for you. Fire in the hole!" Her giggle turned into a snort then more laughter.

"Darlin', ain't no fire ever going near that hole. I can promise you that."

She couldn't help more laughter as she slapped him again. That ass was just begging for it! She wondered if her glutes would ever get that tight. Just…wow.

Tex gently jostled her on his shoulder. "Say, I like this fairy-tale theme. Have you ever seen the porn version of Cinderella? The prince never wears pants."

Bree smiled at his dimpled butt. "Oh? Do tell…"

Chapter Nineteen

BREE COULDN'T BELIEVE HOW MUCH FUN SHE'D BEEN HAVING. Tex and she laughed as they took yet another shower, this one taking longer since she'd dropped to her knees to show him how their first date might have gone had he really been Prince Charming wearing no pants.

After praising her up and down as the best girlfriend ever, he left her to finish cleaning up while he looked after Bubbles. The poor thing had been neglected and whined at the bathroom door.

Bree finished, in no rush, and still in a fun mood. She dried herself, her hair still okay since she'd kept it out of the spray, using Tex to block the showerhead. Instead of dressing in her clothes, now out in the hallway, she decided to give him another treat. Rummaging in his closet, she found a blue uniform shirt.

She put it on, leaving it unbuttoned, and walked out into the hallway. He'd changed into a pair of jeans and a T-shirt, his back to her as he stood, arms akimbo, staring at something she couldn't see. Probably Bubbles.

"How about something hot for you, cowboy?" She gripped the sides of his shirt and opened it wide, showcasing her body and glancing away to let him look his fill. She liked to call it her playful model pose.

"Jesus, Bree."

The voice didn't come from the man in front of her, which had her jerking her head up.

And staring at a stranger.

She whipped the shirt closed, grateful it covered all her lady parts, hitting her high on the thighs, and gaped at a man who looked enough like Tex to be his slightly older twin.

And, oh Jesus, slightly behind him, a younger version of Tex, this one wearing boots with his jeans, a Pabst Blue Ribbon tee, and a very large grin. "Well, hot damn, cousin. Now I know why you moved to Seattle."

That had the hunky, older Tex in front of her giving her the Big Bad Wolf's own grin.

Then Tex was shoving him out of the way and hustling Bree back to his room while the men behind him whistled, clapped, and laughed.

Now that wasn't an awkward way to meet the family. Not at all.

Tex was doing his best not to laugh hysterically while cringing in horror that his brother and nineteen-year-old cousin had gotten an eyeful.

"That—that wasn't you."

"Nope. But that was all you." Tex sighed. "Too bad we can't play put out the fire now that the family's come early." And thank God his momma hadn't been with them. Only his brother, Wyatt, and cousin, Josh, on this particular trip. He left to grab her clothes from the hallway, returned, and closed the door behind him.

Bree was beet red and biting her lip. "I am so embarrassed."

"Don't be. Hell, with a body like that, you never have to be ashamed of anything." He handed her her clothes, regretting that she handed him back his uniform shirt. He'd never seen it look so fine.

Afraid she might burst into tears when she finished dressing and bent over at the waist, her hair hiding her face, he moved closer with care. "Bree, honey. It's okay, they won't—"

She erupted into laughter and straightened, laughing so hard that she cried. "Oh my God. I flashed your brother and your cousin. Welcome to Seattle!"

She kept laughing as he frowned—it wasn't *that* funny—and dragged her back down the hallway, where Wyatt and Josh were stroking Bubbles, who looked as if she'd gone to doggy heaven. On her back, her feet in the air, she pawed up at Josh to keep rubbing her belly.

Seeing her like that, Bree started snorting and laughed even harder. "They even got Bubbles!"

He rolled his eyes when Wyatt looked her over and wiggled his brows.

In a deep Texan drawl, Wyatt said, "Darlin', I don't know why you're here, but please, don't ever, ever leave. Not unless you're comin' back home with us in our pleasure bus."

"It's an RV," Tex said flatly, not liking the look on Wyatt's face. "And you," he said to Josh. "Not one word to anyone at home about this."

"No, sirree." Josh absently crossed the right side of his chest, staring hard at Bree.

"Other side, moron."

Josh bit his lip and crossed the left side of his chest.

Bree, still pink but not laughing so hard anymore, wiped her eyes. "I'm so sorry. I obviously thought you were Tex," she said to Wyatt. "From behind, you look similar." She held out a hand. "I'm Bree Gilchrist."

Wyatt, of course, kissed the back of it. "Wyatt McGovern, at your service."

"Nice to meet you."

Not to be outdone, before Tex could introduce the youngest McGovern, Josh popped up as if he had springs in his ass and crossed the room to her. "How do, lovely Bree." Josh kissed the back of her hand as well. "I'm Josh McGovern."

Tex sighed. "You realize kissing her hand in the same spot Wyatt did is like kissing Wyatt."

Josh quickly let her hand go and wiped his mouth. "Gross."

Wyatt smacked him in the back of the head. But his gaze didn't miss how Tex laid a possessive hand on Bree's shoulder. *Good.* "So, this is the woman who has little brother's...tail...in a knot."

"Little brother." Tex snorted. "I'm taller than you, asshole."

"But not as wise," Wyatt said.

Bree looked between them back and forth. "You two sound exactly the same."

Josh snickered. "You should hear when all four of them are together. Liam and Oliver sound alike too. Just like Uncle Pete. It's weird."

"I'm sorry. Why are you here?" Wyatt asked as he turned to Josh.

"Yeah, why?" Tex asked.

Bree, Tex noted, was trying not to laugh. Hell. They did sound alike. And the fact they all looked like family didn't help either.

"Hey." Josh sounded hurt. "Quit picking on me. I came to save a dog."

"Oh. Bullies." Bree pushed past Tex, but not before turning to kiss him on the cheek, and took Josh and Bubbles into the backyard, where Josh threw Bubbles's tennis ball for her.

The minute she left, Wyatt turned to Tex and fanned his face. "Holy shit. She is, ah, how to put this. Fuckin' hotter than a fur coat in Marfa."

Tex had to grin. "Ain't she, though?"

"No wonder you been skippin' church and helping your photographer at all hours. Momma and Daddy want pics, just letting you know."

Tex might have mentioned Bree to his family once or twice since their first disastrous meeting. Apparently, they hadn't seen his terrible dates with Bree as just amusing but assumed he had some interest in her as well. Which he clearly did.

"How does the rest of her match up?" Wyatt asked.

"She's smart, owns her own business, and just got a showing

in some fancy art house to hang her photographs. And those she took because she won a big old grant from the city."

"Well, damn. Sounds a little too good for you, bro." Wyatt winked. "Now get me a beer. It was a long drive."

Tex had to stop himself from rolling his eyes. He loved Wyatt, but as soon as Wyatt saw Tex, he jumped into big-brother mode. And Tex had stopped liking playing the fetch game ages ago. But hospitality dictated he at least show his brother where to find something to wet his throat.

"Little early for that, isn't it? How about some coffee instead?"

Wyatt snorted. "Shut it, boy. I'm a grown man needing a grown-ass drink. Now do you have any sarsaparilla or not?"

"Not. It's root beer. Get it your own damn self. It's in the fridge, bottom shelf."

After Wyatt grabbed a bottle of quality Virgil's, he sat at the kitchen island across from Tex and stared in awe at a plate holding a stack of pancakes.

"Want some?" Tex offered. Personally, he found the idea of pancake syrup and root beer disgusting, but Wyatt liked his sweets.

"Hell, yeah. Any bacon?"

"There's…" Tex paused. He could have sworn there were a few strips left. But no, the plate was empty. "Bubbles?"

"Ah." Wyatt grinned. "That cute little pup outside stole the bacon. I like her already. Not as much as your girlfriend, but she's adorable. No question."

"Who? Bree or Bubbles?"

"Yes."

Tex laughed and grabbed a cup of coffee, still heated in the carafe. "So great to see you guys. But I thought you were coming next week with Oliver."

"Yeah, we thought so too. Turned out Dad wanted Oliver for some project he's working on. And Josh has boot camp starting next month."

"So, that's a for-sure thing?" At his brother's nod, he grinned. "Josh is staying true."

"Well, according to Uncle Owen, it was touch and go with the Navy. But Josh saw the light." Wyatt grinned. "He's USMC all the way."

They toasted their young cousin, who was animatedly smiling and chatting up Bree outside.

"Going in as Intel though. Had some high ASVAB score." The Armed Services Vocational Aptitude Battery test determined how a pending service member might serve. The higher one's ASVAB score, the more latitude the candidates had to select their own specialty.

"He's a brain. I'm so proud."

They had gone infantry, uncaring of test scores.

"Glad you could make it out here," Tex said.

"Me too. Never been this far north before. Damn, son. It's cold out."

Tex grinned. "At least it's not raining. Yet."

"You always did like the rain."

"It's lush. The vegetation's thick, the dirt's a rich brown. No clay, no red. Black dirt, brother. Great for apples and cherries."

"Oh, my favorite."

Tex nodded. "We need to see about getting you some Mt. Rainier cherries from the farmer's market. They're yellow and red and so sweet. My favorite."

"Speaking of yellow hair and sweetness."

"Huh?"

"Your girl, Bree. So how serious is it?"

Tex heard her laugh and looked out to see his cousin and Bree running around with Bubbles, who followed, barking with more excitement than he'd seen her show in a while. He smiled, loving the sight and sound of all that joy.

"Well, hell. It's that bad?"

Tex blinked and turned back to his brother. "What?"

"Nothin'. Tell me about Bubbles."

"She's seven years old, near as we can tell. I got her to help out a friend. Remember that guy, Oscar, I was telling you about?"

"Brad's little brother?"

Tex sighed. "Brad's *younger* brother, yeah." Sometimes the word "little" brought out the stigma of growing up the youngest in a family of troublemakers. "Oscar's in AA and doing great. Like you?"

Wyatt nodded. "Still sober, thanks for asking." They clinked bottle to mug.

"Nice. Anyhow, Oscar asked me to grab Bubbles from a troubled guy. I did. The dog is a real beauty, just decent and sweet as can be. But she was ignored for years. She's shy but coming out of her shell. I'd love to keep her." And it hurt, deep down, that he knew she'd be better off without him. "I just can't give her the time and attention she'd get on the ranch."

"I know." Wyatt must have heard his sorrow. "I feel ya. Don't worry. Bubbles can hang out with Momma at home or Daddy in the barn. And if she gets to liking more excitement, she'll be just fine outside with the rest of us."

"Good." One burden off Tex's back. "She's so great. I was worried she'd get a family who wouldn't understand her."

"We'll get to know each other on the way back. Don't worry."

"How's it at home?"

While Wyatt filled Tex in on the hometown gossip, Tex laughed and pestered his brother for more details, missing his family a little less now that he had some of Texas making his house a home.

But as he peeked outside again, he realized that home had started to feel warmer the moment Bree had walked through the door.

Bree laughed at Bubbles's antics, thrilled to see the older dog acting almost like a puppy again. "Josh, you're really good with animals."

"And older women," the flirt said shamelessly. "I mean, you're not that old. But mature. In a good way." He sounded so earnest.

She chuckled. "I'm so glad you came with Wyatt. I was hoping to meet some of Tex's family." She hoped that didn't sound too forward.

Josh's eyes gleamed. "Oh, well, we've all been *real* excited to meet you."

"Oh?"

"Yeah. Li'l Pete has been telling everyone about you for a long time. Like how he messed up on your first date. And how that fire happened to burn his phone." Josh laughed. "I mean, that's all kinds of screwed up. Talk about bad karma. I can't believe you gave him another chance."

"Trust me, I didn't plan on it. But Tex is good at his job and showed me sights I might not have been able to capture without him." She paused. "Okay, I have to know. Li'l Pete?"

"Little Pete," Josh enunciated. "On account of his name being Roger Peter McGovern. He never would answer to Roger, so Uncle Pete and Aunt Sara Ann started calling him Li'l Pete."

"Not Tex?"

"Down in Texas? We're all Tex." Josh chuckled. "That could get confusing. Besides, I think he got that name in the Marine Corps. He used to have a pretty thick accent. Now he sounds like he's from California or something."

"Not to me." Bree thought Tex's accent charming, but not as thick as his family's, for sure. Little Pete. Oh, man. What a golden nugget that would turn out to be. She'd have to carefully mine this particular source of information for all he was worth.

Except at that moment, Wyatt and Tex left the house to join them.

"Hey, quit hogging my cousin, Bree." Tex frowned at her. "The poor kid ain't got but another month until he joins his fellow recruits in San Diego." His grin broadened, and he grabbed Josh for a huge hug. "Congrats, Josh. Let me know when it is, and I'll be sure to show up for your graduation." He let Josh go, gave Bubbles some petting after being nudged to do so, and frowned in thought. "I wonder who's on board at the recruit depot. Wonder if I know any of them."

"What's that?"

Tex turned to her. "I might know a guy or two who's doing his tour at Recruit Training in San Diego."

Wyatt laughed. "Get ready for Mount Motherfucker." Then he glanced at Bree and flushed. "Sorry."

"No, what's that?" Bree wanted to know.

"It's a huge hill you're forced to march when you're in boot camp. It's a rite of passage, you could say." Tex grinned. "Oh, yeah. Good times."

He looked at Wyatt, and the two of them said as one, "Not."

Josh cringed. "Aw, man. Don't ruin the mystery for me."

"Whatever you do, don't watch the airplanes flying away or the DI's will make you chase after them for fun." Wyatt cracked up. "Man, that shit was funny."

"Long as it wasn't you." Tex groaned. "I made the mistake of wishing to fly out to Hawaii and got caught by Sergeant Leonard. Guy almost ran me to death."

Wyatt rubbed his cousin's head. "Enjoy this hippie hair while you can, boy. In another few weeks, you're gonna be bald as a cue ball."

Bree shook her head. "And I wonder why more people don't join the service. Sounds like a blast."

Tex dragged her into his arms for a kiss before throwing the ball for Bubbles. "It's the military. They break you down then build you back up. You have to be a good follower to be a good leader, Bree. Besides, when graduation day comes, you feel like you can do anything. And of course, you know you're better than everyone else."

Wyatt nodded. "That's true."

"Even if you get out or quit?" she teased.

Tex looked sad. "Woman, we need to talk. You never quit the Corps. Well, I mean, you can get a dishonorable discharge, I guess. Ain't no quitting till your time is up. But once a Marine, always a Marine."

Wyatt agreed. "There's no ex about it. We say former or prior Marine. Not ex-Marine."

"Got it." She gave him a salute.

He cringed. "Come on, now, Bree. I was enlisted. I worked for a living. Don't be giving me a *salute*." Wyatt said the word with such disdain.

"Worked for a living? Maybe then." Josh smirked. "Now Wyatt shovels cow shi—ah, poop."

Wyatt turned on him. "Is that so?" The big man dashed after his cousin, who though taller and heavier than Bree, could run like a deer, and finally caught the quick teen, forcing him to say uncle while tickling him without mercy.

Bubbles barked and danced around, licking whatever McGovern on the ground she could reach.

Tex put his arm around Bree and shook his head, but she could see him smiling. "Now imagine four boys—like them—in a wrestling death match while their daddy is doing his best to keep the barn cats from killing the new puppy who got loose. Meanwhile the horses need tending, the eggs need collecting, and the dryer just broke for the third time that month."

"Your mom is a saint, is that what you're saying?"

He chuckled. "She's got a first-class ticket to heaven. No doubt about that. None at all."

―――――――――――

Tex hadn't realized how much he'd missed his family, but having Wyatt and Josh around filled the void. He spent the day with the guys and Bree, whom he'd insisted stick around. To his delight, she got along as if a part of the family. Wyatt and Josh treated her like a sister, though he could do with a little less ogling from the younger McGovern.

Bree had left an hour ago, needing time to get ready to head back to work on Monday.

Now, Tex sat with Wyatt and Josh around a small fire out back while Bubbles snoozed by his side. Despite enjoying the hell out of his brother and cousin, Bubbles still came back to him.

That closeness touched him, and he stroked her while he sipped from a bottle of root beer. Normally, he'd have had a real beer, but with Wyatt still sober and Josh only nineteen, he enjoyed a cold carbonated beverage instead.

He sipped and stared, loving the crackle of fire in the small, self-contained pit. "I talked to the guys. They know you're here."

"Hell. Can't remember the last time I saw Brad, Mack, and Reggie. Two and a half years ago, maybe?" Wyatt tugged at the brim of his Stetson.

Josh did the same, snuggling into a sweatshirt Tex had lent him. Thin-blooded Texans having a tough time with the great Pacific Northwestern summer season.

Tex nodded. "Must have been when the guys and I met you in Vegas for that concert. Remember? It was right after you left the Corps. Had a hell of a time. Talk about a party."

Wyatt sighed. "I don't think I remember."

"Oh, right. Well, this time you will remember, Mr. Sober. I want you to meet Oscar."

"Your other brother?" Wyatt asked, sounding a little bit... jealous?

"It's okay, big guy. Don't worry. No one can replace you."

Josh chuckled.

"Shut it, Josh." Wyatt mumbled, "I'm not jealous. But you do talk about him a lot."

"Only to you. To him, I talk about you."

"Oh, that's okay then."

Tex grinned. "You guys are a lot alike. But it's funny he looks so much like Brad."

"And you look so much like me." Wyatt smiled. "A chip off the old block."

Josh cut in, "Technically, you're referring to Uncle Pete."

"Let me bask in the glory of finally not being the youngest with Li'l Pete not around." Wyatt sighed and held out his arms to the darkening sky. "Ah, feels good."

"Wish I could feel that." Josh let out a loud sigh. "I'm always the baby."

"That you are." Wyatt grinned and clinked bottlenecks with Tex.

"But it's not all bad," Tex said. "Momma dotes on us young ones."

"That's true." Josh nodded. His mother had passed away years ago due to a brain aneurysm. There one minute, gone the next. Josh had been four at the time, so while it bothered him, he'd done much better than his father dealing with that long-ago grief. And he'd grown up under Tex's mother's loving eye.

"So," Wyatt said, breaking the silence, "we're here until Friday. Think we can have some fun until then?"

Tex smiled. "You came at the perfect time. I'm off until Thursday. On for twenty-four, then off again Friday. Between the guys, the city, and the mountains nearby, we're gonna have us a great time. Finally, I can listen to country music and not be made fun of."

Wyatt scoffed. "What? Please. I'm still going to make fun of you, but not because you listen to country. Where the hell is your hat?"

Tex flushed. Hell. He'd left it in the house.

"And you call yourself a Texan."

Chapter Twenty

BREE ENJOYED HER TIME WITH TEX AND HIS FAMILY. THOUGH she'd spent much of her time working while Tex showed his brother and cousin around, she enjoyed being asked to dinner and dancing with the handsome McGoverns. She hadn't yet gotten any more one-on-one time with Josh, but she'd learned some interesting things about Tex by watching him with his family.

Tex showed them every courtesy, a truly generous host. They stayed at his home in his bed and in the spare room while he took the couch. They had all needed a break from the RV, which she admitted felt tiny when she'd walked in. The house, in the meantime, looked as if a tornado had hit it.

Wyatt appeared to create messes just to watch Tex freak out.

Her boyfriend had an obsession with neatness. He liked order more than cleanliness, but she could handle that.

He also enjoyed her cooking but wouldn't let her cook for them, knowing how much work she had to do all day. Instead, he'd invited her out with the guys. Monday night, they'd gone dancing at a fun club that had featured Two-Step Taco Night. Hurray for dinner and delicious taco trucks parked outside.

Tuesday night she watched him go head to head with Wyatt playing darts and billiards while she and Josh enjoyed sodas at a nearby table.

Before they'd arrived, Tex had pulled her aside to confide a few things.

"I wouldn't break a confidence, but you should know my brother is a recovering alcoholic. Feel free to get whatever you want to drink, but I usually just get tea or soda. And Josh, no matter what he might tell you, is only nineteen."

"I'll just follow your lead." She'd paused for effect, ending with, "Li'l Pete."

The look on Tex's face was worth a lifetime of sodas.

Sitting with Josh, she watched the brothers battle over a pool table.

"It's a brother thing. They go for each other's throats," Josh explained with a grin. Then they watched someone try to muscle in on the brothers' game, and the McGoverns quickly rallied to throw off an interloper. "Yep. They can call each other names, but nobody else can." He shot her a look. "That means you too, you know. You have girlfriend privileges. Feel free to call Wyatt a horse's ass. Go on. I dare you."

She didn't, trying instead to subtly get some dirt on Tex. But Josh saw right through her. He promised answers if she could beat him at darts. Then her own competitive nature took over. Unfortunately, the kid could talk trash better than she could, and he trounced her.

Wednesday night, while she sat at home trying to relax after a long day, Tex and his brothers met with Tex's Station 44 buddies for "Guy Night," whatever the heck that meant. She stared at the television with shuttered eyes, exhausted.

Just as she started to fall asleep, her cell phone rang.

She answered with her eyes still closed, after blindly finding her phone. "Yeah?"

"Bree? It's me."

Bree opened her eyes, suddenly awake. "Carrie?"

Carrie sighed. "Yes, it's your ex-best friend. I was wondering if we could talk."

"Just us? Or do you feel the need to invite Melissa as well?" Damn. She hadn't meant to sound so bitchy. It had slipped out, along with a yawn.

"Just you and me," Carrie's answered in her cool, lawyer voice, the one that hid her reactions under placid conversation.

"Okay, talk."

"I meant in person, dumbass."

Bree smiled without meaning to but tried not to sound amused. "Real nice. When and where?"

"I'm slammed this week with work. I'm actually at the office as we speak. But we need to talk."

"Yes, we do."

"How about Friday, late afternoon?"

"Happy hour at Curran's? Can you do five thirty?"

"That works. Plenty of time for wine and appetizers while we make up and you realize how wrong you are. See you then," Carrie signed off, sounding way too chipper.

Frustrated and now no longer tired, though her body felt sluggish, Bree ran a bath and settled into the hot water with a sigh.

She had no idea how to feel anymore.

Though she missed Carrie, she'd hadn't hurt as much as she might have, pleased to have Tex and his family filling her need for companionship. Being with Tex, seeing him so happy, showed another side of the man she feared she liked more than she should. And even saying *like* felt like a lie. Heck, she'd fallen for the man. Hard.

He was so careful and gentle with Bubbles. She could almost see him building memories with the dog every time he touched her, counting down the days until she left.

He seemed so proud of his cousin, bragging about him joining the military and treating him like a grown-up one minute while still teasing him for being a teenager the next. But it was a brotherly teasing, not mean-spirited. Josh belonged.

As did Wyatt. She'd seen the older brother giving her some speculative looks, but he hadn't tried to talk to her without Tex near. He was charming, quite the ladies' man at the dance club, and as polite and reverential as a Southern boy should be. A slightly older clone of Tex, but without that something that made Bree's heart race.

She let the bath bubbles cloud her vision, staring into them as they popped and settled into the water.

Her project was coming along nicely, her selection of photographs firm, the matting and framing her next steps to getting everything ready for the public showing in another month. So close yet still far enough away that she could hold off the nerves and panic that hit whenever she thought about showing her work to everyone who believed in her. If she tanked at the city unveiling, there was no way she'd retain that invitation to have a showing at IAG.

Bree sank below the water, easing her big fat head from the worry saturating her brain.

She surfaced and wiped the water from her face, focusing on something other than her work.

Tex.

She groaned, missing him a ton. She'd just seen the big guy last night. But they hadn't done more than kiss or hold hands since Sunday. She'd become addicted to such satisfying sex. But it was so much more than the physical.

In Tex's arms, she felt cared for, could almost believe he loved some small part of her needing that affection. Craving it.

And that allowed her to feel okay about loving him back. He hadn't said he loved her, but he treated her the way she had always imagined being treated by a special man in her life. And technically, he did fill the role of *lover*.

Images and remembrances of how he'd held her, kissed her, and touched her had her going from relaxed to bothered and overheating.

Adding some cold water to the tub helped, as did the exhaustion from all her stress.

After draining the tub and drying off, she double-checked her locks and settled into bed. But she couldn't stop the nagging need to tell everyone the truth, to shout to the world that she and

Tex McGovern belonged together. No matter what anyone else thought.

Memories of her father's warnings, of his intent to hurt any man he didn't deem worthy of his daughter, mingled with dread in her sleep. She had nightmares about losing Tex and her father to a hungry, sneering Melissa while she swirled down the drain, drowning in a mire of worry and self-doubt, alone and unloved.

Tex missed the hell out of Bree, though he hid it well. Earlier in the day, he'd finally introduced Oscar to Wyatt, and as he'd expected, the two got along like peanut butter and jelly. Josh had taken to Gerty, the pair playing video games and laughing so hard he'd wondered if they might be on something.

Meanwhile, he spent the afternoon playing with Bubbles. They went on a walk in Fremont, ate at a bakery that catered to humans and their canines—providing Bubbles with her own pet-friendly frosted carrot cookie—and spent time playing fetch with a brand-new ball he wanted her to have so she wouldn't forget him.

His eyes burned as he walked her back to Oscar and Gerty's, and he told himself it was the wind and not tears at the thought of her leaving.

I do not have the time she needs, he kept telling himself, knowing how loved she'd be by the McGovern clan. Hell, Wyatt crooned to her when nobody was looking, and Josh acted as if he'd never played with a better dog. She got treats, attention, and some quality brushing that made her look like a fancy show dog.

But he still felt guilty, as if he were letting her down in some way.

Bucking up, he left the dog with his friends, grabbed his brother and Josh, and drove them to Reggie's for a barbecue and some game time. Like his brothers at Station 44, the McGovern clan was hell on wheels when it came to games.

As expected, everyone remembered Wyatt and took to Josh as if he were already one of their own. Hearing he would soon be standing on the yellow footprints at San Diego, Brad took Josh aside for some man-to-man Corps talk. Tex watched Josh's chest puff with pride at being included.

Wyatt nodded, seeing the same. Then Tex watched as Mack proceeded to get under Wyatt's skin in under five minutes. *Come on, Wyatt. You're better than that.*

Before Wyatt could pound him one, Tex shot his brother a disgusted look.

"What?" Wyatt snapped. "You can't tell me you don't want to beat him on a daily basis?" He turned back to Mack and smacked his fist into his palm. "One more word about the Cowboys and I'll flatten you, friend or no friend of my little brother."

Tex sighed and took out a ten-dollar bill from his wallet. "Everyone wants to hit Mack at one point or another during the week."

Reggie grinned. "Preach."

"He's a little too smart for his own good sometimes." Tex handed Mack the bill. "Here. Now be nice. Wyatt's not used to playing in your league."

Mack neatly pocketed the ten. "Yo, Wyatt. Sorry, but Tex thought you'd be a lot tougher to crack than you are." Mack shook his head. "You need to work on that thin skin, man."

Wyatt's eyes narrowed, then he laughed. "Okay, you got me. But when I nail your ass and take all your money later, remember, you brought this on yourself." He turned to Tex. "You still crushing him and Reggie at Spades?"

Reggie looked pained. "What? Do you tell everyone we suck?"

"Just family."

Reggie sighed. "Fine. But never tell my sisters about our losses, or I will eat you alive."

"Roger." Tex nodded.

Brad looked over at him. "Are you talking to yourself or what?"

Tex frowned. "I meant 'roger that.' As in, I get it."

Wyatt snickered. Then the others laughed.

If he calls me Li'l Pete in front of the guys, I will kill him.

Josh had been told to keep it quiet as well. God, Tex still couldn't believe Bree had that stupid name to hold over him now. Damn Josh and his big mouth. Show him a set of amazing breasts and he'd say anything.

Thinking about Bree's first meeting with his family made him grin.

"What's so funny?" Reggie asked.

"Ah, nothing important. Maybe I'll tell you sometime."

"I will somehow learn to live without knowing," Reggie deadpanned.

Tex slung an arm around Reggie's dense shoulders. "Have I told you how glad I am to be back at work around your smiling face?"

Reggie groaned. "Please, no."

Wyatt watched and laughed. "Yeah, bro. Without me and the others here, you need someone to lean on. Like Reggie here." Wyatt moved to the other side of Reggie and slung an arm around him, holding Reggie hostage. "What do we say when we need a friend, Tex?"

They broke into song, singing Luke Bryan's "Blood Brothers," to which Mack added the singer's vocals from his phone, patched through Reggie's sound system.

Reggie looked to be in sincere pain, so Tex and Wyatt sang louder, which encouraged Josh to join in.

"No more country music," Reggie pleaded, laughing as he tried to escape the grip of the McGoverns.

"Too late, Reggie. Once you're in, you're in." Tex planted a huge wet one on Reggie's cheek. "Now you're family."

Reggie growled and wiped his face, shoving Tex aside. Wyatt and Josh were laughing too hard to be of any help when Reggie put Tex in a headlock, making him swear to never do that again.

Brad wrangled Mack's phone away from him and played some classic rock through the speakers.

Reggie sighed. "Thank God. Now, can we please get to work on what we've been waiting to talk about?"

"What's that?" Wyatt asked as he dug into some chips set out on the counter.

Reggie answered, "How to get Tex to stop being such a pussy and invite the new love of his life over for game night?" The entire room froze, all eyes turning on Tex, some Doobie Brothers the only noise in the room. "But did you guys hear why Tex is taking things so slow?"

Wyatt and Josh looked at each other then at Tex. "No," Wyatt said. "Tell us, our newly adopted brother, Reggie. Why is Tex being so damn slow with that gal?"

"Why, because—"

"Don't say it," Tex begged.

"She's the daughter of our battalion chief, who promises to cut off the balls of anyone who dares look at her wrong," Mack helpfully provided.

Wyatt blinked. "Well, now. That does put things in perspective, doesn't it?"

Josh shook his head. "That sucks."

"My new motto," Tex muttered. "Thanks a lot, Reggie."

"Hey, I'm just looking out for my brother." He smiled, showing too many teeth. "That's what you get for playing country music in my house."

"He's lying," Mack said to Tex sometime later.

"What?"

"Reggie. He loves country music. Has an entire collection of Kenny Rogers and Darius Rucker's latest album. I saw it in his bedroom."

Tex chuckled. "Thanks. I think. Though you really can't argue with his choices. I still listen to Darius Rucker's 'Wagon Wheel.'"

Best damn song anytime you play it. And don't get me started on 'The Gambler.'"

"I don't even want to know what you're talking about." Mack stepped away.

Reggie took the initiative to gather everyone at his dining table for some poker. "Finally, we have enough for a real game. Six men, cards and poker chips for everyone. Twenty-dollar buy-in, gentlemen." They'd each ante up with twenty bucks, play with colored chips at one-, five-, and ten-dollar amounts, and at the end of the night, the big winner would get to keep the cash pot, regardless of what the chip value actually came to.

Tex enjoyed the hell out of his night. At least, until Wyatt started offering his opinions on Bree. Because he got the guys interested in getting their take on Tex's girl.

The problem was, once that happened, and they met and fell in love with her, the way Tex had, he'd have no more excuses not to claim her in front of his friends and everyone—including her father.

Now how would Bree feel about that?

———

Friday morning came too soon. Tex stood by the RV with his brothers and Bubbles. He'd taken them by the station Thursday morning when he went on shift. After introducing them to the other guys and gals at the station, he'd given them his truck and warned them not to break it.

The hours had flown by, several accidents making the shift both exciting and exhausting. Riding with Brad again in an aid vehicle had felt like coming home, and they'd done some fine work helping some hard-luck diabetics assist with their own insulin, splinted two fractured arms and one broken ankle, and thankfully, delivered a potential stroke victim to the hospital, only to later learn she'd had a false alarm.

Now, standing by his brother, cousin, Bubbles, and to his pleased surprise, Bree, Tex felt full. Happy, sad, and confused at his loathing to part from any of the group. Tex always missed his family when they left, but it had never seemed so hard to say good-bye before.

When he looked at Bubbles, he knew why.

He felt like a total douche for getting teary-eyed, but as he knelt to hug Bubbles one last time, he couldn't help it.

"Aw, damn it." Wyatt stormed away.

Josh sniffed. "Gotta hit the can. I'll be right back."

Bree stood by his side, waiting for him. He made the mistake of looking up, and she saw his face. Hers gentled. "Oh, Tex. I'll let you say goodbye and wait for you over there. Okay?"

He nodded, wiping his cheeks. He had no idea why he was crying. Hell. She was just a dog.

Just the best, cutest, most loving companion. He could tell she didn't understand. Or maybe she did, because she whined and licked his cheek. Which made it damn harder.

Jesus. Let her go. He patted her. "Love you, gal. I'll be down to visit, so don't be a stranger when I swing on by."

She just looked into his eyes, hers so dark and soulful, so sweet.

"Well, damn." He stood and wiped his leaky eyes again. He hurried to his brother and cousin, who'd returned, and hugged them tight. "Let me know when you get home, okay? And don't forget, she likes a can of the good stuff no later than seven. More like six. And you need to pet her and throw the ball for her. Easy at first with the others. I'm not sure if she'll be okay with the ranch dogs."

Wyatt rolled his eyes. "Easy, bro. We've done this before." In a gentler voice, he said, "We'll take good care of her, Li'l Pete. I promise."

"I know." Tex sniffed and cleared his throat. "Get out of here already, would you? And tell Momma I'll call her next week."

"Will do. Expect to see you soon." Wyatt's gaze shifted to Bree. "Both of you."

Tex sighed and muttered, "God willing."

Josh was hugging Bree goodbye, a little longer than Tex liked, but Bree was laughing.

"I promise. I'll write you a letter. But no pictures!"

"Pictures?" Tex frowned.

Josh glanced over his shoulder at Tex and hurriedly entered the RV. "Bye, Li'l Pete. Come on, Wyatt. Bubbles, come, girl."

Bubbles gave one more longing glance at Tex before slowly climbing the steps into the RV.

His heart gave a final lurch and settled. It was the right decision for the dog. And for him, he kept telling himself.

Wyatt gave Bree a hug and a kiss on the cheek. "See you at Christmas." He left soon after.

Tex stood there watching them go, heartbroken yet hopeful.

Bree walked next to him and took his hand in hers. Without saying a word, she turned and took him in her arms.

And like a freakin' baby, he hid his tears in her shoulder and hung on until the sadness passed.

———

Bree couldn't believe how emotional it was to say goodbye to Bubbles. But feeling Tex cry on her shoulder wrenched her heart wide open. What kind of man could make love to a woman like a stallion, had the ability to lose and laugh at himself, then cried, all because he missed his dog?

A man worth loving, that's who.

She stroked his hair, giving him time to collect himself, glad to feel needed.

Tex sniffed one last time and straightened. "Well, that was fuckin' awful."

She gave a watery laugh, not surprised that she'd cried with him.

"I know she's only a dog, and I didn't have her long, but—"

"Tex, stop." Bree refused to let him bury honest feelings. "She's not even my dog and I'm sad."

"I…hell. I know I look like some loser, but I don't care. She's a great dog." His voice cracked a little at the end, but he just cleared his throat as he regained his bearing. "She'll be so happy at the ranch, Bree. It's a terrific place."

"I believe you."

He drew her with him into his house and left for the bathroom. Returning a few seconds later, he still looked as if he'd been crying, but his breathing had evened, and his face was dry.

"Thanks for being here."

"Of course."

"No, I mean, for meeting my family." He paused. "It meant a lot. And, I, ah, I'd like you to meet the guys too. I mean, you know them. Sure. But I want us to all hang out together. Then you can see what being with me is really like."

"Why? Are there secret handshakes or something? Do you guys perform rituals?" She brightened just thinking about it. "Are you all naked?"

"What? Hell, no." He laughed. "You're a goof."

"No, I'm a blond *artiste*," she said for effect.

He sighed. "Never going to live that down, am I?"

"Nope…Li'l Pete."

"You can never tell anyone that name," he said, sounding serious.

"Why not?"

"Bree, do you have any idea what it's like to work and live with a bunch of people who all think they're comedians? We still call Brad 'Ken' because four years ago, one of the guys at our old station said he looked like a Ken doll."

She blinked. "He kind of does."

"See? That kind of stuff stays with you. You call me Li'l Pete, suddenly, it's not Lil Wayne or Lil Baby, it's Lil Pete, the country rapper. They'll have pictures of me with gold chains, rapping. And Bree, I can't rap." He looked horrified. "Or even worse. Peter Pan dolls everywhere with Lil Pete shirts or name tags. I'll be known as a big, green fairy. And it will get ugly, because then I'll be a lost boy, or a found boy, or a…"

"Okay, okay. Reel it in. I solemnly swear to never tell anyone your name. The name your family calls you, anyway."

He sighed with relief. "Thank you."

"I don't see why they can't just call you Tex at home."

He cringed. "Calling a Texan boy Tex, when he's living in Texas, around other Texans… Well, we just don't do that where I'm from."

"Wow. So many rules for you Southern people." She laughed. "Relax. I'm on your side."

"Thank God for that."

"Now, I have to get back to work. Then I have a date with Carrie at five thirty."

"Just you and her?"

"So she says." Bree sighed. "I hope we can get back together."

"I feel jealous." He kissed her.

"Oh, stop it. Not the kissing. The jealousy."

He laughed and kissed her again. "Thanks for being here today. It meant a lot." He looked into her eyes, and she didn't know how to describe the way he looked at her other than gooey. Affectionate. Maybe even…loving?

Her heart raced.

"Would you like to come back here after your date with Carrie? I could make dinner."

"We'll probably munch our way through happy hour."

"Okay. Then maybe we can see each other tomorrow?"

"No."

His face fell.

"I mean, happy hour won't last forever. And I'm sure Carrie will have plans tonight. That or just getting some sleep. I know she's been working a lot lately. So maybe I could come back over tonight."

His smile brightened up her entire day. "Yeah. That would work."

"I'll see you then."

He kissed her. "See you then."

She left, wishing she could turn down the volume on her heart, because it felt like it had woken up to a brand-new emotion today, something she wouldn't hesitate to call love.

Now what to do about it remained the question.

Chapter Twenty-One

Tex cleaned his home to within an inch of its life, knowing Wyatt had been screwing with him by leaving deliberate messes all over the place. The same way he had growing up.

Tex laughed. *Such a dick.* But Wyatt looked good. He seemed healthy, and he'd been back to his old, protective self, keeping an eye on Josh. And Bubbles.

The sadness remained, but it didn't feel as sharp. He could smile a little, thinking about how much Bubbles was going to love his momma. Sara Ann loved animals, and he knew she'd carry a soft spot for the bright-eyed, affectionate canine. His daddy too would fall all over himself for the dog while acting like he didn't much care. Yeah, not a bad life at all that Bubbles was heading to.

Tex rubbed his eyes and wished he didn't feel like such a heel for crying. He had a right to cry, sad over losing his dog. Not that she ever had been. Technically, he'd been fostering Bubbles. But they'd bonded. He hadn't had a dog in years, not since old Cricket had passed and they'd buried her on Old Dog Hill at home. He'd loved the beagle and cried a river when she'd died.

At least this wasn't a death. But…Bree had seen him lose it. He'd cried on her shoulder. Though most women said they wanted a sensitive guy, did they want one who cried over a dog? Would she dump him and kill their relationship over it?

Then again, in his opinion, dogs were just about the best things on the planet. If she couldn't understand that, then maybe she wasn't the woman he thought she was. But she'd held him. And she'd cried too.

Damn it. Bree belonged with him. They had to get past this holding pattern to the next level. He had to commit to taking her to see the guys. She hadn't said no, but he hadn't made more than a general request that they all get together.

And now they wanted to meet her and talk to her, get to know her.

Reggie worried him the most. Brad would be cool. Mack would flirt a little, but he already liked her. Reggie would be the tough nut to crack, the man still hurting from a hard fall, having given his heart to a woman who didn't want it. What if Reggie said something that offended her? Or Bree decided that dealing with four guys instead of just the one she wanted was too much?

"Fuck."

His phone buzzed. With a groan, he put the basket of laundry down—how many towels had Wyatt used, anyway?—and answered. "Brad?"

"Hey, Tex. You okay?"

Tex sighed. "Yeah. It was tough."

"Missing Wyatt and Josh already?"

"Missing Bubbles." He added, "And them, I guess."

Brad laughed. "She'll be good with your folks. Your brother and cousin looked great. I can't believe Josh is old enough to join the Marine Corps."

Tex smiled. "I know. I guess I'm getting old."

"Yeah, almost thirty, aren't you?"

"Over the hill, you mean?"

"Up yours."

Tex grinned.

"You want to come over to Reggie's for dinner? I'm bringing the beer. Avery's making enchiladas, and Mack's making his mom's famous potato salad."

"What's Reggie making?"

"He said he's hosting, and we should get off his back about cooking and dating—should the subject come up."

"Sounds like Reggie." Tex couldn't wait to give his pal some crap about both. "Sure. What time?"

"Five thirty. Avery wants to eat early, and Reggie agrees."

"Sex marathon later?"

"If she's lucky," Brad said, sounding way too smug.

"Ew. Gross, Brad."

Brad chuckled. "I'll count you in for dinner." He paused. "Unless you were bringing a plus-one?"

"I would, but Bree is meeting her friend tonight."

"No problem. We can meet her next week."

"Whatever." *That will be great. The guys will love her. So why are my hands sweating?*

"See you tonight. And bring some of that root beer Wyatt was drinking the other night, would you? And some vanilla ice cream. I have a hankering for root beer floats."

"Gotcha. See you in a few."

They disconnected, and Tex felt better about life. He had a hot girlfriend with plans to canoodle later in the evening. A great group of friends he happily called brothers. Family caring for each other and his dog, and a job he loved. What more could he want?

———

Bree had no idea why Carrie canceling happy hour bothered her so much. She knew Carrie had been telling the truth about an emergency meeting with a client. Carrie never lied about work, and she certainly wouldn't use such a sad excuse to get out of a personal confrontation with Bree. Carrie would just up and admit she didn't want to do dinner.

But that left Bree with nothing to do until meeting up later with Tex.

She should give him time to be alone. He'd had a long week with his family and a tough day saying goodbye.

But she couldn't get his tearstained face out of her mind. He'd been so open, so vulnerable.

And so amazingly beautiful in that moment. She regretted not having that image on film, because it would have reached into hearts everywhere and squeezed. Just one shot of Tex's tearstained face while clutching Bubbles. Of his face hidden against Bree's shoulder while he let the tears fall.

She would never have taken his picture and shared it, rather she wanted to look at it and remember his pain. To know he could feel so deeply for something or someone he loved.

She sniffed, not allowing herself to cry and ruin her mascara. Geez, even she missed Bubbles. The house would feel so empty without her.

Pausing in thought, she wondered which house she referred to, his or hers? Then realized it didn't matter. She felt at home with Tex in both places.

What the hell did that mean?

At loose ends, she texted Tex. Change of plans. Want to do dinner or are you busy until later?

He texted immediately back. Have plans. Want to join me?

Yes!

Great. Come to this address. Hope you're hungry.

Hmm. Maybe she should have asked about his plans before blindly agreeing to join him.

An hour after she'd arrived, she seconded that idea.

"So," Reggie Morgan said, scrutinizing her from head to toe. "What have you been up to, Bree Gilchrist? And why has it taken you this long to run the gauntlet?"

What the hell have I gotten myself into?

Reggie didn't often interfere in his friends' personal lives. Oh, sure, he teased and generally tortured Mack on a daily basis, but that was all in good fun. He and the guys knew they had each other's backs. He loved them all. Brad with his stern approach to life, now regularly easing into chill mode thanks to his family and Avery.

Then there was Mack, the happy-go-lucky prankster without a care in the world other than his Chevelle. Everyone loved Mack. Everyone also loved to get one over on Mack. Of all their crew, though it would kill Tex to admit it, Mack was the man the other teams *always* accepted as a substitute. Simply because, of the four of them, he was the most affable. Tex, despite his easygoing temperament, could be a real hardcase. Probably why he'd made such a good Marine.

And speaking of McGovern, the aw-shucks master of understatement, the fast-moving Southern boy who laughed and loved with abandon, girls here and gone on a weekly or monthly basis, was smart at his job, could "charm the dew right off the honeysuckle" (he'd once heard Tex's mom describe), and strong—physically, mentally, and emotionally—the guy was nervous, Reggie could tell.

Reggie had been through heartbreak. He still hadn't fully healed. No way in hell he'd let Tex suffer that same fate, not when the guy had been head-over-heels for Bree Gilchrist from the jump.

In all the years Reggie had known Tex, he'd never seen Tex get so smitten for so long. By Reggie's calculations, Tex had been bonkers for this woman for nearly a year. *A year.* That was a new record, considering the longest Tex had ever even dated a woman was for maybe a few months.

He studied Bree, knowing at once what Tex saw in her. On the surface, she had long legs, boobs, a face that had literally graced magazines, and a quick intelligence. But beyond that, Reggie saw compassion, laughter, wit, and an elegance not often found in the young and beautiful.

Oh, yeah. This woman had the power to crush his friend's soul, no question.

"So," he said, scrutinizing her from head to toe. "What have you been up to, Bree Gilchrist? And why has it taken you this long to run the gauntlet?"

She just looked at him. "Gauntlet?"

He nodded. "You know what I'm talking about."

"I do?"

"Pick your poison." He nodded over his shoulder at the open game cabinet, waiting.

She tensed before spotting Mack waving at the open cabinet and doing his best Vanna White.

"And what do we have here, Pat?" Mack asked the crowd. "Why, we have Scrabble! We have Parcheesi. Hmm. I see Monopoly and Clue. And, what's this? Pictionary. What a night for game play!"

Bree laughed. "He's such a goof."

"No kidding." Reggie turned to see Mack wiggling his brows. "Would you get off the cabinet door, you idiot? It's not meant to be hung on. You're not a kid, you know."

"Words hurt, Reggie. All I'm saying."

Tex and the others laughed. The Texan eyeballed his woman, saw she was handling everything just fine, and turned back to his conversation with Avery.

"Okay. Let me see." Bree went to the cabinet and pulled out one of Reggie's favorite games tucked behind the others. She raised a brow at him. "The gauntlet, hmm? Well, Mr. Morgan? Time to play."

Two hours later, the scary woman had beaten them at Rummikub four times out of five. The game was played with two to four people, so Brad and Avery had paired up to make one team, and Tex and Bree to make another, leaving Reggie and Mack on their own. Each team picked numbered tiles and hid them in a tile rack that only they should be able to see. The teams played in turn, the goal to set down all of one's tiles first for the maximum number of points, eventually playing off the opponent's tiles.

The guys and he never played for points, just to see who could go out first.

But between many rounds of beer, nachos, some ugly table talk—thank you, Avery and Bree—and some ribald humor even Reggie found hilarious, Reggie was having a blast.

Like Avery, their newest addition to the group, Bree liked to win. She had smarts, and she could manipulate her opponents by acting one way while playing another.

He liked that in an adversary. He also liked the way she and Tex argued about little things. They didn't agree on everything, which he'd never considered healthy. Avery and Brad got along but not so much they didn't snap at each other occasionally, keeping their relationship tight.

He watched, as did the others, though they were less obvious about it. Tex didn't let Bree have her way with everything, but he did cave to many of her decisions, allowing them their wins.

"Seriously, you guys have to be cheating." Reggie frowned. "No way you keep getting all the good tiles."

Tex chuckled. "Reggie, even if I wanted to, there's no way I could be cheating. First of all, you scrambled all the tiles so much that even Brad couldn't get what he wanted. I know, because I looked."

"Hey."

"And second, Bree has her meaty claws hooked so hard into the rack, I can't get close enough to play *our* tiles any more than I could play yours. Oh, and by *our*, I meant hers." He nodded at his scowling girlfriend.

"Back off, cowboy. This is my game. You can have the next one." She added under her breath, loudly enough for them all to hear, "If you can manage to win without me helping."

"*Ha.* I heard that," Tex growled at her.

"All bark and no bite. Play like you have a pair," she growled back then stuck her tongue out at him.

"Oh, you'll pay, Goldie."

She blushed. "Would you shut up and quit stalling the game?"

He gave a dark laugh and drank more beer.

Reggie hated to admit it, but they balanced each other nicely. One seemed to know when to give so the other could take. Conversation, game play, just being there for each other and enjoying the other's company. It was clear.

Tex might be mooning over the battalion chief's daughter, but she was mooning over their Texan Romeo right back.

Mack leaned close as if to whisper and said in a loud voice, "Aren't they just the cutest?"

Tex spit beer over himself, making Bree and the others laugh.

Reggie groaned. "Why does the mess always happen at my house?"

Everyone pointed at Mack, who shrugged. "What? Something I said?"

Reggie couldn't help but laugh. "Go get a rag."

"I hear, and I obey."

"If only."

By the time the night wound down, everyone but Tex and Bree had left. As they started out the door, Reggie pulled Bree back. "What? No hug?"

"Hug?" Her eyes brightened. "Are you kidding? Heck, yeah." She smiled and held onto him with the grip of a grizzly before easing away. "Thanks for such a fun time, Reggie. You guys had me laughing so hard, my stomach hurts." Then she leaned closer and whispered, "So did I pass the gauntlet?"

"With flying colors." He kissed her cheek. "Try not to hurt him too much, okay?"

She looked puzzled.

"You'll fight and make up and fight again. He's from Texas and has a hard head. It'll happen."

She chuckled. "Okay."

Tex had stepped away and returned. Reggie didn't want to think the guy might have been pissing on his lawn.

With a leer at Bree's legs, Tex asked, "What'd I miss?"

"Nothing, cowboy. Go wait in the truck, okay?" She clicked the fob of his keychain. "I'm driving."

"Sure thing, sugar lips." He laughed as he walked on unsteady feet to the truck.

"Sugar lips?" Reggie tried not to laugh and failed.

"That's a new one. Courtesy of your many bottles of beer."

"Hey, I was having root beer floats." He sighed, not wanting to have to say it but needing to. "Bree, we know the pressure you two are under to keep this quiet, but if you're going to get serious, it can't just stay between you two. Unless you become hermits. Or hobbits."

"Hobbits?"

He grinned. "Sure. On your journey to Middle Earth, may you find love and happiness. Live long and prosper."

"Mixing up your fantasy and sci-fi should be a crime against nature."

"Aw, man. If Tex doesn't stick, remember my number," he teased, knowing he'd never date a brother's ex. It went against the guy code.

She knew it too, because she rolled her eyes. "Oh, sure. Tease me, why don't you." Then she grew serious. "I know we have decisions to make, but it means a lot that you guys care. Thanks, Reggie."

"Drive safe."

She nodded and joined her drunk, now singing cowboy in the truck.

"Friends in Low Places" drawled down the street as they left, and Reggie watched until the truck's lights vanished.

"Good luck, Tex. You deserve to be happy." He sighed, rubbing the ache in his heart, feeling alone once more. "Because the alternative is such a bitch."

Tex woke in the morning with the absolute worst hangover. It tasted as if something had died in his mouth.

"Well, look who's awake? Hello, princess."

He groaned at all the damn noise. Was she using a megaphone or what?

"It's eight o'clock in the morning." Bree laughed and bounced on his bed. That didn't have that kind of bounce.

Her bed?

He blinked up at her sitting on her knees over him, unfortunately dressed. The sight of her weird chandelier-looking overhead light fixture clearly told him he was in the wrong house.

"I'm not…home?"

"Man, did you have a lot to drink. What, was that two cases that took you down?"

"Five beers too close together, I think." He groaned again. "Why do I feel so terrible?" He left the bed for the bathroom and, after doing his business, decided to shower. The hot water felt good, as did using what felt like half a tube of Bree's toothpaste as he brushed his teeth with his finger.

The night's events started to filter back. Having so much fun with the guys and Avery. Watching Bree fit in as if she'd always been a part of the group, a part of him. Letting her drive his precious truck while he sat next to her and marveled at her beauty.

Then coming into her home, taking forever to pee in the bathroom, focusing super hard on not hitting anywhere but the actual toilet.

Her putting him to bed while he told her how incredible, lovely, and sweet she was. Talk about being a lovin' kind of drunk.

And then waking up to her smiling, super cheerful, *annoying* face. Hey, he could love the hell out of her. Still didn't make him a morning person.

Now feeling minty fresh and awake, he toweled off, wrapped the towel around his waist, and walked back into the bedroom.

Only to find a topless Bree lounging on the bed.

A woman he hadn't slept with in *way* too long.

Tex dropped the towel and felt his dick swell, as if the caress of her gaze wrapped around him and squeezed.

"My, my. Someone sure seems pent up."

He walked toward her, watching her watching him. Her gaze seemed glued to his dick. Perfect.

"Is this the part of my dream where you prove what a good girl you are?"

"Is the part where you lick me until I scream?"

"Am I hearing a shout-out for a sixty-nine?"

She laughed. "Maybe."

"But, darlin', panties don't work in a sixty-nine."

She scooted back on the bed and shimmied out of her panties. Then she spread her legs and fingered herself.

I'm in heaven. "Oh, yeah. That's it. Get nice and wet."

She moaned and showed him just what he'd been missing. But before he could dive in, she put out a hand to stop him. "No way. You said sixty-nine. Stick to your guns."

"Hey, I'm happy to make you scream. I can wait."

"Maybe I can't." She crooked her finger at him and, when he neared, yanked him down for a kiss. Her lips destroyed him, and her small hand wrapped around his cock. Thoughts became too much. She could lead him anywhere she wanted if she'd squeeze a little harder.

She pulled back to nip at his lower lip. "Turn around. Let's race."

"Fuck, yeah." He kissed her again, so in love with the woman, it wasn't funny. "Winner gets to torture the other for a while longer."

"Deal."

He moved on top of her and turned around. In seconds he felt hands on his cock then a warm, wet mouth sucking. It wouldn't be long for him at all.

Desperate to please her, he zeroed in on her sex and started kissing, licking, and sucking in time to the magical mouth between his legs. Her drive increased his own, and they were both soon moaning and gyrating as passion overwhelmed any sense of a challenge.

Her groans vibrated around his cock. And then the little witch started dragging her fingernails over his inner thighs. She cupped his balls, playing with the taut sac, sending him right to the edge as her tongue worked its own magic.

He thrust a finger inside her, working her with his mouth and hands, so close, he couldn't stop. And then she was coming, taking him right along with her as she sucked and wouldn't let go. Tex let the release wash over him, drowning in her scent as he shot down her throat. Ecstasy entwined with the love he felt for this woman who could take him places he'd never before been.

When she gave him a gentle push, he withdrew from her mouth and pulled away from her swollen clit. With a last kiss, he crawled off and collapsed beside her, a sudden shiver of sensation working its way out of him.

"Oh my God." She put her head on his chest, her breaths coming in soft puffs over his nipples, stirring him anew though his body demanded a rest. "That was so good. I needed that."

"You and me both." He blew out a breath, contemplating the glorious morning. "You need more protein though."

"Oh, do I?" She laughed. "You must have been pent up. I nearly drowned."

"That's because I'm hung like an elephant. I'm my own fireman, putting out fires with the mighty power of my massive hose."

"Okay, I've heard enough."

He laughed. "Good, because I was starting to gross myself out. So, who won, do you think?"

"I did come first, so technically, you won."

"I really did. You sucked so hard, when you came, and I was just...gone." He kissed her hair then pulled her over him, bringing her close so he could access her mouth. After a while, he sighed and ran his fingers through her soft hair.

"Does it bother you?" she asked, her cheeks rosy.

"What?"

"Tasting yourself on my lips."

"I think it's sexy as hell. Does it bother you when you tasted yourself on my mouth?"

"Not at all. I'm amazing."

He smiled. "Bree, I feel so damn good when I'm with you." *I don't want the world to interfere. But I know one of these days it will.* He didn't want to have the future talk with her, not now. But they'd need it soon. "What do you say I try to make *you* breakfast this time? After I get up and get dressed."

"Sounds great." She leaned back to kiss him again. "And by the way, next time you go down on me, brush your teeth again first. The minty thing you were doing was out of this world."

He smirked. "So, I guess we're both winners."

"Sure, sure. But if there's no number one, we just have a lot of number twos. And I'm not awarding you a participation trophy anytime soon, so keep working on your game."

He barked a laugh and left for the bathroom.

After darting into the hall bath to do a quick cleanup, Bree hurriedly dressed in loungewear for the day in a pair of loose, cotton shorts and an oversize sweatshirt and skipped into the kitchen to make a pot of much-needed coffee. She'd love for Tex to try to make her breakfast, but she was taking no chances on her caffeine.

After downing a cup, she poured him one and started to take it to him. What was he doing back there, anyway? She listened and chuckled. Another shower? My, he certainly did like getting dirty and cleaning up. She wondered if she messed her man up again, would he go for a bath next time? Maybe he was part dolphin. Or a merman who liked seducing mortal women.

He'd surely seduced her out of a few brain cells.

The doorbell rang.

She glanced at the clock on the mantle. Eight thirty on a Saturday? What the heck? Sure, she'd normally be up and moving by now, but it seemed a little early for someone to be calling on her. She put the cups down and moved to the door.

The doorknob twisted.

Frozen, she watched in horror as the door slowly opened, not sure what to do. But she had a six-foot-four fireman not far away.

Then her father walked through with a tray of coffee in one hand and a paper bag clenched between his teeth, his hand on the key. He saw her and smiled, the key in his pocket once more, the bag and coffee in hand.

"Hey there, sweetheart. I'm sorry to barge in on you like this but…" John Gilchrist trailed off as a whistling, bare-chested Tex walked down the hall towel-drying his hair. He wore shorts at least, but the happy grin on his face and lack of clothing spoke volumes.

"Bree, did you—" The sight of her father stopped Tex in his tracks. To his credit, he didn't bolt or turn pale. Instead, he nodded. "Morning, Chief. Bree, uh, could I talk to you for a sec?"

"Sure. I'll be right back, Dad." She darted down the hallway, following a fast-moving Tex, and shut the bedroom door behind them. Her bedroom. With Tex. Probably not the best move she could have made.

"So, um, that's your dad."

"Yep." She tried to figure out what to do. "He saw us. You. Me. Well, really, first me, then you." *I'm twenty-seven, for heaven's sake. Why do I feel like I'm eleven again, caught getting my first kiss?*

"Bree?"

"What?"

Tex gave her a soft kiss and smiled. "I think the cat's out of the bag. Why don't you go talk to your dad while I put a shirt on? I'll be right out to back you up."

"Are you sure?"

"I am."

"Okay then." Time to confront the dragon guarding his nonvirgin of a daughter.

Won't this be fun?

Chapter Twenty-Two

TEX LOOKED FROM CHIEF GILCHRIST TO BREE AND BACK, wondering what he'd missed in the scant seconds he'd been looking for his shirt. Fortunately, it didn't smell too bad. A little like alcohol, but probably better to be fully dressed than shirtless with the chief's daughter.

Well, so much for keeping secrets.

He sat next to Bree across from her dad at her dining table, in full view of the sunny backyard, the promise of yet another warm June day. The chief sat hunched over a cup of steaming coffee he must have purchased from the café down the street. He munched on a croissant and stared from his daughter to Tex, his glower darkening.

Bree smiled as if nothing was amiss and encouraged Tex to have one of the delicious-looking pastries the chief had brought. For his daughter.

"Nah, I'm good." He hadn't touched the store-bought cup either, accepting the mug Bree had made for him.

No one spoke until the chief said, "We're all going to pretend this isn't happening? Is that it?" He looked pissed.

"This?" Bree asked, frowning. "What exactly is the problem with *this*?" Before the chief could answer, she added, "And why the heck did you use your key, Dad? You scared the life out of me."

Chief Gilchrist turned red. "Sorry. I texted and called, but you didn't answer. I thought I'd pop over for some dad/daughter time. We haven't shared breakfast in way too long."

"I can leave…" Tex started to offer before both Bree and her father shook their heads.

"No, you stay," Bree said.

"Oh, please, stay." The chief smiled through his teeth. "You're already here, aren't you?"

Already fucked your career, you mean. Tex stifled a loud sigh. "You know what, I think I will have a pastry." He chose an apple tart and sunk his teeth into it. Time to see just how ugly the chief would get about Tex dating his *grown daughter.*

"I'm having a cherry one," Bree said. She chewed and stared at her father.

They all sat chewing and stewing in silence. Tex saw the humor in it and did his best not to laugh.

The chief didn't look amused. "What's so funny?" Gilchrist snapped. "That you're corrupting my daughter?"

"Oh my God. Corrupting?" Bree clapped a hand over her eyes.

Tex coughed to cover the laughter that escaped. "Sorry, sorry. It's just… We're all sitting here in silence, chewing, while you're glaring me to the depths of hell. And it's so surreal. Chief, look, when I was at dinner with your family, we—"

"Were you taking advantage of Bree back then? Lying to me in my own home?"

Tex swore he could see steam coming out of the guy's ears.

"Dad, enough."

All eyes turned to Bree. Hmm. Tex hadn't been treated to that particular voice before, though they'd had their share of petty arguments. Hell, he liked tussling with Bree, both in and out of bed. But he wouldn't want to be on the receiving end of that tone.

"Bree," the chief started.

"No, Dad. This is beyond ridiculous. I'm twenty-seven years old. Who I sleep with or date or do anything else with is not your business."

Tex frowned. Sleeping with or dating he understood. What did "anything else with" mean, exactly?

Her father frowned as well. "I don't ask much from you. Just this one thing. I'd like you to steer clear of firefighters. It keeps personal and professional lives from crossing and creating this kind of dynamic."

"*Your* personal and professional lives, you mean. When Tex was helping me around the city, he did everything by the book. No flirting. No goofing around. He did his job. Period."

The chief seemed to ease back a little. He shot a look at Tex. "That right?"

"Yes, sir. I'm proud to wear the uniform. I was on duty and did what I was told to do. Bree got her pictures because I showed her different parts of the city and our station houses. She saw two fires. You were there for the one."

The chief nodded.

"I have nothing to apologize for then, or now."

The man's eyes narrowed.

"Dad, he's right. I'm sorry if you feel that my dating Tex violates some weird work code, but the plain truth is that it doesn't. Tex hasn't been working with me for a while now. This relationship is ours. We're dating."

Tex reached for her hand on the table and held it. He glanced at her with a smile. "Exclusively."

"Yep. Exclusively." Bree gripped his hand. Hard.

Her father looked at them, then at Tex. Tex couldn't read the man's expression. "I told you not to get involved. You did. I told you, Bree, to stay away from a life you think you know, but you don't."

"Dad?"

The chief stood. "Well, you've both made your decision. I hope you can live with the consequences."

That didn't sound threatening. Not at all.

"Dad, you can't legally force Tex out of a job for dating me."

"That's illegal, sir," Tex agreed. "I do my job well. And I love it."

"But do you love her more?" the chief asked, turned, and left.

They sat, shell-shocked, still holding hands. Tex would have loved to answer the chief, but he didn't know, exactly, what to say. Did he love Bree? No doubt. Enough to give up his job for her? To give up the thing that made him happy, that felt like a part of his makeup? Being a firefighter wasn't just a job to Tex. It was his life.

But why the heck should he have to choose between the two?

"He is acting so weird," Bree said, her voice a little shaky.

Tex turned his chair and leaned close to kiss her. "You okay?"

"I don't know. I'm so sorry. He has no right to threaten your job."

"Shh. Honey, it's not your fault. Your dad ain't acting sensible about this. But you know what? I'm glad it's out now. No more hiding."

"No." She gave him a tremulous smile. "So at least there's that." She sighed. "You let me know if he does or says anything to you at work. He can't interfere with your job."

"I know."

"Not if what he's mad about has nothing to do with work. I mean, obviously if you mess up at work, he could…"

"Yeah, it's sticky. But we'll handle it." Should he confess how he felt now? Yet it felt wrong, somehow. "Bree, I care for you. I want us to work. But I don't want to come between you and your dad."

She blinked. "You want to break up?"

"*What?*" He leaned back and stared. "Hell, no. Why would you ask that?"

"Oh, good." She let out a little sigh of relief. "I feel bad about this. You and I did nothing wrong. We shouldn't be punished because my dad has a stick up his ass."

"Don't worry about it. I'll be fine. And yes, I know, I can talk to my union rep if I have any problems."

"I was just going to say that." She smiled.

"I know. So, is today ruined, or can we still enjoy it?"

She huffed. "He definitely changed the vibe, that's for sure."

"And I was so hoping to ride that last orgasm for a while. Dang." Tex pretended to mope then snagged another Danish from the plate in front of them. "Would be sad to let these go to waste."

"That's true." Bree grabbed a donut. "I'm stress eating now. I should probably stop." She licked the frosting off her finger, and he couldn't look away.

"I like stress eating." Tex took one of her fingers, dug through the frosting, then brought it to his mouth. Watching her while he sucked her finger clean, he saw the arousal she couldn't hide. And smiled. "Maybe the two of us should get this stress out of our systems. You know, stuff our faces full so we're relaxed for a while."

Bree's wide grin encouraged more sucking. "Are you trying to get back in my shower?"

"Huh?"

"Every time we have sex, you need to get clean."

He chuckled. "No, no. I just find the hot water over my body rids my hangover faster. No idea why, it just does."

"Good to know."

"Now can we have some kinky donut sex, or are you going to harangue me about your water bill?"

"Hmm. I wonder if there's a way you can pay it off."

"Well, you know, I have been known to play in the tub with half-naked women. So, tell me, the first time you rode this fine body, was it because you'd deliberately flooded your bathroom or what?"

She gaped. "Seriously? Water damage just to ride the Tex love train?"

"That's a no then?"

"You're an idiot."

Who loves you. "So, what does that make you?"

"A woman who should know better but doesn't care."

"Just my type."

She smacked him. They laughed and play-fought back to the

bedroom, where problems didn't exist, and tomorrow could wait to rear its ugly head.

———————

Sunday at work went off without a hitch. They had a few calls but nothing major. The guys seemed on edge, Tex having told them about his situation with Bree. Though the chief knew, Tex was still keeping his dating life private. The guys agreed that to be a smart move.

But before Tex left the next morning to start his ninety-six hours off, the lieutenant snapped from inside his office, "McGovern, a word. *Now.*"

Shit.

Wash and Hernandez had been hanging out in the commons with Mack and Reggie.

"What's up with Tex?" Hernandez asked. "Ed sounds pissed."

Reggie groaned. "Nothing good, apparently."

Tex looked at his friends, sighed, and took the beating sure to be coming his way. It couldn't be that bad, could it?

———————

A week later, Tex sat with the guys at Seward Park, staring at the water and feeling glum. Well, Gilchrist had said there would be consequences. But ripping Tex not only from his crew but from Station 44? Tex hadn't seen that one coming. Not at all.

"This is bullshit," Brad said. "He can't do this."

"He can." Mack sighed. "He hasn't done anything disciplinary, Brad. It's a personnel shift. He's the battalion chief. He has that power."

"How are the guys at your new station?" Reggie asked.

"Okay, I guess." Tex shrugged. "Pretty understanding, actually.

The lieutenant in charge isn't as together as Ed or Sue, but he's okay. I do my job, take all the shit work like I'm some newbie, and don't complain. But man, Gilchrist made it clear as day that anyone so much as looks at his daughters in any way, they're gonna get what I'm getting."

It hurt. Tex missed his friends. They were his family, damn it. Gilchrist had no right fucking with that. "How's the new guy?"

Mack snorted. "The son of somebody with money and power in the city is playing at being a firefighter, you ask me. That bullshit about pairing us with the FNG because we're a stellar crew who can teach him something is crap. I mean, sure, it's true. We're awesome. But this guy... He's a real prize. Thinks he can do no wrong, and he's barely out of diapers."

"Hernandez and his team can't stand the guy." Reggie snorted. "I can see why. Within two seconds of joining our team, he started mouthing off like he had a right. And he was wrong about procedure, which Wash had been trying to show him. Guy's barely been with us for two days and acting like he's one of us. He's not."

"You can't blame him for that." Tex felt tired. "For being an arrogant ass, sure. But not for being new."

"No, we blame *you*," Reggie growled.

That hurt.

"Reggie." Mack shook his head.

Brad frowned. "Come on, Reg. Tex doesn't want this."

Tex scowled. "You think I like working with guys who know I'm the station fuckup? Who enjoy disc golf and art flicks in their spare time rather than having a beer and playing ball?"

"Oh, that's harsh." Brad cringed.

Reggie leaned back and shrugged. "Well, you wanted the girl."

"Reg, stop." Brad frowned at him.

"Gilchrist is fucking with you," Mack said to Tex, cutting in. "Trying to see if you're serious about his daughter."

"Who knows?" Tex wished he did. "He hasn't done anything

wrong, exactly. I do the same job. Same pay. Just in another part of the city."

"Station 44 isn't the same," Brad said. "Everyone feels it. Ed's been bitching at all of us."

"Especially our crew," Reggie said, glaring at Tex. "Why, man? I get that you like her. But we're your brothers. Would you rather be with her than with us?"

Tex blinked. He hadn't realized how hard this would be for all of them. "Of course not. I love you guys. I'll get back eventually." Somehow. "I think Mack might be right."

"I'm always right."

Tex had to hand it to the guy. Even this disaster hadn't killed Mack's sense of humor, which Tex appreciated. He winked at Mack. "Of course you are. My point is, I think Gilchrist is trying to make me to back off with Bree."

"You think?" Reggie shook his head. "What he did isn't right. But it does make you think. Is leaving us worth it?"

"I love her, Reg," Tex admitted aloud for the first time.

The guys quieted and stared at him.

"You do know what that word means, right?" Mack asked.

"Shut up, Mack." Brad scowled, but Tex saw him work to hold back the grin that threatened. "Such an asshole. Look, Tex, I'm glad you finally found someone. I think what Gilchrist is doing is shitty, but you have to do what's right for you." Brad stood and crossed his arms over his chest, looking like a fucking superhero as he claimed, "We're not going anywhere. And *your* spot, not that dickhead Gornutt's, is waiting."

"We call him Goat Nut. He hates it," Mack confided.

"Goat Nut," Brad corrected, "is just filler. Keep it together, and before you know it, you'll be back with us. But in the meantime, when our schedules mesh, we keep doing what we're doing. Working out together, hanging out together, remaining a unit, in or out of the firehouse."

"Roger that." Mack grinned. "Get it? *Roger* that?"

Tex grinned despite his heartache. "Can I hit him? I've been missing that a lot."

Reggie finally smiled. "Please do. Then we can get back to this run. I think I'm getting faster, Tex. In fact, I'm pretty sure I can beat you now."

"It's on, Navy. Let's race." *And hope I don't pull so far away, I can't ever come back.*

———

Ed O'Brien glared at a man he'd been friends with for years. "This is bullshit, and you know it."

John Gilchrist sighed and rubbed his eyes. His daughter had been on his ass the past week, claiming he needed to get over this overprotective instinct. His wife had called him a few choice names and was only grudgingly speaking to him. The station staff had been tiptoeing around him, all except for his assistant, who didn't care what the hell he did so long as he kept to his schedule.

"You have a point to make?" He liked Ed. A lot. They were old friends, but they also had a particular role to play in the hierarchy of the fire department. Took a lot of balls for Ed to stand up for McGovern.

"This is horseshit. Come on, John. Tex is one of my best. He's fun, makes the department look good, and makes C shift as good as it is. Those two crews are strong and making my job easier. Then you grab Tex and stick me with Gornutt? They hate him."

Hell, John hated him. But the governor's friend's kid needed a place to show his stuff, and he'd passed all the tests and gotten into the department on his own merit. Gornutt had earned a right to be in the department. Maybe not at the new station, however.

"They call him Goat Nut," Ed said as John had taken a sip of coffee.

After choking and nearly spitting up over himself, he glared at Ed as he finally swallowed. "Stressing the new guy is not going to help."

"Neither is taking one of my top firefighters because he's dating your daughter."

"He needs to learn flexibility. Responsibility. How to handle tough situations and push through."

"He does that every day. And he's been dealing with you without breaking down."

"For a week. Give it a little time, and we'll see how things roll. So Goat Nut, ah, I mean, Gornutt, what's his status?"

Ed sighed and reported his findings. He gave John a rundown of some issues to look into, including lowered morale, then left with a disgusted look on his face.

John watched him go, wondering if he was making such a bad choice after all.

But no, he knew what living with a firefighter had done to his first wife. Recalled all the pain, the tears, and the heartache she'd had to deal with. He didn't have much of her left, only the memories he carried. The guilt.

And a daughter he loved more than life itself. In time, she'd understand why he'd done what he'd done. And if Tex McGovern was the man his daughter insisted he was, then he'd make his choice and choose a life with Bree over his job.

Sometimes you had to hurt the ones you loved to help them.

Chapter Twenty-Three

BREE GLARED AT TEX, WHO GLARED BACK. HE'D BEEN WORKING with another fire station for the past two weeks, and the guilt for his situation and blame sat heavily, weighting her down. They still enjoyed each other, still loved spending their spare time together, but she couldn't face his friends with what her father had done. So, they'd been apart more often than not on his free days.

Work had resumed, still polishing her project so it would be ready for the city unveiling in two weeks, but at least she had her assistant to help. Her nerves felt stretched thin, on edge because of how important her work was and because her personal relationships seemed to be struggling.

At least she'd mended fences with Carrie. Though they had yet to really sit down and discuss why the hell Carrie had tried to involve herself in Bree's relationship with Melissa, Carrie hadn't pushed it again. She had apologized, and that was all Bree had needed to hear.

But some tiny kernel of…something unpleasant remained between them. Unfortunately, Bree didn't have it in her to dig deep and rip it out. Not yet.

"I'm not talking to your father about this," Tex said, spacing his words evenly.

"Tex, it's my fault, I—"

"You can deal with your dad however you like. He's your dad." He drew her closer as they sat in her living room, trying to enjoy a movie night at home. "But he's my boss. I can't talk to him the way you do. I won't. He can pull all the crappy things he wants with me, and I'll take it. I won't break for that bastard." He blinked. "I'm sorry. You're in a bad place with this all around."

"I know." She tried not to cry. But her father made no sense! "I've talked to him. Charlie's talked to him. I heard even Ed talked to him."

"He did?" Tex blinked then smiled. "Good old LT."

"My dad isn't reasonable about this. I know it's affecting you and your friends. I feel like it's my fault. Maybe if we broke up for a while…"

"But don't you see? That's what he wants."

She frowned at the vehemence in his voice. "Um, you're not just staying with me to stick it to my old man, are you?"

"What? No. That's stupid."

"I'm stupid?"

"Fuck, Bree. You're not hearing me."

The argument went downhill from there. Date night turned into time alone for both of them. Tex left. Bree stared at her empty home and burst into tears.

Her father was being such a huge ass. She called him. When he answered, she said again, "Why are you doing this?"

"Why, hello, daughter. How are you this evening?"

"You are ruining my life, Dad. And you're ruining Tex's. You have no right to—"

"I have every right," he interrupted. "I make decisions about my battalion all the time. Your boyfriend is no more special than any of my other people. I won't make concessions just because he's dating you."

She took a deep breath, knowing she was getting nowhere. "Dad, I understand that you're trying to control my personal life for some reason. I think it's out of love, but you're coming across as controlling and frankly, uncaring. I really don't understand why."

He sighed. "Honey, when your mother was alive, the man she was in love with broke her heart."

"Yes, then she met you."

"No. I broke her heart. First her ex did, then I did. Firefighters live hard lives. It's not glorious, and it's not easy. We do it because we want to help people. But helping sometimes leaves scars. The divorce rate is through the roof. The propensity for our people to turn to drink or drugs to deal with this life is high. I've lived it. And so did your mother. I don't want that for you. I promised my Allie I'd take care of you, and I will until the day I die. You might hate me for it, and you might think I'm being a real bastard. Maybe I am.

"But I'm only in charge of a small part of my world. It's not like I'm telling Tex he can't date you. If you're that important to him, why can't he give up his job and try something else? He's smart, capable. Why not find a stable occupation and settle down?"

"Dad, are you hearing yourself? You want Tex to marry me? We've only been dating a few weeks."

"I'm not saying marry him now," he hurried to say. "I just mean that you should always come first, before the job. And if he can't see that, then who am I really hurting? It's his choice. I love you, honey. I'll talk to you when you're not so upset. Okay?"

He disconnected.

Much of what he'd said made sense…if she and Tex had been dating for four years and planned to settle down. But by her dad's admission, if Tex couldn't commit to Bree after being together for—she did the math—one month, then he should be tossed aside?

For that matter, what did that comment mean about hurting Bree's mom? What had that been about? Charlie, unfortunately, couldn't explain John's actions, nor could she get through her husband's thick head, though she'd been trying.

What the ever-living fuck?

Baffled, annoyed, and heartsick, Bree just sat there, staring at the blank television screen, trying to get up the energy to pour herself a glass of wine she didn't want.

Someone rang her doorbell.

Just great. She hoped to see Tex but didn't know if she had the energy to argue with him. She kept trying to help him. He kept telling her he'd handle it. And when she suggested taking a break to help him get back to his friends, he insisted on them not giving in to pressure.

She sighed and made her way to the door, only to stop in shock as she looked through the peephole.

"You know it's me. Just open up already."

She opened the door, just to see what would happen. "Melissa?"

Her stepsister walked inside and looked around. "Nice. I like the changes. What's it been? Four years?"

"About that. Melissa, why are you here? To gloat because Dad is causing me grief?"

Melissa grinned. "There is that. But no. I'm here because of Carrie."

"Why? Is she okay? What's wrong?"

Melissa studied her.

"Well?"

"I just… Hell. Do you have anything to drink?"

"Help yourself." Fed up with not getting answers, Bree went back to the couch to brood. At least Melissa's unwelcome appearance might give Bree the fight she needed.

Because anger and hurt and confusion kept swimming inside her, threatening to drown her under the weight of so much chaos. Bree liked her life scripted. A life she controlled. Yet lately, nothing seemed to make much sense.

Melissa sat down with a glass of wine. She pushed another at Bree. "It's a nice Merlot. You have good taste."

"Why are you here?" Bree stared at the wine. Then thought, what the hell, and drank some.

"Carrie is busy at work lately. Too busy to talk to me or you, really."

"Your new best friend is ignoring you?"

"Oh, bitchy. I like this new you."

Bree flushed. "Melissa, I would be happy to yell and scream at you. But I don't need that, and I know you don't. So, please, just say what you came to say and leave."

Melissa sighed. "Fine. I'm sorry John is being such a dickhead about Tex. I like him. And I know you do. And I don't think he deserves this bullshit, whatever it is."

"Thank you." The first nice words Melissa had said to Bree in a long time.

"I also think you owe Carrie an apology."

"I what?"

"I know you guys made up. And she's happy about that, because she loves the hell out of you. You're like sisters."

"There's no like. We *are* sisters."

Melissa nodded, her eyes thoughtful. "Then why would you ask her to choose between you and me? Hell, between you and anybody? Why should Carrie have to give up something to love you?"

"What are you talking about?"

"When you made such a big deal at her place, about her taking my side. You acted like it was either me or her, and when she didn't shove me out the door, you stormed out."

"That's not what happened." Bree glared at her then blurted, "And she should have booted *you* out the door. She's *my* friend."

Melissa gave a harsh laugh. "Oh my God. You are so like John. What the hell is the difference between what you said to Carrie and what John said to you about Tex?"

"I..." Bree blinked. "It's not the same."

"Why? Because I'm not as important to Carrie as Tex is to you?"

"No. It's..." *God. Did I do that?*

"Right. Like John trying to make your boyfriend choose his job or his girlfriend. I bet if Tex left the fire department, John would welcome him to the family."

"I doubt that."

"No, I was talking to Mom about it. John's a little off his rocker about you. It's not even losing you to the man you marry, but it's something to do with firefighting and relationships in general. Mom admits he has some issues."

"Are he and Charlie okay?" She couldn't bear it if her rocky relationship with her dad affected Charlie in any way.

"Oh, they're fine. Or rather, Mom is okay. John has some groveling to do. But he loves her, so he will."

"Good."

"Do you understand what I'm saying about Carrie?"

Bree nodded. "I do. I was angry and hurt. You didn't help."

"I know. I'm good at rubbing people the wrong way." Melissa paused. "I've always been jealous of you. There. Happy now?"

"Why would I be? I only ever wanted a sister. I didn't want to be better than you. I just wanted to be close to my stepsister." *I just wanted to be loved.* The tears came, harder this time, because she'd hurt Carrie without meaning to. Tex had left in a huff, and her father had put a wall between them, something she'd never before had in their relationship.

"Jesus, why me?" Melissa crossed to Bree and pulled her in for a hug. "I'm a bitch, I know. I'm sorry for all the shit I put you through. What can I say? I'm screwed up, but I do love you. Deep, deep down," Melissa teased. "Come on, Bree. I'm sorry. I was kidding. I do love you, you know. Go ahead and cry it out."

She did. And when she stopped, she felt worlds better. Enough to wipe her snotty nose on her sleeve deliberately in front of her stepsister.

Melissa grimaced. "That's disgusting. And annoying that you still look pretty even with all that snot hanging off your nose."

Bree laughed through her tears and found a box of tissues. After blowing her nose and wiping her eyes, she returned to find Melissa on the couch, sipping wine.

"Thanks. I needed that."

"Yeah, you did." Melissa put her glass down and toyed with her hair, something she'd always done when she was anxious. "Let's get this out there once and for all."

"Okay. Let's."

"My mom married your dad. I loved him right away. He became my dad. Charlie became your new mom."

"Yep."

"You were everything I'd always wanted in a sister. And it was good. At first."

Bree nodded.

Melissa sighed. "I... I was used to being the pretty girl. Then there you were."

"But—"

"Stop, I know you're going to tell me I'm pretty too. I am. I know. But back then, you didn't seem to realize how pretty and nice you were, how much every fucking body seemed to love you, which made it worse. So, yes, I had a hard time trying to deal with a new life where I had to share the spotlight. I missed my dad so much. And then I just grew unlikable.

"I hated myself, and I wanted to feel better. So, I started doing things to make people like me. A lot of it had to do with boys and being popular. I'm not proud of it, but I know why I acted out now."

"I'm sorry."

"Me too." Melissa shook her head. "I know we can't go back and undo the past, but you and I don't have to be enemies. I did things to hurt you and never apologized. You kept me at a distance because of it. It was my fault, I know, but—"

"I'm sorry. You're right. You hurt me so long ago, and I built walls and kept you out, even when you tried to reach out to me. I did keep that charm bracelet you gave me though." Melissa's atonement back then had been to offer Bree her favorite bracelet.

"You did?" Melissa flushed. "I felt so bad after I kissed Kurt.

But I wanted to hurt you. So I did, and I hurt myself worse. But trust me, I did you a favor with Doug in tenth grade. He was such a jerk."

"Then thanks." Bree smiled.

Melissa gave a hesitant smile back. "High school was so many years ago, but sometimes you can feel it as if it happened yesterday."

"I know. But that was all the time we really had together. Since then, either you or I am always gone."

"Until recently."

"Yeah."

A pregnant pause.

Bree needed to know. "How is Carrie, really?"

Melissa sighed. "She was fire-breathing mad at me after you stormed off three weeks ago. I put Carrie in an unfair position, and I'm so sorry about it. She hasn't been trying to avoid you though. She's been seriously busy with a new case at work. But I know it hurt her when you just left and acted like she'd betrayed you. You should never make a person choose between friends, Bree. I mean, that's something the old me might have done. You're supposed to be the nice one."

Bree flushed. "I know that. I never meant it, but I was angry, and I took it out on Carrie, which was a stupid thing to do."

"As stupid as John asking Tex to choose between loving his career and loving you. Why can't he love both?"

"We never talked about love." Bree shook her head, baffled. "We've only been dating a little while."

"That's not what Carrie told me. She said you guys have history."

"Technically, we do." Bree thought back to first talking to Tex on the phone and smiled. "He was so smooth, so handsome, full of Texan charm and swagger. I fell for him. But then we had a bunch of problems, over before we could get started. He never quit though. Every time we ran into each other, he pursued me."

"Even volunteered to show the hot photographer around, despite the mighty battalion chief's warnings."

"Yeah." She blinked to clear more tears. "I just don't see what my dad gets out of this. Making Tex miserable? Making me unhappy? All that talk about couples who divorce, yet he's the one making me and Tex fight. We don't always get along, but this stress is ridiculous. And unnecessary."

And something she intended to put a stop to, once and for all.

"I think I need legal representation to help me deal with my father." At Melissa's raised brow, she clarified, "For moral support, you goof. I'm not suing Dad anytime soon."

"I know a good lawyer." Melissa grinned, downed the rest of her wine, and stood. "Let's take my car."

"Let's take mine. You just shotgunned my Merlot."

"You know, we're not just going to be besties and start doing whatever you want because I apologized," Melissa said, her tone lofty.

"Oh, cram it. Carrie's my best friend, and she rarely does what I tell her to."

"That's true."

"What are your intentions regarding Carrie?" Bree asked on the way out the door.

Melissa blinked, and a hint of pink dusted her cheeks. "I don't know what you mean."

"Uh-huh."

"Nice try. But we're dealing the mess of your life right now. Not mine."

"It's not going to be a mess for much longer. Not if I have anything to say about it."

"There you go. That's the spirit. But if the first words out of your mouth when we see Carrie aren't 'I'm sorry,' I will straight up yank out your hair and punch you in the face."

Bree huffed. "I'd like to see you try...Smelly Melly." Melissa's loathed nickname. Immature, yet it had a weird kind of cachet.

"Sometimes I do hate you." Melissa was trying not to laugh.

"I love you too."

———————

Tex hated arguing, and he and Bree had been damn near perfect partners until now. It made sense they'd have some fights. Hell, they argued all the time about little things, but that's what gave their relationship zing. Tonight had been bad. Not fun, and more than troublesome.

Was this woman, who could possibly think he only wanted to be with her to hurt her dad, someone he should risk his career over?

Firefighting was his life. His passion.

But…so was Bree. He loved her. She meant everything to him.

In a world where he could live without firefighting or without Bree, he'd choose her any day. But why should he *have* to choose?

He went to bed feeling tired and sick and woke up for work early the next day. He exercised, his appetite nonexistent, and did what he was told. A brief bright spot in his day was a small teaching moment at the local elementary school, where the kids could check out the engine and ask questions.

Not the best assignment, but much better than cleaning the ladder truck and checking inventory while everyone else went out on a call.

He finished his shift and decided to talk to Bree, face-to-face, because not being with her felt wrong.

But as he drove home to clean up, he wondered if maybe they should take a break. Would distance bring them closer or prove what the chief wanted to happen? That they'd be better apart?

Tex spent the better part of the day dithering over his choices. But by early evening, he'd cleaned up and had just finished brushing his hair when someone knocked at the door.

He walked to answer it and saw something sticking out from under the couch.

Bubbles's toy duck.

Great. Now he felt all kinds of down.

The one good thing about Bubbles being gone was that she hadn't been affected by his new schedule. Or his need to be doing something, anything, to keep his mind from the mess his life had become. He'd lost weight, growing leaner. And meaner, according to Mack.

Man, he missed the guys.

Work had always been a job until he'd found his calling fighting fires and helping people. A job he loved.

Now, not so much. And he hated that as much as he hated missing Bree.

He reached the door and opened it to let Bree inside.

"Hey." He wanted to kiss her.

She looked tired. "Hey."

He stepped back so she could enter. Would she break up with him now? Break his heart after her father finished his career?

Did he care anymore?

Dumb question. Hell, yeah, he cared.

"Let's talk," he said.

She sighed. "Fine. You're in charge."

"Damn skippy."

A hint of a smile. Progress.

"Something to drink?" he asked.

"No."

They stood facing each other in the living room. Nothing at all comfortable about this moment. And none of it made any sense. But Tex felt like it was time to lay it all out, go big or go home. He had choices, and he was about to make the biggest one of his life.

"This whole mess is confusing. It should be between a guy and his gal. Not between a guy and his gal and her father."

"I agree."

"Bree, let me say this, okay? Just, wait till I get it all out."

She nodded. Her hair didn't seem as shiny. She looked pale, her eyes bloodshot. And still, his heart felt so full with her in his life in any way.

"When I met you, it was as if something clicked inside me. I've been alive for twenty-nine years. Been around the world, lived in different parts, met all kinds of people. But none like you. I love how you look. I won't lie. But there are a ton of pretty gals out there. You have what they don't. I don't know what it is, but I know it when I see you smile, hear you laugh, watch you take pleasure in beating me at mini golf or trying to beat me in a race," he added and saw her smile. "I've never felt for a woman what I feel for you. And I don't know if it's right or wrong, I only know when you're not around, everything is a little less bright."

His hands felt cold, and nerves kept him off-balance, but it had to be said. "Bree, I fucking love you. I don't know when it first happened. It might be too soon. It might be too late. But it just is. And when your daddy tries telling me I have to pick between the woman I love and my calling, it don't sit right." He took a deep breath then let it out. "But if I had to choose, I—"

She put a finger over his lips, her eyes shining. Then a tear slid over her cheek, and his heart cracked.

"Damn, girl. Don't cry. Bree, I—"

"Tex, do you mean it? Do you really love me?"

Nothing mattered but this moment.

He stared into her blue eyes, seeing in them a reflection of the man he wanted to be. "I surely do. With all I am. And I choose you, Bree."

She smiled and wiped her tears. "Well, if someone asked me to choose between my photography and you, what do you think I would say? I'll tell you. I'd say no."

His heart crumbled. She didn't love him back?

"Because no one should have to make that kind of choice. There's no life-ending decision to be made. No good reason you shouldn't do the job you've been born to do while enjoying life with the woman you love. And no reason I should have to give up my passion in order to be with the man I love." She looked up at him and smiled. And it was as if the sun shone on them.

Until he realized it really was. The blinding glare came from the sun spearing through a cloud. He smiled. "I think we got the go-ahead from whoever's upstairs."

She laughed and hugged him as he lifted her up for a heartfelt kiss.

When they parted, they were both breathing heavy.

She gave him a peck on the lips and told him to put his shoes on. "Why?" she repeated when he asked. "Because I'm done dealing with this. And so are you. No, I know you told me to let you handle this. But we both know a union rep can't do anything about treatment that's fair and legal, but underneath, in the spirit of being a good boss, it's really not. We're going to fix this. And if my father thinks he can dictate my life, he's in for a world of hurt."

"I don't want to come between you and your dad, Bree."

"Well, you are. And I wouldn't have you anywhere else but right next to me."

He gripped her hand and brought it to his lips. "Best thing I ever did was swipe right, huh?"

"You got that right, cowboy. Now let's fix this mess."

"Guns drawn?" he teased as he found his sneakers.

"You bet your tight, sexy ass."

Chapter Twenty-Four

Bree arrived at her parents' to see Carrie's car in the driveway.

Last night, Bree and Melissa had visited Carrie. And while Bree had been apologizing through tears, Melissa had stood by, showing support for them both.

Bree had discussed her situation with Carrie, and Carrie had helped her frame her argument so she could tenderize her dad before going in for the kill.

"Is that Carrie's car?" Tex asked.

"Yep. My lawyer is present."

"Your lawyer?"

"Come with me." She grabbed his hand, went to the front door, and knocked.

Charlie opened the door, looking relieved. "About time you got here. The blockhead is in his office." She glanced at them holding hands and smiled. "I see you nabbed yourself a hot firefighter."

"I did." Bree was proud of herself for finally getting the stones—as Tex would say—to make things right. It was one thing for Bree to have to deal with an overbearing father. Another for Tex to the pay price for it. "If you'll excuse us, we have a score to settle."

"Don't be too hard on him, Bree. He loves you."

Which was what made this entire situation so bizarre. She would have asked after her father's mental health if she hadn't seen him performing just fine at work and knowing at home with Charlie, everything remained normal.

Carrie and Melissa nodded at them, watching something on television.

The gang was all here for backup.

Bree wanted to laugh at the notion of going up against her father with her posse in tow. She froze for a moment, the worry of damaging her relationship with her father a real threat.

"You okay?" Tex asked.

After taking in a deep breath, she let it out slowly. "Yep. Let's go."

She knocked on her dad's study door.

"It's open."

She pushed through with Tex and saw her dad drinking a scotch while looking at old pictures.

Of her mother.

He looked startled to see Tex with her but covered that with a look of indifference. "What can I do for you two?"

Tex took a seat across from her father and crossed his arms, giving Bree the floor. "Oh, I'm just the backup. The star of the show is your daughter."

Her father sighed. "It's been that kind of day."

Bree thought he seemed fragile. Her tough, reliable father had a shattered look in his eyes.

"I love you, Dad. And I love Tex." She continued, ignoring his scowl. "I am twenty-seven years old. Not a young girl with a crush or a starry-eyed young woman being taken advantage of by some cowpoke trying to get back at his boss."

"I take offense at cowpoke, but go on," Tex murmured.

"What you're doing is wrong. It's cruel, and it's not something my father would ever do to support his daughter. Whom he supposedly loves."

Her dad snapped, "I do love you. You know that."

"Actually, I don't. Dad, I went to Paris as an eighteen-year-old. By. My. Self. If you could trust me to do that, why don't you trust me to fall in love with a man of my choosing? Why punish Tex for wanting to love me?"

"But does he? That's the problem. Your mother fell for a man who didn't love her. And it broke her heart. Then she met me, and I broke it all over again." He looked down at a picture of her mother, and his eyes welled. "You're young. You don't know how this job can grind on your soul. He thinks he knows, but he doesn't."

Tex closed his mouth, and she appreciated that he didn't interrupt her dad. *Finally,* she might get some answers. She sat and waited.

"I have to be strong to keep my family together. To keep my unit together." He pointed at Tex. "You think you're strong, but life will kick you in the teeth one too many times. You'll watch a baby die from smoke inhalation. You'll see a teenager beaten to death by an abusive parent and have to sit with him while you struggle to get a pulse on the way to the hospital. You'll watch your best friend run into a burning building and never come out again.

"It'll happen, and you'll be powerless to stop it. And you won't tell anyone how much it hurts, because you'll be seen as weak. And you can't be weak on the squad when they need you at your peak. To be there for your brothers and sisters in your house. People as close to you as your family, because they *are* your family.

"You'll drink or take a few pills. Then you'll do what you said you'd never do." Her dad angrily wiped his cheeks. "And you'll feel lower than dirt. You'll—"

"Dad, what did you to do Mom?" Bree asked, feeling his pain.

He paused, and she didn't think he'd answer. But he seemed lost in the past when he spoke. "I never meant to. But I'd been drinking. And the woman at the bar next to me didn't ask questions. She was just there for me. I could be ugly and find a place to let that out that didn't hurt you or your mother. And when we were done, it meant nothing. One night, a mistake. But the damage had been done."

She just stared. Tex reached for her hand and held it against his knee.

"Mistakes happen," Tex said in quiet voice.

"And they can destroy lives. Allie was never the same after that. Oh, we made up. I got help. But I hurt her so badly, and I never, ever forgot that. She said she forgave me for everything, but she shouldn't have had to do that. If I'd loved her a little more, maybe I would have given up this mess of a life and been a different man."

"But that's love," Tex said when Bree would have. "My parents have been together for over thirty years. They fight, laugh, cry, and then do it all over again. You think a firefighter's got problems? Try ranching when the drought comes or feed prices go up. Try feeding a family of six on a poor man's salary. Hell, people everywhere have problems."

"But we have more," her dad said. "And that's something you don't understand because you're young and you think you have all the answers. I want more for my daughter."

"You don't get to decide that for me, Dad." Bree smiled sadly at her father, understanding so much now. "And really, if being a firefighter is such a bad thing, why did you marry Charlie and put her through all the pain you keep saying comes with marrying a firefighter?"

Her father flushed. "It's not like that with Charlie. I learned from my mistakes. But I was older when she and I married. You're young, and so is he." He nodded to Tex. "You don't understand how this job can make you hate yourself. I struggle every day to be someone Charlie and you girls can be proud of."

Bree sighed. "Dad, you made a mistake. You learned from it, and Charlie loves the heck out of you. I love that you want to protect me, but all you're doing is hurting me. And hurting Tex and his station. Your decision to take him away from his family isn't right."

Her father winced at that.

"Yes, you hurt a lot more people than just Tex."

"That wasn't my intention."

"But it happened," Tex said, his voice sharp. "I get why you want to protect Bree. Hell, we want the same thing. But you ripped me from my team and replaced me with a shithead."

"Tex."

"It's true." Tex glared at her father. "It's not about being with my team. You put a man in there that won't have their backs like I will. That won't protect them like I will. We work together as a team. Me and my crew. C Shift. Station 44. We're *all* a team. Just like me and Bree. You said I had to choose between my calling and the woman I love. And that's horseshit. Bree is everything, worth more than a pain in the ass father-in-law."

All three of them froze.

Tex hurried to add, "Not that we're anywhere close to marriage, but you know what I mean."

Bree stared at Tex, seeing the flush creep over his face.

"You can't control everything, Chief. And before you start telling me I don't know shit, this ain't my first rodeo. I've been a rancher. I've been a Marine. I've dealt with life-and-death decisions way before putting on the uniform here. But this isn't just a job for me. Being a firefighter is who I am. And if you can't understand that, what the fuck have you been doing the past thirty-plus years?"

The sudden silence grew deafening.

Her dad studied Tex for so long, Bree worried her father might get violent. She could easily imagine a no-holds-barred fight between her dad and her boyfriend. Wouldn't that go over well?

"You love my daughter that much?"

"I don't know what 'that much' means, but yeah, I love her. I'm a lot of things, Chief. I make jokes. I like to have a good time at work and at home. But I've never felt for anyone the way I do Bree. But none of that really matters. What matters is that you deal with your issues and let Bree and me live with ours."

"That. Right there." Bree wanted to clap. "Dad, I'm sorry for what happened between you and Mom. But I know for a fact she loved us both very much." She could feel her mother in the room with them just now, and her love burned so bright. "She'd want you to stop feeling guilty for something that happened a long time ago. You and Charlie are happy, aren't you?"

He blinked. "Yes. Or at least, we were until I started bullying your Texas puppy here."

Tex's mouth firmed.

Bree quickly said, "Then why do you have to feel guilty? You love Mom. You made mistakes. Everyone does."

"Some hurt more than others."

"Yes. And Tex and I will argue and hurt each other, I'm sure. But that's our life. Not yours. I wanted to talk to you about this long before now. But Tex told me not to. That you're his boss making work decisions that aren't my problem. And he's right. Except the decision you made to pull him from him team wasn't about his work ethic or the fire house. It was about me. And that's got to stop. You know it, I know it. Heck, even Ed O'Brien knows it."

Her dad sighed. "Well, hell." He sat there looking down at his glass, tossed it back, and stood. "I guess I—"

"No." Bree stood as well.

Tex looked from daughter to father and remained seated and quiet.

"Don't guess anything. This can't happen again. I don't care if Tex and I get married and have four babies, a dog, and live in a house with a white picket fence or if we break up next month. Our life has nothing to do with decisions you make about his job."

"I think—"

She cut her father off. "I will go above your head. I'm still friends with your boss, and if he knew what you did and why, he'd step in. I know he would. And don't even get me started if I have to go outside the station to my friends in the mayor's office."

On fire now, she waited, full of nerves and ready to make that next big step. The one she didn't want to make. Where she cut her father out of her life to make her point.

Her dad frowned. "I—"

"And if you think—"

"Bree." Tex yanked her back to her seat. "Let the man talk before you threaten to pull his legs off one by one."

"Thank you," her father said wryly. "You've said your piece. I've said mine. And I need to apologize. To you, Bree. But more, to Tex." He stood before them, a big man with broad shoulders carrying a lot more burdens than Bree had ever realized. "I don't know how I got so turned around when I only wanted to do the right thing. But I never thought how everyone around you would be affected by moving you. You're right. I let sentiment screw with your job. But son, this is my daughter. I'd do anything for her."

"I understand."

Bree looked at Tex, who smiled at her.

"I'd do anything for her too."

Her dad sighed. "I'll make it right. When do you go back on shift?"

"To which house?"

"Station 44."

Bree wanted to cheer.

"Tuesday, sir."

"I'll make some calls. Report back to Ed Tuesday morning. I'll move Goat Nut from your team."

Tex coughed.

Bree stared. "Goat Nut?"

"The guys really don't like him," Tex said.

"Neither does Ed." Her father sighed.

Tex and she stood as her father rounded the desk. "I apologize, Tex. My personal feelings toward you won't affect your job again. Your relationship is not my business."

"Good." Bree nodded. "You keep saying that, Dad."

He ignored her and stuck out a hand.

Tex shook it. "Thank you."

"No, thank you for putting up with me." Then her dad yanked Tex close and had her boyfriend's neck in the crook of his very thick biceps. "But I'm never going to be so old I can't protect my daughter, son. So if you think you can hurt her and I won't come after you for it, think again."

"Dad."

Tex laughed. "I get it. You're not so old you can't kick my ass."

"Exactly."

"Oh my gosh. Dad, stop."

But Tex and her dad were laughing now, so that had to be a good sign. Especially since her dad finally let him go.

"You ought to meet my momma. You think you have strong arms, you should see hers. She'd kick your tail if she caught you threatening her baby boy."

Her dad grinned, finally looking like his old self. "Would she now?"

Bree let her dad hug her tight, and she kissed his cheek.

Tex, smart man that he was, made himself scarce.

"Honey, I'm so sorry."

"Dad, what you said about Mom..." Her father unfaithful? Drinking too much? She'd never seen that side of him.

He looked sad. "I never wanted you to know. Neither of us did. It was one time, back when you were just a baby, but it showed me I needed real help. I hurt her and have regretted it every day of my life since."

"Do you really think Mom would hold a grudge?"

He sighed. "No."

"Dad, let it go. You messed up. You learned, and you loved Mom and me. But I have to tell you, you two and Charlie taught me right. Because if Tex ever cheated on me, I'd kick his butt right out that door. And I'm not ever going to support a man who's into drinking all the time either. That man has a tough road ahead of him if he wants me."

"Oh, he does." Her dad smiled. "And you know, I really like him. Don't tell him that. But he stood up to me, and not many do."

"I'm sure it's because of the hat, Dad. You can't mess with Texas."

———————

Twelve days later, after watching the community's positive reaction to her work on display, Bree wiped tears from her cheeks. Happy tears, so full of joy she was overflowing.

Her dad and Charlie were gaga over her work. So were Carrie and Melissa, who had arrived together but not *together*.

"But I'm working on that," Melissa said as an aside.

Bree had never thought to see Carrie in the role of the person being wooed, considering she usually initiated her relationships. How amusing to see her on the receiving end of a slow but methodical courtship. She seemed uncertain of what do to with the rose Melissa handed her.

Bree bit back a laugh.

Stefanie from IAG swung by to compliment her on her presentation and wanted to discuss moving up a timeframe for a gallery showing in New York, at another of her showrooms. "I can't wait, Bree. This is more than I was expecting. Just…amazing." Her eyes lit on Tex and his friends by the food table. "Any chance you can work with any of them? Your shot of the tall one with the dark hair and cowboy hat was inspiring."

"No kidding." Bree grinned. "That's my boyfriend."

Stefanie glanced from one particular photo to Tex, looking gorgeous in a suit and tie, and nodded. "Ah, I see. Still, he's got a face for the camera. And you have an eye for angles."

Sometime later, Avery caught her in a free moment. "This is

incredible, Bree. I'm so excited I'm friends with an art*eest*. Tex keeps calling you that, by the way, with that Texan twang."

Bree chuckled.

"Coffee next week? I need an in-depth interview for work, but that's just an excuse. I have to tell you what's been going on with the guys that you've missed. I'm so excited to have a girl in the group."

"I'd like that." *In the group.* Bree was now a part of something more.

It seemed like forever before the night started to wind down.

Tex pulled her aside to hand her a bouquet of roses. "I've been carrying these around all night. Darlin', you are incredible. This is your night, and you're a star."

She smiled and pulled him close for a kiss. "This has been the most amazing night, Tex. I feel like I'm dreaming."

"Well, you could be. You look like a dream in that dress." The tasteful cream-colored gown flowed from her strapless bust down to her ankles, a slim-lined piece created by a friend with an up-and-coming clothing line out of Milan.

He frowned. "Are you wearing underwear?"

"Would you like to find out?"

"If I say yes and flip your dress over your head right now, think your daddy will skin me alive?"

They glanced over to see her father watching them with a big grin on his face. He really did like Tex, though it was taking her Texan a while to warm up to her father again.

"If he doesn't skin you alive, I will." Bree kissed him once more. "But I bet we could make a break for it. I've put in my time."

"Thank God. My feet are killin' me in these shoes."

She laughed as he complained about his dress shoes.

Once in his truck on the way home, he turned down the music and asked, "So does it have to be four kids, a dog, and a white picket fence? Or are you open to options?"

She stared, wide-eyed.

"I mean, maybe the dog could come first. And I'm not one for picket fences. They take a lot of painting or staining for upkeep. You know?"

"I—I, well…"

He laughed. "If you could see your face! I'm teasing. We'll get to the hard questions down the road. But what would you think about visiting a canine pal of mine? Maybe flying down to Houston when I put in for vacation in December? Think you could work me in?"

"I bet I could. IAG wants to push up my timeline. Once I have those dates, we can go together."

"Just a warning. You're gonna have to meet my momma. And if you thought your daddy was a bear, my momma's a cross between a grizzly and a dragon." He grinned. "But don't worry, Goldilocks. I'll protect you."

"Aren't you funny."

A terrible thought struck her. "You don't think your brother and cousin told anyone how they first met me, do you?" When she'd flashed them wearing nothing but Tex's shirt.

He grinned wide. "Well, now. Maybe that's why my oldest brothers keep asking to meet you."

"Oh my God."

Tex grinned. "Oh, yeah. Meeting my family is going to be so much fun."

"You know, if you want to see me naked anytime soon, let's drop this conversation."

"You got it."

He put his foot down on the accelerator. And soon found she'd been telling the truth.

She didn't have on anything under that dress.

And she did love her cowboy. A little more each day.

Read on for a peek at the next book in
Marie Harte's fun and spicy Turn Up the Heat series

HOT FOR YOU

Coming soon from Sourcebooks Casablanca

July in Seattle

"I HATE THESE THINGS," REGGIE MORGAN MUTTERED TO HIS
partner as they readied to give a presentation to a full crowd of
eager firefighting enthusiasts.

"Relax. You'll do fine." Mack ran a hand through his always perfect hair, the guy vain enough to always wear it styled. Then again,
the new fire station *had* used Mack's chiseled chin, golden tan, and
laughing, bright-blue eyes on a lot of the promotional material for
Station 44.

"Why aren't *you* giving this stupid speech? You're on all the
posters."

"You could have been." Mack grinned. "Your sister said you're
no Idris Elba, but I disagree."

"Shut up."

"Well, maybe Morris Chestnut but with hair."

"Mack, come on. You're good at talking." He added under his
breath, "You never shut up." When Mack frowned, he hurriedly
tacked on, "*You* really represent Station 44."

"So do you and the rest of C shift. What's your point?"

Reggie had been stress sweating for the past half hour, thankful his dark-blue service uniform hid any unfortunate pit stains.
Hell, put him in the middle of a roaring fire, in a submarine having
technical difficulties eight hundred feet below the surface, or at a
family dinner with his father and sisters giving him dating advice.
All traumatic experiences.

But none of them could beat a Monday afternoon lecture at

the local library in front of a ton of people, the majority under the age of ten.

Reggie tried again. "You're the station's wonder boy."

Mack smirked. "That's true. I am the most talented, best-looking, and—"

"Biggest mouth."

Mack shrugged. "And yet, the lieutenant wanted *you* to give the class. Go figure."

Reggie wished he'd never confessed to the LT how much he hated public speaking. Now the guy made it his mission in life to get Reggie over that nagging fear. "Yes, but he never said you couldn't help."

"And take any attention away from the great Reggie Morgan? No thanks. I'll just stand by, clicking slides, and look pretty while the *brains of the operation*—that's what you're always calling yourself, isn't it?—takes center stage."

Reggie did like to remind the rest of his four-man crew that he was the brains of their unit. And the brawn, come to think of it. Sure, the other two on duty had some muscle, but none of them could out-bench him. Mack might be faster on a distance run, but Reggie could break him in half without much effort. Of course, since his free time anymore consisted of lifting weights when not hanging with the guys, that did explain—

"Quit stalling. You're up." Mack shoved him from behind the stacks where he'd been hiding, exposing him to a bazillion stares.

Reggie caught his balance, glared over his shoulder at Mack, then plastered a smile on his face and walked toward the large screen, which would display the slideshow presentation the station had put together for events such as these.

He looked out over the crowd of close to fifty—*hell*—children and a few parents, all waiting expectantly for Reggie to regale them with stories about firefighting and life in the station.

He cleared his throat and said, "Hello there," at the same time the librarian in charge of public events introduced him. Reggie ignored Mack's chuckle and watched his future ex-friend walk to the other side of the screen, pick up a remote for the slideshow, and wait.

The librarian was saying, "Reggie Morgan, one of our wonderful firefighters from the new station serving the Beacon Hill, New Holly, and South Beacon Hill neighborhoods. Reggie's here today to tell us what it's like to be a firefighter. He's got pictures too."

Mack waved at the crowd, at ease with being in front of people the way Reggie would never be.

"And I see that Firefighter Morgan's brought along an assistant," the librarian, old enough to be Reggie's grandmother, said with a smile.

"A handsome, *single* assistant," Mack said with a huge grin. "I'm Mack."

"Mack," Reggie said under his breath. "Behave."

Several of the parents with their children gave Mack a second look.

"I'll give you my number when we're through," the librarian teased and continued when the laughter had died down. "Welcome all, and let's get this show on the road." She turned to Reggie. "And thank you for agreeing to do this."

The lieutenant had carved out an hour for the lecture, part of the fire department's public relations and a way to engage the community. Reggie loved the idea of the station getting to know their neighbors, but not if he had to be the one doing the talking.

He gave Mack another look.

The bastard ignored him.

Reggie turned back to the crowd of eager faces and knew he might as well get started. "Hi, everyone. Thanks for coming out on a sunny summer day. I know you'd probably rather be swimming or playing than hearing me talk."

"Not me," one little girl said. "I have a lot of questions."

"Me too," a young boy agreed.

"Okay. Great." Reggie cleared his throat, not comfortable with such scrutiny. The little girl had dark eyes that seemed to look through him, not at him. She couldn't be more than five or six, dressed to look adorable in matching pink shorts and a T-shirt showing off her tan, holding a fuzzy grizzly bear.

But that cuteness packaged a small, intense, and scary kid.

He swallowed and pointed to the screen, now showing a picture of a fire truck and the number 44 emblazoned over it. "I'm Reggie. This is Mack." Mack nodded. "We're with Station 44, and we work C shift. Our station has four eight-person shifts—A, B, C, and D. And we have two lieutenants, who are our bosses. We—"

The little girl cut in, "How come you only have two lieutenants but you have four shifts? I know my math, and I think you're missing two."

Reggie contained a sigh. "Our lieutenants cover two shifts each."

"Oh." The little girl nodded.

"We have pretty much the best job in the world, because we get to help people when we can, and we get to meet new people all the time."

"But what if they're burned? That's not great." The little girl frowned.

Behind her, a well-dressed man, in slacks and a polo, rolled his eyes.

"That's a good point," Reggie agreed. "And maybe this job wouldn't be good for someone who hates fire or is afraid of blood. But we—"

"Blood?" The girl's eyes narrowed. "What blood? Do you make people bleed?"

Mack coughed but didn't quite muffle his laughter.

A few adults grinned.

The girl's father—uncle?—shushed her. "Emily, let him speak. Sorry."

"No problem." Reggie mentally thanked the guy. "Well, we as firefighters in the awesome city of Seattle have to do a lot more than put out fires. As you probably know, there are thirty-four stations in the city, including Harbor View Medical Center. All of them run twenty-four hours a day, seven days a week."

Mack changed the slides, showing the layout.

"We have five battalions, and each battalion has a chief."

One boy raised his hand. Not the intense Emily, thank goodness.

"Yes?" Reggie said.

"Do you mean battalions like the Army? My dad is in the Army."

"Are you in the Army?" Emily asked. Without raising her hand.

"Actually, I was in the Navy. Mack was in the Air Force, and two of our crew who aren't here were in the Marines."

"Semper Fi," a woman said from the back of the room.

Semper Fi—always faithful, the Marine Corps motto.

Reggie grinned. "I'll tell them you said that. But you know, we live with an always-faithful mindset when we work too. Firefighting is a lot more than using a hose with water to put out a fire. Does anyone know what 'lifesaving' is?"

A little boy in the back answered, "Saving a person so he doesn't die."

"That's a great answer."

The boy beamed.

"Every firefighter in Seattle must first be an EMT—an emergency medical technician. We do something called basic life support. That's like taking your pulse or listening to your heart. We can splint your arm if it's broken and take you to the hospital to get fixed. Has anyone ever seen an ambulance?"

Mack clicked the slide to show them an ambulance, and everyone's hands raised.

"That's what we drive when we're not in the fire truck. Actually, most of what we do is help people get better. We help them in our ambulance, what we call an aid vehicle, and let them go see their own doctor when they want. But if they're really bad off, we might take them to the hospital."

"Do you wrap them like mummies?" a little boy wearing a superhero shirt and cape asked.

"No, not like mummies." Reggie wanted the kids to understand. "The ones who take the really hurt people to the hospital are called paramedics. They do advanced life support. So, if you had a heart attack or got shot or had a really bad break and were bleeding all over the place, the paramedic might treat you in the back of the ambulance. And you know what?"

"What?" asked a girl wearing blue frames with thick lenses. Her eyes looked huge behind them.

"We don't really have that many paramedics, which is kind of weird, if you think about it. We have paramedics in our fire stations, but we only have seven medic units in all of the city. The medic unit is what the paramedics drive. Remember, I said that we EMTs use aid vehicles, like the ambulances. The medic vehicles look like ours but inside, the paramedics do the fancy stuff, like give IVs, intubate, and handle acute sickness and trauma. They go to a special school for that."

"Did you go to school?" Emily asked, her powerful gaze burning a hole through him.

"I did."

"Do you shoot people?"

"Ah, no."

"Do you stab them?" a boy sitting next to her asked. "So, you make them bleed then you patch them up?"

"No." The boy's identical twin shook his head. "He doesn't make them bleed. The paramedic does."

Reggie bit back a groan. "No, the paramedic doesn't make anyone bleed."

"Does he stab them with a sword?" another child asked.

"No, we don't stab or shoot anyone."

"Do you have a gun?" another child asked.

Mack's face had turned red with his effort to hold back laughter. And the class went downhill from there.

By the end of the lecture, Reggie had regained control, only barely, but enough to answer questions from the adults as well. He and Mack showed everyone slides of the inside of an engine truck, explained how the different stations had different equipment, and how their SCBA (self-contained breathing apparatus) gear worked. They'd brought a clean one for a live demonstration, and the children had a lot of fun looking through the mask and trying on a helmet.

The class turned out to be informative and entertaining.

Even though Emily continued to try to stare into Reggie's soul.

She walked up to him at the very end despite her parent trying his best to get her to leave. The man held up his hands in defeat. "I give up."

Reggie noticed that she carried a stuffed brown bear, a cute and furry little grizzly with an ax strapped to its back. Apt that she carried a stuffed predator considering the girl's ferocity with questions.

She looked from her bear to him. "You use an ax like Brownie. And you're brown like Brownie."

Reggie nodded. "I am."

"I think you're pretty."

He blinked.

Mack guffawed behind him.

"Ah, thank you. I think you're pretty too."

"P-R-E-T-T-Y. I'm a good speller."

"I see that."

"I wish I had teeth and claws so when Marty Binker hits me, I could carve him up." She curled her fingers and pretended to claw his arm.

"After the fight, you could heal me by doing BLS and I wouldn't have to go to the hospital." She leaned closer to whisper in a loud voice, "Uncle Doug had to go to the hospital because he was pooping a lot."

The man with Emily, Doug apparently, turned bright red. "Okay, Emily, we need to get you back to your mom." In a lower but still audible voice, Doug added, "She owes me big for this."

Emily continued, "But then they gave him ivy and he had more fluid and got better."

"Ivy?" Mack asked.

"I think she means an IV." Reggie stared at the little girl who said ivy and fluid in the same sentence. "It must have been pretty serious if Uncle Doug needed an IV. I'm glad he's better."

She nodded, solemn, and Reggie was struck by how cute she was when not grilling him. She reminded him of Rachel, a little girl he'd been doing his level best not to think about while surrounded by so many children. The sadness that had never left him returned, though he refused to let it show.

"I'm glad he's better too." Emily smiled. "I'm Emily." She held out her hand.

He shook it, conscious of how much larger than her he was. "I'm Reggie."

"I know. I was paying attention."

"Emily, we need to go," Doug reminded her.

"Okay. Thank you for the stories. Maybe you can come over for dinner with me and my mom. She's really nice and makes macaroni with hot dogs in it. And she hardly ever poops. Well, sometimes, but—"

"And we're done." Doug scooped Emily up in his arms and tickled her. As she laughed, he said to Reggie, "Thanks for the class. And really, you did great. Especially in front of the terror of John Muir Elementary." He nodded to Emily.

Reggie grinned. "Thanks. Today was harder than running the gauntlet when I was in the Navy."

Doug laughed. "I'll bet. Thanks for all you do. You too, Mack."

Mack nodded. "Anytime."

They left, and Reggie was sorry to see them go. Though the little girl had been a tough sell, he felt as if he'd won her over by the end.

"You know, you should have gotten Emily's mom's number." Mack rubbed his chin. "She doesn't poop a lot, apparently. That's pretty much your speed, right?"

"Shut up."

Mack laughed.

They drove back to work just as a call came in.

"Thank God." With any luck, they'd get someone they could help to take Reggie's mind from cute little girls he'd never see again. Adorable Emily and her brown bear, and Rachel, the daughter who might have been.

About the Author

Caffeine addict, boy referee, and romance aficionado, *New York Times* and *USA Today* bestseller Marie Harte is a confessed bibliophile and devotee of action movies. Whether biking around town, hiking, or hanging at the local tea shop, she's constantly plotting to give everyone a happily ever after. Visit marieharte.com and fall in love.